You are about to embark on a grand adventure . . .

"Swaggering pirates, friendly dolphins, hot Caribbean nights filled with passion. A sensuous hero and a loveable hellion. What an adventure!"

—Bestselling author Kat Martin

"Riveting! *Tradewinds* is a splendid debut novel as lush as its exotic setting!"

—Bestselling author Raine Cantrell

Turn the page and see why these authors are raving about this extraordinary new book!

HE'D BEEN SENT TO FIND A
RESPECTABLE YOUNG LADY. . . .

A piercing screech tore through the air. Savage. Enraged. Human. Human and female.

Mast's gut twisted. The thing sounded like a cross between a tigress and a harpy. It couldn't be, he assured himself. It wasn't.

But the shriek sounded again, this time sending a drove of frigate birds into the sky. Mast looked down at his feet in amazement. The sound was sending vibrations through the veranda floorboards, too.

It was coming from inside the mansion.

"Damn."

He made his way inside. There was a small study. Just as he was about to venture farther into the house, the door flew open. Then there was only the sound of the wind, and the deep gasps of her breathing. A wild animal's breathing from a wild, openly hostile human face.

Mast had never seen a woman like her. *Golden . . . Golden . . . no wonder they'd named her that.* Eyes golden like the sea in a Martinique sunrise, and such shining, gilt-colored hair, it looked spun from the gold mines of Guinea itself. And her skin, like blazing white silk.

She was bewildering.

She was beautiful.

She was going to be trouble.

She stepped forward. "Maybe, *m'sieur,*" she snarled, "you were expecting a doll with no brains and no back bone? Well, fancy this. She doesn't exist."

He paced forward and circled her. He regretted it at once.

"You will remove your filthy hand from me at once," she said, "or I will bite it off and spit it out for the monkeys."

He had a glaring, fuming hellion to deal with.

Ah, Christ, he thought. *This voyage is going to be hell.*

IT WAS ONLY THE BEGINNING
OF A BEAUTIFUL RELATIONSHIP. . . .

TRADEWINDS

ANNEE CARTIER

PINNACLE BOOKS
WINDSOR PUBLISHING CORP.

PINNACLE BOOKS are published by

Windsor Publishing Corp.
850 Third Avenue
New York, NY 10022

First Printing: February, 1995

Printed in the United States of America

For the real
mast beneath my sails—
my husband, Kevin . . .
Thank you for your strength, your smiles, your love.
We did it!
And
to the person I'm proud to call my best friend—
my mom, Judie Locke.
Thank you for making me see the stars,
even when I couldn't.

With special thanks to
some special friends—
Kat Martin . . . thanks for everything, Sis.
Meryl Sawyer . . . for every hug, smile and kick in the pants.
Chris Pacheco . . . for being there since the beginning.
Judy Barton . . . for caring about Nirvana.
And Shelley Bradley . . . just for caring.

Prologue

January, 1770
Off the coast of His Majesty's Royal Colony, the Isle of Saint Kitts, the West Indies

The world was chaos.

The sea's most feared predator clawed its way into the *Gabrielle's Hope*. The talons of fire were everywhere, greedily feeding, scratching charcoal black death to the planking, skids and decks of the vessel that had been home to seventy-four passengers and crew members who now swarmed at her rails, a mass of panic.

"Pirates!" went the horrified gasp through the passengers. Women fainted, to awaken to the news that the brutes had boarded, looted the captain's private hold of what they wanted, and left, apparently not interested in anything—or anyone—else.

"Nay, they just left us here to die, is all!" came a sharp wail.

The chaos rose to a crescendo. Screams permeated the air more rampantly than the smoke. A stampede surged across the main deck and back again. A brawl broke out on the quarter deck; two crewmen fought over the last jug of ale.

But the most terrified cry of all wasn't a roaring bellow

or a piercing wail or a deafening sob. It was the barely discernible call of an eight-year-old girl, clinging unnoticed to the side of a stairwell as the crowd bumped and jostled past her.

"Mummy?" Golden cried through the smoke and noise. She was jarred loose from her hold on the stairwell, and fell what seemed like a mile to the rocking deck. "What's happening?" she wondered in a whimper as she reached to push herself up. "Where's Mummy? And why is everyone crying?"

She'd wandered off for a moment, just long enough to gaze at the pretty red flag on the other ship off the bow Daddy called port. She'd hoped so badly to see another little boy or girl standing beneath that grand banner, looking for a friend like her . . .

And then she'd heard the first shriek, and the smell of smoke had invaded her nose. She'd turned back to Mummy— but Mummy wasn't there any more. And the world had gone topsy-turvy.

"Mummy? Where are you?"

Golden's stomach knotted when she still couldn't find the tapered, ladylike hand she knew so well. It was the hand with the sapphire ring on it—the one with the stones shaped like a fish. She had named the fish Nirvana, the pretty word Daddy told her meant "paradise." That's where they were going, he'd told her, a paradise in the New World to start their new life together.

Where was she?

"Mummy, I can't find you!" Golden chewed her lower lip, struggling to be brave. She gulped back the stinging tears, feeling them burn her throat along with the smoke and soot. Daddy had been so proud of her, calling her his "good little sailor." Good sailors weren't afraid of anything—and they didn't cry.

But she couldn't help the scream that escaped her as the ship lurched, a mighty groan of timber calling out the death throes of the lower decks. Crimson flames ate their way up the mainmast and ignited the sails into a huge wall of fire. Things were a frenzy now; everything was loud and confusing and hot, so very hot.

"Mummy, Daddy, where are you?" Golden pushed out as much volume as her lungs would allow. "Mummy, I'm here . . . I'm here! Please, I can't find you. Daddy, help me! Help me!"

A resounding crash sounded somewhere below. The ship groaned, jolted, and shuddered again. There was screaming, more and more screaming, until it filled Golden's ears. It was all she heard. Arms shoved and jostled her as people wrapped themselves around bulkheads and each other to counterbalance the worsening slant of the deck. Like them, Golden stretched out with all her might, praying for something, anything, to latch on to. But her arms were too short . . .

With the next lurch of the ship her worst fear came true. Golden lost her footing and thudded clumsily on her rump. She slid down the incline.

Until there was no more deck below her.

"Mummeeeee!"

The water closed around her like an endless black monster. She opened her mouth to scream, but the liquid beast invaded her insides, as well. She flailed out, fighting, struggling with everything she had within her. Her blood raced; her head was going to explode. *No . . . no! You're not going to eat me alive. You're not going to kill me. You're not going—*

"Help!"

She inhaled on the sooted air greedily as she came up, then repeated the shout. The sea water came back up her throat; she spluttered while desperately reaching for a passing piece of driftwood. Then she clung to it. Chips of white paint came off on her hands. *"—lle's Hope,"* she read across the wood beneath her. She twisted her head from the sight, and the gruesome feeling it made in her tummy.

Only then did she see the atrocity before her.

Never in her wildest nightmares, even after Mummy read her scary stories from the Bible, had Golden imagined a scene this dreadful. The flames reached and ate at the sky, their ravenous roar second only to the wails and shrieks that came from what was left of the *Hope*. She stared, horrified, at the burning things that were cursed enough to still live, racing aimlessly about, finally plummeting to their black water graves. And then she could stand it no more and she squeezed her burning eyes shut, hoping it would all disappear if she ignored it, like a nightmare.

But it didn't. The screams were proof of that. She wouldn't—couldn't—ignore the screams. "Hail Mary, full of grace," she begged to the roiling, smoke-filled air. "Pray for us—oh, please just hear me, sweet Mary. I need you, I truly need you now!"

"Golden?"

Like the miracle she pleaded for, it came. Golden snapped her head to the sky, her heart pumped with hope.

"Mummy?"

"Golden? Oh, Golden. My baby. My little girl."

But Golden's elation was slashed by the way Mummy's voice sounded. It sounded like she was crying, so tearful and sad. Even more horribly, Golden realized, it wasn't coming from the sky at all. Or anywhere near her in the water.

It was coming from the ship.

"Mummy!"

But the volume she forced was for naught. She watched helplessly as Mummy picked a stumbling step along the one remaining deck of the *Hope*, still using that awful, sad voice.

"Golden . . ."

"I'm right here. *Here*. In the water—"

"Golden, I love you."

"No, Mummy. Don't say it like that. Don't say it—Mummeee!"

She lunged toward the fiery shell of the ship as the ocean swallowed it.

Golden didn't stop screaming until her throat dried into a rasp.

And then the awful silence came.

And with it, the sea monster.

It sneaked up behind her with a clickering noise that sounded almost friendly, and a gentle nudge. But when Golden turned, the long, slimy grey snout was another matter. Her gasp of horror went down her throat like a rock. She was so petrified she could only stare back at the big thing, wordless. Daddy had chided her against believing in such silliness as sea serpents, but as Golden took in the big fins along its back and sides, the long tail flipping up as it circled in and out of the water around her, the two round blue eyes watching her, all she could think of were the stories the town bullies had tried to scare her with before she'd left Shropshire. Dear God, she pleaded again, she'd take back all the equally nasty insults she'd issued with her fists if only the slimy grey monster would go away.

"Ohhh no," Golden gasped. The monster did just the opposite. It dipped under the water, slow, then glided a smooth line toward her. Her whole body went numb, except for the horrible throbbing in her chest.

A hole in the beast popped up and blasted a spurt of air at her. She screamed and thrashed back in the water.

The serpent followed her.

"No! Go away!" she cried. The grey snout defied her, and came rising from the water just beyond the reach of her legs. Not that she could move them much; she was horribly tangled in the layers of her dress—and the numbing grip of fear.

The beast submerged just before it got to her. Then came silence. Awful silence. All she could hear was the ruthless pounding of her heart.

Until the slimy thing lifted her out of the water.

Golden shrieked and tried to escape. All the air left her body as she slapped the water and began to sink. Once again, the beast's snout nudged her and brought her to clear air.

She took a few deep breaths before she blinked her eyes open again. The serpent was still there, watching her with calm blue eyes, waiting for her. Something deep inside of Golden told her to reach out, to touch the creature's smooth grey skin, to hold it.

She tentatively wrapped her arm around the large top fin.

The beast made another clickering sound in reply. It seemed a very happy sound, she thought.

She smiled. She wrapped her other arm around the fin and rested her face against it, closing her eyes contentedly.

But when she opened them again, seemingly moments later, her friend was gone. She was no longer wet. All she could think of was "white." White, clear sun. White, sandy beach. White, white eyes that gazed down at her from a face of dark, dark skin.

Golden bolted up. She shoved at the face with what she could manage of a shriek, jumping to her feet.

A soft chuckle rained down on her as she fell down again, dizzy. She rolled over and glared in the direction of the sound.

Her anger quickly turned to wonder. *Mercy.* The black skin covered the form of a—*man.* A very thin one, Golden noted with just as much interest, so tall and gangly he reminded her of Daddy's pipecleaning wires. He had funny, clumped-together hair, like a black bramble bush atop his head. She scrambled to her feet again, transfixed. Her fear changed to consuming curiosity. But she stopped short when she noticed more of his kind behind him, pointing at her. Golden frowned back. They were awfully rude, whoever they were.

"Staring is impolite," she snapped.

Most of the strange men ran to the edge of the jungle, just beyond the rocks. Only the first man stayed, leaning against a long, fancy-looking walking stick with a pointy end on the top of it.

"Forgive dem, little one," he said in a gentle voice. "Dey not see many like you before. You come from far, ah?"

Golden nodded slowly, stared directly at him again.

"You be safe, no worry," he said after a moment. Golden burned with wonderment again—how did he know exactly what she was thinking? "I am Guypa, dee Arawak leader." He pressed a proud hand to the string of seashells around his neck. "When I see dee dolphin bring you, I ask Yani, dee shaman, what he think of this. He says a good sign, maybe a holy sign, he not know dat yet. Dee dolphin bring you. Is good for Guypa now."

"The dolphin?" she pondered. "The . . . the big sea monster?"

The man's smile was big and made Golden feel warm inside. "Ah. Yes. He would seem like dat to you, little porpoise."

"No. My name is Golden," she protested.

"Fine. We call you Golden. But to some of dee people you be always porpoise girl, dee sea goddess. You have dee hair of sun, dee eyes of precious yellow stones." He grandly waved his arm toward the water. "You come from dee fire on dee ocean."

Golden gulped as he said the words. "The fire on the ocean," she repeated, blinking back the tears that threatened again. She would not cry, she vowed with all her heart. Good little sailors were brave . . .

Again as if knowing just what she needed, the man put his hand on her shoulder with a gentle squeeze. "I know, little one," he murmured. "We watch dee fire from dee mountain and we pray for your people. We pray to Agwe, the great god of dee water and dee boats. We even dye dee ram blue and sacrifice it to him, a thing dat is very long and—how you pale people say it?—ah, yes, costly. Then we pray to Ogoun, dee god of war and of fire, and we even make prayers to your god Jehovah."

He stopped with a long sigh that drew Golden's face up to his. He looked like someone had showed him the pain of her own heart, the kind eyes now pinched and hard as they gazed out over the ocean. "But notheeng works, little Golden," he continued softly. "Notheeng can destroy him."

"Him?" Golden stepped closer to the man and yanked urgently on the soft animal skin that draped his skinny hips. "Him who? The one who took Mummy and Daddy?"

"Him, Golden," came the suddenly hard tone of reply. "Yes, dee one who take your ship. Dee one who takes all the ships. Dee one who terrors on all dee islands, takes from all our people. He start four moons ago and does not stop yet. For dat he makes us fear the moonlight now, instead of dancing in it." He drew in another long breath before uttering the final words. "He is dee evil one, little Golden. Dee Moonstormer."

"The Moonstormer."

She repeated it in a slow whisper. For even in her eight-year-old's mind, Golden knew the word had changed her life forever. Even in her eight-year-old's heart, she understood the commitment that name had assigned to her life.

For deep within her eight-year-old's soul, Golden had just learned how to hate.

One

January, 1782
The Gaverly Villa, Grand Abaco Island, the Bahamas

"God's rot, I hate nights like this."

Mast Iverson looked up as his friend mumbled the expression for the fiftieth time this evening. Wayland, Lord Gaverly, Earl of Pemshire, made an impressive sight standing at the window of the hilltop villa. His large masculine frame dominated the alcove. But tonight the man seemed out of place. His tone was as hollow as the Caribbean wind that gusted outside. That tone, Mast admitted, was frighteningly out of character for his normally robust, outgoing friend.

Aye, something was out of kilter. But Mast had known that three weeks ago, when he'd received the note entreating his presence here as fast as the sails of his brigantine, the *Athena,* could carry him. He'd not wasted a moment. He owed his captainship, perhaps his life, to this giant with the face of a bull and the loyalty of a basset hound. All Mast knew of the sea he'd learned from this man when Gaverly had been his captain . . . and that knowledge had given Mast the hope to consider a better life for himself.

So he'd come, straining the limits of his canvas and his men in the name of his friend and mentor. Once he'd arrived in Abaco the urgency had become confusion. His friend had greeted him personally at the dock when they'd arrived, despite the fact that Wayland had been forced by his king's decree into hiding here as the French-English conflict in the West Indies intensified—Wayland's true home of Saint Kitts, several hundred miles south, was the next likely hot spot. The man guided Mast up the path to the villa as if he weren't King George's closest confidant and a top target of the enemy, but instead some merchant with not a care in the world. Once there, Wayland escorted Mast to a luxurious drawing room and filled crystal tumblers with Jamaican rum for the two of them.

Thus passed the afternoon. A crier in the town below called out one, two, then three o'clock. Not a word regarding the ominous missive. Dinner was served. Still not an utterance. Five o'clock; a two-hour accounting of Wayland's latest letter from "that nervy fop across the ocean," as he affectionately termed his king in private. England was fine, thank you, Wayland continued in a peculiar voice, though the only thing anyone in London agreed upon these days was the need for overseas conquest and that everyone's mistress had gone too far in copying their Paris counterparts. Coiffures had started to measure three feet high.

Seven o'clock. Wayland cursed the weather for the fifty-first time. Mast forced down his fifty-first urge to scowl. He took a mannered swallow of rum, resolving to leave when the tumbler was empty if Gaverly didn't come up with something more engaging than court gossip by then.

And just then Gaverly turned and met his eyes. Eerie, was the first word to come to Mast's mind. If Wayland's voice had been peculiar, then his friend's face, normally vibrant as that of a man half his age, was surreal.

"Mast . . . you know you're like a son to me, lad."

This was perhaps the only statement that could leave Mast speechless. It was the kind of mush a man like Gaverly saved for his deathbed, not for an evening of tossing back rum with the friend who'd once been just a dock waif begging for work aboard his ship. But Mast found it impossible to believe this bull of a man would be dying any time in the next century. So what the curses was Wayland babbling about?

"Wager you're wondering what the curses I said that for."

Wayland beamed a grin of victory at what must have been an affirming look on Mast's face. The older man poured more rum for both of them. Wayland's glass was half empty the next moment. Mast didn't follow, watching his friend's features color with intoxication for the first time in the eighteen years he'd known the man.

Something was definitely wrong.

Gaverly proved that troubled instinct all too correct as he looked up at Mast again, backhanding the alcohol from his lips, the confident smile coming off with it. The man's face grew years older in the dim candlelight, drawn to a plane of hard lines overshadowed by a brow folded in anguish.

"I told you that, Captain Iverson, because I can entrust to no other what I'm about to entrust to you."

Mast's confusion shot its way to his eyebrows. "Captain Iverson?"

"I know what I said." The chair legs scraped noisily across the floor as Gaverly pushed up from the table. "I used the rank because I want the rank, Mast. I want—I need—the best bloody seaman in the Indies today. I just thank God it's you."

Mast couldn't take it any longer. Wayland's exit from the table was a pin drop to the tumult he made as he stood. "Wayland, this obscure nonsense is wearing thin. Get on with it before I throw your pickled hide to bed and hoist full sail tonight."

To Mast's irritation, Wayland broke into a soft chuckle then. "Well, isn't this an occasion? The famed Iverson composure at an ebb."

"At an end. What the blazes is going on?"

Gaverly sighed again, running a slow hand through his hair. "You're right. You've honored me with the patience of Odysseus, and I owe you the truth.

"Here it is, Mast. The situation on Saint Kitts isn't good. Not good at all. You know as well as I, that the island's fortress, Brimstone Hill, is the finest stronghold in all the islands. The French want it, and they're coming in force to get it. My right eye says de Grasse and de Bouille are pulling their fleets together as we speak."

"Aye." Mast nodded. "We spied plenty of the French fleet on our way here."

"Damn. The noxious worms are moving quickly."

Suddenly Wayland's gaze pinned Mast. His eyes were glossy and intense, his lips taut and dry. "I must ask something of you, Mast. A deed of a magnitude you could never fathom. And I am imploring you on our friendship, please . . . say yes."

Finally Mast was able to put the evening's events together with his friend's words and actions. He righted his chair and sat back down, squaring one leg across the other. "Are you telling me my next destination is Saint Kitts, Wayland?"

He didn't know why, but the answering smile of gratitude put Mast's senses on full alert. As he accepted his friend's outstretched hand to seal the bargain, the alarms rang louder.

It was stupid, he tried to tell himself. As silly as the flappings of a fretting hen. The assignment was simple enough. Wayland wanted his treasures and gold off his home island before the French could "put their slithering gizzard hands on any of it," in Wayland's words. But King George would have Wayland's head on a platter if he so much as stuck his toe into Abaco Bay. Therefore Mast would see to the deed in his friend's stead—at the astounding rate, Wayland insisted, of fifty percent of the booty.

Once over that shock, Mast even agreed to Gaverly's command for absolute secrecy regarding the commission—though he was perplexed—it gnawed at him why the confidence stretched to exclude even the loyal seamen of the *Athena*. But any other way, Wayland replied with an almost theatrical urgency, might very well be seducing trouble. The Earl of Pemshire's proximity to the Crown at a time like this was something the French would slaver all over each other to get at, even if it was only Mast and his crew as the man's envoys.

Yet Mast had no trouble grasping that reasoning. As a matter of fact, the trouble with the French made the most sense of all so far. No, there was something else . . . something about this agreement that continued to drive nails of uneasiness through his conscious . . . something besides demon rum which set that weird glow to his friend's eyes.

"Christ!"

Mast bounded up so explosively his chair slid and crashed against the wall. But his friend, obviously reading his mind from across the room, ignored the havoc. "Now, lad—" Wayland prodded, rushing across the room with hands outstretched and entreating.

"That's not all you want me to get, is it, Wayland?" He formed the question slowly. Hesitantly. Hoping to God and all the angels he was wrong.

Wayland dropped his arms. "Nay," he replied quietly. "That's not all, lad."

"A woman."

"God's balls. I'm not sending you to the Sahara desert—"

"A woman!"

"A *girl*. For the love of God, Mast, just a girl."

"What's the bloody difference?" he exploded. "A plumper-filled corset? A softer pair of lips? A more willing spread of thighs?"

"Damn you!" came the sudden and vicious roar. Mast whirled to confront the most violent expression he'd ever seen on his friend's face—and Wayland was flying straight toward him. "Damn you, Mast! It's not like that!"

"Oh no?" he sneered, standing his ground.

"You had better say, oh no!"

Gaverly halted a few inches short of Mast before releasing a furious huff and locking his jaw hard.

Then he slowly, almost painfully, said, *"The bloody difference is that she's my daughter."*

For several moments all that marked time was some distant window shutter banging in the night. And Mast's heartbeat hammering in his ears.

"Daughter?" he asked. Surely he must have heard Wayland wrong. But then his friend confirmed the query with a slow nod.

Mast felt his lips open on a laugh as dry and caustic as the surrounding wind. He couldn't and didn't want to control the similar tone of his voice. "But you have the life *I* want, you bastard. No complications. Nothing to stand in the way of your honor, your respect . . . your dreams." Another accusing snort burst past his lips. "At least nothing like a woman. At least none you gave a damn to apprise me of. Especially not some hidden chit of a daughter."

"She's no chit." Again, the vehemence of Wayland's voice was like being jolted to consciousness from a pleasant sleep. "She's . . ." The older man's gaze again filled with that faraway light as he looked toward the window. "She's a very special person, Mast. Hell, maybe even a gift from those barmy island spirits, I've been inclined to think on occasion."

"Then that must have been some tryst in the rain forest," Mast quipped. He folded his arms across his chest as he leaned back against the table.

"There was no tryst," came the quiet answer.

He jerked a brow. "Sir?"

"No tryst." Wayland shrugged and barely held back a grin. "Golden and I . . . well, we just happened upon each other deep in the forest one day." At that the man did smile. "I'd never seen such hair on any native before . . . but a native was what she was. It was bloody unbelievable, Mast. Her whole family was wiped out when she was eight . . . so the Indians took her and raised her themselves. Some even considered her a goddess." The silvered head raised heavenward. "I only knew God had somehow given me a second chance on life. Four months later George granted me the special license to adopt her."

When Gaverly lowered his face, harsh lines again vanquished his features. He returned to the window. "Gor and hell, lad," he muttered. "You don't know what it's been like these last weeks, without her . . . not knowing whether she's alive or—" He cut himself off with a sharp cough. "I didn't know she wasn't aboard until we were well out to sea. Everything was so confused that day; we had to leave so fast . . . When I found out she'd been left behind, it was as if a piece of me was torn away."

His voice faded into a tight, thick silence. And for several minutes Mast welcomed that. He'd never heard such things out of his friend's mouth before. He'd never *seen* Wayland so off keel before. It made for chaos in his mind and mayhem in his instincts. Most of all, it made it all the more gut-wrenching to voice his next statement.

"Wayland, as much of a damnable broadside as this story is, I give my credence and my respect to your feelings. But you know, as well as I, the highest law of my ship, voted on and adhered to by every member of my crew: *No females on board. Ever."* He paused, letting the ultimatum sink into the air. Then, calmly, "Now how do you expect me to not only break that code, but keep my word to you for secrecy at the same time? I'm sorry, Wayland. It would be impossible. Impossible."

He should have known better.

He should have known Wayland Gaverly would bide his time until the most crucial moment to deliver his most shocking blow of the evening.

"I suppose adding five thousand pounds to that commission wouldn't inspire you to attempt the impossible?"

The bastard.

Saying it so calmly. As if Wayland didn't know what that kind of money would mean to Mast. As if he didn't know it was precisely what he needed, even after fairly dividing the sum with his men, to put himself over the top. To complete his plans. To finally realize his vision of the sign, reading in elegant letters, "Iverson Shipping," in the clear Caribbean sun. A man of honor and integrity. Respected. Accepted. At last.

As if he didn't know it was the dream come true.

The bastard.

Mast echoed the sentiment aloud as he pushed to his feet, stomping to the window to confront his friend squarely in

the eyes. Wayland didn't make things easier with his returning stare of admiration, affection . . . and respect.

"You're the only one I can trust, lad," his friend reiterated
in a husky choke. "She's the most precious thing in the
world to me. Please, bring her back."

Mast yearned to look away. His gut wouldn't let him. So
he stood there fuming at this man. Some inner voice cursed
Wayland with every expletive he could remember, while
another voice couldn't stop thanking him for the opportunity of a lifetime.

"All right," he finally growled. "All right, Wayland. I'll
bring your treasures and your daughter back to you."

"And . . . keep my secret, as well?"

Mast nodded hesitantly. "All right. Yes. From the men,
of course, if that's your wish—"

"No!" came Wayland's adamant protest. "No lad, from
Golden as well. Dear God," he blotted sudden sweat dots
from his wide forehead, "especially from Golden."

"What?" Mast's fists bunched at his sides in disbelief.
"Good Christ. You're insane. I can't swoop in, stow her
away on the *Athena,* then transport her hundreds of miles
without telling her something!"

"Then tell her *something!"* came the equally vehement
shout. "Tell her anything, except who you really are and
who sent you for her. Mast—" His friend's voice faltered
to a weary rasp; Wayland's fingers dug into his shoulder.
"You just don't know Golden. She's—"

"A bloody gift from the gods," he grumbled. "I know."

"No. It's not just that. It's . . . Mast, the girl's got a will
of iron, yet a heart of snow. The combination could be dangerous—very dangerous, if she were to trust just one wrong
person with all the right information." The grip on his

shoulder intensified then. "The results would be . . . well, I'm certain you can envision the atrocities."

"Aye, my friend." Experience underlined his tone—entirely too worldly experience. "I can imagine it all too well." At that Mast drew in a deep, yet ragged breath, before he turned his eyes back to meet the sharp green Gaverly stare. "Very well," he conceded. "You have my oath of secrecy and my promise of honor—even for your Indian goddess of a daughter."

The older man's eyes closed for a long moment. "Thank you," Wayland said on a relieved sigh. "Dear God, thank you Mast."

"Ah hell, Wayland," he muttered awkwardly. "Maybe you should have told me that *was* one spectacular tryst in the rain forest."

Six weeks later, Mast reflected on those words, that scene and that whole strange Bahamas night, and wondered if those island gusts hadn't taken off somewhere with his good sense. He was sweaty and aching and exhausted. His head pounded as incessantly as the cannon booms that shook through the dense Saint Kitts foliage. But the French and British forces didn't care, continuing to blast away at each other into an amber island twilight that begged for rest from war.

He jerked up in the chair he was leaning in against the simple-styled archway as a particularly loud boom shook the whitewashed veranda of the Gaverly plantation manor. He couldn't wait to get away from this insanity. And out of these clothes. He'd stolen the uniform of a man who must have been the most slovenly captain in the French force. The gold-braided blue jacket smelled like liquor, women, and something he couldn't place . . . probably pig offal.

He still couldn't believe he'd gotten himself into this. He should have turned Wayland down, no questions asked, fortune or no. He knew better than to stake his future on a woman, of all things. A *woman*. A creature no better than the trade winds that teased at him even now, first blowing in from the east, then the west, enough to throw a ship off course for days—or a man off course from things that truly mattered.

He should know. He'd experienced both catastrophes first hand. Aye, the trade wind had learned her craft well from the female. As fragrant as island wildflowers. As sweet as ripe sugar cane. As enticing as spicy sea salt. Yet as fickle as a will o' the wisp when a shinier trinket called, a more handsome profile, a court rumor of greater sexual prowess. Even death.

"Mum? Come along, stop your teasin'. Open your eyes now. It's me. Masterson. Mum? Can't you hear me, Mum?"

Another cannon boom coincided with Mast's fist pounding into the door frame. The explosion crackled through the surrounding tangle of gommier and wild plum trees, finally dying away across the waves of sugar cane on the opposite side of the mansion. The lull only gave rise to another tempest as a green vervet monkey swung down to the veranda rail, cackling at Mast as if he were the prosecuting bailiff for the entire forest.

"Guilty, your honor," he snapped at the animal. "Now go away."

"I just got here, ya ape."

The weathered but brightly accented voice behind him didn't startle Mast as it sometimes did. He knew Dinky had come inland a good two days ago; the smiles plastered to the faces of the few village wenches he'd seen had given him ample notice this time.

"About time you showed up."

Dinky Peabrooke paused as he sidled around his captain. "Temper, temper, perty boy. Wasn't my decision to come here in the middle of a war, or whatever they're callin' it nowadays, much less tryin' to pass my captain off as a Frenchie fopdoodle, to boot. I was perfectly happy on Martinique, swimmin' *a la naturale* with the natives, drinkin' those co-co nut dobbers—"

"Dinky . . ." he edged with growing aggravation.

"And the stars on Martinique. Crimey, in all my days I never saw such a night sky—"

"Dinky!"

"What?"

"Shut up."

The older man scraped a match along the rail and touched it to the end of a precariously hanging hookah in his mouth. "Damme, Ive. Yer wound up tighter'n a hippo out on a yardarm." He blew out the pungent smoke carefully. "Wanna tell yer first mate what the hell's goin' on?"

Aye. God in Heaven, aye. I want to tell you everything, you loony old sea dog.

"No." Why the hell had he promised Gaverly he'd include Dinky in that secrecy clause?

"God blarst it." Though the scraggly man only came to the middle of Mast's chest, Dinky squared off and gave him a painful jab there. "You tell me what this is all about, kid, and you tell me now. Something's goin' on, and don't ya think I don't know it. The cargo's been aboard and secured for two days now. The men've gorged themselves on so much fruit they can barely stand watch. The *Athena*'s right as rain, ready to fly to the moon . . ." Dinky moved closer, purposely staring with his more penetrating azure eye rather than his duller green one. "What the hell are we still doin' here?"

Mast only clamped his jaw in reply. Damn it, he'd promised Wayland. Men of honor only gave their promise if they were willing to back it with their life. So Dink would remain in the dark about why, and exactly what, they were here for—no matter how much Mast hated himself for it.

Despite his deliberation, the decision was whipped from his hands the next moment. A piercing screech tore through the air. Savage. Enraged. Human.

Human and female.

Mast's gut twisted just like the appalled expression on Dink's face. The thing sounded like a cross between a tigress and a harpy. It couldn't be, he assured himself. It wasn't.

But the shriek shrilled again, this time sending a drove of frigate birds into the sky on their seven-foot wings. Mast looked down to his feet in amazement. The sound was sending vibrations through the veranda floorboards, too.

As if it were coming from inside the mansion.

"Damn."

"Damn what?" Dink retorted. "Ive, don't you dare tell me that thing is—"

"Hide."

"Ive!"

"Curse it, I said hide, Dink. Here they come."

Dinky just managed to pull behind an overhanging clump of Spanish oak when a thin French lieutenant paraded down the opposite side of the veranda.

"Mon capitaine." The little man snapped a grimy hand to attention. When Mast nodded, he flung it down as swiftly.

"La wench?" Mast's imperious tone was still working to frighten his "subordinates" so much that they didn't ques-

tion his god-awful accent. He reinforced the effect with an iron stare.

"Ah . . . oui. Dans le château." The lieutenant bravely directed a trembling finger toward the inside of the mansion, but retracted it as another screech sounded from that direction. He gulped, turning to Mast with a look begging for dismissal.

"Assez," Mast growled. The lieutenant bolted away before he'd blinked.

"Stay put, Dink," he said then, with just as much command, already second-guessing his devious first mate. The answering groan from the oak clump trailed him as he made his way inside.

There was a small study just beyond the doors to the veranda. Mast covered the length of it in three strides. Just as he was about to venture farther into the house, the study doors flew open. The wild screams sliced through him. Then he heard only a muffled din as the doors slammed shut. Nearer to the commotion now, Mast also discerned the French expletives his "men" were grunting . . . and the clank of the chains their prisoner struggled against.

"Chains." Bitter bile invaded his mouth with the word. Grimacing on it, he hauled back on the doors as if to tear them from their hinges. "You imbeciles put her in—"

He was vaguely aware of his voice dying in the echoes of the hall as it died in his throat. Then there was only the sound of the wind—and the deep panting gasps of her breathing. A wild animal's breathing from a wild, openly hostile human face.

Mast had never seen a woman like her before. More aptly put, he'd never felt a force like her before. *Golden . . . Golden . . . no wonder they'd named her that.* Eyes golden like the sea in a Martinique sunrise, and the intensity behind

them to match. They were curtained by a bedlam of such
shining, gilt-colored hair, it looked spun from the gold
mines of Guinea itself. She snarled at him from behind a
huge mass of it, baring a hint of the coral heat that undeniably existed beneath those beautiful lips.

Yet her skin . . . her skin mesmerized him the most. Mast
reached and fingered away the clump of hair to see the
glowing texture of her skin better. Silk . . . her skin seemed
like blazing white silk, as if her defiance were shining right
through it.

She was bewildering.

She was magnificent.

She was going to be trouble.

"Saint Christophe." His tongue felt pasted to his teeth as
he struggled with French grammar. *"Un erreur. Un error
très gros. She—ah, ell, n'est—she ees not—"*

"The dreaded Saint Kitt's sea fury?" She stepped forward
as she finished for him in musically accented English.
"Maybe, *m'sieur,"* she snarled, "you were expecting a
black-skinned voodoo doll with no brains and no backbone?
A marionette you could buy to your will with strings of
worthless baubles?"

Mast fought to keep his face set as she surged even
nearer, lifting her face a few breaths from his. "Well, fancy
this, French pig. She doesn't exist. I am your sea witch.
You must contend with Golden Gaverly now!"

The shock joined cacophonous sensations already raging
through Mast. Her closeness was a torture he thought he
was hardened against long ago. She was inches from him
now, enticing him all the more with her delectable aroma
of island lilies and feminine salt. He tightened every muscle
in his body to avoid reaching up and touching her.

And how he wanted to touch her. He wanted to caress

that sweet skin until it glowed with more than anger. He wanted to make that coral mouth smile, make those hating eyes sparkle . . .

He wanted to kiss her. Hard.

The thought was intense and completely unfamiliar. *Kiss her?* He could feel his lips twitching as his brain struggled with the terror of it. She was just a woman. *A girl,* came Wayland's words to haunt him. *My daughter.*

"Pig!" she spat at him, noticing the movement of his mouth. "Laugh all you want, French swine. Do not think it will change a thing. You can take our island back to your precious king trussed up and shining on a gold platter, but I will never dance on your puppet strings. I will fight you until you kill me!"

She was unbelievable. Dressing him down, even in her rags, as if she were the blasted Queen of England . . . as if the shackles at her wrists were diamond bracelets. But along with all that female haughtiness, her jaw ground with the ease of a seasoned sailor's and her nostrils flared like a practiced barrister's. She was a crowd of people in one body.

Mast locked his hands behind his back. Tightly—furiously battling the message of desire his body was pounding at him in no uncertain terms. So this was why Gaverly had told him so little beyond the essentials, he thought. "Ask the natives for help," his friend had said cryptically. "They call her the porpoise girl—the sea goddess." At the time Mast had been too ecstatic about the money to wonder beyond that.

The money. Damn it, the money!

It took every strain of his will to hold himself in character. He managed to fake a suggestive grin and hold it steady on his face. There were approving sniggers from his "men" until he silenced them with a look. He paced forward and circled her slowly.

He regretted it at once.

Ankles as spellbinding as her face peeked out from beneath the worn cotton skirtings she wore. The slant of her hips was distinct and graceful—the lines of her legs slender and high. Sweet saints, he swore, while mentally assessing her dimensions, legs like a damn thoroughbred.

He moved around to face her frontward again. Not much torso, but that wasn't surprising, considering her legs. Fought it as he did, his gaze traveled downwards, over her chin, down her long ivory throat, and . . . there.

Damn her exquisite existence. She was shaking, ever so slightly, beneath his study. The rise of her breasts between the haphazardly tied laces of her vest corset tempted him, making up for their moderate size with a texture so creamy Mast found himself craving a bowl of strawberries to dip them in.

Maybe she really was a witch. Sensations like this couldn't be natural.

Against his better judgment, he looked back to her face. She still held her gaze firm, but her eyes were wider and her upper lip now trembled. She shrugged, and rounded her shoulders, trying to push her kerchief further into her dress to better cover her breasts.

Mast didn't know how he kept his hand composed as he reached and gently pulled the covering closed for her. Then in the space of a single heartbeat, he found he couldn't pull himself back. Her lashes fluttered as she looked down at his fingers, her breaths rapid, desperate. Ivory heat, he thought, as he pressed the balls of his fingers to her pulse.

She winced as he moved his touch lower. He stopped— but didn't pull away.

He paused, setting his finger in the crook of her throat. Their gazes were still locked, sight and touch their new language. He questioned with a slight pressure of his fingers. Her answer was a fervid quiver, radiating warmth into the whole of his hand.

What the hell was happening here? How could she suddenly look so defenseless like this? When had the tigress transformed into a delicate, shivering kitten? And why, *why* was he racked by such remorse when this dangerous charade was for her benefit?

"M'sieur," she rasped. Mast felt the following gulp as it swelled through her throat.

"Mademoiselle?" The huskiness in his own tone jolted him. Hell, maybe the *romantique* approach would work better, after all. Maybe this Saint Kitts sea witch wasn't the madwoman the natives warned him of.

Maybe this was going to be easy.

"M'sieur." It was even sweeter the second time as she sidled closer to him. She dropped her lashes demurely; raised them again. The raw topaz stare sparkled with a renewed lustre, spearing him straight through.

"Oui, mademoiselle . . ." It sounded more and more like another man's voice. Mast decided then and there to lock her in the cabin farthest from his on the ship. God, how he wanted to plunge his mouth . . . right there . . . over the fullest part of that dark coral pout . . .

"M'sieur."

Her tone had hardened so abruptly that it took a moment for Mast to realize it. Then it was too late to ward off the accompanying snarl. "You will remove your filthy hand from me at once, or I will bite it off and spit it out for the monkeys."

His "men" suddenly turned traitor on him, howling ruthlessly at the jab. The defiant hellion basked in their laughter, straightening her shoulders with a smug yank.

Mast's control returned with an invigorating rush of fury.

In one swoop he grabbed the wench by her nape, anchoring his grip there. In another he drew his pistol and fired it without blinking. The shot whizzed inches over the heads of the soldiers, setting them to petrified, blanched-white attention.

"Report to General de Bouille at Sandy Point immediately." He let as much of his anger seethe into the thickly accented words as possible, knowing he was as furious at himself as at the trembling morons. "Do it now. Before I kill you myself."

The idiots actually glanced at the girl, as if for support. Involuntarily, his hold on her tightened. She winced. Good. Wayland's daughter or no, Lady Golden Gaverly would learn her place, and learn it quickly.

"Go!" he shouted, storming toward them with her still in tow. "I said leave me now!"

The soldiers bolted, tripping and grunting their way down the wide stone stairwell to the ground floor. The oak door crashed shut behind them. A sweep of cool evening air whooshed up behind it, rustling the potted plants along the mahogany-floored hall, tinkling the drops of the chandelier over the entryway.

"They're going to be imprisoned, you know."

Her voice was low and accusing as she twisted around in his hold to face him. The sunset was disappearing fast beyond the beveled windows at the end of the hall, but her eyes still glowed brilliantly at him—mesmerizing, man-destroying eyes. It had to be a sin in a holy book somewhere, that unearthly power she wielded with them—like Christ "just taking a stroll" on the lake, or Arthur "just out looking" for a new sword.

Well, he wasn't going to let the crafty chit win. Mast forced himself to return the amber assault, no matter what temperature his nerves broiled to. Torture, he thought. Even if she slept in the depths of the hold, this voyage was going to be torture. *Thank you very much, Wayland.*

"They are buffoons." He relished the way he could draw out his fury on the richly inflected tones. "I doubt they will even find their way to de Bouille."

"So you're turning them out to the wilds of the island, instead?"

He cocked an eyebrow at her. "You press me, witch. Do not press me."

"You're a beast." She spat the final syllable at him.

"And you are a prisoner. A very intriguing one. So you will come with me to the study, *s'il vous plaît.*"

He steered her in front of him, pushing her through the doors with a force not to be questioned this time. He shoved one door closed with his hand, and smacked the other shut with a swift kick.

Only then did he release his hold. Mast watched the hellion immediately bolt toward the veranda, then saw her face fall as she remembered the heavy shackles at her back.

When his own chest wrenched in reply, he cursed silently again. It was the chains, he tried to reason. Aye, the chains. To get his hands on the mongrels that did this to her . . .

Just a little while, longer, hellion, he implored silently while trying to channel his tension to the more useful purpose of lighting some candles. I'll have you out of those things and on your way to your dear papa, faster than the wind can change.

Suddenly, a succession of cannon booms rumbled across the valley. The faint sounds of human screams were quick to follow. Mast watched Golden's shoulders sag—she fought back a sob—then jerked up with equal swiftness as she spun around on him.

"You French monsters will never get away with this!"

He avoided her blazing gaze. She was getting restless again. If he could only win her trust. Her trust—or her fear.

He painfully admitted that it would have to be the latter. He stepped past her with that same heel-to-toe pace that he somehow knew terrified her. He stopped at the outside threshold of the room, and planted himself there with a stance that spoke domination.

"Brimstone Fortress is lost to the English, sweet." It killed him, but he spoke with deliberate coldness. "We have advanced hundreds of yards."

"No!"

It was filled with so much anguish Mast felt like he'd slashed her soul open. He also felt something slicing into his bottom lip. It was his own teeth.

He didn't dare turn to her. He did anyway.

"Oh, God. *Chérie,* do not cry. For God's sake, do not cry."

Bloody hell. She wept like she fought, with every inch of herself. Her body shook with violent, racking sobs as she drew her breath in deep, loud gulps.

What the blazes was he supposed to do? Mast hurried toward her, stopped, rushed a few more steps, and stopped again.

"Damn it, don't cry." It was his own voice and he knew it. Blast the accent, he swore. He wanted her to hear him. Blast the act. He sprung to her.

"Now, sweet—" He attempted something like tenderness, but it sounded more like watered mud. Mast felt as clumsy as a cow at a tea party. Indeed, her shoulders felt like fine porcelain beneath his cupped hands as he yearned to meld his strength into her. "Sweet, you've got to stop crying."

If he could only tell her who he was—why he was really here. Blast it to hell, why had he given his *word* to Wayland?

"You don't understand," she moaned. It was an awful sound, a dirge of heartbreak and grief. A sound Mast knew all too well.

He squeezed on the slender shoulders tighter. "I *do* understand, damn it."

But she was too far gone to hear him. "He's dead. I know it. Heroic fool. French bastards. Papa's dead and I'm alone."

"You're not alone!" He resorted to shaking her. "You have got to trust me. Look at me. And God in Heaven, stop crying!"

"Alone, alone," she chanted on, "I'm all alone—"

"You're not alone!"

"But aye, I am. So alone. So alone . . ."

Mast growled lowly through his teeth with frustration. He wanted to toss her out the window. He wanted to hurl her against the wall. He wanted to—

His arms slipped down her back before the thought was finished in his head. "Christ," he grated. "Oh Christ, sweet, don't make me do this."

Her singsong had become an incoherent babble as she fell further into her grief. She barely noticed as his finger slid beneath her chin and lifted it. He strained to douse the fire that surged through him at the feel of that soft curve, at the silken heat of her skin.

What the hell was possessing him to do this? She was his best friend's daughter . . . *the most precious thing in the world to me,* as Wayland had put it. There were other ways. Colder ways. Less dangerous ways.

But his other hand came up before he knew it, to explore the pain-twisted contours of her cheeks. So beautiful. But it wasn't a face made for sadness. It was a face made for—

With that, images painted themselves across his mind. Those gilt-fringed eyes, gazing up at him through a haze of pleasure. Those lush coral lips, parted and whispering words of welcome to him. That smooth swan's neck, arching back with each surge of his passion . . .

Mast jerked his head. Sweet Christ. He was falling into madness and delusion as quickly and completely as she. This had to end, damn it. It had to end now.

"This is for your own good, hellion."

He bent and took her lips.

He was determined to be bold and swift about it. Perhaps even brutal, if only to jolt her out of her hysteria.

But he was lost the second he tasted her. Her mouth was a sweet tang of strawberry and passion fruit, an ambrosia that nearly undid him with a strange and frightening hunger. She was so unsuspecting of him that it made her lips all the more yielding . . . and pliable. Her lips molded beneath his with a reactive, instinctual response of their own.

The returning pressure shook him off his axis, and set his senses crashing around him. Terror raced through him as he found his head losing the battle with his body's desire to deepen the kiss. She felt wonderful against him, wonderful and sleek and . . . totally untamed.

The shock vibrated through her body not a moment too soon. She pulled back from the kiss as roughly as he'd started it.

Her eyes snapped open. For a moment all she did was stare at him and breathe, that same panicked animal rhythm of hers. Mast's heartbeat drummed through his ears and he realized he was matching her breath for breath. He eased his hold at the same instant she bolted from it.

"What—on—earth—?"

It was exactly the reaction Mast had expected from her.

His traitorous body's throbbing, burning turmoil stole the breath from his lungs and gave it over to the terror churning in his gut. *Remind me to pay you back for this, Wayland,* he growled inwardly. *With something like a keelhauling from here to Africa.*

But before he could have that satisfaction there was one glaring, fuming hellion to deal with.

Ah, Christ. This voyage was going to be hell.

Two

A moment passed that felt like eternity. Golden couldn't get any more words past her lips; the ringing in her ears and the shivers still vibrating to her toes seemed to have seen to that. Great Goddess Erzulie, who was this supposed *enemy* who could touch his mouth to hers and make her feel as precious and vibrant as a jewel thrown into the sun? Who was this stranger who could intrude on her tears and turn them to liquid fire?

Blast him, anyhow! She'd taken particular pride in those hysterics; this performance was perhaps the best she'd achieved yet. Yet it was as if this French brute had seen straight through her. *Who was he?*

The possible answers terrified her. But she bravely stood her ground as the French swine gaped at her, up, down, then back up again. She fought the urge to return the scrutiny only because she couldn't take her eyes from his dark and mesmerizing face.

Tension worked in his jaw like rigging shifting beneath a taut, tanned canvas; his mouth was a tight slice through the middle. Above a nose seemingly held straight and prominent just for the expression, his eyes, deep and ominous, were of such an intense blue they reminded Golden of a place on the ocean she had rowed to with Guypa, who told her the unusual shading of the water meant that a fathomless pit lay below.

Strange, she thought. This Frenchman was very strange. He set her curiosity to a rapid simmer. And her suspicion.

His handsomeness was just the beginning. Aye, he was much too handsome—not dandied up in one of those powdered wigs they all seemed to wear. The waves of his ink black hair were terribly distracting, sweeping in that teasing way across his temples and around his ears. Then there was the way he moved. He was as graceful as a pacing panther, beginning to stalk before her, turning, then stalking again on long, tight-breeched legs neatly sheathed by high black boots. To finish it off, she'd noticed his sudden drop of the haughty French accent in favor of a more understandable, charmingly accented English for her.

It was then, as if the gods had given her a vision, that realization dawned on Golden.

Captain Swine was acting, too!

The conniving shark bait. Took her for a feather-headed ninny, did he? Thinking he could woo her allegiance simply with his intriguing looks and his play of innocence? She'd show him!

"M'sieur!"

The sharp-toned crack certainly got him to stop and look. Oh, she had to give his performance accolades. His expression was as compact and ominous as any real irritation she'd ever seen. For all she knew, that was part of his charade.

But she had to put this handsome worm in his place— quickly. The sunset was ready to part its deep red curtains to the night any moment; she would need every available moment of that blessed darkness to negotiate her escape out of here, then off Saint Kitts completely . . . and to Papa at last. To tell him firsthand what these horrid soldiers were doing to their home, and to see revenge taken upon the French bastards at last.

If it wasn't too late.

Her heart skipped a beat. No, she rebuked herself. It wasn't too late. Papa was safe. He promised he'd never leave her. And he'd never gone back on a promise, from the first time he swore King George would let him adopt her and through every minute of the three years hence. He was alive. She knew it.

"M'sieur." She even dared a step forward now, hoping to find the chink in that hard armor of an expression still staring down at her. "I have chosen to overlook that—that—" *what was that wet, whirling lip-touching thing?* "that intolerable liberty you dared take with me, but I will not overlook the flagrant injustice of this situation." She raised her chin, searching harder. Still no chink. "You, sir, will either cite the charges on which you summoned me here, or release me."

He answered with silence.

Curse the unnerving pismire back to the mud hole he came from. Golden dropped her eyes from his unnervingly calm face, searching for a respite in the front ties of his shirt. But that became an equally unsettling ordeal when her gaze tangled in the thick, curly, night black hair pushed up between the loose laces.

"What?" he finally said. Lowly. Accusingly.

"You—you heard me." Where had all the moisture in her throat gone? "Convict me or release me, Captain. It—it is ethics."

"Ethics?"

Golden couldn't believe it. The bastard laughed at her as he said it. He turned away and began to pace again. "Good God. A half-savage island wench preaching to me about ethics."

"I am not preaching! I am making you aware of the facts—"

"Ohhh. Now she's 'making me aware.' "

"Stop that."

"Stop what?"

"Talking as if I don't exist. As if I'm not right here."

One side of his mouth quirked up, but he didn't look at her. "Oh, little hellion, believe me. I know you're there."

"Stop that!"

"For God's sake, now what?"

"You're mocking me!"

He spun away again. Golden felt as insignificant as a mouse and doubly as helpless, standing there gazing at the muscles working in his high, broad back and thinking they looked like liquid steel.

This is an atrocity, she told herself—another jest in the long, cruel joke of this senseless Europower conflict. Why did anyone have to "rule" Saint Kitts at all? As if a crown of any size could ensnare the spirit of the islands . . .

She turned her gaze past the veranda, out to the hills of her home. The deep green slopes had bedded down for the night in a nightgown of lavender and blue shadow, nestled under a quilt of endless stars. Her soul went out to them. They were alike, these hills and her. Free, yet not free. Of one soul, yet of a million souls. Belonging to everyone . . . belonging to no one.

Oh, it was not worth raging about any more, she told herself. No amount of pain, of anger, was going to drive the French pigs away—or get her to Papa any sooner.

She set her mind to the problems she *could* figure out. Just when had she gotten careless enough to be caught? Or worse yet, who had betrayed her to these pigs? And how had she ended up at the mercy of the most towering, infuriating pig of them all?

The bastard himself broke into her thoughts as he suddenly pivoted back upon her. "My lady." The honorific form of address seemed too bloody gentle. Golden stepped back despite his courtly approach.

"I'm not mocking you," he told her. "I'm not laughing at you. I'm not trying to confuse you."

A breeze as soft as his voice made its way inside the room, whisping at the ends of his dark hair. Golden fumbled through her mind for words of defiance, but not a sound came. She thanked the heavens when the captain opened his mouth to say more.

But the words were slapped to a halt by an elflike man who sprang between them from nowhere, as if conjured there by a shaman's spell.

"Lord and rot it, Ive, if yer gonna take her, take her. Toss her over yer blazin' shoulder and let's get goin'!"

Golden jumped back. Primitive instincts of alarm added lightning points of adrenaline to her nerve endings. "Who are you? What's happening? Get going where?"

"Blast you, Dink." The captain's hand seemed to swallow the elf's shoulder as he whirled him to face her. "I was getting her to trust me, you fool. Now look at her. You think she's going to go quietly now? Do you?"

"What the hell difference does that make?"

"Use your head for once. I don't have the *Athena* hidden in that back cove for the scenery, damn it. You want her screaming for our heads with the whole island at our backs, or do you want her compliant and willing—"

"All right, all right. I get the bleedin' point."

"Compliant and willing?" Golden interceded. She cocked her head in perplexity. This French bastard wasn't acting like a French bastard any more. "What under the stars is going on here?"

And then her gaze locked with his. Golden's throat clutched as the dark blue depths reached out . . . and engulfed her.

"Dear God," she gasped. She began to look at him—truly look at him. Words crashed in on her . . . all the words of her childhood, the words of fable and folk tale, of fear and of hate. They collided with the image of the towering man before her, and the truth dawned like the first piercing shaft of a new sun.

"Compliant and willing," she heard herself repeat as if through a mist-filled tunnel. "Ship . . . hidden . . . back cove . . ."

"Now, sweet—"

"No! I'm not your sweet! And you're—you're not even French!" She backed away. Deep intuitions of danger pulled her into a low, circling crouch. "You're—you're—"

"My lady—" He continued to inch toward her. Long muscles tightened and tensed in his spread arms; big, rope-roughened hands prodded his way. "If you'll only listen—"

"Your eyes." Amazement raced through her with terrifying speed. "Your eyes. They're the color of midnight."

It all added up, Golden told herself. Lord, it was obvious! "And your hair . . ." The barely perceptible sheen of dark blue in the black waves was blinding now. Why—how—hadn't she figured it out sooner?

"Sky in his eyes, wind in his hair," she murmured incredulously. She knew the rhyme by heart, could recite it by rote since Guypa had taught it to her, so very long ago. "Catch the dark night beams, and you'll find him there—"

"Don't," he demanded tightly. "Lady Golden, this is not what you're thinking."

"He towers like the heavens, with the moon on his chin—"

He reached to the crescent-shaped scar like an ashamed youth covering a blemish. "Stop it."

"Moonstormer, Moonstormer—" She could only whisper the finish, "—the master of sin."

She inhaled a broken breath on a throat constricting with shock. "Oh, God. You're him, aren't you?"

"You're insane—"

"You're lying!"

The monster came closer, seeming to grow until he dominated the room. His stature pushed at the confines of Papa's study. Golden scrambled back and slid down against the wall. She crouched there, unable to move, or think.

It was the moment she'd waited for. She'd prayed fervently, on her knees each morning in the damp sand of the beach where Guypa had first found her. Every day she'd implored the spirits of the ocean to return the sea beast just once more to the scene of his evil, so she could avenge the fate he'd given her parents.

The spirits had been gracious. Her time had come.

And she couldn't move.

"Blarst it, Ive, look what ya've done now. She's gone to jellyfish goo."

"Be quiet, Dink. That's an order." He was still staring at her. Like a supernatural net coming out after her, those mysterious blue eyes reached out to engulf her. Then suddenly, he was looming closer over her.

"No!" Golden screamed. "Get away!"

"Golden—"

"Get away!" She struggled to the corner, where she battled to make sense of the turmoil in her head. The chaos. The confusion. *Mummy, Daddy, where are you? It's so hot, Mummy—come and get me, please . . ."*

Oh, God. It was happening all over again. She was drowning . . . drowning! The smudged linen shirt and gold-braided jacket became her earth and sky. A spiced masculine smell surrounded her. Hard legs pressed to either side of hers; through the haze of her lashes she peered at muscular thighs dwarfing her trembling ones. She scratched out at the monster, but the shackles rendered her powerless. Her lungs ached for air, but she couldn't breathe.

The Moonstormer was swallowing her whole!

Primal instinct overrode the last vestiges of civilized control in her head. With wild relief, Golden let it take over. She broke into a long, low growl from the deepest part of her. Heat blazed through her head as she focused the power to her eyes. Her sight darted everywhere and nowhere at once. All of the old intuitions were there, as if Guypa were teaching them to her all over again, whispering to her to suspend every thought and only feel . . . feel the power of her own senses.

Golden rocked backwards and her feet exploded into his chest.

After a curse, the wall of flesh fell away. Golden looked up. The Moonstormer flopped into the air like a wounded grasshopper. She almost felt sorry for him as she indulged in a tiny victory grin.

Her triumph was short-lived. The Moonstormer recovered from the fall with pantherlike moves. He rolled smoothly to regain his balance. This time he didn't hesitate in his approach. His face was dark and furious as he stalked toward her.

Golden watched him in awe. Great God Puntan. She'd anticipated his swiftness on those legs, but not such fluid, quiet agility.

She tried to disorient the beast by feigning the offensive.

A snarl fired off her lips and she punctuated it with a long, feline hiss.

But he didn't stop. "Temper, hellion," he drawled, yet the thunder of impatience was discernible behind the rain-soft tone.

"I'll kill you." Golden crept up the wall, all the while trying to keep her vulnerable shackled hands as far away from his reach as she could. "I swear by all the *zeme* spirits of earth and heaven, I'll kill you."

Again the Moonstormer said nothing. He merely continued matching her movements with his feral grace. Golden watched him, but tried not to look at his eyes, now shadowed to near black. She tried not to scan the form of his arms straining against his jacket as his tension mounted— tried not to feel the power harnessed beneath the smooth heel-to-toe rhythm of his step.

But her effort backlashed, for there was nothing left to look at but the foreboding white crescent that gleamed from his chin. The Moonstormer's mark seemed to pulse with her own heartbeat.

Her heartbeat grew so loud she didn't realize how close she'd gotten to Papa's bookshelf. She slammed into the side of the tall case, now trapped in the tiny corner it made against the wall. The Moonstormer gave a hint of a victory smile as he approached closer.

"Beast!" Golden cried. "You arrogant, heartless beast!"

His face flickered surprise—

Just before the rest of the world detonated.

Cannons blew, one after another, bellowing through the darkness. Golden's heart fell to her stomach as she thought of friends, of loved ones on the receiving end of those blasts.

But that noise was a drizzle measured against the downpour of chaos which ruptured through the walls around them. Gunfire rang. A door crashed in. Shouts roared and gruff voices barked out commands. Glass shattered, paintings were ripped; furniture toppled, soldiers on the floor below yelled in glee.

"Ive!" The elf appeared again, racing in from the veranda. "They're onto ya, kid—they're on but good. One of them is carryin' on about slashin' that jacket from you himself."

"What? How did they—" A look of blinding comprehension widened the Moonstormer's features. "Good God. The two idiots I let go—"

"They're totin' the hangin' rope."

"The morons actually went back to de Bouille."

"Can we make anon with the prattle, kid? You're outta time."

They were words of prophecy. The tumult grew, de Bouille's troops came pounding through the halls, and were closing in on the study. Golden looked furtively at the closed doors, then back to the Moonstormer's profile. What was she to do now? The chained weight pulling on her shoulders was reminder enough that she couldn't fight the Moonstormer and win—not the way she demanded to. And the French swine were the ones who'd shackled her like this to begin with.

Now more than ever, Papa was her only hope. Lord Wayland, Third Earl of Pemshire, King George's most trusted emissary in the Indies, would know what to do. She had to get to Papa!

Golden took a deep breath before daring a small step to the side. Another. She stole a furtive glance at the Moonstormer. Fates be thanked, a door crashed somewhere below, distracting him for a perfectly timed moment.

She whipped her gaze back to the veranda. Papa's beloved chinaberry tree curled lovingly against it much like a beckoning finger.

No more time to waste. She had to act. Now.

Great spirits help her. God help her. Anything in the heavens help her.

She shimmied over the veranda rail and began to slide down the fat branch, shackles and all.

Three

"Oh, Lord," she groaned, struggling to her feet.

The tree was now a foreboding tower over her head. The curving slope of the hillside—in addition to the stilts every house of the islands needed against the annual hurricane floods—made the veranda much higher than it had originally appeared.

Golden wouldn't forget that fact again. She hurt, everywhere. The shackles weighed heavily on her arms and cut into her wrists. Her arms and face stung from where the tree had lashed her. Most of all, her backside throbbed like a giant bruise, pumping pain down the lengths of her legs.

To make matters worse, a hearty break of wind had fallen over Saint Kitts along with the night. The damp blasts slapped Golden's hair to her face as she raced through the garden. She was nearly blind. Flaming poinciana petals and deep red Barbados lilies tangled around her heels. Flying debris pelted the rest of her body.

"Ive!"

Horror assailed her, as well. From the veranda behind her the elf's voice was sharp with astonishment and urgency.

"Ive, I found her. But jigger me, how'd she get—"

"Damn!" the deeper voice cut him off, resonating across the garden and through Golden like a flying spear. Her burning chest begged her to stop but she didn't dare. She flew over the brook that separated the manicured lawn from the dense rain forest as though her legs possessed a terror-inspired will of their own.

"Damn!" the Moonstormer exclaimed again. "That caballing little chit!"

"Those Frenchies have already torn apart the cellar and front hall. Our only chance is the back stairs."

"Let's go."

Golden bit back a sob. The back stairs! They'd be on her heels again in a minute! She dove into the thick underbrush, yet knew it was only a temporary safety. She had to get up and move again, but her determination was slipping fast, giving way to the pain, the fear, the exhaustion.

And then the touraco called.

It was the subtlest of sounds, a tentative little bird cry at best, but Golden rejoiced as if the king himself were being heralded. Her heart soared; her nerves came alive. Please, she implored to the heavenly powers just once more, let it come again.

The touraco trilled a repeat.

She smiled. Touracos didn't live on Saint Kitts.

Maya did.

Golden softly repeated the bird call.

Long, dark hands whipped aside the foliage behind her. A gleaming smile followed from the cinnamon-colored face Golden knew as that of her beloved tribal "sister" and life-long partner in mischief. The native maiden stepped forward, wielding a bright torch.

"Golden!"

"Oh, Maya, I've never been so happy to see you!"

But the broad white grin took a fast plunge as Maya caught sight of Golden's bound wrists. "By dee stars in da sky, sister! What dey do to you?"

"Explanations later. Do you have your skeleton key?"

"Do da leopard have spots?"

"Then hurry!" Golden held in her wince of pain as she pulled the chain between the shackles tight so Maya could get to the keyholes. "We've got to get out of here!" More crashing and French outcries from the mansion underlined the urgency of her appeal.

"But sister—" Maya's eyes became white circles of shock as she maneuvered the shackles free "You hurt! You arms as purple as dee marble rocks!"

"Ssssh!" Golden hissed it as loud as she could, while glancing back across the lawn. "He'll hear you."

"Who? Golden, who done dis awful thin' to you?"

"By the heavens, sister! I told you to be quiet."

Maya seemed to think that merely meant lowering her voice. *"Who* is going to hear me?" she rasped.

As if the question had been a magical chant to summon him, a familiar tower of a figure sprinted into the garden, jumping wind-toppled furniture with feline fluid ease. Golden cursed the breath her lungs wouldn't surrender with the sight of him. The man-panther stopped as gunshots erupted from the mansion. He stopped and whirled back. His hair was blowing in a dark tumult behind him, but he bolted forward again when a smaller shadow emerged unharmed.

"Get back to the ship and make ready to sail fast, Dink. I'll be there. *Soon.*" Then, looking directly at the spot where she and Maya crouched, "Lady Golden! For Christ's sake, it's dangerous out here!"

"Dear God," she heard herself groan.

"Golll-dennn." Maya's unquenched interest permeated her voice. "Who is he?"

Just thinking of the answer made Golden shrink further

back. Confusion and terror and a whirlwind of other un-
nameable feelings welled up inside her until, before she
realized it, she gasped, "The Moonstormer. He's the Moonstormer, Maya."

"The Moonstormer!"

"Sssshh!"

"My stars, the Moonst—"

"Lady Golden! I'm coming in there if you're not coming
out!"

"Oh, God!" Golden cried.

She yanked Maya and the torch up as she bolted deeper
into the rain forest. At a frenzied run they plunged through
vines and ferns and overhanging flowers. Over slippery
moss and through foot-sucking mud, they jumped fallen
logs and angrily cackling night creatures. Golden willed
herself to keep moving—anything to distance the demon
now onto her scent.

Just when she thought her legs would break off with another step she spotted the silhouette of the rope bridge
through the trees ahead. The forest ended on the other side
of the crossing, then it was just a scramble down the cliffs
beyond to the beach. To freedom at last. Freedom and Papa.

They stopped on the small rise where the bridge began.
Golden heard the gulp in Maya's throat coincide with the
one in her own as they looked across the long expanse of
intertwined vines, ropes, and wood. The bridge swayed back
and forth on the wind like a taunting fiend from a child's
bad dream, the creak of the suspended floorboards supply-
ing the ogre's foreboding howl. But thirty feet below was
the true nightmare. Inescapable rapids became a plummeting waterfall onto razor-edged rocks.

But Golden would rather take her chances on Barbe's

Falls than consider what fate awaited her with the gunfire that echoed through the trees.

"Those soldiers comin' this way!" Maya exclaimed. "And dey gettin' closer!"

"They're following him," Golden replied in a whisper. "And he's getting closer."

Getting closer . . . going to get you . . . the Moon-stormer's coming . . .

She whirled back to the bridge. "We have to get away. We have to do it now."

"Sister, no!" Maya exclaimed. "We go dee other way, through dee cane field!"

"No. Too long. It'll take too long. He's almost here." Golden looked down at the bridge's boards as she said it, but she didn't really see the swaying planks. They were of another world now. Danger that no longer meant anything. All that mattered was escaping the doom of that midnight dark gaze—the way those bottomless eyes probed her for every vulnerability. That demon knew her every secret, forbidden feeling.

"Don't you hear him?" she cried, hurrying out onto the bridge. "We have to get away, Maya, now!"

The wind rushed down from the heart of the forest, moaning around Golden, jeering at her with its eerie tune while it played havoc with the ropes beneath her hands. But she clenched her teeth at the enemy and held on, dragging one foot in front of the other, then another, until the crashing of the surf beyond the cliffs began to drown out the cry of the wind, and freedom was a glorious handful of steps away.

Maya's shriek brought her head snapping up.

Golden would have matched the outcry of terror, but the

air left her lungs at the same moment her stomach dropped
to her toes.

There on the embankment ahead of her, hands on hips
and legs braced wide, the dark embodiment of her nightmares stood waiting.

"You idiot," Mast growled. "You're going to get yourself
killed!"

"Go away!" she snarled back, though Mast caught the
tremble of her chin as she did. For the love of Christ, he'd
never met anyone, much less a blasted woman, so determined, so reckless.

So insane.

"Sweet." He forced a calmness he didn't feel to his voice.
"If those French bastards don't get you, this farce of a
bridge will!"

"Anyone—anything—but you!"

"Listen, you impudent little—"

"Go to hell!"

Her words wrenched. Mast swore at the feeling as if it
were a sucker on his senses. He was rationalizing with himself as he had done just thirty minutes ago inside the mansion, pushing off concern for her exhaustion and her
bruises . . . and the fact that he somehow needed to get
this creature to her father in one piece. No thanks to the
exasperating chit herself, thank you very much.

"Blast it," he hissed, as much to that strange new feeling
as to her. "This has gone far enough, witch. Come here
and let me talk to you like a civilized human being. If you
know what that means."

But the demand was like a fire under her kindling. In an
instant she spun on the rickety bridge and dashed back toward the other side—without a care. Before Mast could

think or move she stepped on an older board too hard. Down it, and through it.

"Golll-dennn!" the Carib screamed.

Golden's own startled wail pierced the air as she plummeted between the slats. She was at the last moment before certain doom when her arms snapped out and locked around a thick board to her side.

Mast regained his breath in an exhilarating rush.

And expelled it furiously. "Stay still!" He spared no harshness on the command. "Don't brook me on this, woman. Just do it."

The topaz stare turned and riveted to him with wide, frightened intensity. Mast tore his eyes away from the fatally glittering depths, only to notice the exhaustion already trembling through her arms.

He tentatively stepped onto the bridge. He damned the insanity of tender emotion that again threatened to overcome him. *Useless frippery. Irrational nonsense. Throw the chit into the brine and be done with it, for God's sake.*

"Sweet." Again, he wanted to cut his vocal cords out with the gentle tone which seemed lodged in them. But Golden had dropped her head as if the rushing water below appeared more inviting every second. "Hang on," he stressed. "Grip the board with all your strength and don't let go. Just hang on!"

She raised her head. Mast dared a step forward as their gazes connected—and melded. Was that uncertain amber shimmer the light of acceptance?

"I told you to go to hell, Moonstormer."

Definitely not acceptance.

"Damn it," he snapped. "I'm not going to hurt you!"

But even if she'd believed him, it was too late. A cacophony of high-pitched howls erupted from the forest and before Mast knew what was happening a gang of half-naked natives followed their war cries. Golden raised her head and returned the animalistic yowl. Mast's gut twisted just like the first time he'd heard that otherworldly sound, on the veranda at the mansion. Some untethered instinct had risen in him at that moment; a primal longing to protect . . . and possess.

He ran down the bridge for her.

He never saw which board double-crossed him, but he sure as hell remembered the pain as his leg fell farther and farther through the hole, until—

"Ah, God."

He witnessed the ensuing scene like a faraway nightmare through the blood that hammered in his ears and the agony that roared through his suddenly crunched groin.

He remembered a collective whoop of victory going up as she was lifted and passed, literally, over a chain of dark brown flesh that extended down the bridge to her. Hands and arms cradled her and fawned over her. Singsong voices chanted like she was a precious ceremonial offering cup.

Or a living goddess.

The second she'd landed back on the embankment, the human rescue line coiled back with a grace that under other circumstances would have impressed him. Mast fleetingly wondered if any of them could be enticed to join the *Athena*'s crew before he pulled his leg back through the jagged hole and pain cut off his thoughts.

The night shadows blended with the mass of mahogany-skinned bodies on the bank. He peered harder into the darkness, seeking only one glint of amber sunshine in the blur of greys, browns, and blacks. But it was as if she'd melted into their midst.

"Bring her back!"

The words cut through the forest and across the sugar-cane field, where they stopped Golden in her tracks. The Moonstormer's command had the same muscle-clenching effect as before. She froze, movement as dim a concept as rational thought, her mind held prisoner on one side by hatred, and fear; on the other by perplexing awakenings in her body and soul . . . by memories of long masculine legs in black boots, of those legs pressed against hers, searing a new kind of heat through the core of her body as warm lips demanded her breath from her mouth . . .

"Oh, Moonstormer," she uttered across the whipping green stalks, "what kind of a spell did you woo over me?"

"Lady Golden!" came his thundering bellow on the wind again.

"Oh, my goodness," came Maya's frightened outcry next to her. "Sister, you got to move!"

Still Golden couldn't force her body into motion. Confusion whirled through her like the trade winds that whipped around her. She wanted to stand and face the murdering beast. Nay, she couldn't. To confront the hard, merciless judgment of that spread-legged stance again . . . the blue-black power of those eyes . . .

Oh Papa. Papa, I need you so. You'd know what to do.

"Sister!" Maya reprimanded. "What now?"

"I must get to Papa. As soon as I can. I must go. Now."

"Papa?!" the Carib railed. "You be a ninny, girl? Golden, look at da sky! Look at dee clouds and dee wind! There be a storm comin' in! The French, dey all around the island like bees to honey." The native wagged a disapproving finger at her. "And girl, you *not* dey favorite flavor of honey right now."

"Bosh," Golden huffed, stepping around Maya determinedly. "A few supply boats, Maya. So I burned the swine out of some new blankets and a few kegs of ale."

"Ah. I believe you. That's why dey lock you up in chains until you turn blue in dee fingers, ah?"

"Enough," Golden countermanded as they reached the rise where the field sloped and gave way to the full wind and embracing salt air of a wide, white beach. From here she fully surveyed the tumult from which they'd come. To the right, near the rock grotto, the torches of the tribe's warriors darted through the night like earthbound comets. The lanterns of the pursuing French militia formed their flickering backdrop. Guns crackled; birds cawed and rodents scattered; and above it all the Arawak cries grew higher and more threatening across the wind-whipped island.

It was odd, Golden knew, but it was suddenly the most comforting sight in the world to her. Her people were there for her again. Once more, when the rest of the world threatened to break them apart like something no more lasting than a loaf of bread, these people she didn't share a drop of blood with became more her family than any in her native England could.

"My mind is decided," Golden said gently to Maya. "As you well said, sister, the French are everywhere. And the Moonstormer will not leave here until I do. Stop glaring at me like that, it's true. I don't know how I know it, but I do. You're all in danger because of me."

"You shush. Shush right now," Maya commanded. "Golden, it is simple. The boat, it cannot go in the waves. Look. Dey gettin' bigger! Dey'll roll you over like a turtle on dee sand!"

Golden gave her sister a sideways glance and a half smile. "Who said anything about a boat?"

Maya choked. Then gasped. "By the mighty Agwe! You not goin' to call that dolphin *now!*"

Golden's reply was four high-pitched squeals that emanated from the deepest part of her. She repeated the sequence as she walked down the hill toward the water, shutting her eyes and letting the sound of the sea envelop her, call to her as she called to it . . .

"Golden, dis is crazy!"

"Ssshhh. I have to hear him over the waves."

"There nothin' to hear! That porpoise won't come in these waves!" Maya crossed her arms against herself.

"No. He'll come. He always comes when I call."

"You'll never make it!" Now it was a dread-filled plea.

"Pig's posh." Golden kicked at the water in angry punctuation. "Nirvana is an excellent swimmer. You know that."

"Fool. Not dat good. The Bahamas are many suns an' moons away."

Golden knew she wasn't helping matters by laughing, but she couldn't help it. "Oh Maya, I'm asking my friend for a favor, not a death pact. We'll go to Nevis for the night. Look—it's so close you can see Powell's Hill from here. In the morning, I'll find passage to Nassau from there."

"I still don't like it. Not a bit."

A riot of faraway squeaks cut Maya's words short—her fears went soaring. Maya followed the line of Golden's sight out just beyond the wave break. Sure enough, a gleaming, light grey snout bobbed in the current there.

"By the moon an' dee stars," Maya whispered.

"I told you he'd come." Golden's eyes were radiant, her smile even more so. She ran into the water as if she were merely frolicking in a pond. Maya looked on with an expression she tried to keep disapproving, but as she watched the waves frame Golden, she knew it was a more fitting picture of her sister than any haughty white man painter could ever capture, no matter how fine the gown or lovely the canvas, and she smiled.

"Well, don't be gloatin' aboot it," she called. "Go, sister . . . go."

"Run Maya, *run!*"

But Golden could see that Maya didn't hear her horrified scream. The warning was lost in the pounding crash of a wave against the rock formations close to the shore.

Golden could only watch helplessly as he came further down the sand, his white shirt billowing in the wind, his powerfully honed legs assured and steady as they stalked in long strides. She watched in helpless horror as the Moonstormer turned his bloodlust on her sister.

Four

If he lived to be a hundred, Mast would never forget Golden's scream. Wild, intense, unnatural—he knew it could only be from the lungs of Wayland's heathen-goddess of a daughter.

But the only one standing on the shore was the nervously pacing native girl. He made his way toward the maiden. Panic was a foreign and frightening companion across the wind-whipped sand.

The wail came again, even more piercing and strident. This time, the sound froze him in his tracks.

It couldn't be. He warred with himself, denying seldom-wrong intuitions. It was impossible. Ridiculous. A dangerous manifestation of his exhausted senses.

But he'd no sooner hurled the idea away than the Indian whipped her head toward the roiling sea—confirming all his shocking suspicions in one moment.

That unmistakable cry had come from those man-smashing, eight-foot-high waves.

"By the Almighty." He'd remember the dread beneath his murmured words forever. "Golden!" The despair when nothing responded but the crashing surf.

"Dear God." He dropped his head, watching the tendons of his arms as they powered his coiled fists. "Dear Jesus God."

Dread so inundated him, Mast didn't hear the angry shouts until they were perilously close upon him.

"Imposteur!"

"Lyeeng bastard!"

"Kill heem!"

Each was punctuated with the crack of a gunshot. De Bouille and his men.

Mast deliberated which course to take, but the Indian maid's scream decided that in a swift second. He ran for her. She bolted away just as quickly, eyes wide with terror.

He caught her elbow just in time. She shrieked again, writhing like a hooked fish in its death throes. Mast ignored her flailing. He hauled the girl close, then dived with her as the deadly points of lead whizzed over their heads. "It's all right," he told her as loudly as he dared while pulling her to the shelter of the trees. Despite his reassurances, she never stopped screaming.

They were both breathing hard when they reached the foliage. The native's eyes glowed huge and white at him. "You," she stammered, gulping deeply. Mast's throat burned as he remembered her "sister" doing the same thing. "You saved my life, Moonstormer," she murmured in awe. "Maya is forever in your debt. Maya must—"

"No. No, there's no time. Just tell me where she went." He gripped her shoulders. *"Please,* Maya, just tell me she didn't—" He jerked his head free of the gnawing, despised thought. "Where did she go, Maya?" he demanded through tight teeth. *"Where?"*

In reply he received another scream, as the gunfire streaked twenty feet closer. With a grunt Mast shoved Maya into the thick foliage. "Run!" he ordered. He did the same in the opposite direction. Bullets went whirring past his ears as he sprinted up a familiar hill, across a jagged crest of rocks. He paused only a second before arrowing his body down the twenty-five-foot drop into the lagoon where the *Athena* lay in full-rigged splendor.

He patted a quick check of his body as he flung himself over the top rail of his ship to a rousing cheer of welcome from his crew. Divine intervention alone seemed to have kept even a shard of the French bullet barrage from catching up with him. His men agreed. Cries of "lucky bugger!" and "kissed by the bleedin' leprechauns!" punched the air.

Until the cannon boomed from the shore.

The ball gave an eerily loud plunk as it came down just right of the starboard bow.

"Sweet Jesu!" Rico swore. Mast's burly South American boatswain grabbed the wooden rosary hanging from his neck and crossed himself with it.

"They be a little riled, aye, Cap'n?" A withered, but kind-eyed face leaned forward and beamed a crooked leer at Mast.

"Yes, Ben. They're rather upset."

Mast turned to everyone then, calling to even the farthest reaches of the two-hundred-foot brigantine. "Hoist away! Secure the hold; steady man at the helm. Ben, pack those guns well." He ran a hand over the remaining water on his face and hair as he strode beneath a jungle of ropes and pulleys, while adding over his shoulder, "But I don't think we're going to require them."

"What?" Robert yelled incredulously. The *Athena*'s master gunner could be taken for a cannon himself. He was lumbering his huge frame across the bustling deck. "Mast, you wanna take another look at that shore? They're not invitin' us to a picnic!"

In direct contrast to the big man's tirade Dink popped up, offering a fresh shirt with the leisurely gesture of a

London tailor. "Welcome home." He smirked knowingly. "Where's the wench?"

"We're setting sail, Robert." Mast waved away the shirt. He scooped up a long glass and peered through it for an updated assessment of the force on the beach. "As expeditiously as possible." *And never coming back. Never.*

"Ive, where's the wench?"

Robert's wave at Dinky was more forceful. "But we can rout them! Easily! Mast, what the hell are you thinking?"

Mast whirled then, glaring his master gunner to silence. "Robert." His voice was equally intense, yet low with the tight rein of leadership. "I have my reasons."

Reasons. Poseidon's blood, reasons. Mast swallowed hard as he finally took the dry shirt from Dink, nearly punching his arms into the sleeves as *she* came to life in his mind again. Snarling at him. Cursing him. Staring at him in that unthinking, vulnerable way. Wildness and freedom, ivory and topaz, texture upon texture of that beauty which seemed to well and glow from the inside out . . .

"Mast . . . Mast! Damn it, I'm talkin' at you!" Wood chips flew from the rail Robert punched into. "God's codfish, where'd you chop your head off and leave it?"

"Asked the same thing afore he went off with the wench," Dinky said caustically. Mast shot a dark look at him. Dink returned it with an innocent shrug.

"The wench?" Robert swung his head between the two of them, but concentrated his incredulously cocked eyebrow on Mast. "You had a wench? Why?"

"That's what I'm tryin' ta figure."

Dink's quip was the knife that finally cut Mast loose. Abandoning his battle with the ties of his shirt, he stomped forward and pounded a gut-blasting glare into his first mate.

"Mr. Peabrooke." His lips barely moved and his throat

twisted painfully from the pressure of keeping the words
composed. "I don't want to talk about the *lady* any more.
I don't want to hear another word about her. I don't even
want her whispered about on the decks of this vessel. The
lady is gone. That is that. Understood?"

Dinky's scowl said he didn't. "Gone?"

"Yes, damn it, gone!" When he repeated the word something snapped inside him. He couldn't tamp the burning fury
any longer. His hands coiled into Dink's shirt as the sick
dizziness surged in his gut . . . as Wayland's grief-stricken
face loomed in his mind. "Gone," he snarled. He swallowed
as he forced himself to say the next word. *"Dead.* Do you
understand now?"

His hands shook as he released Dinky. Then he turned.
He didn't feel worthy of any human contact. Silence fell
like the first heavy raindrops that spattered upon the deck.

"Blimey," Robert cursed.

"Christ, Ive," Dinky muttered. He squirmed uneasily, at
a loss for anything to say to his friend. He had sensed something askew about the kid since the moment Mast came
back aboard. That spitfire of a wench had done something
crazy to Mast—but just what, Dinky supposed, was going
to be as impossible to figure as the direction of tomorrow's
wind.

He wasn't quite sure if he wanted to try, either.

But suddenly the dark wet head jerked up—and the Mast
Iverson he knew was back again, full force, and full fury.

"Let's get out of this hell hole," his captain bellowed,
breaking a determined stride across the deck. "Tighten the
jibs and secure the topsails. I have a feeling this storm will
surprise us. And Ramses, Dack—" he whipped back around
just before leaping to the quarterdeck, "give those bastards
a few good rounds as a going away present."

The crew let up an approving cheer, Robert's howl at its crescendo. The *Athena* was off with a fury of wind and a blaze of glory.

Glorious, Golden thought, everything was finally glorious. She couldn't believe the French had arrived to save Maya from the Moonstormer, but just before Nirvana turned and she'd lost sight of the shore, that was indeed what the swine seemed to be doing. She just hoped they didn't kill the monster. Nay, she wanted that delight for herself, when she returned with Papa and the glory of the English Navy. She hoped the French would chase him and his long legs just far enough for him to hide in some cave, where he'd have to starve for a good fortnight or two before she returned to finish him off. Not that she'd taken particular notice of his legs.

Thankfully, Nirvana's squeal cut off those unnerving thoughts. Golden eeked happily in answer, and smiled, feeling free and strong and invincible again. Even her body didn't throb and ache so much any more. The ocean currents were cleansing and invigorating her as she and her friend sped closer to Nevis—and the first step to finally reaching Papa.

Aye, everything was glorious. Nirvana was the most magnificent dolphin in the sea, sleek and graceful and swift, as he carried her along through the cool water. They were invincible!

"Storm?" Golden laughed to her porpoise friend. "Oh, Nirvana, if Maya could only see how we've conquered her little storm!"

The first wave didn't throw them off as much as the second, third, and fourth that followed it. The wind frothed the water over them, pounding them from every direction at once. The waves churned right, left, then backward and forward. The mighty Agwe was stirring an angry stew tonight. It was after her tenth gulp of water that Golden fearfully realized that she was part of the recipe.

"I can't see a thing," she cried, blinking back the lash of saltwater on her face. Nirvana wasn't answering her now; she knew he was drawing on dwindling reserves to keep her afloat . . . and alive.

"My friend, I believe we are lost."

A deafening roar sounded to her right. Golden looked up. There was nothing but water—a wall of it, collapsing straight toward them.

She heard somebody screaming. She thought it curious, as the blackness came in to engulf her, that a pair of deep blue eyes would suddenly appear in her consciousness . . .

And warm her so.

"She's a hot one, all right."

Rico bellowed over the din of the waves as he and Mast struggled at the wheel, guiding the *Athena* clear of the Narrows, the aptly named strait separating the islands of Saint Kitts and Nevis.

"Aye," Mast called back, and left it at that. Talk was the last thing on his mind. His thoughts were as chaotic as the waters. Every detail of the ship demanded his attention.

Every detail of her face demanded his remembrance.

"Fasten down those buntlines on thee staysail!" he yelled, glancing at Dack wrapped around the mainmast, and instantly remembering *her* body wrapped around that fat tree branch as she'd actually dared the impossible, escaping the way she did. He cursed at himself and directed his attention forward, only to be assaulted by the brave face of the fig-urehead on his bow. Her bold breasts jutted into the tempest, as the lithe curves beneath her carved gown guided them through the broil.

His Athena, he thought. His goddess. Gone.

His fault.

Christ, Wayland. She just disappeared. She was running from me and she threw herself into those breakers and she disappeared and I'm sorry—I'm so sorry—

He wished he were one of those blasted waves now. Then he'd bash something as hard as the tempest beating his hull.

"Call Ben up!" he shouted to Rico, stepping out from the wheel. His body clamored for motion—for furious en-ergy—for escape from the sight of that proud wood figure he seemed certain would turn to flesh any moment now.

He traded places with his grizzled gunner's mate and gave him a sound slap on the back. Rico and Ben grinned wickedly at each other and set to their task, both welcoming the challenge of a feisty sea as much as a good battle. Knowing the helm was in capable hands, Mast left the two men and jumped into the vigorous distraction of the activity on the main deck.

His men nodded in respect and appreciation when he jumped into their midst. Every face and body was as wet as his. They bent to the spokes of the revolving capstan at his order, racing together to bring down the two topsails before the force of the gale did. The *Athena* bucked beneath them, pitching the deck nearly vertical at times. His crew slid and scurried around him and soon Mast was calling out orders every minute, as well as trying to help.

He was hoisting a tub of water over the port rail when the gleaming fleck appeared on the waves below.

He flung his head away, struggling for air. His gut rose

to his throat in the space of a breath. There was no way it could be real . . . not now. Not in this fury of a storm.

He was overtired, he reasoned to himself. He was letting his exhaustion play tricks on him, letting his misery and guilt conjure the blazing gold vision out on the rocking sea. He just wouldn't look that way again.

The lad Dack staggered up with a fresh tub of bilge. Mast reached and helped him toss it over.

"Good God."

"Ex—excuse me, Captain?"

"It got closer."

"Captain?" the youth repeated in an unsure voice.

"It got closer."

"Ive?" came the more confident tone of his first mate. "What is it?" Dink asked. "Blarmy, what's pulled yer eyes outta yer skull like that?"

But Mast didn't reply, now bending farther over the rail and squinting into the rain, not believing his eyes—yearning to believe his eyes.

"Ive, what the hell is it?"

Still not answering, Mast left Dack and Dinky standing there peering into the darkness while he pushed himself back inside the ship's rail.

"Rico!"

Heads shot up across the deck at the power of it. Eyebrows followed in due course at the force of their captain's stride.

"Two degrees port, Mr. Sanchez."

"What?" The South American's voice cracked with shock despite its booming volume.

"Mast!" Robert seconded the protest with a shout from the main deck, "We're in the middle of a bloody chaos!"

"I'm aware of that, Master Gunner. Two degrees, Rico. Port."

"Captain!"

"Now!"

His crew traded wondering glances with each other as he pounded back through them to the rail. " 'Od's blood," someone mumbled. "Somethin's lit Mast's fire."

"Lit it but good," another replied.

"Something over that rail," said another.

The curiosity climaxed to torment. They surged as one to the port rail.

They choked as one when they saw it.

The mass of hair was the first thing to catch the eye. It gleamed even against the inky water—a flash of light framing a delicate, but otherwise undiscernible face. Closer study revealed the long and slender arms, stretched out over the waves like a bird's against the sky. It was a beautiful sight for its grace alone.

But then came the fins. Sleek, just like the creature's arms, shiny and strong as they lifted for a terrible second of recognition, then fluidly slipped back beneath the waves.

The seamen traded looks of question and terror. Each face only confirmed the horrifying answer.

La Sirène.

They turned as one to their captain. Mast was several feet aft, quickly tossing rope into the longboat. The biggest of the group, Rico, the boatswain, walked forward and placed a foot on the opposite edge of the ten-man sloop.

"Captain—"

Mast looked up. His brow furrowed. Rico's normally robust and round face looked pinched and agitated; the balance of the men behind him looked no better. Their thoughts were clear. He'd become possessed, or worse. The wild thought swept into Mast's mind that he quite possibly agreed with them.

"Rico," he said. "Good. I'll need your help to pull her in."

"Nay, Captain."

Mast stopped. He turned, still in a crouch over the oar box. The wind slapped his hair into his face. "What?"

His crew moved around the big man to signify their support. Rico folded his arms across his chest, folding the flesh there in two. "I'm not goin' out there, Captain, and neither are you."

Mast's eyes snapped to the others. "Blast it. There's more at stake here than all of you think!"

"Captain, do you not see?" Dack blurted. The young man rushed forward, impassioned enough to fight the restraints of the others. "By the blood of the saints, *look* out there. It's *La Sirène!*"

"The bitch'll eat ya alive, Mast!" someone else followed.

Mast blinked at them, and blinked again. After a long moment, the meaning of their looks and their warnings finally sank in. He laughed with the incredulity that struck him. "For God's sake. You all believe this, don't you?"

"But Captain, it's true." Dack all but climbed into the longboat as he emphasized with urgent hand motions. "Please listen! I didn't believe it myself, you know the good book tells us not to; but it's her. Legs on land, fins at sea, so the legend says. You can see her fins out there, can't you? And beautiful, they say. Like a carved madonna. Traps poor sailors with her face and then eats them. Eats them alive, Captain. Arms and legs and all."

"Dack, stop it."

"But it's legend, Captain. The legend says—"

"For Christ's sake, stop it!"

He climbed out of the longboat and pounded across the deck. Even Rico moved back as Mast came at the group of them, eyes burning with fury.

"Legend," Mast gritted lowly. "I suppose you all believe in the snow fairy and the Sherwood Forest phantoms, too. And I've no doubt you go to sleep nights worrying about the Moonstormer!"

He shoved through them like a storm in his own right. He marched straight to one of the *Athena*'s cannons and leapt atop it.

"Here's what I think of your bloody legend," he called.

He paced to the lip of the cannon. Before any of them could stop him, Mast dove off the gun and into the tempest.

Five

"A dolphin!"

Mast hoped repeating it would dim the amazement. It didn't.

He blinked at the slashing rain that drove into his face; shook his head to confirm he hadn't gone unconscious somehow and was only dreaming the sight.

Yet there before him in the frothing tempest was a soaked and unconscious Lady Golden—draped over the back of a god-blasted dolphin.

Six thousand, Mast thought furiously. He should be getting *six* thousand pounds for this absurdity of a commission.

Despite his frustration and the turbulence of the waves, Mast approached the animal as gently as he could. The dolphin was depleted of all energy, the alarmed glare to its eye the sole display of any resistance it could muster. Surprisingly, Mast found himself taken back for a moment as he matched stares with the graceful sea creature.

"Easy." He placed a hand to the slippery grey flesh. "She's going to be safe. You've done the lady well, my friend."

The dolphin clickered weakly in reply as Mast moved to inspect Golden. He clamped down the bitter burn to his throat as he pushed back her hair. He saw her face, her features, but there the similarity to the blazing savage he'd known on the island ended. Her spun gold hair was now strings of dull and matted yarn, plastered to shoulders that barely supported her soaked clothes. And her skin . . . he tried not to think about her grey, clammy skin. Mast had forced himself a long time ago to will away the memories of that distant Irish morning until they no longer stabbed his chest in two.

"Ye piss-headed brat. I told ye to move away from her, di' I not? Ye mum's dead, brat. Dead! Lookit her bloomin' face, blast ye. Grey like that means just one bloody thing. Aye, she's gone, well enough . . ."

"No!"

It was a moment before he recognized his own pain-filled bellow. His body responded in kind. Another will seemed to take over. He fiercely hauled the pale girl from the dolphin. He locked her against his chest before lunging into the first painful stroke that would take them back to the nebulous hulk on the horizon that was the *Athena*.

It was an agonizing forever before the hulk took on the definitions of rigging, masts, and stays. Mast forced himself to ignore the screams of protest his limbs assailed him with, concentrating instead on the shadows of his men as they valiantly held the brig steady in the tempest. Almost there, he told himself through the wall of exhaustion.

The attack came without any warning. The wall of water conquered him from behind, pummeling around him, roaring through him. In a burst, the world was turmoil, confusion, stinging salt and tears as Mast and the lifeless body in his arms careened further down into the churning tumult.

Just when he was certain they were in the pit of hell or damn close to it, his head broke the surface again. He gratefully gulped air while jerking Golden up by the only thing he could secure his hand to—her hair. Muttering some kind of an inane apology, he pulled her up until her chilled cheek pressed next to his.

With his free arm he struggled for balance, clawing out at the darkness that had taken over the horizon, the sky, everything. He whipped his head upward, trying to determine, in this forsaken blackness, which way was up.

His hand flung against wood. Wood strung with rope.

Poseidon's teeth. He was at his own front gate.

Mast fought back the tremors of his arm as he pulled himself and Golden and all three hundred pounds of the water they'd soaked up onto the first rung of the *Athena's* rope ladder. He stopped, hanging there, gasping in the dank smell of the tar and the wood, feeling his body shake joyously with the thundering pace of his heartbeat.

"All right, sweet," he grated into the clammy skin next to him, "now it's your turn."

Nothing.

"Breathe, goddamn it."

Nothing.

"I ordered you to breathe!"

It was then that he felt it. He crushed her body tighter to him, and felt it again to be certain. There was warmth beneath her skin. Just a tiny ember of life, of hope, but it was there.

Mast pulled away a few inches and stared at the woman in the crook of his arm. The unintelligible ache came over him again, the same pain that had assaulted him when she'd wept in his arms on the island. Only this time, he didn't fight it. The pain was strangely empowering, he realized, throbbing through him with a drive he'd never felt before.

He threw his head back and yelled with all the magnificent strength of that ache. "Dink!"

A line of faces popped into place across the rail above him.

"Ive! Crimey, you idiot, we thought you'd done and—"

"Yes, I know, Mr. Peabrooke. Now make ready. Cargo coming aboard."

"Cargo comin' aboard?"

His first mate's repeat lilted with incredulity. Mast was still too far down on the ladder to hear the exact things to follow, but a lantern was swung over the rail in swift time, accompanied by Dink's low whistle of amazement.

"Blarst me eyes. You got her."

"You thought I'd be back else?" He climbed up the last rungs with renewed vigor.

He'd never been so happy to see the top rail of his ship. Torrents of water dripped from them while ascending the ladder, but his limp little hellion refused to wake up. Mast made stops to look at her, to feel her, to assure himself the increasing warmth to her skin wasn't a trick of his exhausted mind. By the time he got to the top, visions of hot stew and dry clothes started to invade his senses.

But as he flipped over the rail with Golden in one final grunt and heave, Mast saw that the ordeal had just begun.

His crew awaited him with the lust of a hanging mob.

Their resentment hung thicker than the light rain which still hung in the air. He could feel it with each labored breath, as he crashed to the deck and helped Dink tow in the ladder.

Then he slowly rose to his feet. Despite the fatigue which racked him with each stiff move, Mast honored his men with a direct, serious stance.

Even so, he refused to release Golden. With every movement he kept her to him. He cradled her in his arms, gathering her as close as he could without betraying his burning desire to sweep her close, until she snarled at him to stop smothering her. For now he had to settle for tightening his grip and hoping it warded away the wind and the rain—and the lethal lung infections they could bring—just a while longer.

"Captain."

Rico was once again the first to step forward. This time Dack was with him, but the younger sailor cowered behind the South American like a calf at its mama's udder.

"Captain, we're—we're glad you're safe 'n' all, but—" Rico faltered in his obviously rehearsed speech. The big sailor's eyes kept flitting back to Golden. His composure was waning as he discovered some new proof of mortality with each glance: the blue tint of her fingertips, the chattering of her teeth, the tiny shivers starting to tremble through her. "Oh . . . Captain, it's like this—"

"You noddy, you've floundered it to high hell." With that Dack shoved Rico away. His voice was high with rising hysterics and his limbs were visibly shaking. "This is it, Captain," he shrilled. "You're a fool. Do you hear me? A fool! We don't want the witch here, Captain! She's trouble. Trouble! Did you stop to think she might have even cursed us already? Which hex will she give us, Captain? Scurvy? Plague? Pox? They say your member can fall off with the pox."

"Oh, for Christ's sake," Mast growled. "Dack—"

But the youth was already charging at him, eyes gleaming as bright as the rosary he whipped out and waved in front of Golden's inert face. "We cast you away, sea witch! Away, do you hear? Back to your witch's brew! Back, back!"

"Dack!" Rico shouted. "Lad, you've given to mush!"

"Look at her!" Mast thundered at the surrounding crewmen, gambling on the perplexity and misunderstanding he saw creeping over their faces. "Look at her, all of you. Oh aye men, here's your deadly sea witch. I wager she'll tear the ship to splinters with her blue fingers and toes. Tell me, has anyone here ever witnessed an unconscious witch casting a spell over a ship?"

A round of uncomfortable chuckles answered him.

"Quiet," Dack broke out in a hiss. "Quiet. She wakens!"

"She what?" Mast dropped to one knee and leaned over her face. "Golden?" He knew the crew could hear every inflection of tenderness in his query. For some reason, he didn't care.

But it was another matter when Dack shoved his face between him and Golden. Some unrecognizable instinct prodded Mast to pull her sleek form closer as the lad stared down at her. Dack's scrawny chest shook with uneven gasps. "You hold her, Captain, and I'll suck her," he decreed in a fervent whisper.

At that he yanked Golden even closer. "What!"

"Aye. We—we must take her breath from her before it burns us with its fire."

And then Mast noticed the weird glow to Dack's eyes.

The unnatural sheen thickened and glistened as the youth lowered himself over her, breathing more rapidly, swinging his rosary wide and high. "We must draw it out of her," he huskily rambled on. "Strip her naked of it."

If a man's senses could ignite into fire, Mast was certain his did in that next moment. All he could see was Dack's fuzz-bearded face smashing down against the smooth, pale plane of Golden's cheek, and the youth's hand, that greedy, rammy little hand crunching around a wet and helpless breast, groping her before them all.

The fury was wild and strange, like no anger he had felt before. It was deep—primal—frightening.

He leapt to his feet with a growl that exploded from within. "Get the hell away from her!"

A slash of distant lightning illuminated the stunned stares of the men. Mast was certain his own features were no less haunting as he breathed hard to contain them. From somewhere in the turmoil of his mind he perceived Dack's struggling form held back by Robert and Dink, and he forced himself to issue a rasping, but controlled order.

"Take him below, Dink." He had to stop for a moment to reclamp his jaw, reharden his voice. "Take him below until he's reflected on the proper way to greet a guest."

The deck fell into silence. Even the wind seemed to blow with a hushed murmur in the draining end of the storm. Mast watched and waited as all eyes slowly turned from where Dink and Dack disappeared below, back to him— and, most definitely, to the being in his arms. Their faces were full of questions—eyes wary—frowns cautious.

"I am taking my guest below before the pneum takes us both."

"Nay!" the men chorused. They rushed toward him.

He rushed toward them.

Mast didn't know if it was frustration or anger he felt looking at these grown men skitter away like frenzied mice. Christ. This was the bloody eighteenth century. Sea witches were things of a world that believed the earth was flat and bathing was unholy; a world of wives' tales and lunatics' rantings—such were certainly not the fears of modern, logical seamen as these.

"Gentlemen," he declared lowly, "That was not a request."

A terrible sense of foreboding washed through him.

* * *

Golden wasn't quite sure where she'd been sent when the wave hit her. It all collided together like a dream, this jumble of half-beliefs her life had become.

At first she was certain she was in heaven, the way Mummy always taught her. She was eight years old again and nothing was wrong with the world. Peace and contentment filled her. She could even see Mummy, ever so clearly, and Daddy was there, too. They were kissing on the deck of the *Gabrielle's Hope.* They were alive and no fire was going to destroy their voyage this time.

Then God turned his back on her, just like He had before. She was dancing with Guypa on the great raft holding the sacrifice for Agwe, the god of the waters. There was happiness and smiles and color, so much color. A conch shell blew loudly as they chorused their praises among the offerings of sweets and wine, pigeons and mutton, and the beautiful seven-tiered cake. Then they threw the sacrifices into the water and somehow she'd become one of the oblations herself, diving into the blue water, away from the chants and the music and into the spirit world, where there was finally peace among the fathoms of the sea.

Until the fathoms became eyes. Park blue eyes that carved away her senses until there was nothing, yet everything was left to feel. *Moonstormer, Moonstormer, the master of sin . . .* His carved face loomed before her. His murderer's mark was curling as he smiled at her, and stretched out a hand to her. Long, dark brown fingers came snaking closer.

Golden knew it for certain then. She was in hell.

She welcomed the blackness that came with the echoes of her scream. When sensation returned, she ached all over. In addition to the consuming discomfort her wrists throbbed incessantly, and she could feel they were slightly swollen.

Hell hadn't wanted her, either, came the first dismal thought. Golden fought to go back to the sleepy abyss where she could forget it all . . . the running, the storm, the fear . . . and the monster who had put her through it all. She shuddered and squirmed. Just thinking of the Moon-stormer made her insides twist and her heart fill with rage. His touch still seemed to linger on her skin. She wondered if he had defiled her forever with it.

Oh great spirits, her heart pleaded, *let this all be a nightmare. Let me wake up with the sweet smell of oleanders in the air, the island finches singing at my window, and Papa calling to me for breakfast.*

The only voice that called was consciousness. Golden struck out at the enemy. She was surprised as her arm actually carried the thought through. It came down against something very soft.

More surprise—but pleasant this time. Golden's eyes opened despite herself. Rich tapestry pillows lay around her. She pulled one close, to breathe in its warm, yet distinctly savory scent. Very nice, she decided.

She gingerly ran a finger across the amber-and-cinnamon-colored pattern. She found the pillows laid atop a down coverlet in a shade of similar, but deeper hues, next to a wall paneled with polished, red-tinted wood.

Golden started then. The wall was rocking. And she was rocking with it.

A barrage of wonderings assaulted her as she rolled over in the bed. Where on earth—she quickly amended that, on sea—was she? Who had saved her—cleaned her wounds—bandaged them up—kept her safe and dry?

And changed her clothes, for heaven's sake. Golden ran a hand across the intricately stitched flowers of a camisole that was most definitely not hers. It was the deepest red she'd ever seen, and of the sheerest, softest fabric.

She sat up straight in the bed, burning for the answer to every question at once. A wave of dizziness sent her swiftly back to the pillows. The soft cushions reeled around her and she felt horribly ill.

"Ohhhh." She reached and pulled a pillow against her, curling herself around it as if its downy interior could take the place of her innards. "Ohhhh . . ."

"Rrrraaack!"

"Oh!"

She jerked up in bed at the sharp sound. The wood paneling cracked as her head slammed against it. Golden yanked another pillow to her along with the covers, wielding it all like armor, preparing her lungs for a battle cry.

The only thing that attacked was the room itself. Images floated before her eyes in shimmering triplicate. She blinked hard, making out the shapes of a small writing desk, a dark wood dressing screen . . . and a gently swaying bird cage, with a turquoise and green blob flapping in it.

"Rrrraaack!" the blob screeched at her. After she blinked a few more times, it coagulated before her into the form of a cockily grinning macaw. "Hello-hello-hello," it rambled on. "Beautiful goddess. Hello, goddess. Hello."

Despite the awful way she felt, Golden found herself smiling. The bird's sound brought images of the rain forest to her mind, awakening a deep part of her soul. She swallowed a heavy lump in her throat and answered the creature in a soft croon. "Well, hello, pretty one."

"Pretty." The macaw latched on to a familiar word. It excitedly bobbed on its perch as it launched into a well-rehearsed repartee. "Pretty damn foolish. Damn fool woman. Damn fool—"

"Caesar!" A door whacked open above. Long legs sheathed in ebony black breeches descended the small, nearly vertical stairway. "Caesar, quiet! You'll wake the dead, you daft headed—"

He stopped when he noticed her sitting there. Golden gave a small, shocked cry. The Moonstormer was even more powerful than she remembered. His height was conquering the cabin. His dark stare was swallowing her whole. His bare chest gleamed with bronzed sea spray. The waves of his dark hair were windswept back, as if he'd been flying across the night sky on a terror run. The same tightly reined tension ticked beneath the same telltale jaw scar.

She'd never been to hell at all.

Satan had merely come and found her.

She screamed. "You beast! You hideous, heartless beast!"

He rolled his eyes, fists on his bare waist.

Golden gasped.

He dared to press his lips in an arrogant, mocking scowl. "Oh, no, sweet. We're not going to start that again—"

It was as far as she let him get. Golden flung herself at him with a war cry that would have done Guypa proud. Pillows and blankets went flying with her. The demon would curse the day he stalked this quarry!

The Moonstormer's shocked face loomed before her as she struck him. "By the love of Christ!" he thundered at her, eyes flashing blue combustion. Then the stunned features whipped away as they toppled across the desk together.

His body beneath her took the blow. Flesh slammed to wood with a harsh *whump*.

He groaned out in pain. Golden froze amidst the bedclothes. She was shocked and furious with herself at the same time. A sick feeling twisted through her stomach and her skin turned prickly and cold. She'd . . . she'd hurt him. The realization struck her like her first standoff with a wild boar. Like that time, this was exhilarating, and then nauseating.

But she'd never hurt a human before.

Hurt? she retorted back to herself. This was the Moon-stormer! What the bloody hell did he know of hurt? What did this beast know of Mummy's screams in the fire—in the flames he ignited—as she shouted out Golden's name until she could shout no more? And what did he know of the silence as her mother and father sank away, gone forever?

This wretch knew nothing about hurt. Nothing at all!

She exploded, shrieking with the agony and the pain that flooded her. Golden flailed herself into the demon with teeth and nails, knees and elbows. The dizziness hit her like a gale wind but it didn't matter. She beat through the orange haze with every ounce of her strength.

She began to tear at the mounds of bedding next, searching for that disgusting, dark brown face. She longed to be laughing in it as she sent his soul to the abyss it belonged in. He grunted in protest and she followed the sound. She could feel his legs trying to wrap around hers but she kept herself in perpetual motion, squirming free every time he gained a hold.

"Would you calm the hell down?" Mast finally got the lung power to yell. But it came out as muffled bilge, even to his ears. If this wasn't happening he'd never believe it. This soft, slender, supple barbarian was attacking him with his own bedding!

One of his arms at last met air. Mast reached for the first thing he could get his hands on. And he wasn't going to let go.

A silken shoulder writhed in his grip. He didn't let go.

"Lady Golden," he shouted at the small opening of air,

"As captain of this vessel, I command you to—Aaggh! Goddammit!"

The barbarian was trying to eat his hand off.

Mast tried to break free but her mouth held to his wrist as a wolf to beef. Her tenacious teeth clamped down harder with every wrench and turn. He could feel the vibrations of her growls down the length of his arm and through his crushed chest.

By the pittance of breath left in my body, he vowed then, *not another female will desecrate the decks of this ship again.*

As for this one . . .

Mast gathered the strength left from the farthest reaches of his body and powered it to his legs. He kicked up and out. They rolled from the desk in a sprawl of limbs and bedding and confusion. He flung the cloth away and sprang to a crouch, expecting anything at this point.

Her mouth popped free from him, in its place a piercing cry of surprise. Then came the cursing, or so Mast supposed, it was in rapid-fire Caribbee and came from a mound of blanket that was scurrying away from him. He watched as the lump fumbled around, as disoriented as a rat caught under a tavern rag. He sensed she was close to collapsing altogether. Damn fool woman. She'd pushed her body too far. Not to mention his.

"All right, sweet." The growl was octaves away from being an outright command. "Now we're going to play by my rules."

He started by whipping away the down coverlet.

The lump froze.

"Ah. That's better." She really was just a kitten, he thought, as he lowered to his knees and started to inch toward her. Find the right way to stroke the animal, and the rest was purrs and compliance.

He dragged on the silk sheet next. An ivory foot and ankle came into view, but snapped away again into the mound. "Aye. That's it," he prodded, scooting closer. "You see, hellion? 'Tis a simple thing. Learn to keep your place, and we'll get on just fine."

The explosion came just as he reached for her. "Go—to—hell! My place will never be with you!"

Golden hurled the blanket at him and didn't look back. The insidious, cruel beast! Tricking her with that act of gentle words and softness! *And you,* she assailed at herself, *falling for it like a bug in a Venus flytrap. Silly, trusting fool!*

Well, this fool could sit with King Solomon now for what she'd learned. Golden tore across the cabin, searching out new and better munitions to fire at the pirate monster. She heaved several quill pens, a rather well-flying flute, and, to her delight, a small bookcase of heavy books. From the sounds of his fierce grunts and gritted oaths, she'd made a few dead-on hits, too.

But she couldn't ignore her rapidly waning strength. Sweat ran along the sides of her face, and it was difficult to discern just where her feet ended and the floor began. Everything was horribly blurry.

Clarity! It returned in one glorious moment. Color and texture pressed into view just as her shin exploded in pain. The sound reached her ears just a split second later. "Whack!" went her leg against the bottom riser of the stairwell.

But even the pain was bliss as Golden was struck by inspiration. With a triumphant smile she dashed up the steps until she gauged herself at a perfect attack level. She reached to steady herself along the wall—and was suddenly slammed into it, instead. Another wall, one of towering flesh, surrounded her.

Golden shrieked. The Moonstormer remained horrifyingly silent. She writhed, she kicked. He gripped, and subdued. The demon was overpowering. Eventually he'd lowered her flat against the stairs. Her aching wrists were bound over her head by a single one of his. His tall, powerful body came next. He straddled her, surrounding her with the warm, hard feel of his chest, and the iron grip of his thighs.

He lowered his face directly over hers. Inches away. "Check." It was soft, tauntingly soft. "And mate, my lady."

By the great Puntan. The feel of him . . . the look of him. Golden's heart pounded in her ears like a war drum as she became lost in the inky depths of his stare. He was swallowing her with his eyes again, pulling her into the pit of his dark soul.

"No!" she cried, writhing against him. "You can't do this to me! You won't!"

The Moonstormer didn't move. He let out an exasperated sigh. "My lady," he stated softly. Golden detected the rich aroma of brandy on his breath. "My lady, I haven't done a thing. You have brought all of this on yourself."

"You're mad." She worked her gaze away from his, tried desperately to keep things that way, but was drawn back to the hypnotic blue depths despite herself. "That—that's the most inane—"

"Proverb?" he offered.

"Lie I have ever been defiled with. How dare you!" she railed. "I have done nothing to warrant this capture or this torture. But I suppose that's what fires your guns, Moon-stormer. Preying on people when they're most vulnerable,

most helpless to fight you back. The times when you can inflict the most fear and pain!"

Golden broke off as the beast's stare hardened even deeper, impaling her like two blades of cold blue steel. Golden tensed, half expecting him to strike her.

His words might as well have been the blow he held back. "It would serve you well to dull that razor-edged tongue of yours, sweet. A syllable more from it could, quite possibly, insure you a captivity more vile than this."

Golden seared him with a glare. "I beg your pardon?"

"Begging is not necessary. A mere 'pray you' or 'thank you' would be sufficient, if it's accompanied by the customary female decorum." He cocked an eyebrow at her. "You *are* familiar with decorum?"

"You're a monster," she seethed. Before she knew what she was doing, she bunched up her lips and spit at him. "I'll truly kill you when I have the chance!"

Mast managed to beat back the fury well enough to reach up at the goo on his cheek. He glared first from where her spittle slithered across his finger, then to her rebelliously uplifted face.

But it wasn't that insolent glare that piqued him. It was that the chit didn't even try to conceal her pleasure at his indignity. Spitting in his face, and looking as if she wanted to flaunt it to the world: nostrils dilating, eyebrows arched and preening, lips set stubbornly . . . and so damn sensually.

The fire finally flared too high. Mast seized her again, digging one hand into the small of her back and the other into her nape. "Kill me, shall you?" he drawled, curling up one side of his mouth just enough to tell her he noticed the color draining from her cheeks. "Perhaps, sweet, I should have rendered the same to you when I had the chance."

"When you had the chance? Aye, when you stole me

from the French on Saint Kitts, only to stand there in Papa's study and—and put your lips all over me, and insult me like I wasn't even standing there!"

"Something like that." His voice was bitter. The little heathen was going to hear him out this time. "Something like saving you from those bastards so your precious neck wouldn't hang next to Papa's laundry the next morning, darling. Something like dodging bullets from those same bastards because I decided to traipse after you in the middle of the night, across a rather painful bridge, not to mention the hike through the rain forest behind an army of your banshee friends.

"Yes, my lady," he continued more slowly, relishing the revelation and shock that started to inch across her features, "it was all smashing fun, but the highlight had to be nearly drowning ten yards from my own ship, just to pull you off the back of a half-dead dolphin."

Lady Golden Gaverly went slack in his arms.

"No," she blurted. "It couldn't have been."

"Think again, sweetheart," he sneered.

"You came and got me from Nirvana?"

"Nirvana?"

"Answer me."

"Nirvana? You gave the damn fish a name?"

"Answer me!"

Silence. Golden beat at the arms and shoulders that entrapped her, but the Moonstormer didn't budge. He only continued staring at her, long and hard, continued surrounding her, close and big.

"Fine," he finally growled. "Yes. I was the one who came and got you from—" his lips tightened and his eyes rolled, "Nirvana."

It was very well near an apology.

It crashed in Golden's ears like a proclamation of doom.

What was she supposed to feel now? To do? It was her turn to stare at him. Golden's eyes moved down, across the dark chest with its slight matting of black hair, to the breadth of the arms that held her. The arms that had plucked her from death, she thought. The heart that had risked its pulse for her own.

"Why?" she whispered. "Why would you—why did you—why did a monster like you do that for me?"

"Oh, for Christ's sake." His scowl reminded her of Mount Misery's sinister spring storms.

Mast broke free of her and shoved himself to a standing position. He thought if those damnably lush lips called him a monster one more time he'd prove the accusation correct. He breathed in and out, counting to ten each time for ten times, before he turned and gazed down on her again.

"All right, sweet," he ordered. "We are going to settle this right now. I command it, so you listen well."

As he supposed she would, she tried to jump up again. Defiance dominated her features though she wobbled like a cross-eyed drunk. "You . . . command me . . . to do nothing," she faltered.

"I command whoever and whenever I like, my dear." His tone was deliberately smooth and detached. Even so, the next moment he stepped to her and gently helped her back down. "You see, that's the way it works on a sailing ship. Especially this one. I am the captain. I am the law."

She snapped a hazy, but clearly disbelieving look up at him. "The what?"

"Captain. Mast Iverson. And though I'll probably live to rue it, I welcome you to my brigantine, the *Athena*."

"Just like that?"

"Just like that."

"Because you command it?"

He met the confrontation in her upturned eyes as he did the challenge in her tone of voice. "Because I brought you here. It didn't need to be commanded."

Her nostrils dilated. Her lips tightened. She was, at least temporarily, silenced. Mast fell wordless, too, just looking at her. Cor and hell. She was adorable. Fiery eyes gleamed amidst that shining mess of hair. The ugly crimson nightshift Dink had come up with was playing against her skin like the strawberries he'd been craving of late. She was chaos, madness, frenzy; a full-fledged rebellion against the order—and blessed, uncomplicated celibacy—he'd fought so hard to win for his life. Until now, hadn't realized how well he'd done so.

"And so, Captain Mast Iverson, what is it you want from me in return?"

Mast regarded her as carefully but as blankly as he could. If any time he needed that well-honed skill of discarding the useless baggage of emotion, of concealing the thoughts which truly dominated his brain, it was now. Wayland was depending on him to stay that way. He'd given his word. *Damn it.* "Are you always this suspicious of seamen who save you from storms?"

The rebuttal knifed through Golden. At this moment, that was the last thing she wanted to remember. She'd show him where his dodging would get him! "I'm suspicious of you, Captain. The only thing that's kept my hands from your neck—"

". . . is that you're beginning to realize I'm *not* the Moonstormer?"

Choked silence was all she could answer him with for an interminable moment. Golden's throat clamped shut and her lips cracked dry. Then she found her voice. "That's impossible."

"Nay." To compound the confusion, he was so blasted assured about it—even arrogant, as he swooped back down next to her. "Highly probable."

"No!" she protested. She grabbed a stray strand of hair over his forehead just as she clutched in her head for the comfort of logic and hate. *"No.* Look at you. Look . . ." Despite her efforts, Golden heard her voice softly trailing off. Strangely, frighteningly, she didn't find the sound unpleasant.

"Your hair," she murmured, "so black it's almost blue." *So full it's like an ocean in my fingers.* "And your eyes. So dark they're almost black." *So deep they swallow me with a glance.*

"Stop." The captain clipped short her words and her touch, catching her hand as she trailed it down the side of his face. It wasn't difficult for Golden to notice the murkier depths his eyes slid to or the tension quaking just beneath his grip. It was a subtle change, one her mind couldn't identify at all but her instinct sensed that it was meaningful.

"Books are not their covers, Lady Golden," he said in a resonating murmur. "Just as folk songs do not a sea demon make."

She didn't respond to that. Instead she tried to make sense of the cacophony in her body and in her heart. None of these hot and trembling feelings made sense. Nothing about this experience felt right, or recognizable—especially this man. This dark and mysterious and scarred man.

Golden forced herself to lift her other hand to his face. She couldn't bring herself to touch the curving indentation on his jaw, but she managed to force her shaking fingers within an inch of the scar, just below the taut corner of his mouth.

"He rides through the night," she whispered, "with the moon on his—"

"Stop!"

They both fell silent. Golden heard his heartbeat pounding as if it would drive a hole through his chest.

Then he began to force her hand farther towards him—towards that mark!

"Nnooo . . ."

"Touch it, Golden. It's a scar, damn it, not a burning coal. Not the bloody moon. Satan didn't claw it on me; the wrong end of a knife did during my first sea battle. Touch it."

"Please," she protested, "no!"

"I'm not asking."

And he showed her then and there just what was expected of his commands. He pulled her fingers to his jaw and she wrenched her head away, crying out. Golden vowed to hold her breath until the ordeal was over, but he relentlessly held her there for a minute, then another.

Somewhere through the pressure of her lungs and the screaming in her brain, the amazement gripped her. Then the realization of warm, strong smoothness. Oh yes, such incredible smoothness . . .

Golden let out her breath. She inched one eye back over to his face, then the next. She was touching him, feeling his mark, by herself!

"Who *are* you?" she whispered. "Why are you suddenly everywhere in my life? Why—what do you want with me?"

His thick eyebrows lowered, so somberly he might have been Yani, the shaman of the tribe at home, contemplating yet another of her impossible questions. "You're tired," he replied, playing evasion in genuine Yani style, as well. He stood up, unexpectedly towing her with him. "Right now, all that matters is seeing you recovered from your ordeal. I'll have some food brought to you, then you'll sleep."

"Captain's orders?" She tilted a challenging look at him.

"Something like that." The corner of his mouth also tugged up.

Several quips should have come to mind in retort to that hasty dismissal, but Golden failed to recall any of them as he helped her into the heavenly, spice-scented sheets. The assault of exhaustion was a humbling reminder of just how right Captain Iverson was; she'd taxed herself too far. She caught a glimpse of herself, bedraggled and pale, in his direct gaze. Then those midnight depths fogged over again with some unreadable thought and he turned, bounding back up the stairs, two at a time.

She was left alone with her foggy and jumbled thoughts. Good Lord, where could she begin to make sense of this chaos? Of this man who'd seemed to bring that turmoil to her life single-handedly? How did it happen that he'd just popped into her life from . . . well, nowhere? What did he want that he snatched her from doom not once, but two times, first from the French, then from the sea? *And who was he, that he knew where to be and what to do at all the right times?*

The mystery pressed her mind to its limits. But how or where to find the answer? Certainly not from his dark and scowling captainship himself. The man answered her questions with a glare that said she must be insane or insolent or both.

The missing link was nowhere and everywhere at once. It permeated Mast Iverson's voice, rumbling in the gentle thunder at the ends of his commands. It was explicit in his infinite patience with her, even when she threw herself at him and pummeled him to within an inch of his sanity. And it was in each moment of his touch . . . the touch she sensed, somehow, she'd only begun to know the magic of . . . the power of.

It was all there, just beneath the surface, waiting for her to grasp it!

And that was just what Golden intended to do. By the fates, she'd have the answers to her questions, even if it took a few days of patient, creative persuasion to accomplish. She'd learn the truth, even if it meant learning everything about this whole new world of a ship first.

And yes, oh yes, she'd uncloak the staunchly elusive Captain Iverson . . . whether he liked it or not.

Six

Golden fought the nemesis of sleep with a vengeance. Her renewed determination was humming through her veins and fear gnawed harder at her mind. Images of the most recent twist her nightmares had taken were still terrifyingly fresh.

But eventually, her struggles came to no use. Not even her will could ward off the wearied call of her body. Her stomach was full of the turtle soup and sea biscuits a cabin boy had brought. And with her mind soothed by the rum in the accompanying mug of bumbo, she succumbed to a deep and thankfully dreamless slumber.

It seemed but a moment before her eyes twitched again. She blinked once. Twice. The light was now mated with a balmy, breezy warmth, and Golden drew the back of a hand over her cheek, glorying in the feel of it. Opening her eyes completely, she realized the light was a high midday sun, streaming down through a wide, slanted window, from a bright, cloudless blue sky. The accompanying wind lent a crisp feel to everything as it went whistling through the shrouds and whipping canvas to yardarms. The ship clipped along at what she could tell was an impressive speed.

The ship!

Golden sat up with a start. Good Lord. The ship.

Memory returned with more blinding force than the unfettered sunshine. Golden lay against the pillows and tried to sort through all the images that circled through her head, as if to place the order, so far, of this remarkable experience she'd been hurled into.

But no matter what the memory, one likeness remained the same. The powerful, mysterious face of Captain Mast Iverson.

That sight whirled her into absolute confusion.

By the stars above, what was she to think of this riddle of a man? It was simple enough mere days ago; Mast Iverson was the Moonstormer, and she was destiny-bound to kill him. Now he was the most unscoundrelly sea scoundrel she'd ever met—and she owed him her life.

It brought a bounty of curiosity to ripeness in her head. Only which crop to glean? The buds of the frustration and anger which had germinated in her for so long, demanding reparation for the parents she would never hold or love again? Or the softer, more womanly blossoms this man had awakened inside her for the first time, pulling her close to him in Papa's study that night, touching his lips to hers in that warm and wet and amazing way. What *was* that mesmerizing lip-touching thing, anyway?

Golden sighed heavily. To loathe or to trust . . . either decision terrified her; neither seemed more right or wrong than the other. She couldn't loathe Mast Iverson, not after the astonishing bravery and kindness he'd shown to her—yet because of those feats she didn't trust him, either. After all, pirate or no, what seaman jumped into a roiling tempest for a complete stranger of a woman?

Blast the perplexing dastard!

"Well, Golden," she at last ordered at herself. "There's only one way out of this dilemma, you ninny. And sitting here in a mope is not it."

She kicked back the covers and swung her legs out of the bunk. Her overworked joints and muscles gave a protest of soreness, but Golden reveled in the feel of the fresh air blowing through the chemise to her skin.

A few minutes later, she discovered that the pleasant sensation was but a hint of the magnificence that awaited her up on deck.

Golden lifted open the hatch and instantly peered high, higher yet, into the canvas forest over her head. Its majesty took her breath away as fully as the green-leaved wilds of home. Shrouds and backstays were vines and branches; masts, spars and sweeps, the trees the ropes grew upon. And throughout it all clamored the creatures of the forest— the ship's crew, swooping and flying around their world just as the mongooses and monkeys of the rain forest did, if not easier and swifter.

Indeed, the large sailor who easily swung then jumped from a tangle of ropes before her brought the same laugh Golden awarded to her favorite vervet monkeys back home. She followed with rapid applause.

The seaman jumped in surprise and snapped a glare at her.

Golden's laugh caught in her throat. "I'm sorry." She attempted a small smile. "I didn't mean to startle you. I just—you were wonderful, swinging on all those ropes." A wayward giggle broke free. "You reminded me of the animals in the trees on Saint Kitts."

To her relief, the man's broad shoulders loosened— though the relaxed mien didn't reach to his face. "Well, now, I imagine I did, my lady."

Golden tilted her head. "You know me?"

"Ah . . . aye." A strange light flickered in the sharp hazel gaze that quickly swept down her body. "Your arrival was quite an event around here."

"It was?"

"My lady, does the captain know you're up here?" he responded instead.

But Golden's eyes had now lowered to the intricate motions of the man's hands. Her previous question, and his, were lost to the new fascination before her.

"What are you doing?" She padded closer to eagerly study the length of rope he made into complex loops and knots.

"Uh—well—" he stammered, "Nothin' that would interest you, I'm sure. Just securin' the lines."

"Securing the lines," she repeated slowly. "And what's *that?*"

To her surprise, the man chuckled. Golden had a feeling he didn't chuckle often. "Blimey. Don't miss a thing, do you? It's a belayin' pin. You wedge it in the fife rail—like this. Then when your line from the mast comes down, you lock the rope in with the pin—like this."

"I want to try." Golden grabbed the dangling rope from him, noticing she made the big man laugh again. She carefully emulated the seaman's motions, pulling on the line as hard as she could. She beamed a victorious grin when it stretched as taut and straight as he'd done.

But suddenly her lips dropped into a small *O* of wonder.

Her hands halted on the rope as she stared across the deck.

She knew him the instant she saw him. There, on a high plateau, stood the king of the ship's forest. The black panther. Lean-muscled legs braced to the roll of the sea—strong profile etched against the sky—terrifying and sinewy, yet graceful and . . .

Beautiful, Golden thought. He was utterly, unspeakably beautiful.

Though the weather had been graciously clement since the storm, Mast felt the silence take over the deck like a sweep of fog. His hands tightened on the spokes of the wheel. He was manning the helm for Rico. He'd taken on this duty by his own request hoping to unknot the kinks in his senses. They seemed permanently snarled since last night's encounter with Wayland's daughter. As he noticed Dink frozen halfway up the yardarm in front of him, with his face locked in a wide stare down at the main deck, Mast knew his gut hadn't begun to know the true art of knot-tying.

He slowly turned.

"Good day, Captain Iverson!"

God save him. She greeted him with such a warm smile she could have been calling across the lawn at a croquet match—only the woman held the buntline to the mainsail, not a harmless wooden mallet. Worse, she was still half-naked, in that nearly transparent red chemise. Still captivating, from the way the men were as much as swabbing the decks with their tongues. And her, utterly mindless of it all.

The knot in his gut didn't get a few new twists, it got yanked out completely—and strung tight across his ribs until Mast was certain he heard a few crack. Control was unreachable any more. After handing over the wheel to Dink, Mast made straight toward her.

"Great spirits," Golden muttered in amazement as the captain jumped from the upper deck to her level in one leap. She attempted a friendly smile as he stalked toward her, but the rigid way he held his hands at his sides and the straightforward bent of his head as he charged at her made her feel like a mouse in the boar's path.

His immediate presence didn't help matters one bit. His

spotless white linen shirt billowed from his upper body, making him appear all the more overpowering. His dark brown breeches were of a matching crispness but an exact opposite fit, hugging the contours of his legs in a way that made her eyes widen and her chest flutter. And still he came closer, closer, until Golden thought he might tie *her* to the fife rail—then he forced her tightly back against the wide wood pole.

"Your . . . your ship is gorgeous, Captain." She ventured another smile in an effort to ease the uncertain air between them. "Even the belaying pins."

His retort reminded her of a snake's soft, but lethal whisper. "The what?"

"The . . . belaying pins." Bloody uptight ape; what was he scowling at now? "Your gracious crew was just teaching me all about them," she asserted, lifting her chin. "Mister—um—"

"Robert," the big monkey man supplied with a reassuring wink.

She returned the gesture with a grateful smile. "My new friend Robert even let me secure a line for you. I think I did quite well, too; don't you agree, Robert?"

She never received her answer. The captain's long fingers coiled around Golden's elbow like hawk talons. "Below," he ordered.

"I beg your pardon?" She trumped it by daring a stare straight into his eyes, though nothing met her frown but gloom. Level upon level of dark blue shadow.

"You'll beg my pardon below." His white-linened arm shot out, motioning toward the hatch. "Get down there. Now."

"My dear *Captain,* you may think you can act the ogre to me just as you can to your crew—"

"I am not an ogre."

"The hell you aren't!"

"Below! Now!"

"Go secure a line around your *neck!*"

Golden was at a loss to comprehend the indignation she felt. The overbearing ox. She might kill him yet, no matter who he was! The feel of her nails as she drove them to his chest was delicious; she dug in, twisted hard, then pushed as vehemently as she could, hoping the railing was conveniently close by.

But this time Captain Mast Iverson was ready for her. He absorbed her attack with no more than a grunt and a step back for balance. In a single swoop, Golden found herself hurled through the air and landing soundly over his shoulder.

"You requested an escort, my lady?" he sneered, his jaw rough and his breath hot against her thigh.

"You bastard!"

Horrified, humiliated, she lifted her head one last time in hope of rescue, but the last sight Golden saw before they bounded down the steps were a sea of gargoyle-like male faces staring after her in paralyzed awe.

She was doomed.

She was infuriated.

The silence seemed to stretch into eternity as he stood there gazing upon her, as if, were he to glance away from where he'd tossed her on the bunk, she'd disappear in a whoosh of magic smoke. 'Twould serve the brooding ape right, Golden thought with a huff.

She ground her fist tighter into the sheet, still trying to regain her composure from the degrading ordeal. Oh, to be anywhere on earth right now except here, subject to his rock hard scrutiny, feeling like a pebble beneath his wide-legged stance, feeling utterly helpless to—

To what?

Golden knew far too well what. She was helpless to resist that ungodly force about him, she admitted furiously. His eyes could peel her like a banana, leaving the soft, malleable part of her exposed and vulnerable. How did he do that?

Of course, the brute picked that very moment to step closer to the bed. She cursed her flip-flopping stomach, railed at her jolting nerves. She outright condemned her rising gaze.

How did she do that? Mast raged inwardly as that sunlight-spectrumed stare stopped him cold next to the bunk. How did she seem to see so deep within him? He could swear his gut had been carved out fifty times today alone.

He yearned to thrash the chit, or kiss her soundly. But he could do neither, damn it, making the admission as her father's tender gaze and trusting handshake filled his memory. The pictures did nothing to ease the fury Golden had ignited in him above.

"My lady." He forced himself to stamp each word with control despite the tempest raging through him. "You are on the *Athena* now—and, as such, are part of an entirely new world. A world where certain laws must be obeyed, without fail, without question."

"Then I suppose," she snarled, "you're going to dictate them to me now?"

"You suppose correctly," he leveled back. He wasn't going to let her get at him. Wasn't going to . . . wasn't going . . . to . . .

"Number one." He planted each foot to the floor in emphasis. "Any fire on board will be attended and controlled at all times."

Especially that fire in your eyes. That maddening, mesmerizing amber glow, searing me every time I look there. Filling me, burning me even now. Stop it. Stop it! Not going to let you do this to me!

Golden waited in the tense silence with growing perplexity, as she watched what looked like a power play across Mast's dark features. His jaw clenched, his scar turned an angry white, then his brow and temples fought back, furrowing with hostile intensity. His eyes never left hers. The dark shadows were roiling with layers of blue and black conflict.

Then suddenly, he huffed once—just once—and whirled on his heel; so swiftly, Golden caught a draft from the movement. He didn't stop until he got to the stairwell. He braced one boot to the bottom step while whipping his head back her direction.

"Rule number two." His voice had dipped even lower and more ominously commanding. "If I ever see you on my deck in that kind of attire again, I assure you I'll do more than embarrass you in front of my crew." He stormed up the steps. Then he was gone.

Warring emotions raged through Golden. To her chagrin, none prevailed. She ended up frozen there in the middle of the bunk as she listened to his furious bellow above. "Dink! Get this savage some proper clothing."

After that horrifying meaning sank in, but not long enough for Golden to bar the hatch, the weathered little elf man she'd first seen in Papa's study scuttled into the cabin, his arms laden with an array of satin and brocade.

"Fit fine mood he's in," the man grumbled, as he dumped the lavish heap onto the bunk.

But Golden barely heard. As if floodgates had burst open, the frustration and hurt poured free from her. She gathered the clothes up and furiously hurled them at the startled elf man. "Get out, and take all of this with you!"

"Now, darlin'—"

"And tell your wretched monster of a captain that I do not need a lickspittle lady's maid pawing his greasy hands over me. I will wear whatever I please, whenever I bloody well please!"

The elf sighed, looking around at the puddle of material he was trapped in. "And just what do ya mean to dress in, darlin'? That chemise is charmin', if ya ask me, but I don't think Ive is too fond of it. I don't claim to know what he'll do if ya take to the main deck in it again."

Golden stopped for a long, deliberating pause. "All right, all right," she mumbled, dismally seeing his logic. She tentatively fingered an elaborately embroidered hem. The rich feel of it sent a shiver of excitement up her arm. She lifted her eyes to meet the startlingly two-toned, but infinitely friendly gaze of the elf. She smiled. "They—they *are* lovely."

They truly were. The pile was the most gorgeous treasure trove of fabric she had ever seen. Her simple and often petticoat-less clothes at home bowed to the demands of tropical heat rather than the latest dictates from court. But she responded to the textures with a deep female lust for frills and finery. There were fancy-cut bodices with embroidered ribbon and lace, and more daring necklines with rich silk fichus to tuck into them. There was satin of such deep sapphire blue she could have been holding the ocean in her arms. And there were brocades with flowers as lovely and intricate as the orchids and heliconias of the islands. Yards and yards of material went flowing through Golden's hands like the milk and honey of Mummy's Bible stories.

"Well," the elf man interjected into her awed perusal, " 'tisn't the absolute finest, but—"

"They're gorgeous," Golden countermanded fiercely. A good-humored chuckle was her reply, and she looked at him again. Weirdness of those dual-toned eyes aside, Golden decided she liked the little man. "They're gorgeous," she repeated, softening her tone in way of apology. "Where did you get them?"

The man's weathered face broke into a haphazard grin. "Ah, missy, the spoils of the sea are curious at times. Let us say they were gifts. Aye, gifts."

"Well then," Golden said, unsure what to make of the peculiar way that made her feel. "You have generous friends, Master . . . um . . . ?"

"Mister," he corrected. "Peabrooke. But don't insult me by callin' me that. It's just Dinky, my lady. Just Dinky. Ship's first mate. Blarsted proud o' it, too."

Golden couldn't help but giggle as Mr. Dinky Peabrooke tugged arrogantly on his breeches, acting the stalwart seaman, all the while standing in a pile of costly ladies' gowns.

"I thank you for your kindness, Dinky. And please don't insult *me* by using that 'my lady' rubbish. My name is Golden. Just Golden."

" 'Fraid not, darlin'. My apologies, but accordin' to Ive's orders—"

"Ive can toss his bloody orders to the gulls!"

Dinky was surprised the timbers didn't come down on them with the plenteous gift Lady Golden made of her voice. It was an effort to stand his ground there, watching the girl's rage pull her shoulders tight as she whirled from him. Hell, she sure was a passionate lick o' fire.

No wonder Mast had been smolderin' like a live coal lately.

"Now calm down, spitfire," he soothed. "Why don't ya go try this on. You'll feel better arftah we get ya pretty."

"Pig's posh I will."

"Now, cut that out! Get behind that screen, missy, and that's an order."

Try as she might, there was no way Golden could frown at the little man. Her smile grew wider as she took the pink brocade gown Dinky offered her, running her hand lovingly over the exquisite flower-patterned material. "You're as awful as your captain," she laughed over her shoulder as she trudged behind the dressing screen.

"I'll take that as a compliment."

"Then you're as daffy as a cuckoo."

"Now fireball, I know he hasn't given ya much cause to think elsewise so far, but Ive's not as terrible as all that. Give him half a chance. The lad's been very . . . well . . . tired lately."

"Oh, aye." Her tone reflected her frustration as she struggled into a silky chemise, then a fuller garment she didn't recognize, but ventured a good guess was an underpetticoat. "Tired enough to haul me up like a potato sack and throw me down into this dungeon."

There was a telling pause. "Ya mean down here into his own cabin?"

"His—?"

Golden's hands froze where they fumbled at the gown's hooks in the middle of her back. Her arms dropped completely when she started to study her surroundings; truly study them.

Good Lord. The man's presence was all around her—and she'd never even noticed. Why, right there before her stood a gleaming porcelain washbasin nestled in an impeccably kept shaving stand, with a bronze razor at the ready in its slot. A matching comb kept it company—its bed a soft, clean drying towel, perfectly folded. Even Mast Iverson's toilette was a command.

His cabin.

"Crimey, darlin'. He couldn't put ya anywhere else. Everyone was rantin' 'n' railin' at him when he pulled ya aboard that night, carryin' on about la Say-rene this, and sea witch that. Ya weren't lookin' too chipper, either, I may add. I almost believed 'em myself, but not Ive. He just marched straight down here with ya, and that was that."

Dinky had to admit, after his eloquent speech on Ive's behalf, the spitfire's reaction was not what he'd expected. Golden looked haunted as she exploded from behind the screen, gown connected all wrong, underpetticoats a haphazard train on the floor behind her. She dropped into Mast's burgundy velvet reading chair, looking around the cabin as if seeing it for the first time.

"But how did he—where did he—Dinky, where did *he* sleep?"

"Like I said, we didn't think ya'd weather it through the night," he quickly filled in. "But Mast insisted on stayin' with ya. Just stretched out in that very chair you're in—"

"What?" She jumped up. "You mean I took his own bed, while he slept . . . there?"

"Berth. Ya took his berth or his bunk, darlin', not his bed."

"He tended me . . . watched over me . . . ?"

"Well, it was the fever that really pulled some tricks. Wasn't very high, but blarst me if ya didn't thrash like it was a blacksmith's bellows inside ya."

"But why? Oh Dinky, why? After all I put him through . . . stars, I nearly sent him over Barbe's Falls!" She plunked back into the chair, hands coiling together in her lap. "Oh, God."

Praise God, Dinky thought, watching the girl. At first he'd thought it too incredible to be true, but damn 'n blow him if all the signs weren't there: her glazed and troubled eyes, the lip she well near chewed off in front of him, the fingers she nervously tapped on the chair. Aye, it was all there, etched across the confusion-crinkled face that gazed past him as if he weren't there any more.

Praise the saints, indeed! Mast's spitfire was smolderin' right back for him!

There was just one Goliath problem left.

"Mr. Peabrooke!" Mast's bootsteps matched the thunder of his bellow over their heads. "Dink, I said to give her the blasted things, not press and tailor them for—"

Dinky watched Mast as his friend's voice and body froze on the stairwell. It had been a long time since he'd seen Mast's features widen so uncontrollably. An even longer time since the grooves of tension around those stern eyes and mouth fell away like that, surrendering to something damn near resembling—at the thought, Dinky grinned—desire.

His gaze swerved to Golden, who rose from the chair on the other side of the cabin. Her eyes shimmered as they locked with Mast's, her lips slightly parted, as if to speak any moment . . .

"You . . . look better," the captain stammered.

Golden didn't reply.

Dinky managed to hold back his chuckle until he'd excused himself from the gaping pair and climbed out into the bright Caribbean afternoon. "Goliath of a problem?" he murmured happily to himself. "Ah, lizard spit. Blarsted Israelite David knocked over that stubborn giant with just a stone.

"And that little spitfire's sure as hell got more than stones."

Seven

If not for Dinky's interruption, Golden imagined, she and Mast still would have been locked in each other's gaze: she, absorbing this intensity of a man in a wondrous new light; and Mast, gathering every inch of her in his dark and tumultuous stare, then not knowing what to do with what he had.

"Why?" she finally asked into the silence. "Why?"

Mast frowned. "What the bloody hell did I do now?"

"Stop that," she snapped. "Dinky told me. Not only did you dive into that storm and save me, but the crew wanted to throw me back after you did. And you didn't let them. Why?"

"You definitely look better." He regarded her question as much as he'd consider a dog bark. He cleared the cabin length between them in three strides. "Proper clothing becomes you," he rushed on, "even if you look as if a hurricane was your lady's maid. Turn around."

"No. Not until you answer me, blast it. You not only saved me from the storm *and* your crew, but you brought me here, to your own cabin. Then you stayed by me, helping me to rest and heal. Why? *Why?*"

He just scowled distantly. "The corset. That's it. Your corset's backwards. How the blazes did you do that? Don't they make you wear a corset in that godforsaken wilderness?"

"Answer me!" Golden locked her feet to the floor and

her hands to his elbows. "You stayed by my side the whole time, didn't you? Even after I nearly killed you back on Saint Kitts, and attacked you again last night. Didn't you?"

She moved to him then, and slid her hands around the hard muscles of his forearms. "Please tell me, Mast Iverson. Why are you doing this for me?"

The straight line of his mouth didn't falter. But the tendons which coiled and hardened beneath Golden's hands spoke to her just as clearly as words. The flexions felt like a gentle whisper and a powerful shout at the same time.

But then . . . he touched her back. Words of any kind suddenly didn't matter any more. His hands, strong and commanding, curled around the ends of her elbows. His fingers, gentle and revering, slid down the underside of her arm. Golden gulped back the sigh in her throat. Her arms were no longer flesh and muscle. They'd been transformed into rivers of languid, liquid warmth.

"My lady." His murmur was low, intimate. "Do you remember our little talk on the stairs last night?"

She nodded. She wanted to scream. To make that wondrous lip-pressing magic with him again.

"So you remember when we spoke about books and covers? About the importance of trusting what you can't see as much as what you can?"

Again, her head bobbed dumbly. Oh, his voice. Like the sudden gust of a trade wind, it swirled gently around her, forming, for one exquisite moment, a world of its own, where the only two people who existed were her and this dark, seductive mystery of a man.

"Then turn around . . . and let me fix your corset."

She moved without thinking, as if her spirit were now taking directions from his. Indeed, his hands felt of another world as they grazed her skin, and guided her arms from the sleeves of the gown. Her eyes closed and her senses stopped as he adjusted the wayward corset around her hips with one masterful pull. Then the gentleness came again. Mast slowly, silently glided her arms back into the pink brocade. Golden didn't know if she breathed during the entire ordeal. Surely not even the sparks from a thousand shooting stars could fill her senses with more painful, beautiful ecstasy.

Then he slowly lifted the hair off her neck.

"Christ."

Mast hadn't even felt the oath tempting his lips. He watched his trembling hand as it lingered among the white-gold strands around her shoulders. He seemed certain his arm had detached from him somehow and was touching sunlight itself. She was beautiful. So wild and free . . .

Free. Oh aye, free. Free to the tune of five thousand pounds. Wayland's five thousand pounds. Your best friend. The man you promised her safety and her purity to . . . not this hot, hard madness you're encouraging, Iverson. Not the madness she could so easily infect you with.

He jerked his hand back. With a swallow he grappled for the corset ties. He gritted his teeth against the delicious temptation of her skin beneath his fingers; bit his tongue against the craving to suckle away the goosebumps the tawny flesh responded to him with . . . to know her gasping, hardening reaction if he reached beneath the loose corset to cup those cream-smooth mounds and their rose-velvet tips . . .

"Hold still," he commanded her. His breath was coming mercilessly swift and severe. He rushed to close the whalebone panels together over her back, a resurrected Orpheus fighting the lethal temptation of Eurydice. He grabbed the last length of each tie in his hands, and yanked. Hard.

Golden's lips burst with a guttural groan. Her senses came crashing down from the clouds. The brute not only forced every last breath from her body, but fastened her in that way, permanently! Her eyes felt ready to pop from her head as the captain adjusted and buttoned the gown over the torture device, then jerked her around to face him again.

In spite of the discomfort and the dizzying lack of air, she found herself biting her lip in anticipation. Of just what, Golden didn't understand. She found her eyes rising to Mast's, searching the endless midnight depths as she gulped deeply.

"Well. It appears you can be a human being, after all."

She couldn't have been struck more speechless had the harsh indifference of his voice been a tub of cold bilge water. She watched, numb, as Mast turned and briskly ascended the stairs.

The hatch thudded ominously behind him.

"Wretched, insufferable ass!" The words came tumbling furiously, yet achingly. "Arrogant, blood-hungry boar! Lying, rat-swallowing snake!"

Damn him.

How could one man cause so many aggravating, baffling, terrifying sensations at once? Golden paced from one end of the cabin to the other as she pondered that imponderable question. The space was confining, at best, but all she could see was the endless road that seemed to stretch before her. The unconquerable quest. The unfathomable man.

Even as she stood here, surrounded with the things of his private world, she felt more warmth from the richly colored furnishings than she did from the person who used them. Putting her hands on things, straining to receive an aura from any of them, was just as hopeless. The ornately lettered books she leafed through held no tenderly placed markers or well-loved edges. A few knickknacks were granted permission to be on display, if one could call a sandglass, an extra quill and inkwell, and a trio of compasses proper knickknacks. The brass fixtures of the cabin shone with a lustre that was strange, almost inhuman.

An impossible man.

Just then, Golden froze where she stood, next to the writing desk. One paper in particular snatched her gaze—and held it a shocked captive.

Her hand seemed a foreign, faraway entity as it floated down to the desk. Her fingers curled around the hastily scrawled parchment. Then everything snapped back in focus again. Biting, furiously sharp focus.

She clutched the parchment tighter. Yanked it up to eye level. Then curled it up in her fist along with a handful of skirting as she dashed across the cabin, flew up the stairwell, erupted out of the hatch, and still didn't stop. She'd do that only when she found a certain towering, impossible sea captain—and demand the explanation he now clearly owed her.

Yet for all the determination that drove her, Golden almost stopped and reversed herself when she found him. He was standing on the quarterdeck, as glorious—and imposing—as a dark god surveying his dominion. He was leaning into one leg that braced against the rail. The wind blew his shirt against his chest; she could make out the coarse texture of the curled black hair across that high and muscled plane, the dark ovals of his male nipples silhouetted at either side of it.

She sucked in a lungful of air at the sight. She would have retreated completely, but for the friendly face she caught perched atop the captain's far shoulder. She smiled warmly at Caesar the parrot.

The bird recognized her as well, raising his wings with excited caws of greeting. Golden smiled wider, but couldn't bring herself to step forward yet. Though his pet had seen her, Captain Iverson had not, and she couldn't help staring, transfixed, as an unguarded moment of contentment played across the man's features. Even as Mast admonished his pet and tried to calm Caesar's excited flappings, he spoke softly, gently, and a smile flashed across his face for a brief moment.

A smile!

Lord, Golden marveled, the man had *teeth*.

All traces of her earlier trepidation magically vanished. Golden let a laugh fly free as she stepped forward. "I'm sorry, Captain," she called as she walked the last length of deck to him. "I think Caesar's simply saying hello to a friend."

His head snapped at the first word of her statement.

By her last syllable, skitterings of nervousness once again plagued her stomach. All the tenderness and cajoling words Mast just afforded his parrot disappeared like the sun behind a sudden thunderstorm.

"Hello, hello, hello," Caesar broke into their thick silence, bouncing on the broad shoulder and seeming to crack a grin of greeting in accompaniment. "Hello, sweet. Beautiful, sweet goddess. Beaut—"

"Damn it, Caesar." Mast stole a quick look at Lady Golden, locking his teeth until they hurt when he saw the beginnings of curiosity cross her face at Caesar's ramblings. Blast that bird. Blast himself, for spouting that mush in the first place as he'd watched her sleep last night. He'd known that holding her wouldn't make any bloody difference in breaking her slight fever, but he'd done it, anyway. He'd cradled her smoothly curved body against his, staring at those features that were proud even in sleep, and crooned dribble she'd never remember or hear again, if he had anything to say about it.

"Don't speak to him that way." If this frustration wasn't enough, she boldly stepped forward then, reminding Mast at once of that moment when she'd confronted him, on Saint Kitts. That bursting, blinding, wanting moment.

"My lady, with all deference, Caesar—"

"Is a living, breathing soul and doesn't like to be snapped at any more than I do."

He had to add a hard swallow to the tension between his teeth. Snapped at? Any more than she did? It was too ridiculous to even be addressed.

"My lady," he growled, "what do you want?"

Those topaz eyes flared another few carats' worth of brilliance at him as she thrust a piece of paper in his face. A frighteningly familiar piece of paper.

"A bill of lading from Abaco Bay Ropemakers, Captain; Abaco Bay, Bahamas, in case your memory may need to be refreshed."

It was refreshed, all right. Refreshed and infuriated. "You—little—thief." He grabbed the bill and her wrist in one lunge.

"I am not a thief!" She tried, unsuccessfully, to wrench free of him. "It was right there on your bloody desk! I'm surprised Caesar didn't take advantage of it for other purposes!"

Mast willed himself to let her go at that. Cor and blast, she was right.

And by now, she was just as enraged as he was. The flush of anger on her cheeks played up her wild profusion of hair even more, even as she beat the shining mess away to glare at him. Her lips curled, as if fighting back the temptation to snarl.

"You asked me what I wanted, Captain?" Now the coral softness pursed and trembled. "An answer or two would be nice, for once. Mayhap an explanation of how you conveniently happened to be in my papa's mansion that day on Saint Kitts, and are now sailing for the same island he's been relocated to."

Mast forced his body to a relaxed posture as he leaned back against the rail, trying to conceal just how much of a tumult she'd thrown him into, and just how close to the truth she was getting. The truth he'd sworn to keep—for her own good, he drilled at himself—bloody hell, for his own good! The dream was so close now. Oh, so close. All the years of saving every sixpence and pound, of planning and imagining and envisioning—it was all too bloody damn close to lose over a jungle snip with the perspicacity of a hawk and the temper of a she-lion.

"I'm afraid you've found me out, my lady. I wanted to keep it a secret, but aye, I beat off all those other ships bobbing about in the storm just to have the privilege of saving your life myself. Astounding. How did you do it?"

"Stop it!" She pounced toward him, eyes blazing saffron fire. "Stop pretending you don't know and you don't care! You magically appeared in my life two days ago, and suddenly you're everywhere in it. Why? What do you want with me—or my father? What do we mean to you? Captain—" She honed in, tighter, unrelenting. "What am I to you?"

Despite how he'd denied it, Mast knew the question was coming. He had prepared the bulwarks of his will for it—but the plea in Golden's voice made easy work of vanquishing those desperate fortifications. And before he knew what was happening, he was lifting his hand to her cheek. He was possessively brushing the wind-whipped hair from her sun-warmed skin. When she answered that gesture with an inadvertent tilt of her head, it took every force of will he had, to battle wrapping that blond glory around his fist, and drag her next to him, and mold his lips tight and long against hers.

His senses screamed once, then again. When the ungodly sound shrilled out a third time, Mast realized what the sound really was.

Golden's alarmed expression corroborated his dread. That gruesome shriek had originated in the main hold. A rougher, even more terrified yowl now pursued it.

"Dack." The name had the vile taste of blasphemy on his lips. He'd first declined Dink and Robert's recommendations to put the lad in forced confinement, despite Dack's unholy breach of shipboard decorum on that first rainy night. But he had been forced to change his decision after he'd pushed open his cabin hatch later that same night and come face to face with the glaring youth—and his seven-inch dagger.

"What is a dack?"

He turned to see his apprehension duplicated in Golden's eyes. She thought something was wrong with the ship. He would have found himself forcing down a smirk if he hadn't been so afraid of—

Of precisely what happened.

Rico tore up on deck like a mongrel caught in a hornet's nest. *"Ay Carumba!"* he shouted. "You not going to believe this, Captain!"

Dack was just a few bounds behind him. The dirty, sweating youth squinted at first, disoriented by the contrast of the sun to the darkness of the hold, but soon his gaze was alert and tearing around the deck; seeking, searching.

Mast yanked Golden into his side. As if by instinct, she began to shiver.

"You!" Dack screamed. His eyes honed in on her. He raced up the steps to them.

Golden stopped squirming. She found herself pressing tighter to Mast. The brute she'd been preparing to tear apart a moment ago was suddenly her lifeboat in this chaos. This chaos directly bearing down on her.

"You!" came the accusing shriek again. Golden grappled tighter to Mast. His answering clutch was like the warmth of a torch on a starless night. It gave her the courage to peek out at whoever—whatever—was attacking her like this.

Her one eye of concern suddenly became a full gape of astonishment. A mere boy glared back at her. Very disturbed and very infuriated, but a *boy*. Her heart filled with compassion and curiosity at once. She turned to the lad, but leapt back to Mast when the young man lunged at her.

"You caused this, witch!" he hissed. "You and your spells and your evil! I warned everyone. I warned them all. But they wouldn't listen. And now you've summoned another witch from hell to help you. We're doomed! Doomed!"

Pandemonium erupted. Questions, shouts, and accusations shot through the air. Mast tried to leap across Golden at the youth; she barely succeeded in stopping him. Her new friend Robert matched noses and hollers with a withered sea dog and she was certain neither knew what they argued about. The din grew louder and rougher and angrier. By the spirits, there was going to be a full brawl before long.

Then her gaze stretched across the melee to Dinky. He wasn't speaking a word. His face was softened. His eyes fixed on a sight over her shoulder that completely entranced him. One by one, the rest of the crew noticed it, too. And they followed suit. Golden swallowed. She slowly turned her gaze with them.

"Maya!"

Eight

It was not supposed to happen like this.

Mast didn't know exactly what happened in those shock-frozen moments after Golden recognized the Indian across the deck, but he'd remember, well into his later years, what brought him out of that daze.

It was the weight at his feet. He looked to discover a pool of black hair around his boots. An emotion-wrought Caribbee was drifting from the middle of the thick mass. "What—is—this?" he snarled.

The only thing that stayed him from complete frustration was the expression on Golden's face. A bewildered half-smile tugged at her lips. A tender, but knowing expression clung to her cheeks.

"She says you saved her life," she translated, her voice soft, but shaken with amazement. "And now she owes you hers. She says that's why she followed you from the beach the night you left Saint Kitts. The beach where the evil soldiers shot at you."

"Oh, for God's sake—"

"Did you?" But those glittering eyes already radiated Golden's belief in her friend's story. "Captain." She slowly stepped forward to him. "How many times did you risk your life that night?"

Mast imagined a floundering fish would have been more

comfortable. The sight of her before him, wind-filled and smiling that way, was no bloody help. "Would somebody get this wench off me?" he forced himself to growl.

But try as Rico and three others would, they could not daunt the native's zeal. She clung to him as if he were one of her gods come to life. Mast cursed and tried to escape, only to look up into the challenge of Dinky's face. His friend's glare was promising something close to mutiny if the girl were not allowed to remain on board as Golden had been. And if the bewilderment over his first mate's display of gallantry wasn't enough, that wondering, searching topaz gaze still burned into him, petitioning his compassion with as much influence as Dink.

Did he have any decision left?

In answer, Mast pulled Maya up. Then he actually mumbled out a welcome aboard the *Athena* to her. He of course concluded by explaining that his decision was based on the sage counsel of his first mate—*not* upon the long-dormant whispers which had awakened to the call of that hypnotizing amber stare.

Yet the rationale did little to explain why, now three days later, he padded around the starboard side of the galley in intense hope of not interrupting or attracting the musical female laughter coming from the other side. Questing a moment of peace on his own quarterdeck without the torment of watching the coral lips from which that joy spilled—or scrambling in his brain for an answer to the amazing questions which that mouth was also capable of forming.

Her questions. God, her questions. Could a mere seventy-two hours be packed with any more? It had started with Robert's little line-securing lesson that first morning, and hadn't let up since. Even their discovery of Maya brought no reprieve. Golden's curiosity was an insatiable, incurable thing. Once she'd tagged along behind Mast on one duty or repair along the ship, she eagerly moved to the next. She was watching him, listening to him, digesting that information, then asking, to his repeated astonishment, intelligent and legitimate inquiries about the details of everything from tacking against a headwind to slushing the masts with the kitchen grease. Bloody hell, she even talked him into letting her try her hand at some of it—at which, to his further disconcertment, she showed the awkward, but promising touch of a quick learner.

That's when the torture would become unbearable. She'd smile up at him from whatever messy task he'd set her to, eyes twinkling, cheeks smudged but flushed with excitement—and she'd bring him terrifyingly close to a smile himself. Then just at that frightening ledge, she'd nonchalantly glance away as if she had no idea that by learning about his world, she was getting closer to the heart of him.

Dangerously closer.

The observation transformed his hands into fists—for the hundredth time today. "Blast," he gritted.

Damn it, he was not going to allow this. He didn't care if she was the daughter of the *king;* this seditious chit could not stride aboard and turn his life inside out like this! This was *his* vessel—where *his* word was law—and he didn't have to open any of it or himself to her if he refused.

Yes, he thought on a stomp forward, he'd even march up to his own quarterdeck if he desired to. He strode onto the plane of polished wood, welcoming the gusts whipping over it more than he ever had in his life. Mast breathed deeply, filling his lungs, then his mind with the cleansing wind.

A high squeal gashed the reverie as if a machete were slicing rice paper.

"Good God." The words felt ripped from his throat as

he spun around, already seeking out the only person he knew who could emit such a sound.

He didn't see Golden anywhere.

He wasted no time in leaping down to the main deck. He was joined by several of his crew as he stalked the starboard rail like a man possessed. In a way he supposed he was possessed, especially when the shining-haired heathen raced toward them from the other direction and no other feeling permeated him but relief that Golden's shriek pealed with excitement, not distress.

"Maya, come!" she yelled. "He's swimming over here off starboard now!" Golden yanked up her skirt, revealing bare and smudged feet pattering below.

"Golll-denn!" the poor, panting Indian returned as she caught up. "Dis is nonsense!"

"It's not nonsense!" She halted on the other side of the longboat from Mast, but if she saw him, she certainly didn't say so. "Yes!" she cried, lunging into the rail. "There he is! Look, Maya!"

"Golden!"

But the Indian's cry wasn't in reprimand this time. It was a scream of horror as Golden lunged over the rail, arms reaching out, feet jumping off the deck and sliding over the choppy sea.

Mast thanked God he'd seen as much. He cleared the longboat and charged to swoop a restraining arm around Golden just before it would have been too late. "It's all right, Maya," he strained to say past the wall that felt crushed on his chest. "She's not going anywhere."

The brow over Dinky's green eye arched as Mast shot a glance at him. The center of the blue eye narrowed in silent understanding of that look. "Yeah—she'll be fine," his first mate piped hastily. "C'mon, Maya girl, I'll—er—

be delighted to show ya the—um—galley, that's it. Aren't ya hungry?"

Maya wasn't hungry—or much of anything, it appeared, besides stunned. With her large brown eyes still fixed on Mast, the full Indian mouth attempted to break its perfect circle to form words. "You—you did it again. You saved her life!"

"Dinky!" This time he made it a command. Maya had dived into another worship session at his boots and Golden started wriggling in his hold. Mast was on the verge of toppling over into the longboat with both of them when Dink pulled the native girl away with a gentle, yet uncharacteristically chaste touch.

But the intrigue over Dink's new-found chivalry would have to wait. Mast quickly thanked the crew members for their concern. He waved them back to their duties before he spun to Golden. She winced in protest as he secured her yet tighter to him, but he'd be skewered whole if he fell for that play of helplessness as easily as he had on Saint Kitts.

"Now, hellion," he bit out each word distinctly, "do you mind telling me what the damn blazes you've disrupted this entire ship and crew for?"

She actually had the nerve to glare back up at him. "I'd show you what the blazes, if you'd only let me move an inch."

He wanted to haul her back to the cabin without a blink of acquiescence. He gritted his teeth as he did the opposite.

Surprisingly, she didn't even waste a moment to gloat. Golden flashed a genuinely appreciative smile at him, then joined his hand in hers as she moved against the rail again.

Her tender tone of explanation came as another mild surprise. "There." She pointed. "About thirty yards out, and to the left."

Mast was more than a little skeptical. Yet he obliged Golden if for nothing more than the feel of her hand safely pressed to his.

"Wait a minute," he spluttered as a distinctive splash erupted where she'd pointed to. "You don't actually think that fish—"

"Dolphin."

He ignored her correction. "You can't possibly think that . . . animal . . . is the same creature I pulled you from a fortnight ago."

"I don't think. I know. Extra width to the snout, three light splotches past his left eye. Don't gape at me, look at him. It's Nirvana. He's followed us."

"That's preposterous." But his eyes tore back to the sun-dappled waves where the lone porpoise frolicked. The first he'd ever seen without at least one other mate nearby. And the first with an abnormally keen interest in the *Athena* . . .

Because its "mate" was aboard her?

He turned to Golden, not knowing whether to frown or laugh. Her own face was lit by a spirited smile.

"They're much smarter than you 'masters of the sea' think they are, you know." Even the rebuke lilted with an easy joy Mast had never heard from her before. It continued to the extra sparkle in her eyes, the gentle way the wind made love to her hair. He decided he liked the change. He didn't mind when she entwined their hands tighter as she turned to gaze at the dolphin again.

"Nirvana found me when I was eight. He saved my life. He's watched over me ever since, no matter where I am." Her laugh was a tinkling sound as the dolphin leaped in a graceful arc, as if confirming what she'd said. "As a matter of fact," her voice gentled, "I'm ashamed I wasn't looking

out for him to begin with. I should have known he'd be
there."

But by then Mast was only half listening. His mind clung
to the first part of her explanation. For one surprising thing,
the statement didn't end in question marks. For another, it
came from this sudden and probably short-lived peace they
shared, making her words doubly meaningful. But most surprising, it was the first real opening she'd given him about
her world—a world, he knew, that possessed as many shadows as sunlight . . . that harbored the occasional turmoil
he'd seen in those dancing eyes . . . that created the nightmares he'd shaken her free from more than a few nights.
Nightmares, he had the most gut-twisting suspicion, that
were inexorably linked to the hatred that festered inside her.

And for that, he seized that opening gratefully. Greedily.

"Saved your life," he began, almost nonchalantly. He had
to be careful. "You were all of . . . six?"

"Eight."

"Oh. Aye, you told me that, didn't you? Eight."

He nodded, his usual, polite captain's nod. But there was
something very odd about the movement nonetheless, Gold-
en thought. Something very discomfiting.

His profile gave her no answers. Cool composure formed
the same invulnerable wall around the sharp-hewn features
as it had for the last week. The same solid veneer, no matter
how bright she'd tried to smile at him or how hard she'd
labored to learn of his "world," as he called it. That same
maddening combination of courtesy and intensity that met
every one of her questions but didn't give an iota more,
and certainly never asked for anything in return.

Still, this Mast unsettled her. Before, he'd made it a point
to prove just how impersonal he could be. Now there was

interest, however calmly disguised it was. It made her feel very nice—and very strange.

"I suppose," he continued in that same interested but uninterested voice, "That's how the natives came to consider you a sea goddess."

She tried not to look at him, but the subtle light of understanding in his eyes was compelling. Dinky had told Golden of the countless others who had mistaken his captain for the Moonstormer, and the notion made her feel connected to Mast somehow. She smiled despite herself.

"Yes," she answered. "That's when the Arawak took me in. Many of the tribe still call me Porpoise Girl, though they know I'm far from the perfect little goddess."

The captain quirked one side of his mouth. "Isn't immortality a pain in the arse?"

Golden laughed. A few moments of easy silence passed between them before he turned a serious gaze to her again.

"The Arawak," he repeated, brows bunched in puzzlement. "I thought they'd been obliterated a hundred years ago."

"In the true sense of the life they knew, aye. Slavery and European diseases wiped out many of the ancestors of my tribal family. But the islands teach one to adapt, to . . ." Golden thought a moment, breathing in, as if the action could bring a sweet Saint Kitts breeze to help her find the word, "to blend."

"I see." He took a step closer, and Golden could feel her instincts prickling in alarm. His eyes were suddenly fathoms deep and impenetrably dark.

"Tell me . . ." His murmur came low and serious as well, delving unnervingly into Golden's soul. "Tell me, was it the Arawaks who taught you to hate the Moonstormer so much?"

She jumped so fast from him she collided into the edge of the longboat. The lovely, happy moment between them was gone. Nay, Golden amended, it had never existed. All he'd wanted was to bring this torment of remembering again.

Anything but make her remember.

"Life taught me that, Captain Iverson," she grated. "And I'll be happy to pass the lesson on when I take the air from that monster's lungs, scream by scream."

The only reply he gave her then was a hard swallow. But even that simple gesture made Golden feel as if he were reading her thoughts, as if he were battling the loneliness and hate right along with her.

"Don't," she whispered. "This is my pain. Mine. You don't understand. You can't understand."

"Damn it." He came nearer by one heavy step. "I do understand." Then his face lowered even closer. "More than you know, hellion. More than you know."

"Ah." She forced herself to give a steady nod, but her breath wobbled. "But you just can't tell me why, right?"

Now his own jaw clenched and his gaze quickly flew to the water. That dark, uncomfortable look was all the answer Golden needed.

"Just go away," she rasped. She shrank in on herself as she backed away from him. "Please, just go away."

He nodded slowly. God blast him, even that small movement spoke quiet, yet all-encompassing empathy.

What was this man trying to do to her?

But before she could consider the question any more, Mast pivoted from her and returned, alone, to his stance at the helm of his ship.

* * *

"It is all my fault," Maya blurted, her voice thick with threatening tears.

Dinky hurried back across the small but cozy space of his quarters and pressed the stein of ale to her lips. "Now, lovey, we've been through this already. I told ya that was a dotty notion and I meant it!"

"But dee Moonstormer, he angry because of me! If I not follow him dat night from the beach, if I not stewed away—"

"If you'd not *stowed* away, my lovely Maya bird," he interrupted on a chuckle, "my heart would not be trillin' the song it does now."

Her round cocoa eyes glowed at him with grateful warmth, but a hesitant edge still clung to her voice. "Dee Moonstormer, Peabrooke—he look like da black rain cloud."

"Maya," he admonished, "I think you could lighten that cloud if you'd stop callin' him the Moonstormer."

"Golden calls him dee obstinant ape."

He chuckled again, more robustly this time. The sound brought a little smile to Maya's lips. She'd never known anyone as exciting or lively as this man they called Peabrooke. She'd been taken immediately by his entrancing two-toned stare. She felt as if her feet hadn't come out of the clouds since. If only his master could be as happy as he. That Captain Iverson and his constant frown worried her. She heard that he'd all but ordered Golden to continue the living arrangements he'd established for her in his quarters—something about a "recuperation" from her "ordeals" in "accommodations befitting a lady."

Yes, it concerned her greatly—but not only for Golden's sake. She explained this incongruity to the man at her side. "I just don' like it. No way at all. I never see Golden like dis. She so . . . ah, how I say it?—so wound up tight, like dee cobra around da tree branch. And ev'ry time I talk about dee Moon—dee Captain—it get worse. She get more upset. It not good. She got a burnin' crazy temper, Peabrooke. Your Ive may get hurt."

"Lovey." Dinky pulled both her hands into his and smooched a reassuring kiss atop the knuckles. "Stop worryin'! Yer all flummoxed fer nothin', I promise ya. My captain and yer sister are just bein' stubborn about the whole thing, that's all."

"The whole thin'?"

"Aye, darlin'."

"Peabrooke," Maya huffed, cocking her head at him. "What da stars you about?"

"Oh, sweet Maya." He yanked the rest of her close as he breathed it against her cheek. "Let me show ya what I'm about . . ."

And his fingers and his mouth did just that. What an exquisite demonstration! Maya arched into Peabrooke's embrace, sucking hot gasps through her teeth, never feeling anything so natural, so beautiful. This was better than she'd anticipated it would be. Peabrooke was like an inspired music man, playing the chords of her body until they sang out in joyful yearning. His tongue lolled out the harmony along her ear. His warm breaths set the drumbeat it kept time to. And the melody? His sweet, prodding touch, exploring the line of her hips, the swell of her bottom, up to either side of her rib cage, and finally over the two peaks that so urgently awaited him. She cried out as he grasped her there, his fingers kneading—no, compelling—the sensitive tips to taut, tender ecstasy.

"Do ya understand now, my love?" he asked in a rasp, bringing his hands to her face, stroking her cheeks.

Maya nodded into his gaze, knowing her eyes were as sultry with passion as his. "Golden is a cuckoo."

"Ive's an even bigger one."

He brought her tight against him and slanted his lips upon hers. Maya's senses exploded in light and fantasy.

On the other side of the ship, things were a completely different story.

"The vultures take him," Golden seethed. "The insensitive, ruthless beast."

She punctuated it with another whack against the wall with one of the spice-scented pillows. But the action was as effective at draining her frustration as the previous twelve throws.

"Beast!" came a riotous call from the cage a few feet away. "You stubborn, angry beast!"

Golden's lips turned up despite herself when she looked up to Caesar. The bird bobbed proudly on his perch as he rattled off the words she'd taught him behind Mast's back. She envisioned the look on the lout's face when he found out what she'd done. The flash of agitation that would quirk those lines edging his temple and jaw, then the slow roil of those blue depths of eyes that signaled . . .

Her smile faded. What, indeed? *Did you expect something at the end of that other than a question mark, Golden? Did you actually think you'd have "melted" Mast Iverson by now? Well, the man's not an iceberg, Golden. He's a slab of unbreakable, unmeltable iron.*

"Oh, Caesar," she sighed. "If I could only learn the mysteries your captain guards so tightly—learn them as easily as you master those words."

The macaw's deep-throated guffaws seemed to confirm how ridiculous that idea was. Golden sighed again. "Yes, my friend. I'm afraid I agree with you, though I am utterly loath to admit it."

She was drained. So drained and disheartened, and now, more than ever, thoroughly confused. Taking the chance of leaping into the waves with Nirvana, as disastrous as her last journey with the dolphin had been, suddenly appeared an enticing consideration compared to the uncertainty the *Athena's* decks held for her each day . . . or the unanswered questions—and the unabated torment of her senses—provoked by the exasperating captain of this world.

"Rrrrraaack!"

Golden broke into grateful laughter at the bird's blatant preens and fluffs for her attention. "All right, you flirt," she acquiesced. "Maybe it'll be easier to get you to talk."

She rose and lifted the latch of the cage. The macaw eagerly jumped down to her forearm. She resorted to a little flirtation of her own, scratching him along the back of his neck. Caesar went as still as a puppy in the throes of a good scratch.

"You like that, do you?" she teased, though Golden was certain her enjoyment rivaled that of the bird's. Caesar's soft trills, the exotic colorings of his plumage and the feel of his heart beneath her fingers all brought comforting images of Saint Kitts to the front of her ravaged mind.

"Oh, my friend," she said wistfully. "What I would give to be on Saint Kitts right now! You'd love it, Caesar, you truly would, especially at this time of the day. The air is still warm, yet cool enough to run free in. Maya and I would probably take to the cane fields, taking turns hiding from one another, or perhaps we'd be in Basseterre, if Papa had some business there. We'd tell him we were going browsing in the shops, but we'd really sneak away to the docks, where the ocean opens up to the whole world—aye, the whole world, Caesar!"

She settled dreamily into the velvet chair behind her, envisioning the brilliant sights and sounds of Basseterre at sunset. "Maybe, if we were lucky, a ship would pull in," she mused. "We'd be able to see the town wenches parade by on their way to the grand vessel, dressed up in their bright dresses and smelling like jasmine and lilacs, their faces powdery and beautiful as they smiled to the sailors at the rails. Everyone would be laughing and talking with each other, their cares blown away on the wind, and—"

"Rrrriccckk!"

But Caesar's perturbed screech fell on unhearing ears. Golden waved him away as she jolted straight up.

Her own words echoed in her brain. Sweet star fire. The fancy-dressed village wenches . . . the smiling seamen, blurting hours' worth of conversation to those powdered women at the tavern tables . . . telling them anything they wanted to know!

Mast was a man.

And she had gowns. Plenty of beautiful gowns!

A slow smile spread across her face.

"Caesar, I have a plan. A wonderful, glorious plan!"

Nine

It was going to be a magnificent Caribbean twilight. The sunshine had aged through the afternoon like a fine wine, and now the stars awoke early to sup of its bouquet. The breeze was warm and satiny, the water an equally lustrous texture. Puerto Rico shimmered like an emerald off the port rail. Hibiscus blooms were kissing the air with their heady tropical fragrance. It was the kind of scene a man threw his arms open to, bared his soul to, in hope that some of the brilliance might rub off on him.

But the last thing Mast desired right now was brilliance. Alone on the quarterdeck, he rammed his hands further into the pockets of his long vest. He dared nature to shove any more blasted "brilliance" down his throat.

Nay, his mind had done a well enough job of that, thank you. He hadn't seen one lustrous hair of Lady Golden Gaverly today, not a surprising circumstance after he'd sent her skittering away from him like a petrified colt yesterday—but instead of welcoming the occurrence, even being thankful for it, all he'd felt was a burning emptiness.

And, damn it, curiosity. Wondering where the hell she was. What she was doing.

What kind of trouble she was getting herself into.

It would have been easy enough to inquire into—or, for that matter, to find out for himself. But beyond Maya's reassurance that the little hellion was aboard and safe, he told himself it didn't matter. That untamed, disrespectful, overly inquisitive creature of a woman was already more trouble than his most dread dreams anticipated, and he was certain the less he knew of her mischief—short of burning the ship to driftwood—the better.

Aye, it was best that he stay as far away from that fiery-eyed face as he could. And the equally destroying heat in the lithe body below it.

He'd had enough "brilliance," thank you. Enough for a bloody life full.

Enough for a heart full?

He swore beneath his breath. He whirled from the rail, hoping to leave those insane thoughts behind him.

Another mistake. The sky was even more magnificent off the starboard rail. Clouds were trailing across the horizon like ribbons upon the floor of a mantua-maker's: coral and amber, deep orange, burnt copper. It was mere seconds until the most vibrant-hued of them became the ripples of her hair. Long and brilliant and fire-kissed, like strands of the sun itself . . .

"Damn you, Golden," he grated beneath his breath. "Damn you."

The name reverberated along every recess of his body and mind. *Golden, Golden, Golden . . .*

What the hell was happening to him? Mast swallowed deeply as the memories came now, unwanted, yet uncontrollable. He saw the hellion as she was against this sky just yesterday after supper. She didn't just gaze at the azure water and the puffy clouds. She was a part of them, free and flowing and uninhibited. The only thing that had seemed out of place were her clothes. Oh, to rip them off and revel in the passion and glory of her body in the wind, and then, oh yes, to join her there—to form the curve of her womanhood against the hard, throbbing part of him, to part her silken mouth with his own, exploring her softness and heat . . .

But he couldn't. Not under any circumstances. Promises . . . promises meant everything to a man of honor, he forced himself to recite as if the words were one of Maya's sacred mantras. He'd promised Wayland he'd protect her. His friend had promised to pay him well for it.

And there was the promise Golden carried of her own. A vow of revenge for a hate so strong, she'd kill a man for it.

Goddamn it. He needed an ale. Nay, rum. A bottle of it. He turned to descend to the hold when he was jarred short in his tracks by a god-awful noise.

"Ooohhh, on Fridaaay morn as we set sail, it was not faarr from land, there I spied a fair pretty maaaid, with a comb and a glass in her haaannd!"

Mast wondered if His Majesty was in need of some new court criers. Hearing Dink's off-key warble along the alcoves of Windsor might be the thing that would lure him back for a visit.

"Ive!" His first mate swooped upon him. "Been wonderin' where ya were since eight bells. Kee-rist, my watch below night, too." The green eye shakily honed in on him. "Almost thought I wouldn't find ya, but I guess it was too much to hope fer, aye?"

"Too much to hope for?" Mast extended his long glass toward Puerto Rico, pretending indifference to the implication in his companion's tone.

"Yeah. As if ya might, fer once, be takin' supper with someone other than Caesar."

Mast didn't lower the tube from his eye. Lazy palm fronds teased him from the amplified circle of vision. "Mr.

Peabrooke, I'm afraid I must order you to discontinue com-
ments like that regarding Lady Golden."

"Oooooo." It rose and fell with feigned seriousness.
"Now he's orderin' me." Dink cocked an elbow to the rail.
"Blarst, Ive. That wench has gotten to ya more than I
thought already."

"Lady Golden, Dink. Her name is Lady Golden."

"See what I mean? There ya go again." The older man
showed no mercy with his hearty chortling. "No offense,
kid, but nobody, and I do swear nobody, has snagged your
riggin' like this, since the day the countess—"

Mast lunged out before rational thought could stop him.
Some kind of guttural sound escaped him as his hands
coiled into Dink's shirt and he jerked the skinny man up to
his eye level. "Goddamn it, Dink." He faintly realized he
was shaking. "I told you to never mention her again."

A long, unthinking, uncomprehending moment passed.
Mast battled back the inferno of fury that engulfed him.
"Hell," he heard himself mutter. His arms quivered as he
released his friend; he blinked back the hot red fuzz at the
corners of his vision. "I'm sorry, Dink. Christ, I'm sorry."

"Awww, knock it off, Iverson." The tone was practically
jovial. But a sobering cough followed. "Listen, kid. Ya
never told me what happened in Cornwall, and I don't think
I really desire ta know—but damme, Ive, I wager you've
been haunted by that bitch long enough." There was an
all-knowing pause. "I think, in that way of hers, that little
spitfire wagers it, too."

Mast dropped his head between his elbows as he leaned
against the V of the bow. "That little spitfire, Dink, grew up
on an island. She's never seen anything beyond the beaches
of Saint Kitts since she was a child. She's just curious."

"About you."

"About everything."

Dink snickered again. Mast looked over his shoulder at him, a hint of humor forming at his own mouth. "Don't you have a loaded gun to go clean?"

"Captain Iverson! That's no manner in which to speak with your first mate." There was no mistaking the voice of the chastiser. But as the two men turned, they were certain Golden's musical voice had bewitched and gone to inhabit the shell of another.

In place of the hellion was a vision that would make any seasoned courtesan wither with spite. Where wild tresses once roamed free, now a sophisticated golden coil framed a clean and exquisite face. Soft tendrils hugged the proud slope of her neck. A bow of emerald green satin encircled her throat, and Mast found himself wanting to cut the adornment away in jealousy. The ribbon perfectly matched the gown she wore. Or, more aptly, had poured herself into.

"You . . . look . . ."

He stammered into silence. For the life of him he couldn't find the word to complete the sentence. The only thought, the only sensation he knew was fire, that, blast his traitorous body, engulfed his manhood.

What the hell was she thinking?

What in the world was he thinking? Golden silently asked the question as she stood there in the late afternoon glow, sensing the sun on her face but not feeling anything, especially from Mast. She trailed his dark and riveting stare as he studied her up and down. She contemplated his firm-lined mouth, seemingly frozen in its half-parted state. Still, she could determine nothing.

With nervous hands she smoothed down the front of the gown and toyed with the stiff gold lace along the low-scooped neckline, trying to ignore how ridiculous she felt.

Oh, what had she been thinking? That she, backward island girl, would appeal to a worldly, sophisticated seaman like him? If she could only get out of this dress! She wished she had the outfit Guypa had made for the celebration of her *bara*—her first woman's blood. She looked magnificent in the shells and beads of that!

But this was not the time for wistfulness. She had come up here to expose Mast Iverson the man. She came to tear down those frowning, silent walls and discover, finally, just why he'd come into her life—precisely what this voyage and her meant to him . . . and how, oh how he made her blood run both hot and cold; how he made her feel such fury then such longing . . .

This whirlwind had to be stilled! The time for secrets was past due. The moment for boldness and honesty had arrived.

Clinging to that thought as her strength, she forced her legs to move across the deck, despite how they sweated and quivered beneath the layers of the gown.

"Captain." She tried to address him steadily but she made the error of looking up his tall body as she did, and her composure wavered like a gull on a crosswind. He was all wind-blown and rugged and dark-tanned masculinity, breeches scuffed with dust from the day's work, vest and shirt whipping tight against his chest. The sight of him, along with the breath-squeezing limits of her clothing, made her feel languid and dizzy and painfully, exquisitely helpless.

But that was only the beginning. True helplessness was found in looking at the man's face.

Power had met its visual definition. The midnight gaze was more fathomless than Golden had ever seen. Her heart smashed against her ribs as those mesmerizing eyes met—and held—hers.

Great Puntan. She'd exposed something in Captain Mast Iverson, all right. And she was drowning in it.

"He's a poop, girl, never mind him," Dinky cut in. He yanked her hand into his and plopped an enthusiastic kiss on the back of it. "He was goin' to say ya look ravishin'. Whallop-me-in-the-gut ravishin', Golden. Crimey, that frock looks better'n you than it did on Bessy Greenquist, and she was—"

"She was a tramp and that's exactly what you look like."

Mast's words threw her heart back against her ribs. It collided with her spine and sank down, broken and shriveled, to her stomach. But as she had earlier in the day, she couldn't break her gaze from the sight of him—so now, she couldn't stop staring, no matter how effortlessly he lashed that cruel and horrid glare back into her. Her chin remained raised before him as if held by an invisible string, despite how it fought to tremble and wither.

"Thank you, Captain Iverson." Her voice surprised her. Her words were clear, even composed. "Now I can stop guessing just how much of an unfeeling clot you are."

Mast vaguely heard a low, appreciative whistle from Dink's direction. But it was background drizzle to the din in his own head. Lust and need, awe and bewilderment, anger and . . . God, yes, fear, all repressed and pounded down for so long, they were like new sensations to him. New emotions.

Christ. Emotions.

He stepped toward her. His hand trembled as it came up.

Too late. All he grasped was the back of her shoulder as she whirled from him. "Don't touch me," she hissed, flashing him feline-fierce eyes as she wrenched out of his hold. "Just—don't—touch me."

And then she bolted away.

"Well." Dink smacked his lips in loud, irritating time to

the sea against the hull. "Ya were smashin' with that, kid, just smashin'. Truly, I mean it. What I wouldn't give to see ya do that all over again. The finesse, the—"

"Lash it, Dink."

First Mate Peabrooke leaned leisurely over the rail, enjoying the ridiculously rapid departure of his captain. Only when he saw Mast's head disappear below deck did he let the devilish chuckle fly free from his lips. "Maya!" he called on his own way down to the lower decks. "C'mere, ya delicious little thing. There's passion in those stars tonight."

Ten

He pulled the hatch closed so violently behind him that Golden was stunned the ship didn't come apart from the impact. She jerked her head up from where she'd thrown herself onto the bunk, staring at the furious image he made as he landed at the foot of the stairwell. Veins throbbed in his fury-tightened arms. Pure thunder darkened his face. Her own face widened, then froze. She only remembered to breathe when her heart pummeled an aching reminder.

"What the—" he grated. "Why—" Then again, Captain Iverson seemed as competent to complete a sentence at this moment as she. Star's fire, the man was upset.

He lifted a stiff-fingered hand toward her. A long heart-beat thudded by before he curled the fingers back and beat his fist sideways into the wall. "Damn it," he muttered. "Damn it."

Iverson, you grand poet. Mast thought sardonically. He sunk his head to the ledge he'd made of his forearm, grappling through his mind for something else to say than that, but the words never came. His aching frustration didn't blossom to life on his lips. The confusion never straightened into a string of eloquence that he could turn and spout to her as if he were a hero in a romantic play.

Nay, he determined dismally, that was it. Just . . . damn it. Damn it that this was the first time in a long time that his mind couldn't function properly, that his libido had taken over the duty, instead—and it terrified him to the core. And damn it that it was Wayland Gaverly's god-blasted daughter who did this to him. Damn her ingenious little mind for concocting this dress-up scheme, and damn her entrancing body for carrying the strategy out so well.

Damn every lovely, resplendent inch of her.

He rolled his head and looked to her again with the last imprecation. She sat there, awash in a halo of the day's last glow and he thought, for a single frozen moment, she truly was a goddess. Sad and ethereal, lovely and . . . adorable. Half her elegant coiffure had tumbled into her cleavage and the satin ribbon lay tangled beneath the mess, only one askew loop still intact. And there was the ocean of material she was drowning in: endless yards of satin and underskirts swallowing her and the bunk. In the midst of it all, those gut-stopping, soul-stripping eyes glittered like a gold mine as she looked up to him in shock and even a little fear, but most of all, in hurt.

"Is that all, Captain?"

The query was such a contrast to the hellion he knew, so quiet and potent, that Mast, for a heavy moment, didn't react. Then a slow fury coiled through him, erupting as he pushed off the wall with a fierce jerk. "Blast," he gritted. This was hell for him, too!

Before he knew what he was doing, he swooped down over Golden and pulled her up next to him.

"Nay," he growled into her face. "That's not all."

"I told you not to touch me!"

"And I'm telling you to obey your captain and be silent. If that is possible. *My lady.*"

She hated him, Golden decided once and for all. Hated the

insensitive bastard, with every inch of her that wriggled and fought beneath the layers of stifling clothing that bound her.

Yet minutes later, her head had only accomplished getting away from him by inches. Her fists were at the front of his shirt. From there down, his hands splayed across the small of her back, pressing, binding, molding her to him in a way that felt strange and hot.

"Don't." She leveled at him, trying again to pummel his high shoulders. His hold was like a steel trap. "Please . . ."

But her voice had become as weak as day-old turtle soup. Golden dreadfully realized her legs felt equally weak, especially as his fingers started gathering the material of the gown this way, and then that across her skin. Oh, Lord . . . oh, Lord!

"Please. Don't."

"Don't what?" came the derisive, yet whisper-soft answer. His touch moved down further, further . . . sweet stars in heaven, around her backside, taking the curve of flesh there in his hands, squeezing it.

"Isn't this what you wanted, sweet?" His breath was rough and demanding at her ear. "Wasn't this the result you were seeking?"

"I—I don't know what I wanted . . ."

"Of course you do. Answer me. This is just what you hoped for, wasn't it?"

His words taunted her. His tone caressed her. Golden didn't know which to believe . . . if she was still capable of clear thought. The insufferable brute had turned her brain into a jumble of rocks. The weight was overpowering, pulling her head down, down until she was horrified to find her lips suddenly lodged at the crook of his hard, dark neck. He was moist there, moist and warm and pulsing with strength. Oh, Lord!

He pulsed even more as she felt him drag a deep breath in. The air traveled in a shaking, dominating wave up the length of his body. He slowly exhaled along her neck, just behind her ear.

Golden never knew such a sensitive place on her body existed. She shuddered uncontrollably, cried out involuntarily. The load of rocks in her head shifted again. Her world reeled backwards, but his powerful hand was there, saving her, drawing her back up to him.

"Golden. My maddening little hellion . . . Golden." The hoarseness of his voice denied the mighty grip of his limbs. But Golden found the rasp amazingly powerful. Power was flowing from her as well as into her. "Sweet Golden, you cannot be oblivious to the way you make me feel."

Feel . . . yes, Golden agreed. All she wanted to do was feel! She moaned in surrender to that heated urge as she slid her hands over Mast's shoulders, and her fingers went spanning around the broad curves of them. He was so hard and carved and interesting. His body was as wondrous and overwhelming as his heroic heart and mind. He was an uncharted land she longed to explore and discover . . .

She set sails to her fingers over the line of his collarbone, made daring passage up the tendonous pathways of his throat and neck. At last she delved her hands into the thick, dark waves of his hair. At the same time an insistent force pried her legs apart, sending ever-increasing circles of pleasure spiraling out from her womanhood. The force came from his leg, she managed to comprehend, as he eased her further against it. Harder against it. The sweet torture of it!

"All I feel . . ." she finally managed to whisper, ". . . is you."

"And . . ." A timeless, breathless pause as their husky gazes fell upon each other. ". . . how do I feel?"

"How—how do you feel?"

"Tell me what you feel, Golden."

She took a breath, but no answer came. How did he expect her to put this incredible feeling into words? How could he ask her to describe the sensations he aroused as he pressed fingers between her shoulder blades, raked his touch down her spine, softly circled her waist, then lifted his thumbs to the undersides of her breasts? And his thigh, the most excruciating torture of all . . . how did he expect her to describe that astonishing, yet somehow warm and familiar rhythm he'd awakened in the soft folds of her woman's heat?

Ohhh, how had this happened?

How had this happened? Mast asked it to himself, even as his eyes drank greedily of the flushed face just inches from his. He could almost see the consciousness of her own womanhood bloom to life in her. Every stroke of his hands, every nuance of pressure in this instinctual dance of theirs, brought those enraptured features even more to life before him. Every passing minute marked another consuming tarantism of shivers through her body. And his.

Retribution. It was all he'd wanted. To teach her, to show her firsthand, what a gown like this on a body like hers did to a man. And so he'd grabbed her. Brazenly. Damn near awkwardly, it had been so long since he'd held a woman like this.

He'd expected her to slap him again, and that would be it. Nay, he amended, he'd wanted her to slap him again. Anything, please God something, to help him escape this thickening haze of need, this deepening abyss of hot, hungry desire . . . this dangerous web Golden Gaverly had so innocently, expertly woven around his senses.

But she didn't fight him. No, she wasn't that merciful. She was responsive, and sensuous. Giving . . . open.

"Mast . . . you feel wonderful."

Damn her. She was so breathtakingly honest.

"Golden." He murmured the sparkling word, but inside he screamed at his muscles to regroup and retreat. But she was so soft and so close; her slender fingers felt so good on his flesh and she smelled so damn good. Mast recognized the fresh breeze of his pine soap now mingled with the sweet wind of her island-flowered scent. And it was too much, too much.

"*Golden.*" The firmer tone he forced worked the miracle he needed in his legs. As he moved away he also yanked her fingers from him and constrained them between his in the air between their bodies.

"What is it?" Her eyes glittered over their shaking handclasp. Her voice quivered. "Don't . . . don't I feel good, too?"

"Oh, God." Wry laughter spiked the words despite his best intentions. Mast slowly shook his head. "Golden, don't you know what you do to a man when you dress like this? When you look like this?"

"When I look like this?" she retorted, with a strange and swift harshness. But then Mast saw the tone was only intended to distract from her eyes full of pain. "Well, you certainly don't have to be so blunt about it, Captain. I wasn't such a mess until you insulted me," she snapped. "My hair would have stayed if you hadn't forced me to run down here, and the dress—"

"You make him want to touch you where he shouldn't."

He cut her off as if she hadn't said a thing. But even Golden struggled to recall what had angered her. His words ignited in her mind and his fingers started to kindle new heat in her blood. The flames formed slowly, torturously, smoldering at the tips of her fingers, up her arms, around her elbows.

This wasn't the way this was supposed to happen! *She* was supposed to be enticing *him*.

"Oh, yes." She felt his warm voice against her cheek. "You make him want to touch you, Golden. Like this . . ."

He moved the back of his hand over the curves of her other cheek. Even as his knuckles brushed there Mast wondered where they would trail next, what direction. Another force had conquered him, despite how his mind screamed for its rightful throne over his actions. *This isn't right,* it protested, only to be refused by the mass of feeling and heat and raw nerve endings his body had become. *This is right . . . God, this is right.*

"You make him want to embrace you, Golden. Like this . . ."

And then he withdrew his leg from her woman's curve, replacing it with the pressure of his full male swell. Their chests met, hard nipples mating. Their thighs pressed, long legs shaking and tangling.

Golden's senses burst into blinding intensity. She gasped with the exhilaration of the feeling; smiled when his intake of breath joined hers. A long, shuddering pause became a long, wanting stare.

"M-Mast?"

"What?" The reply was more his breath than his voice.

"Wh-what does the man want to do after this?"

He didn't answer.

That filled Golden with perplexion. She yearned for his response, needed it. She felt it in every inch of his body throbbing against hers, in every desperate clutch of his hand at her back and every insistent stroke at her neck.

Then she looked into his eyes.

His answer, she discerned with astonishment, was there. Very deep within the bottomless ocean depths there lurked—Lord, yes—a predator. A predator called fear.

Golden was too moved to be surprised any more. Without a glimmer of expression other than the wave of tenderness she felt, she reached up and lightly fingered the crescent of his scar. His skin trembled beneath her touch. She smiled. Her fingers explored their way to his lips, over the clean, masculine shape of them, between the soft, parted opening of them.

"Golden—" he entreated.

"Show me," she implored back.

"Golden—"

"Please."

"God save me."

Golden's heart exploded as he pulled her lips to his.

The experience was more exhilarating, more soaring and magnificent than when he did it in Papa's study the first time. For now, Golden comprehended, there was under-standing and emotion with the excitement. Now there was yearning to return the rapture Mast freed in her—to make him feel as glorious as he made her feel, in this fiery mo-ment, in the magic of his arms.

And from the way he coiled his arms around her and crushed every last rational thought from her mind, Golden joyfully gathered she had. She wrapped her hands around his neck, eager to match Mast's ardor with all the longing and need in her soul. His hand grasped the back of her head, bending her even more to his will. She surrendered without hesitation, giving from the deepest part of her. The hot, hungering place, where she never thought she'd find fulfillment . . . until now.

They dragged apart and gulped on air. Mast nearly choked with the sight of her. Her eyes were glazed over in lusty astonishment, her hair . . . everywhere. And her lips. Christ, her lips.

He took her mouth again, engulfing it with even more hungry urgency this time. He wanted to be inside her.

Self-containment was a hopeless cause, gone the way of all his exasperation and fury when she'd not only returned his kiss, but transformed it into pure fire with her precious, vulnerable kind of desire, her honest, untamed affection.

He wanted to be inside her.

Golden whimpered deep in her throat as Mast gently backed her to the wall and pressed his body to hers. She didn't think they could get any closer without climbing inside each other and from the way his lips slanted again and again over hers, he actually seemed to be attempting such an absurdity. She didn't care. She wanted to please him. She wanted to make this magic go on forever.

The first time he prodded her lips apart she supposed it a slip.

The second time was nauseating.

The third time brought outright horror.

His tongue came with that. Delving into her mouth with its wet heat, twirling with hers in absolute, carnal possession. Golden's heart raced to her head. Her stomach plummeted to her toes. Her skin caught on fire, then tingled to prickling ice.

She screamed.

Mast suddenly found himself sprawled out on his bunk, skull crashed against the wood-paneled bulkhead. He righted himself an inch, straining to set his eyesight level. "What the bloody hell?"

"What the bloody hell, indeed!"

The woman was going to drive him to the sharks. "Golden." He rose from the bunk but she dashed away, darting next to his writing desk and hunching low there, as if it were a giant rock she could hurl at him if she needed to.

"Don't come any closer! Oh, I know what you're all about now, Captain! I actually thought my fear was silly. Surely nothing so wondrous, so exciting, could be so horrid!"

"Horrid?"

"I said stay away!"

"Oh, for Christ's sake." Mast forced himself to a stop. His hands strained at his sides as if they were the locks on his self-control. "Golden, this has gone too far."

"You can grill a pig it has!"

"I'm going to grill *you* if you don't get up off the floor and explain yourself to me."

A short and derisive laugh broke from her lips. "You'd like that, wouldn't you? Anything to get me close enough again, aye? Didn't get the prey moist enough the first time?"

That was it. With an exasperated growl Mast stepped across the cabin, hauled the incorrigible heathen to her feet, and secured her relentlessly to the desk with his own body as belaying pin.

He inhaled deeply, trying just as much to dilute the need in his body as the exasperation from his mind before carefully grating, "I have had enough of your mistrust and fear, my lady. For God's blasted sake, I was kissing you, not killing you."

He stopped there, hovering over her face, waiting for her flippant comeback.

None came.

"K-kissing me?"

He had to strain to understand her bare whisper. "Well,

yes," he growled, feeling his patience—and his breeches—stretch painfully taut. "What the hell did you think—"

"A . . . kiss?"

He sighed, a short and exasperated breath. "Hellion, you know kissing."

But his allusion to that tumultuous first embrace they'd shared on Saint Kitts seemed to go right through Golden. Her hands remained as fixed at his neck as her gaze did to his face. Puzzlement curved around those piercing amber eyes. It was a look that, if he didn't know better, bespoke . . . awakening. Wonderment. Damn her, even innocence.

"You mean you weren't preparing me for dinner?"

The utter seriousness of her question only deepened his frustration. "Preparing you for dinner?" he sputtered. "No."

"Not even the last part?"

"The last part?"

"With—with your tongue." To Mast's surprise she blushed and flitted her eyes away. The copper satin of her lashes was captivating against the coral tint of her skin. Christ. It was maddening, the way she did that. Maddening . . . and intoxicating.

Again as if another force swept in and invaded his body, Mast parted his legs and drew her close until Golden's sleek form was couched firmly between his thighs. "That was kissing, too, hellion."

As if for shelter, she burrowed closer to him, grasping the ends of his shirt ties. "Well, in the rain forest it's certainly not," she responded softly. "If a body went around getting that slippery around a tree snake, they'd end up that night's supper."

Mast's hands paused along her spine. Suddenly, it all became clear to him. Damn! Why hadn't he considered it before?

She'd only been a child when the Arawak took her in. Naturally, she'd been initiated with the code and customs of the natives since the time when she could understand such things. On the islands, that meant the code of the wilderness—where man was the visitor, not the king. It was possible for a snake to drench a person through with slather before swallowing their head whole in a matter of seconds.

His poor hellion thought he was spicing her up for supper!

It would have been comical had her horror not been so real. Mast pulled Golden even closer as he thought of the terror he'd just put her through. All he wanted to do was impart his reassurance to her—and, he realized with shock—his apology.

But something went awry between his body and hers. Her sigh was anything but calm as she breathed it into his chest. Her fingertips were none too forgiving as they spread around to his back. Mast couldn't help the breath that erupted from his own lips—or the uncontrollable question which escaped him at the same moment.

"So . . . how would a body kiss in the rain forest?"

Her smile radiated warmth against his chest. "Can't you feel me showing you?"

I am a doomed man.

He was so enraptured by the uninhibited gaze she beamed up at him that Mast allowed her to remove his vest and shirt with nothing more than a deep swallow and a labored breath. Through every moment, Golden's long and curious hands explored every inch of him. Her touch first glided then kneaded, growing in possessiveness. She traveled up his ribs to his chest, down his arms, even making an intricate study of his hands and fingers before she circled behind him and then outlined each contour of his back. A primitive, sensual little mewl emanated from her throat as she finished with each part of him, as if she were memorizing him.

It was pure torture. It was exquisite ecstasy. All the practiced seductions of London, the ardent embraces of Paris, the deep-tongued come-hithers of every port he'd known in his life—they had no right to be called kisses. Not after this. Mast's body opened to her ministrations. His skin hungered for them. Each nerve was inspired with light and sensation, with fire and need.

"Close your eyes," she instructed gently, now standing in front of him again. "Close your eyes, and open your senses. Feel me kiss you."

I am a doomed man.

He wanted to scream. He groaned instead. He moved to protest her motions but she murmured a huskier repeat of her directions and all he could do was obey, praying for deliverance even as he yearned for the sweet damnation of her touch.

Hell's fire came with her lips. A shudder claimed him as he felt the first wet nip at his shoulder. Her mouth was warm, soft, suckling. His hands dropped into agonized clenches as he felt her continue up to his neck, up until he heard her breathing in his scent as she licked him, that same enticing moan echoing softly from inside her. He pulled his fists tighter against the surge of torment that rampaged in his groin. It was very nearly a relief when her hands took the place of her lips again.

Until her palms flattened against his nipples.

"Ohhh," he grated. "Oh, God." His head fell back, his knees started to puddle, his erection stretched beyond salvation. The tension grew even worse as he looked to see Golden examining one hardened half of his chest, then the other. A softly bewildered look adorned her face.

"Our way of kissing pleases you." The statement was eloquent in its simplicity. "Yet I wonder what it would be like if we took your way of kissing, and blended the two."

But before Mast could deduce what she was about, she dipped her head to his breast and formed her velvety mouth to his nipple.

His knees liquified completely. His groan was a primitive eruption as he grabbed Golden and took her down with him. Their lips and tongues mated heatedly, hungrily as he pushed her all the way to the floor.

He stared at her for a long, hard-breathing moment. Her lips were parted and swollen and pleading to be kissed again. Passionate flecks of bronze now darkened the gold alloy of her eyes.

She wanted him. Mast could see it as clear as a signal fire, in every radiant inch of her face, though he doubted she was capable of recognizing it for what it was. Christ. She held nothing back. Her honesty stunned him.

And sobered him. Oh aye, it hit his mind like a cold slap to a drunkard. This couldn't continue. He couldn't give in. What the hell was happening? Where was his proud disdain for this stupid game of tease and tantalize? Where was the terror of losing his treasured self-control? Where was the dread of sacrificing every scrap of self-worth and gentlemanly honor he'd hurdled the overwhelming wall of his nonexistent heritage to attain?

"Mast . . ."

Her pleading whisper suddenly sounded more like the swish of the grim reaper's scythe in his mind.

"Kiss me again."

"No. I . . . can't." *Oh God, I can't.*

"You can. I'll let you. I promise not to hit you this time."

He shivered. She was incredible, lying there before him,

hair a shining sun spectrum around her on the floor, skin glowing and vibrant and warm, so temptingly, wonderfully warm. As beautiful as a sea siren—and as stubborn as a bull. She wasn't Wayland's blood daughter, but she might as well have been.

Wayland. Oh, hell. *Wayland.* He'd shut the man out of his mind on purpose, he realized now, not wanting to connect Golden with anyone or anything else. He'd branded her with his own touch and her passionate responses to his senses.

He'd been a bloody fool. The truth was the truth. And the truth was, here he lay half-clothed on his cabin floor with the daughter of the man who had taken him in, mentored him, damn near fathered him. The man had taught Mast how to scale his walls, to act honorably.

He had to get out of here.

"Mast, *please.*"

"Golden. Ah, God, Golden. I'm sorry. So sorry."

The next half hour passed like a dream. He remembered shoving up from the floor but not being able to leave. His eyes were riveted to the pain-filled look on Golden's face. He yearned for her to jump up and lay one of her infuriated slaps across his face but she didn't move, didn't speak, only impaled him with a stare she must have learned from some wounded forest creature.

He'd turned and slammed his arms back into his shirt. This wasn't his fault, for God's sake. He wasn't the one who'd sidled up to the main deck in a gown that would stop a rampaging elephant! At least thinking of it that way gave him the strength to rise and get up to the main deck without glancing back.

But in his mind he glanced back again and again. His heart, damn that traitor, followed every time. And every time he relived the ache that attacked his head with her frown . . . the wings that carried his senses with her smile . . . the terror that stabbed his entire being with kisses—her kind or his.

It wasn't long before his eyes turned up to the vast night sky, and he realized he might as well have been looking in a mirror.

Great God. He didn't know how it happened, but it had. This hellion Golden, this goddess Golden, this woman Golden, had ripped a hole open inside of him the size of a Caribbean sky. Opened it, and filled it, blowing into his life like an unpredictable gust of wind, clearing away the clouds of his world so the stars in his night sky glimmered again, and the air of his days crackled with excitement.

Aye, she'd shown him the stars. And all he had given her was pain. She'd opened herself to him—almost literally—and all he could offer her was rejection.

But damn it, it was all he'd ever be able to offer her! Mast's constellation was just not for navigating, and the sooner Golden comprehended that, the better. Lady Golden Gaverly, he corrected to himself. The same lady that dear "Papa" probably had a line of suitors dreaming about this very moment.

Conjuring that image only sent his fist flying back into the pile of canvas he lay on. "You owe me, Wayland," he muttered into the silent, cool night air. "You owe me for this ungodly torment."

Eleven

Golden finally found the best word for it. Torment.

Her head felt like a smashed mango. Her eyes fared no better, little helped by the scrap of sleep she'd managed to get in some dim hour just before sunrise. It even hurt to smile, as she was returning the men's banter over the morning soup pot—with a lightheartedness she couldn't be farther from feeling.

That was only the beginning.

The real torment sliced much deeper; agonized much more. To petrifying depths of her soul.

Mast didn't want anything to do with her—even as a woman. He'd made himself perfectly clear this time, whether she liked it or no. And now from the way he sat in the longboat across the deck, his eyes resolutely fixed out over the ocean, she deduced he never wanted to look at her, either.

Well if that was the way he wanted it, she'd not look at him, either. Golden wrenched her gaze back to the simmering pot and threw her concentration into the thick turtle stew. But within a minute the warm moistness that dewed on her skin began to feel just like the hot trails Mast's touch had seared into her neck and her lips and her senses last night. Her heartbeat tingled beneath her breasts and the rising heat of her body pooled in that soft, secret place between her thighs.

Oh, mighty Puntan! How had this all happened? What kind of a trap had she fallen into? She had set out to vanquish this man but had ended up being humbled instead. She felt lost in a sea of wonderment and awakening, longing and need, all at once. She should be exulting over the remains of that gloomy, frowning wall she'd set out to crumble, but this morning Mast Iverson and all his secrets were still locked up tighter than a murderer in Newgate.

His closed expression across the deck completed the dim view. Golden felt physical pain remembering the want and hunger that had stroked those features a handful of hours ago. She struggled to blink back the vision of the heat in those eyes as he'd fanned the embers of need between them both. But suddenly she'd found herself alone on the floor of the cabin, watching his boots disappear up the stairwell with the remnants of her hope smashed across their soles.

Torment, she concluded again. This pain was nothing less.

Golden didn't realize what a death grip she had on the soup ladle until Maya appeared by her side, gently prying her fingers from the wooden handle.

"Sister, maybe you rest a moment."

She looked into the deep brown strength of the native's eyes. "No," she protested softly. "Maya, thank you. But I'm fine. Truly. I just—"

"Goll-denn . . ."

"*I am fine.* Now if you don't mind, the soup's settling, and these men are still . . ."

Despite that earlier resolution, her gaze was pulled across the deck to the longboat, and her heart rose to her throat to cut her voice off. Sure enough, Mast wasn't studying the horizon any more. His eyes were riveted on her. He didn't smile, but he didn't frown, either—which perturbed her even more.

Then he curled his finger in a single gesture of bidding. Golden jerked her head in an irrevocable no.

Mast's expression didn't change. Not even a glower. With difficulty, Golden concealed her further surprise at that.

He beckoned her again. A break of wind teased along the deck, lifting the dark waves of his hair from his face and neck, accenting his powerful features—making it more difficult to refuse him.

No! Golden rallied. He wasn't going to entrap her so easily again! Not this time! She couldn't endure it all this time; not the want, the heat, the *pain* . . .

But when she turned her back on the arrogant bastard, a fresh tureen of soup and a mug of bumbo were shoved at her. Golden's scowl found Maya's determined hands at the two handles. But she didn't raise her eyes up any higher. She knew what would be waiting—a returning glare of near-black Arawak disapproval.

"Dee captain hasn't had his food yet, Golden."

"Fine. Take it to him."

There was an exasperated curse in Caribbee. The thump of Maya's stomp on the deck. A slosh of soup on her wrist.

"Peabrooke is right," Maya muttered. "You scared."

At that, Golden snapped her eyes up. "And since when do you listen to Dinky?"

Her sister's eyes betrayed the blush her dark skin couldn't. This time it was Maya who looked away first. A girlish smile inched across the full Indian lips.

"Maya," Golden gasped. "Maya . . . you . . . and Dinky . . . ?"

Maya's smile grew even wider, and somehow, Golden

thought, wiser. "Oh, Golden." She pressed the tureens of food forward again with the plea. "Golden, go to him. If only for me, go."

Golden deliberated. She looked across the deck again. Frustration gathered and erupted from her in a heavy huff. If only the black-haired brute across the deck wasn't playing the imperious ass to the hilt! Sitting there, elbow cocked on the side of the longboat, all Mast was missing was his crown. So blasted controlled. The cat waiting for the canary.

If only some bird would come along and scratch those unfeeling eyes out.

That sole thought provided her the strength to take the tureen and mug from Maya and begin the trek across that foreboding stretch of deck. Halfway there, Golden twisted her head with a last glare of rebellion at Maya, but her sister only beamed lovingly back, now holding hands with Dinky like the lovebirds they used to scoff at as little girls. Sickening.

"The sight doesn't sit well on my stomach, either."

Though Mast growled the complaint loud enough for her ears only, it was clear he only intended tactfulness, not conspiratorial fun. Golden scowled; but not at the remark . . . at the acute sting of disappointment her spirit reacted with. *Did you expect anything else from a hunk of solid rock, Golden? Solid rock isn't capable of having fun. Solid rock isn't capable of anything. Except inflicting pain.*

"I'm not here to parry words with you, Captain," she countered coolly. "Do you want anything besides this?" She thrust the bowl and mug at him.

He didn't move for a long moment. Berating herself even as she did, Golden gave in to the temptation to glance at him. As she expected, all she saw in that face was a cool lake of composure.

Until she took in his eyes.

His eyes were a furious sea. She had just enough time to gasp before the enraged storm charged up his arms, too, to whip both the containers from her hands. In the same motion Mast tossed the soup and bumbo over the side of the ship. In another he jolted to his full height, cleared the edge of the longboat, and grabbed her arm.

"What do you think you're doing?" she cried, as if her demand would stop the beast.

Golden struggled just to keep up as she tripped along behind him down the side deck. He stopped and turned only when they reached a secluded section of side rail. Still he didn't release her from his unrelenting grip.

"Damn it, Golden," he muttered between his teeth. "You're more maddening than a headache."

"I'm more maddening—" But that was as far as the retort got. The helpless tone of Mast's voice, along with the way he pressed the knuckle of his opposite hand to his temple wreaked their unbearable havoc upon her anger. Blast him, he looked like he truly did have a headache—and she had an urge to tenderly stroke it from his brow. How could he alternate so easily between appearing the dragon about to blow hell's fire, and the tired little boy?

"Please . . . excuse that," he tried to begin again. "My swearing. Using your personal name," he went on in explanation. "They are liberties I should have never commenced with you, let alone have continued like this."

Golden's heart lurched in her chest. The sympathetic urges faded as fast as they'd sneaked up on her. Harsh understanding took their place. "That was why you called me over here?" *Not the way I touched you last night . . . not the way I made you feel?*

"Well, yes." But then Mast squared his jaw and added,

"Well . . . no." He coughed nervously, as if ordering himself to get on with something unpleasant. "Golden—my lady—I . . . also owe you an apology. My behavior last evening was reprehensible; hardly decorum befitting a gentleman." Joining hands behind his back, he took a determined pace along the rail—away, Golden noticed, from her.

"We should arrive at Abaco within the next fortnight," he announced. "Until that time, I assure you I will be comfortable in the forecastle with the rest of my men. I hope this action will make up for my lack of discretion. You have my word that an imprudence such as last evening's will not happen again."

He eased back into his coldness as if into a favorite old rain cloak, she thought. Indeed his face could have been an unfeeling grey cloud for all the emotion it showed. And her heart seemed to be the convenient puddle it filled with its gloom. He had apologized for kissing her. *Apologized.* With one horrid sentence he'd wiped the beauty and magic and destiny of their embraces into the realm of nothing where he was concerned!

Golden had to force air into her lungs. Sharp pain twisted between her breasts, yet the physical torment was a twitch compared to the inner agony of looking back to Mast again.

"Be my guest to apologize until you're as grey as Nirvana, Captain," she said evenly. "But they'll only be words, because I will never, never be sorry for what we shared last night."

"Captain!"

Mast would have welcomed the interruption to that agonizing moment had the call not been so terrified. Without a thought he hauled Golden to him as his head snapped up to the crow's nest. The sudden silence on deck told him the rest of his crew stared the same way.

"Ramses?" he shouted to the young man in the bucketlike perch atop the mainmast. "What ho?"

"C-Captain—starboard bow, two o'clock!" The lad paused to catch his gasping breath. "P-Pirate jack on the horizon!"

"Great stars," Golden choked.

"All hands to battle stations!" Mast bellowed. "Except *you,* hellion. Dink! Find Maya and help her to the food hold at once! Tell her Lady Golden will be along presently."

"The hell I will!" Golden lunged against the strength-filled arm she'd reveled in around her waist a moment ago. She twisted in Mast's arms, hoping her glare proposed brave defiance and not the sheer dread which truly threatened her.

Her opportunity was short-lived. Robert lumbered up with a long glass in hand. "You'd better take a look at this," he said to his captain.

Mast accepted the narrow cylinder and quickly inspected the growing shadow on the horizon. "Bloody damn."

"What?" Golden demanded. The growing trepidation on both men's faces made her heart pound in a terrifying way. "What is it? Mast!"

But neither of them afforded her a glance. "Is it him?" Robert asked quietly.

A new harshness laid claim to Mast's expression as he lowered the long glass. His eyes were slits into the sunshine. The taut lines fanning out from them merged with the grim cords of tension running up from his jaw. "It's him."

"Two gold dragons?"

"On a black field," Mast emphasized.

"Skulls in their claws?"

"Skulls in their claws."

"Bloody *damn.*"

Golden's pulse dropped terrifyingly silent.

She'd heard that description countless times before. On many a balmy summer evening, she'd eavesdrop over the veranda where Papa and his official guests would stroll for after-supper cigars and conversation. To her delight, the talk would inevitably meander to the latest doings of the Caribbean sea scoundrels. Her main goal was always news of the Moonstormer, but the notorious pirate El Culebra was just as often the subject of those early evening curses and threats. El Culebra, with his sinister black jack, gleaming with the dual dragons in a direct affront to England's great "sea knights."

And all too often, a deadly affront, as well.

"Mast!" Suddenly Golden whirled to do the restraining now. "Oh, Mast," she begged on a tight swallow, "please, cry off. I know of this pirate. He's very dangerous—"

"I know who he is, too, hellion." It was an acknowledgement. Nothing more. Yet when he looked to her, his eyes glinted with something almost whimsical. The same something Golden remembered in the gazes of Guypa and his hunters before they went out on a big kill.

"Then I can help you," she blurted frantically. "I know this brute. Papa strategized about him often. He'll force you to cut hard port after the first round, then—"

"Then nothing," Mast cut her off. "I ordered you below, and that's where you're going." Swiftly and efficiently, he swept her into his arms and started through the rising turmoil on the deck with her.

"But you don't understand! I can't. Mast, I can't!"

He tried to ignore her. He battled to shut his ears completely against her cries, but Mast simply couldn't deny the sound was different than Golden's usual protest. Her voice was higher, almost . . . distressed. And she didn't just put up the little soaked-cat struggle he expected—no, she battled him like a frenzied lion. As if she were more than angry.

As if she were afraid.

He condemned even the moment of concern he gave to that thought. Damn it, he'd reestablished the boundaries between them not more than a quarter of an hour ago. Now here he was, letting her tear them down already.

The hatch to the holding decks came into view as cannon fire began to throb through the air. Mast kicked open the portal with one foot.

"No!" Golden cried. Mast drowned in a face full of hair as she looked over her shoulder at the ladder that disappeared below. Just as quickly she snapped her terrified gaze back to him.

Her eyes were the most intense shade he'd ever seen them. Glittering and brilliant, yet dark and swirling with a deep, roiling pain, too. Ah Christ, not now. Not those eyes.

"Hellion—" he managed, trying to reassure her.

"I can't go down there!"

"Golden, this is not a request."

"I'm not hiding in your blasted salt pork!"

But for all the pluckiness of the words, it was near a sob in sound. Mast forced himself to set Golden down. She wouldn't let go of him. Hell. He felt like King Henry sending Anne Boleyn to the tower. But Henry hadn't a friendly visit from a resentful ex-bunkmate bearing down on his starboard bow, either.

"Sweet, this is for the best."

"God take your bloody best!" Her fingers dug deeper into his arms. "Let me stay with you. Damn it Mast, please!"

Golden prepared herself for his refusal. Instead, Mast didn't move for a long moment. He just stood and stared at her there in the middle of all the chaos and confusion, the strangest, softest look overtaking his face.

Hope flickered in her anew. The joyful inkling grew to belief when he reached out two fingers to pull a strand of hair from her cheek. A small, but potent tug inched up one side of his mouth. Golden held her breath.

"She's coming down, Maya."

"Noooo!"

There was a flash of blue—the sky. Was it her last look at it ever? Then the feel of Mast's steel grip, and down she went, into the swallowing, suffocating blackness. Just like the great water beast that had tried to take her that night. The monster that had killed Mummy and Daddy!

"No!" she heard herself scream again. The first ominous, rumbling blast erupted in the air above, just before the hatch slammed down with a sickening boom.

"No! Mast!"

He'd left her! In this choking, horrid dark!

"Damn you!" Splinters from the ladder dug into her fingers as she tried to claw back to the brightness above. But the only light now was an oily glow from the small lantern Maya held as the ship's belly digested them. Shadows, huge and frightening, loomed around her. The weight over her head seemed a pressing, pounding, living thing until her breath no longer came easily and she gasped, struggling for air.

"Sister," she heard Maya implore. Then gentle fingers pried her loose from the ladder and down between two large barrels. "Sister, you be all right down here. Ssshh, now."

"No! It's so dark!" She felt the outcry in the pit of her stomach and the core of her heart.

"You *safe*, Golden. You hear me? Come sit down here. Come . . . sit, sister."

Golden forced herself to listen to the reassurances,

though she didn't know if it was Maya's voice or just the solid weight of fear that buckled her knees. She sank to the floor next to her sister, between the barrels.

Home, came the next disjointed thought, brought on by the assault of smells to her senses. Sharp spices mingled with potent dried fruits, hearty rum mixed with pungent salted pork. She sniffed deeply of the aroma, trying to make it a calming incense of sorts, trying to believe her own voice as she murmured again and again, "I'm safe. I know I'm safe. I'm safe."

But with each passing minute the refrain grew harder to believe. The enticing aroma of the hold was soon vanquished by the stench of sulphur. Smoke held Golden's throat and lungs desperate, stifled hostages. The timbers above voiced the moan she felt, protesting the torment of erupting gunpowder and trompling feet they were victim to. Cannons boomed and pistols cracked louder and louder overhead. Muffled shouts collided with screeched profanities. The battle was in full, terrifying heat—and it was all about to cave in on her!

Then just as suddenly, the din stopped.

But the silence, Golden swiftly learned, was more frightening than the commotion. Not a rope groaned or a spar creaked. Worst of all, not a footstep sounded.

Her nerves wanted to break out of her skin all at once. What was happening up there? Had the pirates surrendered? Had Mast? Was anybody killed?

Was Mast?

A brand-new wave of ice cold fear crashed over her with the horrid vision. Mighty Puntan, was Mast lying somewhere above, choking on his own blood, slowly dying?

Golden's eyes flew wide and her mouth popped open.

"Spirits!" she rasped as a shocking realization grabbed and clung to her mind:

Being trapped in this hold wasn't the only thing that petrified her.

"Mast . . . oh Mast, please don't die . . ."

"Golden, you all right?" Maya reached for her, but the Carib fell short when the ship pitched into motion again.

"A hard port," Golden gasped, figuring the direction. "We took a hard port. Oh God, Maya. It's his trap. El Culebra. We're falling into his trap. Mast is in trouble!"

"Sister! Capt'n know what he doin', girl! Peabrooke and da men helpin' him, too; so you just stop dat—"

But the ship rocked and reeled around them again, as the overhead storm of gunfire rapidly resumed. Golden snapped her head toward the thin lines of light that were the hatch perimeters. "Please, great spirits," she murmured. "Please." If only Mast would come bounding down here to prove Maya's words true. The frowning ape could even call her "my lady," and she wouldn't snort once. She promised; oh, she promised.

But the hatch didn't open. Mast was dead by now, for all she knew. The increasing lurches of the deck only added to the turmoil of that panic, the agony of that fear.

It was too much to bear! She couldn't sit in this black torture chamber a moment longer!

With a determined outcry, Golden jumped up and sprinted to the foot of the ladder.

"By dee stars," Maya exclaimed. "Golden, no!"

"I'm sorry, Maya. I'm so sorry." She gulped. She wasn't used to hearing her voice quaver with uncertainty and fear. "I have to know if he's all right. I have to know!"

Then she whirled and scrambled up the ladder. Before the

finish of Maya's final, feeble protest, Golden had pushed the hatch open and started to boost herself onto the deck.

It was like entering an inferno.

Heat instantly took half her breath away. Black, fetid smoke sucked out the other half. Golden forced her head up through the grimy fog, coughing back the burn on her throat, blinking back tears of irritation.

At first she could see nothing, but images gradually began to take shape. Snaking ropes slithered everywhere on the deck. The edge of a sail flapped aimlessly with no tack. Mast would normally be glowering like a demon about the disarray. With relief, Golden then began to make out human beings through the gloom: the loyal and stalwart old Ben, and big, burly Rico, hastening together to load the barrel of a truck gun.

But no stiffly held shoulders rose next to the two crewmen. No figure paced like the weight of the world was on those shoulders. No hard profile stood out against the roiling chaos of a sky.

No Mast.

Please, great spirits, where was Mast?

Twelve

Ironically, it was El Culebra himself who helped her discover the answer. Golden had scrambled no more than ten steps along the deck when an outburst like the gods' own wrath blasted at them. The air came to life in orange and yellow fury. The hideous black smoke was transformed into an almost beautiful picture of white-blue tendrils for a second.

Golden's senses froze in place as she was overwhelmed by the scene around her. She didn't even realize she'd turned her head until the sight of the *Athena*'s figurehead suddenly flashed before her, a strange profile of loveliness in the rainbow colors that flashed against it.

But it was the face just above the goddess's that knocked the air completely from her lungs.

"Mast!"

She breathed it more than said it, her heart throbbing a dance of gratitude. The uneasy feelings of this morning, even the realizations she'd experienced minutes ago in the hold, were but a taste of the emotion flooding her with the sight of him.

He was dirty and clearly exhausted, but he was alive, and vigorously so. She couldn't make out his face, but barely leashed tension was evident in every movement as he shouted orders and helped carry a few out himself. All the while he kept a constant fix on the opposite ship. He had his long glass in one hand, his pistol in the other.

Golden longed to leap up and run to him. But the sky exploded again, this time with a blast from the *Athena*. Golden shrank behind a crate, and slammed her palms over her ears. When she lifted her head again Mast was gone from where she'd spotted him. Her throat clutched in dread until she found him again, now just a few feet away.

Her instinct warned her not to get any closer. Her heart knotted at the reason why.

Mast's face betrayed as little as it always had. But below his sweat-drenched neckerchief, his hands hung wearily at his sides. He rested back on one leg as he consulted with Robert, instead of rooting himself to the deck with his usual brace-legged stance. His shoulders looked as if the weight of the world was just too heavy to bear any more.

Golden's chest tightened hardest of all when he angled slightly her way, allowing her to hear the conversation he and Robert exchanged.

"The bastard's really got us by the bangers this time," the *Athena*'s master gunner muttered.

"Carlos was bound to get lucky one day."

Carlos? Golden's whirling mind repeated. Mast had apologized for using her first name, but El Culebra was Carlos to him?

"Cor, but he's had it in for you forever," Robert continued.

Mast's expression seemed to age ten years at that. "Feels like it, doesn't it, Rob?" Golden gulped at the undiluted fury of his reply; she gaped at the extra hard stare he drove into Robert. "You'd better send Ramses below now for more cartridges and pistol balls."

There was a leaden pause. "We're almost out—"

"Aye, damn it, I know. But we're going to need that extra

fire as diversion when we let the jibs out and pray for half a chance to fox ourselves out of this."

"And . . . if we don't succeed?"

"If we don't succeed . . ." Mast hesitated, then snorted uncomfortably. "If we don't succeed, Master Gunner Teach, then I want you and Dink on the quarterdeck with me when they board."

When they board!

Golden's fingers flew to her mouth. Her gaze raked the sky in wild disbelief, coming to rest on the menacing form across the water. Like a dragon, the enemy frigate appeared. More vicious orange blasts roared from El Culebra's cannons. She heard Mast and Robert swear in unison. She saw only their backs as they ran off in their respective directions. Her gaze remained on Mast. Her hand followed suit by its own unthinking accord, trailing after him, wanting to haul him back on his long and powerful legs—wanting to hold him and feel him holding her against this hot and confusing insanity.

But he had men to lead. A ship to defend.

A defeat to fight against.

"It's—it's not that bad," she tried to reassure herself as she shakily rose. "Mast loves this ship. He'd never let it go. He must be wrong! Or confused . . ."

That was it. Everything was confusing. Everyone was shouting and shooting at once and the smoke created such a strange, shadowy maze, suggesting things that weren't there, shielding dangers that were. Everything was upside down and inside out. It couldn't be real. It wasn't!

But that was what you thought twelve years ago, Golden.

Her body coiled again and her eyes squeezed shut. "No," she gritted to the screaming voices in her head, the pounding terror in her veins. "No!" Moment by moment, she willed herself to defy the memory, and forced her eyes open in determined victory.

Finally she unfurled her fists. Her head rose to the wind. "I am not helpless any more," she stated shakily, but defiantly. "I am not helpless."

At that she breathed in deeply, surrendering her mind to her senses . . . her thoughts to her feelings . . . her fears to her instincts.

A heart-pounding few minutes later, Golden took an identical breath to reinspire herself as she swung her bare legs over the aft rail. One of the cuffs of Mast's shirt fell out of the roll she'd made of it and she angrily jerked it back up to her elbow. The sash she'd grabbed to secure the shirt about her waist was coming loose, too. She stopped and twisted another knot rather than retie it completely. There was no time for fashion!

She tightened her belt again, straightened her face into the wind, and pushed her body into a graceful arc over the water.

She sliced the choppy surface just where she'd planned. The water tasted worse than the air, Golden came up spitting the sooty stuff and cursing in Caribbee. Yet after a moment she realized that was all the more better—practice for the performance ahead, she encouraged herself. The performance of her life.

A little encouraging was just what she needed at this point, too. From down here, the ships were hulking, overpowering monsters. Golden gasped as much in awe as fear. And though much of the battle now raged at the opposite end of the vessels from where she was, her nerves flowed cold with fear at each smack of a pistol or fizzle of a cannon's touchhole.

That chill turned to outright ice as she made her way through the swells and nearer El Culebra's ship. Demonic cackles pierced Golden's ears between constant shouts and catcalls across the water at the *Athena*. Many of the voices were already slurred from an early victory celebration.

"Agwe, give me strength," she muttered as she looked up to the faces that went with the derisive jeers. She'd not seen a more wicked lot elsewhere. Dirty brown faces flashed gold teeth and leered with missing eyes. Rum bottles passed from greedy mouth to greedy mouth along the frigate's rail.

Except one mouth, Golden noticed. One pair of lips on one dark brown face simply smiled calmly as the liquor flowed by. The expression broke only once, shattering into a fierce grimace just when some of the golden liquid splashed upon his ornate red and gold satin frock coat. The coal black stock atop the jacket looked as if made of the same thick black hair tied neatly back from the man's smooth, almost aristocratic face.

"El Culebra," she gasped. The beautiful, yet lethal snake. *Saints and spirits, I really need strength.*

It was all Golden could do not to cry out thanks to the quick response to her prayer, in the form of the soot-covered grey snout which moved up beneath her.

"Nirvana. Oh, I couldn't have asked for a better friend right now!" She even laughed as the dolphin clickered enthusiastically in response.

With Nirvana's help she was peering up the far side of the pirate ship within minutes. Golden smiled in gratitude as her friend bobbed his snout in support. Then she turned and reached for the carelessly hanging rope that would, she fervently prayed, support her climb to the chain plates above—and the top rail beyond those.

The jib sails unfurled and snapped as they caught the wind. Mast felt his ship's instant response to the new power, as he turned to look while the *Athena* angled back closer to the frigate's stern—and the weakened hull there, thanks to Robert and Ben's aim.

But he was a fool if he thought the increasing pounds of his chest were excited anticipation of the upcoming encounter.

"God," he muttered to himself. If this were any other voyage, Mast would be the first to welcome a face-to-face challenge with El Culebra. He'd even dare the first step up to Carlos Nanchez himself, man to man, and nobody else, and settle all the years' worth of confusion and conflict between them for once and for all.

If, he reaffirmed, this were any other voyage. If his entire body wasn't clenching at the image of Carlos throwing open the hatch to the food hold, to discover a fiery pair of eyes and a snarl of passionate hate greeting him there. If his inner ear could stop hearing that gloating Carlos laugh as he'd order his men to "restrain" the lustful creature, in every sense of the word.

Fury sparked, flamed, and exploded through him. "Robert!" he bellowed with the thunderous result. "Robert!" He whirled through the sweltering grey tumult, ignoring the smoke which caused his eyes to run moist drops with the sweat down his face and neck. He ran faster, trying to forget the hammering pain in his head— and the unrelenting torture of his thoughts.

Robert's hardy profile couldn't have loomed ahead a second too soon. Mast dashed to where his master gunner rammed a shot into a still-smoldering cannon.

"Robert!" he shouted. "Double it! Double the cartridge!"

Robert's eyes bulged with incredulity beneath the elbow which wiped his brow. "You're flammin' me, right?"

"Double it now!"

"Nooo!"

The moan flooded his ears at the same instant a petite body almost toppled him to the deck. Mast angrily seized a pair of thin brown arms, but checked himself when a wide and terrified cocoa gaze penetrated his sights.

"Maya! What the hell are you doing up—"

He choked his own interruption, as understanding sliced icy blades of dread through his body. "Where is she?" he rasped. "What's she done? Tell me, Maya. Where the hell is Golden!"

"I—I don't know! She leave—oh, great Puntan have mercy, she say she got to find you—but I get fear when I hear da big boom—I hoped she here with you—"

"Well, she's not here with me."

"You can bet your balls she isn't!"

Every head on the deck snapped at Rico's astonished bellow, just in time to see the normally unflappable South American stumble a trio of steps backward. Mast released Maya and sprinted to Rico's side. He accepted the long glass from his boatswain, swept it to his own wide eye.

"Saint Chris have mercy." Young Ramses seconded Rico as he bounded up the deck, his keen vision guiding his finger across the waves. "He's right, Captain Iverson. There; on the far side of the aft capstan!"

"Damn her." He hadn't even spotted her yet, but Mast was certain the oath would be appropriate when he did.

He wasn't wrong. God in heaven, she looked hideous.

He couldn't figure out what the hell she was wearing even through the magnification of the glass, but it was dripping wet and encrusted from top to bottom with layers of glutinous black grime. Her legs were also coated with the stuff, as dark as Maya's with the goo. Mast swore again as she scraped more of it from the capstan and smeared it over her face.

"The wench is lo-co," Rico exclaimed next to him.

"Or bloody brilliant," old Ben put in.

"Only what the bejesus does she think she's doing?" Robert stammered, at a loss to answer himself.

"Damn you, Golden," Mast uttered again, oblivious to them all. He never dropped his eye from the long glass, as if he could somehow protect her through it. But his gut knew better, wrenching against his ribs in agonizing reminder of his helplessness.

But the real agony came with the sudden jest the trade wind played, blowing a bank of their own smoke back at them—erasing Golden from his view.

Mast's curse of frustration was drowned out by a terrible screech from the opposite deck. He didn't have to search his memory far to recall where his heart had stopped at that sound before. That first wind-whipped night, when he'd heard Golden before ever seeing her. When the French had bound her like an animal.

Holy God, what would a maggot like Carlos Nanchez do?

"Make ready!" His terror was so unthinking, the order scorched up his throat and thundered out of him before Mast realized it. "Make ready to bring her close! I'm going aboard the frigate!"

"I'm joining you," Robert returned.

"And me."

"And me."

The cries went up again and again. Mast's mind pounded with apprehension, and his body tightened to the bones with the fate he planned for Carlos if the bastard so much as breathed on Golden. Mast stopped and gave in to the tug at a corner of his mouth. Was this the same semicircle of men who stood here a fortnight and a half ago in fear of the murdering "sea witch"? Were these those same skittish "mice" who now smiled back at him . . . as they prepared to die for her?

A new attack bellowed from the enemy ship. A cry of outrage rose from his men. The two vessels shifted closer to each other.

"Dink, you'll lead from this deck," Mast boomed. "Rob will second me in the ropes. Hold her steady!" *Hold on steady, hellion,* he shouted mentally across the waves.

After securing his rapier at one side of his body and his pistol at the other, he whirled and hoisted himself into the shrouds. Robert followed an instant later, just below Mast's left hip. Through the smoke and the noise they climbed higher, higher still. Mast was determined to get the best angle he could get when he swung across to the opposite deck. It could be the only chance he'd get, he suspected grimly.

The conjecture was confirmed when he turned at the crest of his climb and took in the scene below him. Since bitterly leaving the *Athena* just over twelve years ago, Carlos had made it well and widely known that "El Culebra, the new terror of the Main" would accept none less than the dirtiest and deadliest men beneath his jack. The swarm of vermin below certainly lived up to that standard. The animals scratched and beat at each other to get a prime place at their rail for the battle they could smell coming. They were baring mouths of greasy little teeth and daggers of sharpened steel.

"Lucifer's balls," Robert muttered. "Does Carlos toss 'em raw shark for supper?"

"If any of them have so much as touched her . . ." Mast grated. "Damn it, where have they taken her?"

His answer came at once. It was astounding.

First there were only the yowls. Terrified, croaking male yowls, distinct even through the layers of lower decks.

"The gunnery deck," Ramses stated below. Mast nodded agreement, for the relentless storm of cannon fire from the opposite deck had strangely and abruptly ceased.

The silence didn't go long unnoticed by Carlos and his men, either. But they'd barely recognized the hitch when the entire gunnery crew burst out upon them, a mass of bulge-eyed, frantic-limbed hysteria. *"Bruja!"* they shrieked. *"Bruja, bruja!"*

"By the saints," came Rico's disbelieving exclamation.

"What, Ric?" Robert turned and asked. "What they sayin'?"

"Bruja," Mast interceded. His voice was tight and equally amazed. "Witch."

"What!" The whole crew let up the next cry of astonishment.

But there she was, bursting to life before their eyes. A wild, begrimed Golden sprang from the lower decks like a harpy from hell, arms slithering, eyes racing, teeth bared. A supernatural screech exploded from her as she leapt atop a capstan, tearing at her hair and eyeing the terrified crowd of pirates as if selecting which of them to gobble up first. Many refused to stay and find out. They raced to the far railing and leaped over it. The remaining fools pushed and tripped over each other in their efforts to avoid becoming the intent of that gleaming topaz stare.

"I'll be damned," someone said in amazement.

"She's playin' 'em like a jig!" exclaimed another.

"They really believe she's the sea witch!"

"Seems the question isn't where they've taken her, Mast," Robert chuckled, "but where she's taking them."

Mast could do nothing but agree. Surely enough, the opposite deck started to move away from them. Gradually at first, then as the pirate ship's mainsail caught the new wind, Carlos's frigate sliced an anxious retreat away from the *Athena*.

Yet they weren't so far that Mast and his men didn't have the opportunity of observing Golden's finale: a wail that woke every angel in the heavens, a writhing dance over to and then atop the rail, then a screaming descent into the water.

"Damn me and slam me!" Robert bellowed as he began to descend the shrouds. "She did it!"

The men seconded him with a massive roar of victory.

Mast's body followed with a massive rush of relief. Then he ignited with fury. Then he twisted with tender aching, and then battled the burning rage again—all of the torturous sensations channeled on one dripping blond head atop a dolphin plowing through the waves toward them.

She was radiant as everyone clamored to help her over the rail. Several jugs of fresh water were miraculously produced to slosh the last of the soot away from her unbearably sleek curves. Golden laughed in delight and hugged her bathers, soaking them, as well. Rico was next with the blanket from his own bunk, wrapping it around her as if he were a boy with a newborn kitten. Everyone shouted and talked at her at once and she seemed to answer every man at the same time, bestowing upon each a sparkling gaze and a speech-robbing smile.

With every muscle and nerve in his body, Mast forced himself to stay rooted to his spot just beyond the edge of the mob. He coiled his arms farther around his chest, tighter against the conflicting furies which pounded there.

Damn her. She was beautiful—and maddening. He wanted to take that incredible, brave neck she'd just risked for him and caress it, kiss it—then strangle it.

"Where is he?" he could hear her asking. "Has anyone seen Mast? I want to see him."

And then she broke through the crowd and was standing before him. Half-smiling up at him, like a soaked London beggar waif seeking a scrap of food . . . or affection. Her huge topaz eyes were gleaming with anticipation and expectation. Mast swallowed as he met that gaze directly, but then his eyes were dragged down to the wet sheen of her lips, slightly parted in unspoken offering . . . *I did it for you, Mast. For you.*

She hadn't lifted a finger, but the blow was just as physical. Mast stepped back, fumbling, unsure. Terrified. His mind was a tumble, his senses, chaos.

"Damn it, Golden," was all he could think to say, "you've ruined one of my best linen shirts."

Thirteen

Golden sought out the formal clothes first. Yes, there they were, satin waistcoats and embroidered jackets, making a brilliant-colored storm as she hurled them across the cabin with an invigorating scream. After that the rage took over completely. All the doubts and the confusion and the utter futility of the last week crashed over her, consuming her, and she didn't care what she threw next. As long as it was clean—and his.

Mast appeared just before the third armful. Underdrawers. With furious delight Golden stomped closer to assure a bull's-eye.

"Oh, I'm sorry," she jeered as the white cotton mound covered his face, "that was shirts you wanted, my lord? Begging your highness's forgiveness, but we're well out. Seems a mindless little barbarian soiled them all while risking her life for some pirate's ship in the Indies!"

"Golden." His voice was a clenched growl as he stepped across the mess to her.

"Bestow your blessed forgiveness on me again, that was a privateer, wasn't it? We island pagans can be so twiddlepated!"

"Well," he snapped. "The truth at last."

"And just what is that supposed to mean?"

"Don't blink those wild eyes at me." He reached her side

and hauled her up next to him with one fierce pull. "You heard what I said."

"I heard nothing!" She jerked and seethed at him like a wild horse at its tethers. "My ears retch at your words!"

"They aren't gorged on soot and salt water already?"

That image certainly didn't help the temperature level of his agitation. Then again, once a pot was brought to boil, what was more heat? What was more madness to insanity? For lunacy was surely what this was . . . the freezing panic when he'd realized Golden was actually aboard Carlos's ship . . . the flood of gratitude when they pulled her back to safety . . . the fury that came over him immediately after . . . and now this blur of all three—and more.

So much more. So much it slithered around him and into him, tangling through his thoughts and senses, winding faster toward the point of—

No control.

"Damn it!" He had to fight it—to grip her as hard as he could—to make her listen. Golden struggled, but he stilled her by pinning her closer to him. Rico's blanket lost its hold on her shoulders and fell down to her elbows. He didn't care. The less layers to shield those defiant shoulders of hers, the better.

"What you did was stupid, Golden." He lowered his voice as he lowered his head at her, the motion as much a struggle for control as for command. "Stupid and reckless and—" But the fury and the fear billowed up in him, choking him for an endless minute. "For Christ's sake, you could have gotten yourself killed!" he finally exploded.

And there it was. Logic. Sense. So why didn't the merciless weight lift from his chest? Why did his lungs and his heart and his very soul compress harder? Why did Golden's presence next to him—warm and wet and alive—ring increasingly jubilant bells through his being . . .

He inhaled again. It was no use. "Does that make sense?" he rasped. He desperately searched himself for a haven of cold detachment and rationality, but all that materialized was his hand, slow and heavy, raising to cradle Golden's already-lifted chin. "Killed, Golden. Dead. Forever. Do you understand?"

She said nothing for a long moment. Then Mast felt her reply—a single shiver, coursing up her body, spending its echo in her eyes. "No," came the answering whisper. "No, I don't understand. I don't understand you at all, Mast Iverson."

Golden shoved past him, unable to bear the pressure of his stare any longer. The hurt had mounted in her to the point of detonation and now erupted. Her arms flew into the air in a depiction of what her feelings were doing in her chest.

"Understand?" she repeated in a bitter laugh. "Understand what? That frown on your face? That hardness in your walk? That conviction in your stance? For that is all you've given me to understand, Captain. Dub me a witless female, but I don't wish to understand it, either."

Mast dropped his hands from his waist, only to coil them as hard as anchor chain at his sides. He strained to rein in his frustration, his—damn it, he raged, his rising physical need. The way she stood there, half turned to him, was unbearable. His wet shirt was clinging to the curve of her thigh and embracing the one high, rosy breast he could see. His thoughts became a maelstrom, a mutinous whirl of unobeyed commands, unwanted ideas, uncontrolled emotions.

"That has nothing to do with it," he gritted.

"That has everything to do with it!" She whirled at him

again. "You hardheaded ass! How dare you tell me I threw myself into that nest of vipers for nothing! How dare you think that one word, one look of thanks, one gentle touch from you wouldn't have returned my deed a hundred times over!" Her face twisted, as if a spasm of pain shot through her. She exhaled several times, violently. "How dare you afford your bird the smile you won't spare me. And save my life—twice!—then regard my existence as if it doesn't matter. And . . . and then caress me the way you did last night, and then kiss me like that, and then . . ."

"Then what?" Mast cut her off, the trail of her sentence leading to a place he knew all too well. "Then ravish you? Promise you the oceans and the stars and my heart? What happens after that, *my lady?*"

She stepped back, but her chin still jutted defiantly at him. "Well, then—"

"I'll tell you what then. Then we get to Abaco. You wipe my blood off your pretty little dagger and traipse off to Papa without a parting glance. That's what happens."

He was using the image as a symbol, the way the fancy European writers did, Golden realized—but she didn't care. She reclaimed her backward step with a furious forward lunge. "I don't own a dagger."

"The bloody hell you don't." His eyes darkened so much they were the black of midnight instead of the blue. Not that he even saw her with them; as Golden watched, Mast's gaze departed from her, from even the walls of the cabin to someplace filled with unspeakable pain and loneliness.

"Every woman in any place on this earth has the kind of dagger I speak of. Daggers that gleam at a man from behind lowered lashes. Sway at him from low-cut bodices. Seduce him until the poor sot is powerless to resist. Then—" He turned to fall into the burgundy velvet chair that had been his bed for the week. "Then they kill him. They kill his beliefs. His will. His soul."

It was a long moment before all of those words penetrated Golden—and all the pain that had produced them. The pain of loss and betrayal which resulted in—yes, she realized, hate. And the agony of living with that hate. Battling it each day.

For another prolonged minute she couldn't move. Suddenly she beheld each plane of his face, each crease or crinkle that edged his eyes and nose and mouth, in a startling, beautiful new light.

Then she went to him.

Her hand was the lightest feather touch on his knee, but it deeply penetrated Mast's agony. He lifted his eyes. She'd curled down at his feet, gazing at him with a look that was more potent than Scottish brandy. And thrice as inundating.

He stretched his fingers out to her cheek. "Mum had skin just like yours," he murmured. "Smooth and fine, like the Irish mist." A ragged sigh came from deep in his throat. "She was beautiful."

"Is that where you lived before you sailed?" she asked softly. "Ireland?"

He pulled his hand away. The wave of anger was violent and piercing, and he didn't want to chance hurting her. "If living is what you'd call it."

"Mast. It surely couldn't have been that awful."

"It was that hell-damned awful."

Her eyes widened with that wounded animal sheen. He tried to check his voice to a calmer manner, but the words just weren't made for polite conversation. "You see, sweet, I was what they call a mongrel. To the children of my village, a catch-colt. To their parents, a baseborn. Would you like an historical slant? A by-blow. I could bore you for hours on the hundreds of ways to say *bastard."*

He rose then, feeling all the old instincts flooding back; unwanted, but inevitable. It was as if he were standing in the middle of the village commons again about to square off against Sean O'Rooney, the boy who made his sixth through eleventh years on earth more like hell.

"Oh, aye, how quickly one grows by the hand of ridicule," he said. "So at twelve, I was more than ready when Mum packed me up and out to Dublin. 'Go to the city,' she said. 'Go to the docks and find work. Go to school and find knowledge. Show them what my *gossoon* can really do.' " He smiled then, as he always did when remembering the musical brogue he'd loved so well. His heart swelled when he looked to see Golden smiling as well.

"And so I went, determined to march back to that village one day a rich man. I got my job on the docks. But it didn't take me half a shilling's time to see it was on the sea where a man's fortune lay, not next to it. I signed aboard my first voyage ten days later."

But it was there that his smile faded. The memories turned to pain. He swallowed heavily before willing himself to continue. "I came home from that journey wearing a new suit and bearing a new gown for Mum. It was lavender." A clenched jaw joined his tightened throat. "Her favorite. But she never tried it on. She was too weak by then. Pneumonia had taken her lungs and her will."

He could feel his voice darken beneath the foreboding Irish rain clouds in his memory. "I bribed the physician to come," he grated. "I stayed by her side . . . God, I pleaded with her, threatened her. But she'd already given up on me. She died in my arms two days later, in the hut we had shared just outside town."

Wish You Were Here?

You can be, every month, with Zebra Historical Romance Novels.

AND TO GET YOU STARTED, ALLOW US TO SEND YOU

4 Historical Romances Free

A $19.96 VALUE!
With absolutely no obligation to buy anything.

YOU'RE GOING TO LOVE GETTING
4 FREE BOOKS

These books worth almost $20, are yours without cost or obligation
when you fill out and mail this certificate.
(If the certificate is missing below, write to: Zebra Home Subscription Service, Inc.,
120 Brighton Road, P.O. Box 5214, Clifton, New Jersey 07015-5214

Complete and mail this card to receive 4 Free books!

Yes! Please send me 4 Zebra Historical Romances without cost or obligation. I understand that each month thereafter I will be able to preview 4 new Zebra Historical Romances FREE for 10 days. Then, if I should decide to keep them, I will pay the money-saving preferred publisher's price of just $4.00 each...a total of $16. That's almost $4 less than the publisher's price. (A nominal shipping and handling charge of $1.50 per shipment will be added.) I may return any shipment within 10 days and owe nothing, and I may cancel this subscription at any time. The 4 FREE books will be mine to keep in any case.

Name _____

Address _____ Apt. _____

City _____ State _____ Zip _____

Telephone ( ) _____

Signature _____ LP0295
(If under 18, parent or guardian must sign.)

Terms, offer and prices subject to change without notice. Subscription subject to acceptance by Zebra Books.
Zebra Books reserves the right to reject any order or cancel any subscription.

TREAT YOURSELF TO 4 FREE BOOKS.

A $19.96
value.
FREE!

No obligation
to buy
anything, ever.

ZEBRA HOME SUBSCRIPTION SERVICE, INC.

120 BRIGHTON ROAD

P.O. BOX 5214

CLIFTON, NEW JERSEY 07015-5214

"Oh, Mast!" He was vaguely aware of Golden's hand upon him again, but the words had a will of their own now; he could no more stop them than he could the pain. He turned away from her.

"I made a vow on the pauper's grave where we buried her," he continued harshly. "I'd never, *never* die like that. I'd never be laughed at again. By God, when I died, they'd mourn an honorable man, a trusted friend. They'd pay their respects to Mast Iverson, not their pity."

He jerked a book from the shelf next to the bunk, opened it; slammed it. "I threw myself back into my life at sea, determined to work my way to the top as hard and as fast as I could."

"And you did."

"And I did. My captainship came when I was seventeen." He couldn't help the unsmiling laugh that escaped him then. "God, I was a cocky blighter. I strutted from port to port like the peacock with the world at his arse."

"You?" Golden almost echoed his chuckle. "But you're not like that now."

"I should hope to hell not."

"What changed you?"

Mast raised an irked eyebrow at her—a tiny sign of the real discomfort shooting through him. "It doesn't matter."

"It does so matter."

She moved nearer to him then, leaving Rico's blanket back by the chair. Mast was jolted into the present with the moist, beguiling sight of her, moving closer by the heartbeat. Heaven save him, he could see every curve of her body beneath his drenched shirt.

"It matters to me," she said with the most direct and fearless gaze he'd ever seen. "*You* matter to me, Mast Iverson."

God. He shut his eyes, twisted his head, but she moved

and was before him again when he opened them. "Golden. I don't think—"

"You matter because you understand." She stepped yet closer, her hands sliding up his forearms, her touch such a smooth balm on his raw and angry senses. "I thought nobody could know the kind of pain I'd been through, but I was wrong. You even tried to tell me, yet I was so stubborn; I wouldn't listen."

Her waist was so close, it was nothing but a pressure of his hands to secure her in his hold. "Golden," he breathed again. She was moist and warm there, damply erotic . . . softly inviting.

Her sigh echoed his as she arched in his embrace. "You understand this, too, don't you, Mast?"

"Understand . . . what?"

"This feeling I get when we're next to each other. When we touch each other. You feel it, too, I know you do." She placed tentative fingers to his face. Mast couldn't help but respond to the supplication, looking down into her gaze.

A sun-colored gaze was his remuneration. Sparkles of uninhibited desire twirled in the jonquil skies beneath her eyelashes. Mast had seen an infinity of sunscapes upon the seas he'd traveled, but none took his breath away as this one did—burning to the very core of him. The very heart.

He should have looked away.

He couldn't. Especially as Golden moved her fingers from his skin to her own—to the dark place where his shirt closed between her breasts.

"Does it make you ache, Mast? It makes me ache, very much . . . right here." Then she twisted the button out of its loop, slowly drawing the material aside. "And here."

"No," he managed to croak, stopping her just before she exposed the erect, warm peak. What was he allowing her to do? Wasn't it enough that her breasts defied him through the fabric like that? Wasn't the sight too breathtaking already, the deep rose tips of her arousal puckered around the twin white-linened nubs that screamed to be thumbed and caressed and suckled?

"You understand that ache, don't you, Mast?" She transferred her touch to his chest as she just went on, so simply and openly—as if she didn't know the way she was dragging his senses, his world, to the very edge of destruction. "Aye," she agreed with herself. "The thumping beneath your skin tells me so. And the way your chest feels. The way it felt beneath my mouth last night . . ." Her fingers sought the sensitive place she spoke of, as she gently rubbed his nipple to the same excruciating need as before. "They're just like mine, aren't they?"

Mast could only hiss fiercely through his teeth. He was speechless. Terrified. And utterly humbled by the honesty of this animal-woman before him, moved by her wonder, her absence of anything coy or even awkward about the mysteries of her body—and his. Dear God, Mast admitted, she'd already unclothed him in every other way tonight. He was bare before her, vulnerable as he'd never been to anyone . . . and she to him.

Yet it was the way it was meant to be all along, wasn't it? The way Adam and Eve must have sought and explored each other before time corrupted that sweet, incredible communion with the bitter wine of betrayal, the molded bread of deceit. And now this island Eve sought him out . . . this natural, unaffected woman he'd needed for so long, not the "cargo" he'd been commissioned for, not the "Lady" of anything, but the soul who longed to explore with him, to share with him. He had only to respond. To set himself free.

He couldn't think of a higher honor to be given.

He felt as if he were stepping out of shackles as he pressed forward against Golden, then softly kissed her forehead. "Aye," he said roughly. "Just like yours, sweet."

Golden lifted her head. Her gaze darted over his face, recognizing the new, darker way Mast spoke. He looked back at her. She wetted the smile that sprang to her lips. It expanded as his eyes grew even duskier.

"It aches in other places, too," she whispered.

He took in a deep breath. "I know."

"Do you . . . want me to show you where?"

"No."

Disappointment twinged at her until Golden observed the way Mast shook his head at her. Slowly. Determinedly. Sensuously.

"I want to find those places myself."

Her heart stopped with his words. Then burst into a thousand shards of joyful anticipation. Golden closed her eyes, reeling from the sensation, savoring it. She had to blink once when she opened them, for it was as if she still dreamed, watching Mast's face unfold in masculine longing as he unfastened the rest of the shirt then gently peeled it from her shoulders. His eyes didn't leave hers as he yanked at the hooks of his own shirt and vest and stripped free of them.

The dark majesty of his body had never taken her breath away more. He stood before her, offering himself to her gaze . . . opening himself, she knew, in more ways than just clothing coming off of skin. It was delicious torture to acknowledge his gift with no more than her eyes. She wanted to follow the lines of her gaze with her fingers, but she was suddenly afraid.

Thankfully, Mast absolved her of that dilemma. He moved to her again and his arms folded around her body as the deep blue tapestry of his eyes folded around her mind. The need to touch him finally overruled. With a rapturous sigh, Golden glided her hands up the molded planes of his chest, around the taut column of this neck. His caress moved the opposite direction, down to cup her buttocks with big strokes of his hands. They meshed themselves together, entwined in a shimmering new wave of discovery, releasing and fusing all the heat, all the yearning they'd tasted, but denied themselves since their gazes had first met in that hallway of the Gaverly plantation, it seemed so long ago.

"Here," he rasped against her cheek as his fingers raked her bottom. "Is this where it aches, sweet?"

"Yes . . ." She ended on a gasp as he drew her against the center of him. His hardness rose along her woman's cleft with a steady, yet primal pulse. It was the beat of night wind and high seas . . . the sound of two hearts meeting; the cadence of a ritual as old as time, yet as young as new passion. It was a rhythm Golden longed to dance with this dark and beautiful mystery man.

"And . . . here?" came Mast's ragged whisper against her neck then. "Does it even hurt here?" Golden's head fell back to nod the yes her lips couldn't form.

His exhalation was hot and heavy on her skin as his mouth began to descend. Golden thought she'd never breathe again as he laved teeth and tongue down the cord of her neck, feathered kisses and nips into the valley of her throat, and finally brought his mouth up the rise of her chest, to where she stiffened and contracted, tingled and hardened, so poised and ready . . . ready for his wet touch.

"Oh, Mast . . . yes, there."

She saw and felt her words take effect on him. His mouth widened to claim the whole reddened bud of her desire. Golden cried out, curled her fingers through his hair, urging him closer. What a feeling to watch him, what a surge of tenderness and joy, power and surrender—what a feeling of . . . womanhood.

She sighed. Mast moaned. He suckled her nipple deeper. Her fingers nearly tore the hair from his head. "Oh, *Mast*," she breathed.

Finally he tore himself away, only to retrace his lips' original trail until his journey brought him to her mouth again.

Mast breathed in the sea salt that persisted on her skin, mingled with the soft scent of her femininity. The mixture filled him, intoxicated him. "Here . . ." he murmured, just skimming the sensitive top skins of their lips together. "How much does it ache here?"

Her response was wild and whimpering, resounding from the back of her throat and straight into his as Golden thrust lips and hands and tongue upon him. *Her tongue!* Mast would have laughed at the irony of it—if he'd been able to comprehend anything but this ecstasy bursting from the slick grotto where her mouth joined his, drenching his.

He had no recourse but to let her plunder. And to plunder in return. They kissed, wetly and feverishly. They devoured and sucked, licked and fondled until their air came in gulps and pants and their bodies vibrated instinctively against each other.

Golden had only to look in Mast's eyes to know what he wanted then. She lifted her legs around him, surrendering herself to his care as he grasped her to him, then turned and lowered her into the haven of his bunk. She stretched into the soft, spicy sheets as she watched him yank off his boots, and when he turned back to her, she extended a hand of passion-taut fingers to hasten him back to her.

But suddenly those fingertips went limp with fear. Mast didn't respond to her request. He just stood there a long moment, his jaw flexing with something that appeared terrifyingly akin to hesitation. *No . . . no!* her eyes screamed up at him. He was so broad and beautiful and brown, she hurt.

Then in an eye's blink he was upon her. Yes, he was kissing her, grasping her, sliding against her. He curled his shape to hers, eagerly molding their bodies into one passionate being. The motions coiled up into his lips, as well; he took her mouth slow and sinuously at first, then began to thrust and parry with her teeth and tongue, gasping harshly with her in between. With each impassioned stroke and touch, a new wash of shuddering heat flooded Golden, each more intense than the last. She moaned and quivered, she writhed, and kissed him back. Coherent thought was a dim thread in the back of her mind; she struggled to cling to it—but for how long? Nothing Guypa had taught her had ever prepared her for this!

Then when she didn't think this joy could get any more incredible, Mast shifted above her . . . and his fingers were suddenly *there,* unfolding the most intimate part of her; inflaming her to a fevered longing she'd never known.

"Does it ache here, Golden?" His voice came surprisingly strong, yet far away as Golden whirled through stars and sparks of delicious sexual awakening.

"Yes . . ." She dragged her eyes open to the sight of Mast kneeling beside her, with a beautifully profound look on his face . . . an uncommonly large swell to his breeches flap.

She sat up. Mast stilled his caresses, not saying anything as he followed the angle of her gaze. Her dark, curious stare worked into him just like a caress—with no less effect. He looked down with her as the already strained material between his thighs jerked and tightened even more.

"Oh, Mast . . ." She inhaled in awe. Mast didn't think

he'd ever heard or seen anything so enchanting. She made him feel so powerful.

Powerful might have been overdoing it, he realized the next moment. Without any warning, Golden reached out and cupped her hands fully around the bulge of him.

"Ohhh, Christ."

Her fingers stilled at his forceful gasp, but didn't release. "You ache here, too," she whispered in amazement. "Don't you?"

"By God and the angels above . . ."

"Am I hurting you?"

"Oh, God, no—yes—no, don't let go!"

He was, as usual, turning the poetry in his head to complete verbal mush at his lips, but the arousal was now agony and all Mast could comprehend were her fingers, exploring him, opening his senses in ways he never thought possible.

"Yes, sweet," he encouraged. "Now just . . . let me free. Oh, sweet, sweet Golden, that's it . . ."

His hips bucked as Golden released the fall of his trousers. His manhood lay just beyond the hose underneath, pulsing, beating, a mesmerizing swell of power and mystery. Golden reached and loosed the bind of his hose. His swollen shaft erupted into her hand, filling it.

"Yes, Golden," Mast grated. "Take me in your hand. Hold my ache. Hold it tight."

It was the first of his commands she'd ever been elated to appease. Golden closed her hand around the length of him, joining his shuddering sigh with a heated one of her own as he grew bigger, harder, hotter. In little time she could stand the expanding tension no longer. Golden lifted both hands to the sides of Mast's face. She plunged her pleading eyes into his impassioned ones. "You've shown me everything else of your world, Mast Iverson," she whispered. "Now show me this. You've been lonely for so long . . . let me fill it."

Then, after she slowly, softly kissed him, "Love me, Mast. *Please*. Show me the bond we can make as man and woman."

Fourteen

If even a tiny chunk of self-control was left anywhere inside him, in that moment it was pulverized—crushed beneath the beautiful honesty of her plea—devastated by the ardent whisper it had come wrapped in, until all that was left in his senses was Golden—blazing-eyed, daring-lipped, incorrigibly curious Golden. And all that was left in his heart was the demand to fulfill that precious curiosity, for once and for all.

Mast lunged and pulled Golden down upon him. He growled low in his throat with the discovery that they fit even better together without clothes on. Golden sighed, perhaps with the same thought, for she snuggled even closer to him, inadvertently transforming the tight curls of her womanhood into a warm cushion around his sex.

His growl turned into a groan. Her wigglings were uninhibited, unplanned, yet dead accurate on the apex of his arousal. Mast practically clawed his fingers into her waist to stop her, but the action only drove Golden harder against him. She was whimpering into his mouth between the fervent sweeps of her tongue as she molded her mouth to his again.

He finally had to pry her away, so he could drink in the beauty of her passion-flushed cheeks, the bemused glaze of her eyes. "Lay back, sweet," he told her. "I want to kiss you."

"But we are . . ."

"Nay. I said I want to *kiss* you."

She smiled then, a tiny curve of her mouth—yet the most dazzling of any smile he'd ever seen on those precocious lips. With that smile came the trembles which told just how deeply he'd honored her by wanting to reciprocate her native-style caresses.

If she only realized it was all he'd been able to think about. To dream about. Yearning to reach out and touch her skin like this, feeling the flowing lines of her body like this . . . gliding his hands over graceful thighs and hips, lovely shoulders and arms, ivory smooth breasts and lips and neck until his fingertips pumped so much lightning-hot desire into him he trembled from the impact. He couldn't stop. Oh God, he couldn't stop.

Don't stop, Golden silently pleaded. *Don't stop, ever!* She watched, entranced, as Mast's long fingers roamed her skin, alighting it into a thousand streaks of giddy sensation . . . stroking atop and around her breasts, splaying around her rib cage, even swirling into her navel . . . Then he rolled her over and repeated the torture, grazing her shoulders, kneading her hips and bottom, even rubbing the backs of her knees, where, she was stunned to discover, she was deliciously sensitive.

But her breath caught when his fingers began a deliberate path upwards—toward the moist darkness between her legs. Golden gasped and protested but he continued on, into that heated center of her being, seeking and then finding the nub where so much of her pulsed in slick readiness.

She cried out in ecstasy with the first bright tinglings of pleasure. Her fingers curled into the pillows; her heartbeat pounded in her arched neck. It was too much. She was surely going to explode!

"Mast. Oh, Mast, please . . ."

"My sweet," came his reassuring murmur at her ear. "Oh my sweet, it's all right." He kissed the hollow of her nape as if for confirmation, before turning her in his arms again; until they were face to face and kissing deeply, lovingly.

This time when his lips parted hers, Golden surrendered wholly and passionately. Their tongues swirled and devoured, teased and consummated. The glorious sensations poured through her and overflowed the boundaries of her senses. Her hands slid around Mast's flexing shoulders. Her legs clamped around his sinewed waist. Her hips pressed instinctually to him, opening to him.

"Jesus," she heard him utter in a hoarse whisper against her cheek, though she was more conscious of the spasm that followed through the whole of his body. And the hard, hungry knob of his passion warming her womanflesh again—prodding her—promising yet a higher plateau of ecstasy . . .

"Now, hellion," he rasped. "Open for me now . . . yes . . ."

"Yes," she echoed him, as his flesh slid into hers. Their heat became explosion, their passion became lovemaking. Golden gasped and froze. There was a sharp moment of pain, as Guypa had always taught her to expect, but she wanted to capture every second of this new and wondrous moment in her memory forever. This awakening of pure physical need in her body, pure feminine joy in her soul.

But Mast's hoarse whisper at her ear clearly said he didn't share the incredible feeling. "Oh, God. I'm sorry. Golden—I didn't mean to go so fast. I—"

"No!" she nearly yelled at him. "Oh, *no,*" she forced in a softer tone. "Oh, Mast . . ." She tilted a small smile to go with it. "The Arawak woman is strong long before she goes to her man's bed, so that they may share pleasure there, not pain." She tunneled her hand into the thick, dark waves at his temple and pulled him into a fervent kiss. "And I want to give you so much pleasure. More and more pleasure."

"Dear God," he half-chuckled, half-grated. "Ah, *God* . . ."

Then all words and sensations were eclipsed by his pure masculine groan and his full, hot erection. Golden's own sob of desire mated with his. He was more than she ever thought he'd be—more flesh, more sensation, more hot demand. He was exacting every response her body had to give, but restoring it each time he entered her anew, saturating her with his heat.

He was exhilarating and terrifying, both at the same time. Golden reveled in the new awareness that came as his body became part of hers, but trembled at the other feelings coursing through her at the same time—at the way her legs clamped around him and never wanted to let go. Her hips rose to meet him, powered by an unseen force that only gathered more intensity as she struggled to assuage it, tormented her more as she fought the drowning threat of it. It came at her from all sides as Mast moved harder and farther within her. She cried out in fear, wanting to continue, dreading to continue.

"It's all right, sweet," came his ragged, but gentle whisper. "Let it go . . . I'm here."

"Mast," she sobbed. "But it's so . . ."

"I know."

And he did. He altered his pace then to include enticing circles of movement in addition to his sensual plunges. Soon Golden envisioned herself dipping into a pool of exquisite liquid sensation. Each immersion was a little longer than the last, but not quite a full dive. Soon she felt herself straining for the edge—yearning for that blissful submersion—pitching herself higher into Mast's powerful thrusts until he lifted her tight against him and his voice was around her, grating, "Now, Golden. Come with me *now.*"

It flooded every inch of her, seized every muscle, engulfed every thought and feeling in her soul. Golden cried out as sparks of unthinking ecstasy seized her. Not a moment later Mast added a deep, guttural groan as he clutched her and froze, then pushed her back to the pillows as he drove his hot, fevered release into her.

The drums of their passion dance gradually subsided to a soft and easy cadence, but they rocked to the rhythm for a long time after, spending the last notes of their passion song in each other's eyes. That shared gaze spoke thoughts there were no words for, communicated sensations there was no sigh or moan for.

At last Mast slid down next to her, though in truth he was over her. One arm and most of his legs were draped possessively across her body. Golden happily took advantage of the situation. She let her hands roam his nakedness, satiating every curiosity she'd harbored about his hard male build for so long. She raked his thigh, marveling at the power it had even in rest. She found a faded scar on his knee and wondered how he'd come by it. She memorized the cords of his back, the feel of his shoulders as he reached to hold her closer. She smiled at that and moved to snuggle deeper into the curve of his embrace, thinking she'd never felt more complete or free in her life.

The warm palette of twilight was quickly giving way to the cool ink of night throughout the cabin, but neither moved to turn up the lantern. They lay in the darkness, content with their entwined state of nakedness. Together they listened to the evening sounds of the hurting, but miraculously still-floating *Athena*. Canvas flapped somewhere, then halted as it was lashed down. The distinctive scrape of knife to wood told that Rico was hard at work on the Madonna figurine he was carving for his mother. A harmonica started up a peaceful tune in accompaniment. Robert swore loudly.

They joined in a quiet laugh over that last sound, then shifted in each other's arms so that Golden's head fitted beneath Mast's neck. He felt wonderful—warm and strong, yet gentle and smooth as his fingers slowly brushed along her thigh and waist.

"I can feel your heartbeat," she whispered.

"I can feel yours." His touch trailed between her breasts. "Here."

Golden heard him draw his next breath. It was jagged, hesitating. She drew back her head and stared at him.

"Countess Arabella Wincroft," he said before she could ask.

Her brows knitted. "Who?"

The moon had risen enough that she could see his throat constrict with a swallow. "You wanted to know what made me change."

"Yes," she replied with a hint of question to the word.

"Well, her name was Arabella."

He took another long breath, as if summoning up the courage to continue. "I was—God, how old *was* I?—well, I was young. And Arabella was . . . older—beautiful and sophisticated. She'd been places I'd never heard of. We were from two different worlds, but I thought the physical heat we shared equaled spiritual passion, and it would only be a matter of time before she happily gave up her diamonds and silks to run away with her daring young sea captain."

A harsh laugh came from deep within his throat then. "It took her only three months to show me what a fool I was.

With the help of her next rutting toy, of course. I think he was a court page or something . . . I remember the uniform on the floor of the bedroom when I walked in on them."

Golden winced, pressing her chest to his as if to show him how much she felt his pain, too. "How awful that must have been. I'm sorry . . . so sorry."

"I know you are."

And, she knew, he did. Golden felt it in the vibrations of his body as he spoke. She heard the conviction permeating the short, but meaning-filled statement. She heard his heart thumping through his skin to her—the way her own body had shaken so many times in the middle of the night, when there was nothing to protect her from the cold and the dark. From the memories. From the pain.

She bit hard into her lower lip, but the terrifying sting clung at the backs of her eyes. The desperate oath pounded at the door of her heart . . . *Good little sailors don't cry . . . don't cry . . . don't cry . . .*

"Hellion? What is it?"

She couldn't reply to his murmur for a very long moment. She was struggling for words where there seemed to be none, and praying for an easy way to begin, when she was starting the most difficult sentence of her life.

"I . . . was telling you the truth yesterday," she hesitantly began, "when I said Nirvana saved my life. But it wasn't because I'd swum out too far, or gotten caught in a storm. It was because I'd fallen overboard."

"Fallen . . . overboard?" He said the words disjointedly, as if they'd make some sense apart, since they weren't clicking with him together.

Strangely enough, his confusion was comforting. Golden lifted up a few inches to look directly into Mast's face. "My real parents—before Guypa and the Arawak or Wayland

Gaverly ever knew me—well, things weren't so good for them in England. So they decided to make a new start in the Indies. We—" still she vacillated, feeling a physical pressure in her chest as the images collided and reeled in her memory, "we had almost arrived when pirates raided the ship we were on."

"Pirates." Mast's repeat trailed off as full comprehension began to dawn upon his features. "The Moonstormer."

"Yes." As determinedly as she tried, she couldn't keep the bitterness from tainting the affirmation. "Even after robbing the ship, the monster set fire to it. I was separated from my mother in the chaos. I tried, but I couldn't find her. There was so much smoke, and it was very dark . . . Then the deck tilted and I slid into the water. I came up just in time to see her shadow along the deck, just before the fire—"

"Stop." It was a taut, husky command. "Don't go on. You don't have to."

He pulled her back against him, with an embrace so fierce it was nearly violent. "Christ, Golden," he whispered, the tumult of his heartbeat booming around her as its echo. Golden closed her eyes, hardly daring to believe what her own turmoil of thoughts was telling her.

This moment . . . she never dreamed this moment would come—the moment when this pain inside her, this persecuting hate, would . . . begin to heal. She'd always thought that moment would be when she at last stood over the Moonstormer's lifeless body—but that wasn't it at all. No, healing was in the enveloping arms of this man . . . healing was in the way his breath caught as he physically agonized for her loss . . . healing was in his thundering heartbeat at her ear, in the feeling of his words.

Healing, Golden comprehended with a joyous influx of warmth, wasn't in bearing her hurt, but *sharing* it.

She gasped. Gratefully. And with the unmitigated thanksgiving of her new realization, painfully.

"Sweet . . ."

His voice came through the chaos, resonant and smooth, yet laced with a hint of question. Golden opened her lips to say something but trembled against him instead, and whimpered with the frustration of it. Mast cradled her even tighter. The action spoke more reassurance than a thousand poetic words could.

"Thank you," she at last whispered, never meaning anything more in her life. "Oh, Mast . . . thank you."

And then she kissed him. Softly, so softly at first, brushing reverent, breeze-light caresses over his mouth, as if crossing herself before prayer. And then the full supplication . . . she wrapped her arms closer around his shoulders, formed her body tighter to his, offering her lips completely to whatever he would do with them.

Oh, what he did with them. It took but a few tentative urgings of his lips for Mast to realize just how willing she was. He let out a low growl denoting his pleasure at that discovery. Another animal-like sound came as he clutched one hand to the back of her head, another around her waist, and passionately rolled her back against the pillows.

The hand in her hair brought her lips up into his full-mouthed kiss. His tongue followed, storming hotly around and against hers, delving deeper and deeper until all Golden could do was mew her wholehearted approval.

The sound vibrated through Mast like a thousand needles of desire pricking him at once. "Christ," he grated. "I want you again already."

"Then take me . . ."

He rejoiced at how wonderful his choked laugh felt. "You brazen little savage," he taunted, before parting her lips anew.

She only answered with a long sigh of pleasure as he prodded aside the folds of her womanflesh and thrust into her again, his groan of satisfaction harmonizing with her cry, their passions singing and soaring together at the same time. It was glorious, it was triumphant. Yet Mast wanted to be deeper . . . closer . . . harder.

He scooped his hands beneath her hips and pulled Golden tighter around him. Hot sensations surged through his body but her reaction staggered him to his core.

With his first thrust she trembled and whimpered. With the next her head flew back against the pillows. With the third her arms went back and tangled in her hair, and with the next, her legs became yielding and pliable beneath his grip.

She had completely surrendered to him.

He stilled for a moment, just gazing at her. Visually drinking of the tawny lashes sweeping against the passion-stained cheeks, the sleek lips pleading his name, the muscles standing out in her neck as she strained to please him, the sweet-tipped breasts that invited him to please her in return . . .

Words spilled out of his heart and over his lips before he ever knew what they were. "You're beautiful."

Her eyes opened. Even in their hooded and desirous state, topaz fire flashed out at him.

"Love me, Captain," she whispered. "Love me hard and hot." The faintest smile touched her lips. "And that's an order."

Mast realized it then. The little heathen hadn't surrendered at all! She wanted nothing better than to be lost in the power, the hunger, the violence of his need.

The last thing he felt before blinding white oblivion overtook him was sheer, thankful amazement.

Three bells. It must be nine-thirty, Mast mused in some foggy corner of his mind, at the same time cocking one ear for the normal sounds of the ship at this time of night.

Everything seemed somewhat quieter than usual. The men had been keyed up about their dramatic victory over El Culebra, and he expected some kind of lively banter from the forecastle, if not full-scale music and laughter.

But then the crack he allowed in his eyes jerked all the way wide.

The light beyond the window was not moon glow. It was the blush of the rising sun. It was five thirty—in the morning.

"Good God," he mouthed. Since turning to life on the sea he hadn't slept a whole night through since—Mast couldn't remember.

Despite his haste, he made his way out of the bunk as gingerly as he could. As he did, he admitted he wasn't just concerned with giving Golden her rest. There were several other equally intense reasons. There were issues he had to sort through, alone and carefully. Things that tumbled one after another to the crest of his mind as he gazed at her while he dressed. Thoughts rushed to his heart and soul with frightening, maddening urgency.

He needed some air. Preferably cold and bracing. Definitely now.

An all-too familiar coastline loomed off the port bow as he strode up to the quarterdeck and studied the horizon.

"New Providence already, Robert?"

The bulky man turned his head at his captain's voice and grinned. "Aye. And as smarmy and wicked a port as ever, from the look of things."

A nerve tensed in Mast's jaw as he nodded agreement. "I hate to put in at all, let alone here. But it's only going to be for the day. You know how underhanded Carlos likes to be about things. We may have damage we don't even know about yet, and I hate—"

"—to take any foolish chances."

Dinky had joined Robert that moment to help finish the favorite expression of their captain in joking unison. Mast snorted and swore at them, then reached to Robert with a hearty whack on the shoulder.

"Excellent time, Master Gunner. Get some sleep before we put in."

"Willingly obeyed, Captain."

"Oh, and Rob—" Mast momentarily waved the big man back to him. "I'd appreciate your eye on Ben while we're in New Prov. His affinity for the gaming taverns has seemed to grow lately, and the last thing we need as a send-off is any of that rabble from the Blue Gull Inn."

"Understood," Robert gruffly replied. "Noticed the same thing about ol' Bennie myself when we sat that storm out in Jamaica."

Mast expressed his appreciation of that with another rough slap to his master gunner's shoulder. "Sleep well, Rob."

"Right." The burly man quirked a sardonic brow in obvious reference to the forecastle's round-the-clock disorder. "In that case, I'll take your bunk."

"You won't get near my bunk and that's an order."

Robert gave a laughing shrug as he descended toward his own berth in the forecastle, but when Mast turned to

Dinky he instantly knew his first mate didn't share the mirthful reaction. Dink's green eye challenged him without a blink, the greying eyebrow above cocked like a suspicious question mark.

Mast scowled. "What the hell are you looking at?"

Dink gave a few soft pops of his lips before answering, "I'd say a man who had left something—or should I say someone—in his bunk."

Despite his hardest order at himself otherwise, Mast hastened his gaze to the deck. He was flabbergasted to discover that his feet were . . . shuffling.

"I'm right, aren't I?" A laugh grew and bubbled from Dink's throat. "Scale and fry me whole, I'm right!" He rushed to Mast and flung an enthusiastic punch into his shoulder. "Ya stubborn mudhen; I knew Golden would be the one to melt ya down!"

"Dink—"

"This is splendid—spit 'n' damned splendid!"

"Dink—"

"I shoulda known somethin' was up when I didn't see her up here nippin' at both ends of yer dander. Guess the spitfire's a bit fizzled this mornin', eh?"

"Dink, listen to me!"

Mast had to yank his way free from the elbow-rattling salutation. His first mate stepped back and looked up. Both colors of Dink's gaze were darkening at once. Peculiar . . . Mast had never found that two-toned stare the frightening oddity most people did, but suddenly he found himself turning from it like a gaping stranger. Hiding from the things Dink and his eyes would discover in him without even trying—things he didn't want to recognize himself.

"It's not so splendid, my friend," he uttered. He braced himself against the rail, yearning for some magical infusion of his vessel's steadiness. "A bloody mess sounds a hell of a lot more like it."

A half beat of silence passed before Dink sighed, heavily and knowingly, behind him.

"Ya told her about everything, didn't ya?"

He echoed his friend's hard exhalation. Then, almost mournfully, "No."

"No?"' Dink snorted in puzzlement. "Then where's yer mess?"

Mast lifted his head, looking at, but not seeing, the rising blush to the sky. "Christ, Dink." The amazement in his voice was a new and strange sound. "I wanted to tell her. Badly. I wanted to tell her everything."

Another contemplative silence. Then Dinky materialized at the rail next to him, looking out at the horizon with a determined glint that Mast found surprising and comforting at once.

"Ive." His tone was calm, yet carefully so. "We've been friends a long time, lad. And seamates longer 'n that. So you know I'd be a green noddied fool not to notice just how different this voyage has been—or that ya've chosen not to tell me why, either. Now, don't go throwin' a bloody shoe. Ya should also know by now that it's perfectly dandy by me if ya choose to do so. Ya got yer reasons for yer secrets good 'n' fine." The dark furrows of his face deepened in a brood then. "Especially if Lord Wayland, Third Earl of Whatever the Hoochie, is involved the way I think he is."

Mast tensed. He'd avoided that name since rising this morning. He'd been desperately shoving any thought of Wayland toward the safe unthinkingness at the fringe of his mind. Yet now the moment of truth was here. Now the confusion and the remorse were poised and ready to pummel him. He shut his eyes as the cold, hard blows sunk in.

"I wish your instincts were off for once, Dink."

"So what the hell if they aren't?" came the retort and the sigh like a sane man trying to communicate with a lunatic. "Ive, I'd think you'd've noticed by now. Golden is not her father. That spitfire is a person all by herself—hell, sometimes a coupla people by herself—and most of all, she's crazy about ya. Don't gimme that boar face. She is, and I'll tell ya somethin' else. Ya feel the same way back, ya ugly bovine, even if it hasn't penetrated that thick noggin of yers yet."

Mast had pushed *that* gut-twisting thought back to the black sanctuary in his brain, as well—precisely because of what the confrontation did to him now. Images invaded him, body and soul. He had visions of open, giving coral lips and the ardent tongue beyond them . . . of whispered entreaties and unbridled sighs of gratitude and fulfillment . . . of breathtaking nudity, endless lengths of leg pulling him closer . . . of giving in and giving up and giving more because there was nothing else to do with the passion that filled him—

"What the hell does that have do with it?" he snapped a halt to the maddening torture.

His first mate pierced him with another exasperated scowl. "Ive, ya made love with the woman. In yer case, this equals the exodus from Egypt." He placed a fatherly hand on Mast's shoulder. "Now I'm not sayin' there's anythin' wrong with that. But considerin' it all the same, why don't ya take a chance on trustin' someone—and let the truth off yer chest fer once?"

"No." He whipped his gaze over the water. "That's out of the question."

"Damn it, Ive! Ya've kept it a secret long enough. I'm sure England thanks ya, but—"

"No, Dink. You don't understand. It's beyond that now. Far beyond it. It's out of control."

He clenched and unclenched his hands as he turned and began to stomp back and forth across the deck. "We planned it all so simply, Dink. So bloody, blasted easily, without a care. You remember, don't you? You and I, so full of pomp and arrogance when George's men selected us. Us, of all the brigs traveling to the Indies; we were going to be the messengers of England's 'most private and important' communiqués in their 'great Caribbean conquest.' And then our already huge heads were swelling beyond control when we came up with just the plan to accomplish that."

He shook his head. Those long-ago days still seemed so near, so incredibly, crystal clear. "Do you remember?" he said more to himself now than Dink. "Do you remember how damn proud we were of that scheme? 'Why not fly a pirate jack from the mast, instead?' we suggested. 'Bloody brilliant!' they answered. 'Better yet, we'll create a whole mystique,' we said. 'We'll make up stories, tell tales in the sailing taverns, let word of mouth carry us into legend status. We'll concoct such a magnificent monster, nobody will come near us *or* England's confidences."

His feet froze and his fists hardened like ice before he concluded lowly, "And we'll call him the Moonstormer."

The sun started to reach tentative amber fingers over the horizon. They touched Mast's face, but instead of warmth, all he felt was an inundating need to run from them . . . like a vampire, hiding his vile secret from the living world.

"We should have seen, Dink." This time the raggedness of his voice didn't surprise him. The words matched the ripped-apart way he felt. "We should have known what would happen . . . what the others would do."

"The others?" came Dink's perplexed interjection. "The

other what? We should have known what would happen? Ive, yer not makin' sense!"

"Murder." He slammed the word in with a sharp turn of his head. "Does that make enough sense? Aye, Dink, pillaging, burning, and murder—right before Golden's eyes. She was only eight years old. Her parents, her security, her life, all gone—incinerated while she watched from the back of a damn dolphin. And all blamed conveniently on the Moonstormer."

Dink's mouth opened speechlessly, clamped back shut. "Sweet saints," he finally stammered. "Ya mean the things we hear in the taverns, all the elaborate stories we thought were rumors—"

"Are *not* just rumors. Somebody, somewhere on this goddamn ocean is making the Moonstormer a reality."

"No wonder Golden went half-harpied on us that night on Saint Kitts."

"Her hate is well-nourished. She's been carrying it for twelve years."

"Twelve years! Ive, ya mean to tell me there's a bastard who's been terrorizin' like this for goin' on over a decade?"

"And getting away with it in the name of a pirate that doesn't exist." With each word, his fury coiled a slow fire through him with each word until Mast found himself taking short, hard breaths to keep it under control.

"We gotta do somethin'."

"Something, Mr. Peabrooke, is only to be the beginning." Mast looked down to the hatch of his cabin as he said it, knowing the words were as much a vow to the woman that slept beneath his deck as a statement to his friend above. And as the first full patches of morning light winked through the shrouds of the *Athena,* he smiled as he didn't run, but welcomed the crisp and clear sunbeams, instead.

"You gave me something special last night, hellion," he murmured beneath his breath to that closed door across the main deck. "And though I can't dream to acknowledge you for it the way I should, I promise one thing to you before this mess is over. I promise it, Golden, on every speck of the little honor I may have left in my body.

"The truth, my sweet. You'll have the truth, by God, if I have to chop its head off myself and bring it to you on a stick."

Fifteen

"New Providence! All lines secure at New Providence, Captain!"

Rico's bellow was the first thing to greet Golden as she pushed open the hatch into the midmorning sun. She hesitated in the resonating aftermath of the hail, smoothing the front of her simply cut light blue gown for the hundredth time since she'd finally decided it was just the right thing to wear today—and checking her hair for the two-hundredth time.

Still, she faltered. Was it the right thing? Did she look all right?

Nay, she corrected herself, she wanted to be better than all right. She wanted to be perfect.

She wanted Mast's eyes to darken to black, bottomless desire when he saw her . . . the way he'd gazed at her last night as he'd stroked her to passion, longing and finally ecstasy. She wanted him to welcome her to his side with openness and trust—the way they'd at last trusted each other with their deepest and most difficult secrets.

Most of all, she wanted to look up at him in the glorious Caribbean sun; she wanted to look at the wonderful sun-hardened planes of his face and at the wind rustling in his black sea of hair—and she wanted him to look back and smile at her. Yes, the way he'd smiled at her last night, when they'd loved and laughed until the waves of shuddering intensity had claimed them and all he'd been able to do was gasp her name over and over again . . .

As if her reflections made it so, that distinctive timbred voice called out from the quarterdeck, "Very well, Rico. Thank you. Now everyone, let's get to work. Cover every inch of your assigned area. Those bastards may have gotten luckier than we thought. I want first reports and supply orders turned over to Dink as soon as possible."

A hearty round of "ayes" answered, not that Golden noticed over the wild drum dance in her heart. Somehow she willed her feet up the last two steps and onto the deck—

Just as Mast tilted his gaze her way.

He turned hesitantly at first, as if his ear had caught something and he wasn't quite sure what. Then his head lifted, and his stare embraced her completely.

Golden's heart soared. She'd have sworn by ten talismans there was a spark of something reflecting a bottom to those dark blue recesses. By twenty zemis, a smile, however flickering and unsure, twitched the edges of his otherwise firm and official mouth.

Golden softly smiled back.

Mast thought his chest was going to implode.

"What the hell was that?" came Dink's vague voice through the explosions in his senses.

"What?" he snapped in agitation.

"You croaked."

"The hell I did."

"Boar's snot you didn't." But then the older man interrupted himself with an appreciative whistle as he followed Mast's line of vision. "Damn," he said, "I'd croak, too, kid."

Mast made ready for the safe denial that sprang in his throat. But he stopped himself at the brink. What purpose would that do? Make Dink's call any less true? Deter him at all from getting to the answers that Golden's trusting smile impelled him to find, no matter what?

No matter what. "Damn it. We've got to unearth every corner of this hellhole if we have to, Dink." He didn't take his eyes from Golden as he growled it. The desperate notion occurred to him that he might even be pledging it to her. "Every corner," he enunciated in emphasis. "Twelve years ago or not, an entire ship doesn't go down without someone remembering it. Especially in New Providence."

Dinky cupped a hand to his brow as he surveyed the dirty and bustling crowds along the docks. "Whatever you say, kid, but I think it's gonna be a bit like huntin' for dirt in a dung pile." He sniffed in disgust. "New Providence. Pirate Republic, my arse. More like a Derelict's Dungeon."

But his friend's mutterings had faded to a dull buzz in Mast's ears. Instead, a fierce pounding began through his head as Golden stepped, in that tantalizing swish of a dress, up to the main deck. The throbbings rose to an unbearable pitch as every male on the docks locked his attention on her.

Mast cleared the stairwell in one stride, the deck between them in another two. He heard Golden's stunned squeak as he grabbed her and hauled her to the shelter of the galley.

Golden's heart instantly sank as deep as the shadows he'd pulled her into. Not even her journey up to the crow's nest last week had antagonized Mast so quickly.

Now she knew she should have stayed in the higher-necked gown she'd originally dressed in. Or maybe, her deepest fears whispered at her, it wasn't her clothes at all. Maybe last night simply wasn't the precious keepsake to Mast as it was to her.

"Well," she blurted, trying—and failing—to keep composed. If only Mast didn't still loom over her, all half-unkempt masculinity, smelling of spice and sea spray and their lovemaking. "I can see I've disrupted your schedule yet again, Captain. So if you'll excuse me—"

Then, suddenly, everything was exploding white stars and Mast's lips, hard and passionate, on her own. Golden's eyes flew open with the first inundating surprise of his kiss, but fluttered closed as languid heat flowed and gathered inside her. Mast released his hold to push her back against the galley chopping block. Now Golden's hands slid up his torso . . . through the exposed forest of hair on his chest . . . then around his neck and up through his dark and windblown hair.

"Bother me, hellion?" came his intense, husky murmur. "Oh, aye. Feel just how you bother me."

At that he caught her hand and directed it down into the warm space between his legs. He groaned. Golden gasped. Her knees and thighs became liquid fire. The blaze beckoned stronger, crying with primal intensity, until she could resist no more. She braced her body back against the block and her legs forward around his body.

"Jesus, Mary and Joseph." He choked on the last syllable. His head fell forward. His eyes and mouth clamped shut. Golden never thought pain and ecstasy could mold together on one face before. He was a breathtaking sight.

He held her like that for a long moment. His hands were clutching her thighs through the layers of the dress, fingering the slick blue fabric as if fighting a war with himself. Golden waged a contest of her own with each shift his hands made on her skin, shivering with the magical command he'd claimed to her body just hours ago.

"Hell," he finally muttered. Golden felt the unsteady wobble of his fingers as he slid them from her legs and started to smooth the layers of her dress. He extended a hand as if to help her stand. Instead, he pulled her back into his arms.

"We're in port, sweet." His tone lowered back to a business level, though his kiss was a gentle apology. "They'll need me above soon. Repairs . . ." A ragged sigh escaped as his hand trailed down her arm. "Supplies. Peeling terrified Spaniards from the hull. We've got a sea witch aboard, you know."

"How horrible for you, Captain." Golden feigned wide eyes of pristine female shock.

The side of his mouth twitched with a threatening smile, but was vanquished by a stare of dark concern. "New Providence isn't Milan, Golden. Not even Basseterre. It's a viper's nest—and nothing your curiosity can't live without. I don't want to have to order you, but I want your topside time limited today."

"Not even to slush the masts?"

He sighed, battling back the smile again. "Especially not for that. How about a nice afternoon chat with Maya?"

Golden scrunched her face in disgust.

"All right, then. How about Ben teaching you how to ram a truck gun properly?"

She kissed her approval at that—though a playful slap followed when Mast rolled his eyes to heaven as if to ask "why me"?

He regained the leading edge when he lifted his own hand to her face, cupping her chin up so her eyes met his. "One more thing," he growled. "And this time, it *is* an order."

"Oh?" She tried to sift the huskiness out of her voice, but it was impossible with the heat that started to crackle again between their bodies, while his night blue eyes pulled at her.

"Change your clothes," came the equally unsteady return. "Immediately. You and this dress go together too damn perfectly."

With that he took her lips again. And again. When he finally, reluctantly stepped back, he squeezed her hands. His expression was full of desire, with something else Golden couldn't pinpoint . . . a kind of longing, perhaps . . . or pain. Whatever it was, it clutched sweetly at her heart.

But he pivoted and left before she could tell him.

She didn't follow Mast. For long minutes Golden lingered in the shadows. Her mind recounted every second of the moments which had just transpired. "Perfect," she repeated under her breath, hardly daring to believe she'd just heard the word on Mast's lips.

Hardly daring to believe the joy that filled her heart so completely in response.

And even three hours later, beneath a light but thorough coat of gunpowder and dust, the glow inside her burned like a three-tiered chandelier. By the oddly amused smiles Maya and old Ben returned to her through the dim light of the gun deck, she judged that her newfound bliss wasn't just an inner revelation.

"Mr. Gunner's Mate." She addressed Ben while stepping away from the muzzle of the truck gun. "I believe the work is ready for inspection."

The old codger shuffled forward, scratching the few grey hairs he had. "Blimey. Near perfect, too, for a wom—" he hastened to revise himself, "for a greenhead. Cartridge and wad good 'n' tight, shot rammed right well . . ."

"Of course it's perfect," Golden interceded. "It has to

be. Captain Iverson depends on these guns in times of trouble."

"Aye, milady, he does."

The wizened seaman lifted one eye and eyebrow to her. Golden met the unspoken question with a direct gaze that made Ben's stare widen even further.

Surprisingly, the old sea dog cocked a warm smile at her then. Her heart was turning a somersault. Golden smiled back.

"You're a good friend and a loyal crewman, Ben." Without a thought she grasped his hand.

"Oh now, don't be startin' that kind o' mush."

He looked away with a bashful smile. But Golden observed that the expression didn't reach his eyes. There was a sweet sadness in Ben . . . a longing she knew every drop of the seven seas wouldn't be able to fill. So much like that first unfathomable loneliness she'd wondered at in his captain's eyes, that day the cannons had boomed across Saint Kitts—the day Mast Iverson had stomped into her life. The most unforgettable day of her existence.

She wished *all* these wonderful men could have such a day. They deserved it. They had earned it. They had kept Mast alive all these years, so she could experience the joy of loving him now.

The mist of intense emotion clouded her vision for a long moment. Finally, quietly, she told Ben, "Thank you, my friend. Thank you for everything."

"Nay, milady, thank *ye*. From all of us—even the captain, whether ye believe it or no."

"Oh, Ben," she found herself laughing again, "I believe you, I do! Maya?" She whirled to her sister then. "Come to the cabin with me while I clean up."

They stepped out into the companionway. But they were

no more than three steps along when Maya pulled her to a stop.

"And just when were you makin' to tell me, sister?"

The guilt-imposing twist to the question wasn't lost on Golden. Neither was the implied answer. But both only seemed to hold Golden back tighter from the playful retort she'd normally have fired back at Maya. A funny new sensation flooded her. She awkwardly admitted to herself that it could possibly be . . . shyness.

"Tell you what?" she lightly quipped.

"Tell you what?" Maya mocked. But the next instant a giant beam of a smile replaced the glare on the native's face. "You and dee captain," she whispered. "Oh Golden, tell me it be true!"

A well of laughter bubbled and burst through Golden as she nodded and Maya squealed. The last remnants of shyness fled as her sister pulled her into an embrace. Golden's strange feelings were now replaced with happiness, and the fulfillment of sharing it with someone—who understood.

"Well now," came a friendly and familiar accent. "Why wasn't I invited to this soirée?"

Dinky had appeared in the corridor, head cocked with a smug grin. With a wonderful new perception, Golden observed the brightening of Maya's eyes, the quiver of her sister's hand at her breast.

"Maya," she said quickly into the resulting pause, "I believe that lesson at the gun wearied me more than I thought. I've a need to lie down for a while. Would you mind if we talk later?"

"Oh no, sister!" Maya's response was as subtle as a battering ram. Her eyes were already glued on Dinky. "I don't mind at all!"

A self-satisfied smile remained on Golden's face as she

continued to the cabin to clean herself up. She washed her face and sponged her body thoroughly, all the while remembering what it felt like when Mast's hands stroked her breasts and belly and thighs. The memories were so entrancing, she closed her eyes to see them better: the skin-tingling touches, the silken, caressing sighs, the wet and consuming and deep-moving kisses . . .

And she ached for this day to end, so, like the nightbeams to the ocean, her dark-eyed captain would join with her again.

Please, Great Spirits, let him come to me again.

It was then that her eyes snapped back open. They moved to where her sky-blue dress lay lovingly draped over the velvet reading chair—the dress she went "too damn perfectly with."

Golden grinned devilishly as she slipped back into the gown.

She tried to make good on her words to Maya and lay down for a while after that—all the while praying she wouldn't get too much rest tonight—but there were so many new feelings and sensations to revel in that the task was impossible. It was as if her body had thrown a surprise party for her, and her soul was the gift she'd gotten to unwrap.

The restlessness finally forced her up from the bunk. Golden meandered about the cabin, lightly touching the wood and brass, trying to absorb the strength and beauty of the textures . . . thinking about the strength and beauty of their owner. She opened the wardrobe and breathed in the clean cedar scent there. She hummed the little tune Rico had taught her. She straightened up the washstand, refolding the already-straight towels, repolishing the already-shining razor and comb.

The restlessness was driving her insane.

Golden carefully listened to the rest of the ship. Many of the crew had gone into New Providence with Mast, and those who remained were absorbed with a myriad of duties and repairs.

Surely nobody would fault her for a short walk on deck.

She was right. Everyone topside was busy in or about the rigging, rechecking each line and shroud and backstay for a nastier-than-expected bite from El Culebra. If she kept her plain-colored overcloak pulled around the bright gown and stayed along the far side of the ship, they'd never know she was there.

She had no idea just how near impossible that feat would be. Golden let out an amazed breath at her first real view of New Providence. The mosaic of sights and sounds beyond the *Athena*'s opposite rails filled her senses to the brim. She thought she'd retained accurate memories of the London docks Mummy and Daddy and she had departed from for the Caribbean. But only now did she realize how dim those images had grown, in comparison to this spectacle before her.

Shouts and screams, loud laughter, even a piercing gunshot assaulted her ears. Horses, dogs, cows and chickens roamed among the odd-shaped buildings that seemed to have been thrown together out of anything from driftwood to palm fronds. And the humans comprised more color and texture than that: big-bosomed wenches with skin as white as a Saint Kitts beach at high sun, or as black as the hardened lava rocks that bordered it; Spanish rogues strutting like peacocks in their red and gold satin coats; tattoo-covered ruffians who looked like they'd just as soon cut a man's throat before looking him in the eye. It was loud and dirty and chaotic—and absolutely fascinating.

Something stirred inside Golden. With a touch of surprise

she recognized the feeling as her deeper, wilder instinct, usually only awakened in the interior of the rain forest. Yet that same sense told her that Mast could emerge from that crowd any moment. She reluctantly continued down the deck.

Return to the cabin, return to the cabin. She chanted the rebuke over and over at herself. But her excitement and energy were now rampant, and she dragged her feet more and more as she neared the hatchway.

Suddenly she stopped. Oh, a hatchway still filled her gaze, all right: the hatchway to the side hold, fifteen feet across the deck. From what she could gather, it was a barely used space; Golden hadn't seen anyone use the hold since she'd been aboard the *Athena*. Why, Mast hadn't even found the time to show it to her yet. The hold was probably just stuffed full of ship's records and tossed-aside trinkets—old things filled with memories and forgotten stories.

If hatchways could move, the crosshatched square would have grabbed her curiosity in a chokehold.

"Well," Golden murmured smugly. "You wanted me below deck, Captain?"

She took just enough time to grab a lantern from a peg on the mizzenmast before pushing the wood slat aside and slipping beneath.

Questions blanketed her more fully than the darkness. What would she find? Mast had finally told her he was transporting valuables from Saint Kitts for a customer— would they be down here? And did he keep anything else down here? Personal things? Trunks of treasured possessions? Something that would bring her even closer to him? But she didn't think she'd ever be close enough.

She restarted the tune she'd been humming as she pulled off her cloak, laid it aside in a corner, then lit the lantern. The pool of warm amber light first enveloped several kegs and crates, the kegs marked "water," the crates, "gunpow-der." Golden widely sidestepped them. If the ignited oil in the lantern made even the least contact with the volatile powder—she shivered with the horrific thought.

Ropes, ropes, and more ropes . . . patches of extra can-vas . . . wait—a flash of something pink, and green.

She peered closer. The colors were old paint, curling off the features of a carved woman. A large chunk was missing from her left shoulder, contoured in the distinctive round perfection of a cannonball. The former "Athena," Golden suspected, downed in the line of duty for her captain.

She affectionately touched the goddess's nose. So Mast *was* sentimental.

She turned toward the other corner. A variety of un-marked crates and chests answered her gaze. Golden inter-rupted her humming for a murmur of admiration at the elaborate carvings adorning some of the chests. A few were even inlaid with designs of gold and mother-of-pearl. The craftsmanship was excellent. Papa had taught her how to appreciate it. He'd taken her to the attic of the mansion once and used his own prized collection from his travels as examples.

To her dismay, all the containers seemed to be locked. Golden tugged on all the bolts anyhow, praying she'd get lucky.

"Praise to the heavens." The last chest gave up her mir-acle. Anticipation thumped through her as she creaked open the lid and reached in for the first piece of booty.

It was a small item, wrapped carefully in muslin. Golden's breath caught as she unraveled the material to reveal an ornate ruby pendant. Inscribed faintly on the back were the initials W.G.

"W.G.?" she whispered. Someone Mast knew? A friend

who'd rewarded him for some act of bravery? A long-ago love, before that countess had mercilessly broken his heart?

Maybe the next treasure would give her more clues. It was heavier and flatter, also swathed in muslin. A picture? Golden's fingers worked into the tie ribbons more eagerly at that possibility. One, two, three layers to peel away.

Disappointment sank over her like a damp fog bank.

"A plate," she huffed. "Nothing but a blasted fancy-paint plate. Now what am I supposed to do with—"

A freezing grip of recognition twisted her throat shut. Golden had first ignored the garble of lettering on the elaborate shield decorating the middle of the plate—oh, Papa had tried, unsuccessfully, to further what little formal learning she'd had after she came to live with him—yet this was the single phrase he'd demanded she master:

"To God and King, loyalty until eternity."

The Gaverly family oath.

"These aren't Mast's things," she choked. "They're Papa's.

"But what are they doing here?"

There was a logical, reasonable answer to that. Golden was sure of it. She just had to find Mast, and he'd explain. Yes, find him—

Now.

She struggled to her feet, clutching the plate to her breast as if it were armor against the darts of apprehension threatening to destroy her. She'd just go find Mast—she didn't care where she had to go or what she had to do—and everything would be fine again—wonderful and magical again. She let out a wincing laugh. He'd probably frown a thunderstorm at her for ignoring his wishes. Maybe he'd even heave her over his shoulder and then throw her into his bunk again, but that would make the peacemaking all the more explosive and joyous.

She had to get to him! Golden fumbled and hastened to pick up the lantern and then her cloak.

She froze with the things only halfway gathered to her.

The light in her hand now fully illuminated the corner where she'd first laid the cloak. A concisely folded triangle of crimson was tucked neatly there. A flag. A red flag.

"I just want to look at the flag a moment, Mummy. It's beautiful, don't you think so? What a lovely red flag."

Golden tossed aside the cloak without faltering her gaze. Her hand moved out and over the tidy red bundle. Dark, nerve-numbing instinct poured over her with the action. *Horror! Fear! Go back! Don't look!* She swallowed while her throat was thudding and constricting. She blinked, with eyes dry yet stinging.

"Stop it, Golden. Why . . . why England's flag is red. Aye . . . Mast just keeps this one down here because . . . because it means something. The sentimental ape."

But even as the assurances tumbled past her lips, a black border of fringe came free of the fold, falling between Golden's fingers like the icicles she could feel congealing in her heart.

"No," she rasped. "No, damn it. No . . ."

She jerked angrily at the cloth, whipping the crimson length out full, spreading it wide with slashing sweeps of her arm and lunging shoves of her feet. When she was done, she held the lantern high over the carpet she'd laid.

She gurgled out some kind of a cry into the hand she slapped to her mouth. And then convulsed into it with a dry retch. And another.

With the fourth or fifth heave she could no longer hold herself up. Golden fell to her knees above the blood red field, next to the figures that had been emblazoned to the middle of it: a death white mask of a pirate skull, resting perfectly in the curve of a yellow crescent moon.

The flag that was embedded upon her memory forever.

The Moonstormer's flag.

In the *Athena*'s hold.

Not Mast. Please, God, no. Not Mast not Mast not Mast.

Her wail was long and piercing as it surged from the deepest pit of her soul and erupted through the gash in her heart.

Sixteen

After the pain came the fury, consuming her until nothing else existed or mattered. The remnants of the last love or joy she'd ever feel lay scattered upon their crimson deathbed as Golden rose and climbed from the hold—and they could rot there, for all she cared. She'd never miss them in New Providence.

The gangway was just a number of feet away now. She inched yet closer to the ramp that would take her down to the dock, her lips turning up in a grim smile as her gaze took in the shoving, shouting throng of humanity there.

"Well, Moonstormer," she murmured, "I will admit my gratitude to you for one thing." She slid another few steps forward, smiling wider as two men on the quay erupted into a fist fight. "Thank you for bringing me to the one place on earth where I'll find at least a hundred men willing to help me kill you."

Before her sentence was finished, eight more ruffians jumped into the brawl, and a cheering audience formed. Fortunately, the men on the *Athena*'s deck weren't immune to the excitement. Golden sent up a rapid thanks to the gods as she darted across the gangway without receiving so much as a glance from their distracted gazes. She slipped deep into the crowd, and never looked back.

The jam of humanity at the docks thinned as it dispersed

among rows of everything from hovels of mud and refuse to more permanent and even grandiose structures of wood or clay. Many signs along the way had the "New Providence" painted out in them and replaced with "Nassau," the more recent name for the town until the Spanish again took over again last year. Indeed, at least six or seven different languages assaulted Golden's ears as she moved along. The confusion added to the chaos in her already-overwhelmed senses. Her head began to pound harder, and her stomach growled. As if by instinct, her mind's eye brought up visions of long, gentle fingers soothing the pain in her brow, Mast's broad chest cradling her close against the confusion and aching.

"Stop it," she ordered to herself under her breath. The remembrances were hazy, conjured-up images of a man who didn't exist.

Lies.

Golden backed into an alcove to recollect herself. With each breath she was pleased to find the safe veil of anger and hate once again falling over those silly emotions she'd let free. The spear of romantic delusion certainly wouldn't sneak up and stab her again, she vowed. Never again.

She snapped her head up. She smiled at the discovery that from here she had a good view of the rabble venturing down each avenue. After a quarter of an hour in scrupulous study of the throngs, Golden pulled her cloak around her and started down the road the most dangerous-looking brutes were taking.

Her stride was undaunted at first. Head held high and shoulders set, she was determined to seek out only the dirtiest of the dirty—the most lethal pistol shots, the most ruthless knife-wielders, the men whose cutlasses bore the most notches in their hilts. She scrutinized each face she passed with the intensity of a breeder selecting a prize stallion; her crew was going to be the fastest, the hardest—and the deadliest.

Yet she'd only proceeded halfway down the street when her step slowed to an uncomfortable shuffle. Her stomach was twisting in an apprehensive knot. Every face she'd encountered was staring back at her—and certainly not with businesslike decorum. Yes, she concluded, the stallions were hungry—only they were carving *her* up for dinner.

Golden proceeded as bravely as she could. She kept her chin aloft, though now she fixed her gaze straight ahead, not looking anywhere but at the end of the road.

The shock of pain gouged into her right ankle just before the unyielding object stole her balance. Golden's breath burst from her lungs in a stunned gasp as she fell, face first, into the road.

The dirt smelled horrid and tasted worse. Golden spat the heavy brown stuff from her lips even as she gulped on the clot of humiliation in her throat. She gathered her strength and slowly pushed herself up, though she felt more like burrowing into a grave in the lane then and there.

Her shin again scraped the coconut-sized boulder she'd tripped over. A swell of blood started to ooze from the scratch. But that ugly sight didn't displace the flood of frustration rising perilously close to the point of breaking her composure.

"Damn," she muttered, wiping futilely at her face and gown. "Oh, damn, damn, damn!"

"Come now, *querida*. It is only a little dirt."

Her head jerked up at the exotic, but friendly male voice. A hand met her gaze. Well-worn and well-scarred, but strong. The color of sun-bronzed bricks. And outstretched to help her.

Golden hesitated a moment, but just a moment. Tentatively, she lifted her fingers and allowed herself to be helped up. Her stare also ascended, stopping at the man's face. It was of the same dark copper color as his hands, only embellished by a black, well-trimmed beard and mustache. His flat eyes and bulbous nose seemed out of place in comparison, but the majestically tilted feather in his tricorn hat and the violet satin ribbon holding back his grey-flecked hair imparted an unmistakable air of wealth and dignity to him.

"Th-thank you," she stumbled out. "That boulder came from nowhere . . ."

The stranger chuckled from deep in his throat. "Indeed it did. But perhaps it was out warning young beauties away from the streets at this hour so close to nightfall."

Golden attempted to glare up sideways at him, but found herself returning his knowing smile, instead. They shared another laugh.

"I am called Roche. Roche Braziliano."

"I am called many things, but my name is Golden, and you may call me that."

Roche Braziliano swept his hat from his head as he bowed deeply. "I am much honored to be at your service, Señorita Golden." He lifted his body back up more slowly, with his eyes lingering over her in a manner Golden found strangely disconcerting, but couldn't fix upon the reason why. "And perhaps," he drawled on, "my reward will be to discover some of those other identities of yours . . ."

He kissed her hand in the same languorous way he rolled his r's and dipped the ends of his words. Like the man, Golden supposed, the accent had been undeniably South American once. Now both were laced with a strange blend of other cultures. He was a misfit of sorts, came the suddenly comforting perception. Just like her.

"Well, Master Braziliano—"

"Roche."

"Roche." She laughed with him at her unsuccessful attempt to mimick his accent. "I thank you again for your trouble, sir. But I must be going—"

"Ah, I see. A lady with a mission."

Golden stopped. She cocked her head back up into the assured set of the copper face. "How did you know?"

Roche Braziliano chuckled again as he stepped close to her. Very close. One scarred hand came up and brushed a tendril of hair from her face. Again Golden chastised herself for the inexplicable chill that overcame her with the contact.

"Because eyes like yours, *querida,* should be twinkling with joy, not pain."

Self-incrimination or no, Golden obeyed her instincts and turned away then. From the Brazilian's touch—but especially his words. They reminded her not only of why she was here, but of all the moments that had lined her trail. And damn her heart for directly ignoring her earlier command, in every reflection there was Mast. The first awkward, adorable way he'd tried to comfort her in Papa's study . . . then all the hours on the *Athena* he'd spent so patiently opening up the world of a brigantine to her. And then his surprising, yet wonderful *im*patience as he'd kissed her on the floor of his cabin. At last, the sparkling moments of their joining last night . . . the hours she never thought would happen.

Making love to her parents' murderer.

"Hurt, Master Braziliano, is just the start of it."

Though her voice sounded far away, she could hear the force of anger in it. She felt the fury slice through her muscles and bones again. The need for vengeance was driving a relentless beat through her blood. Golden bit down hard on her lower lip to stay the clamoring tears in her soul.

"Who is he, *querida?*"

She started in momentary surprise. The Spanish gentleman had moved very close behind her again. His query was soft and understanding at her neck. This time Golden didn't wonder how this complete stranger had known exactly what to ask. It just seemed enough that he did.

She turned, then slowly worked her eyes up into his face. She wanted to trust somebody again so badly.

"Would you believe me if I said the Moonstormer?"

The bland expanse of the brown eyes widened. A burgundy leather glove slowly stroked the beard below. "The Moonstormer. Really, now?"

Golden drew her fists up to her hips. "I knew it. You don't believe me."

"I didn't say that."

"You didn't have to." She pivoted on her heel.

Roche Braziliano swirled her back, laughing as if he'd merely pulled her up for a dance. *"Santo Dios.* You are a fiery one, my little Golden." He cupped her chin up. "Now stop that frowning. This is just an impressive accusation you make, you know. Many, many have come to this town to claim their victory over El Moonstormer. Many others have come claiming to *be* El Moonstormer—"

"I have proof."

Braziliano's mouth straightened. He lowered his hands and stepped back from Golden. He began to pace a small circle while appearing to casually take in the air with her. But the lightning-fast darting of his eyes told her otherwise.

A half minute later he slid up to her again as if just paying flattery to her eyes. "The evening shadows grow long," he said in a low voice. "And there are too many eyes and ears that hide in them. I suggest we continue this in my salon, *querida*. It is but a short distance up the road."

"Your . . . salon?"

Golden's smile faded. Mercy, standing in the middle of the lane with the cocksure foreigner was nerve-testing enough. The idea of following him inside one of these hovels, behind closed doors, set needles of apprehension darting along the back of her neck.

But what other choice did she have? Where else did she have to go? Who else did she have to trust—especially as the shadows of twilight were, just as the man said, growing before her eyes?

Her apprehensions were ridiculous. She berated herself. She was not the bumbling innocent Mast's gaze always told her she was. She knew a man who respected her when she saw one. And she saw one now in the warmth of Roche Braziliano's face.

"Your salon it is, *señor.*"

The Brazilian smiled his approval at her perfectly-rolled "r."

It turned out that Roche's salon was a very pleasant surprise. Despite her limited experience in New Providence, Golden could see the structure was one of the most grand of the town. Ten shining brass lanterns hung in a row from the front eaves, showing off the gleam of the whitewashed front portico. The main building itself was of rough stucco, but a real stained-glass window was set into the solid oak front door. Golden couldn't help reaching out a curious finger to the colored glass as they entered.

"It's from France." Roche's indulgent smile had returned. "Go ahead," he chuckled, "touch it." Golden obeyed happily.

"You must be hungry, as well," he added as they entered.

As if on cue, her stomach grumbled again. She laughed. "A little."

"Come, then. We will continue our talk in the dining room."

The Brazilian ushered her into a small, but luxurious room off the rear end of the main foyer. An ornately carved dining table sat beneath a shimmering labyrinth of a chandelier. Roche seated Golden in an impressive oak chair at one end of it, then sat in one of the matching chairs to her left. A serious-faced native, in servant's attire, appeared to take Roche's hat and Golden's cloak. Then he vanished after a few hushed instructions from his master.

"Now." Roche returned his attention to her with a serene nod. "About this proof of yours."

Golden had been taken in awe by her lush surroundings, lost in the crystal wonderland above her head. But her eyes dropped quickly at the invitation of Roche's query. "All you need is sitting in the harbor right now," she replied, leaning forward eagerly. "But it will be gone on the morning's tide, so we must act tonight—"

"Wait, wait—*alta, amiga,* slow down." Braziliano caught her gesturing hand in midair and brought it calmly back to the table. "One thing at a time. In the harbor, you say—"

"Aye. On the *Athena.*"

"Mast Iverson's brig?" True surprise lilted the question, and lowered his eyebrows.

"You know him?" Golden returned a similar vexed expression. Well, of course, he did, she rebuked at herself a moment later. Every rake and outlaw in New Providence probably did. They'd probably all, at one time or another, plunked down their ale stein next to him and never fathomed they were drinking to the health of the Moonstormer.

"I marvel more that *you* know *him,* mistress. Mast Iverson and I haven't crossed many paths in the past. But I know how he feels about the *señoritas* aboard his precious ship."

"You're still no less wrong on that account, Master Braziliano. But I swear by all the sea spirits that I've seen what's in that hold with my own eyes."

"And it will tell me Mast Iverson is the Moonstormer?"

"Aye."

"You are very assured of yourself."

Golden fixed her gaze securely to him before answering. "A person doesn't forget certain things in their life, sir. Even after twelve years, they remember those things on sight."

Braziliano rose a thoughtful finger to his beard again. "Twelve years? Hmmmm. That was a long time ago. I don't know if I even remember where I was—"

"Well I can tell you where I was." Her hands gripped tighter to the lion's heads on either side of her chair. "I was clinging to a piece of driftwood in the Caribbean Sea. A piece of the same ship I watched burn and sink with close to a hundred people still aboard—" She let out a heavy breath, "including my parents."

Silence. Golden didn't lower her gaze. Braziliano didn't lower his. His copper finger steadily stroked his beard.

Finally she stated into the stillness, "I want him dead, Master Braziliano."

"I know."

"Will you help me?"

The Brazilian didn't reply. He only reached out and un-curled the fingers of her hand from one of the lion's heads, then pressed his palms around her hand. "Did you know," he murmured, "you are a very beautiful woman when you are angry?"

She tried to pull her hand away. Braziliano held on tighter and kissed her knuckles, instead.

He chuckled. "Relax, *querida*. Of course I will help you."

The rush of triumph was nearly painful in her chest. "Thank you," Golden said on a massive exhalation.

"Of course . . ." That was when the rough sienna hands started to stroke higher up her arm. "There is the little subject of payment to be discussed."

Golden exerted full strength to pull herself free this time. The force caught Braziliano off guard. Her hand flew out of his grasp and Golden bolted to her feet. "You needn't be concerned about that, sir. My father is a leading dignitary in the West Indies, royally sanctioned by King George himself. He will make this honorable act well worth your while."

"Oh, he will, will he?" A full-bodied laugh rocked the black-haired head back. Just as forcefully, Braziliano shoved to his feet and moved around the table to her. "He'll dub me a knight of the realm, eh?"

"Well—yes. Quite certainly, after His Majesty hears of your bravery against the Moonstormer—"

"Knighthood wasn't what I had in mind, *querida*." His voice had transformed to a wolflike growl, his teeth and eyes agleam with the same predatory mien. "At least not from that *cobarde* on England's throne. Now, come here."

He lunged. Golden jumped back with a shriek. She grabbed a poker from the fireplace and swung it with a snarl.

"Oooh, such a little *tigre*, my Golden. But I like that. The fire . . . the passion . . ."

"I'll use this," she threatened.

Roche Braziliano's leer only widened at her. The next

second, Golden knew why. Arms seemed to come out of nowhere and grab her. The poker was whipped out of her hand and disappeared into a closing trap of darkness. And all that remained in the light with her was that leering, lusting flat-eyed face, menacing nearer, nearer . . .

"Very good, men," the curving lips beneath the mustache sneered. "Ahhh, that's so much better . . ."

His mouth pressed hard and lustily against hers.

The scream rose and throbbed to get out of her throat. Golden forced herself to swallow it down. *Think, Golden. By the love of all the spirits, think!*

As much as the act revolted her, she opened her mouth just enough to let his bottom lip in, then—

"Aggghhh! *Caramba! Santa María y José!"*

"Captain!" The darkness had voices. Their volume increased in proportion to the tightness of the steel grip holding her. "Captain Braziliano, *qué pasó?* What happened? Are you all right?"

"The witch bit me." Golden could detect his astonishment as he held his fingers up in front of him, the blunt copper tips wet with his own blood. He whipped his stare at her again, a demonic countenance of fury taking place of the playful gallant who had brought her here. "So it is to be like this, my little *tigre?"*

"Let—me—go." Golden squirmed and attempted to pounce at the gloating-faced Brazilian, but her arms were corkscrewed tighter against her back, and her knees kicked in so she fell to them on the floor. Despite her effort to bite it back, an outcry of pain escaped her.

"You dolts!" Braziliano growled. "Carefully! *Carefully!* We only want to break this colt, not make her unridable."

The voices in the darkness shared in his laugh. A new streak of rebellion shot through Golden; she hissed and tried to wrangle free again. A hand yanked her head back by the roots of her hair.

"Dios, you are a hot one," came Braziliano's whisper on her face. "The pleasure Iverson must have taken from you . . . no wonder he broke that stupid rule of his."

Golden lurched again. For some unexplicable reason, the words sparked every violent and defensive instinct in her being. "You bastard," she seethed.

The back of Braziliano's hand across her cheek was her answer. The blow snapped Golden's head on her neck; white flecks of dizziness floated before the sudden view she was afforded of the fancy-papered wall.

"Shut up," the Brazilian's cold voice said.

From the darkness came a greasy-sounding snicker. "You want we should take her to your room, Captain?"

"No. I have no appetite for Iverson's leftovers. Besides, I cannot know what she may bite off next." Another round of chuckling. "Lock her up in Abby's old room. Alone," he emphasized. "Except for Lilly. Send her in tomorrow to do something with this hair and face."

The last he said as he lifted Golden's chin back up and studied her features with a faint smile. "After all, my bride auctions are the finest in the Indies. And I've a feeling I've suddenly found my prize filly for tomorrow night."

The dizziness washed completely over Golden then. Her head was swimming in disbelief. Her heart was crashing a tidal wave of terror against the dim background of more male laughter around her. Pain came again, too, as the hands behind her forced her to her feet. Despite how her body screamed for mercy, she tried her hardest to wrangle and kick from her bonds. She stretched her head and hands out toward Braziliano, focusing on the copper stub of a neck she'd lunge for first if she had the chance.

"You can't get away with this!" she cried. "You . . . you . . ." But words wouldn't come. She was a fuzz of nausea and exhaustion and fear.

"Or what?" the exotic accent mocked. "Or your father, the friend of the Crown, will have me hanged? Or maybe your friend Mast Iverson will don his Moonstormer's mask and come murder me?"

Braziliano laughed again. But now the sound was far from humorous or warm. He leaned his face over Golden's with a slow and unfeeling smile. "You little fool. Did you expect me to believe that *absurdidad* about your 'father'? And Mast Iverson—" he snorted derisively. "Mast Iverson wouldn't hurt a flea, *querida,* let alone your shipload of people. It is his prim and proper way; everyone in New Providence knows it. Bah! If that stiff-cravat *caballero* is the Moonstormer, then I am the king of the mermaids."

"Pleased to meet you, your highness." Golden's voice was barely a rasp, but she forced her head to stay up long enough to flash the Brazilian bastard a hating glare.

Roche Braziliano stepped away. He waved his hand as if at an annoying fly. "Get her out of here."

Golden awoke groggily to the eerie silence and faded shadows of early morning. She rolled her head on the plush down pillow in the big feather bed they'd thrown her onto last night, but instantly regretted the action as the aftereffect of Braziliano's blow made its presence known up the side of her skull. Besides, the pillow smelled of old cheap perfume and . . . she'd only experienced the other smell once before, in the bedding of Mast's bunk after they'd made love the third time.

Mast. The thought of him pierced sharper than the pain

in her cheek, a surge of agony in this half-awake moment that her heart was unguarded. Golden rolled over and brought the other pillow next to her. She clutched it with all her strength and, for one soul-twisting moment, wished she were holding him. She wished that crimson and black flag had been in any other hold in the world. She recalled Roche Braziliano's conviction that Mast wasn't the Moon-stormer, and wished she could believe the double-faced, lying blackguard.

The blackguard, she suddenly remembered, who was going to sell her into marriage tonight from an auction block.

"Dear God." Her head snapped up. "I have to get out of here."

But the room became a tornado as soon as she tried to move. Golden managed to fumble as far as the bedpost, which she clutched in hopes that the tempest would pass. It didn't. More thoughts rushed in and swirled with the dizziness and the hunger: the *Athena* was setting sail and Maya was still aboard with those criminals . . . Saint Kitts was falling to the French and Papa would never know . . . she couldn't marry anyone—she could be carrying the seed of Mast's baby . . .

"Calm down, Golden Gaverly," she muttered. "Nobody's going to help you out of this, so you need to think very hard and do it yourself. Now take a deep breath, and try again. The window would be a good start. One step at a time . . ."

"Search it again."

Mast's tone was as black as the circles beneath his eyes. But as Dinky studied his friend's intent stare over the early morning light on the water, he knew the last things on

Mast's mind were the events that had put the fatigued shadows there. No, Mast wasn't remembering every cheat and whore and criminal in New Providence they'd spent all yesterday and a good portion of last night questioning about the burning of a ship called *Gabrielle's Hope* twelve years ago, or the remarkable and disconcerting collection of information they had managed to get from them. And Mast wasn't thinking about the *Athena*'s jammed capstan they'd come back to, and the three hours it had taken to fix it, or the hairline fissure in the fore topgallant sail they'd had to address after that . . .

No. Dinky knew that what beat in his friend's mind, was that moment the two of them had parted ways in the wee hours of the morning. Dinky had just turned to head for his own bunk for a few precious hours of sleep himself when Mast's call had come harsh and urgent over the deck.

"Dink!"

"What?"

"Where the hell is she?"

"What the crimey are you talkin' about?"

Within minutes the entire ship had the answer to that. And every man was put to the search for one very-much missing Lady Hellion. Now, two hours later, they'd just finished the fifth sweep.

Mast wanted a sixth.

"Captain," Old Ben wearily said, leaning against the galley wall a moment. "I just don't think she be aboard—"

"Search it again."

"The colleen was a mite misty when I was with her at the truck gun earlier. Most likely she's bolted miles from here by now."

"Search the ship again, Goddamn it." Mast spun around, his face tight with fury and exhaustion. "And this time, look closer. She had to have left something behind—" He looked back away as his voice faltered. "A clue of some kind . . . a note. Something."

"Captain Iverson!"

Young Ramses' shout was shrill, yet muted. Dinky exchanged a swift glance with Mast as they attempted to determine where the lad's hail had come from.

"Captain! Down here!"

"Great God," Mast suddenly gritted. He nearly beat aside Dinky and Ben as he bounded across the deck. "Not the side hold."

Ramses popped out into the air as Mast knelt down at the open hatchway. The young sailor's eyes wcre full of apprehension as he looked up to his captain.

"What?" Mast demanded. "What the hell is it?"

"I—I think you should probably look at this yourself, Captain," the youth blurted.

Mast swung rapidly down into the hold. He spotted the yellow circle of the lamp—precisely where he'd dreaded it would be. In the far corner, near Wayland's crates.

All right, Iverson. He forced his inner voice to reprimand with a calmness his stiff-moving body ignored. *This is not the catastrophe you think it is. So she found her father's trunks in your hold, and it confused her. And, Golden being Golden, she ran pell-mell somewhere to try and figure it out. Probably those rocks out beyond the point to discuss the matter with the crabs and the seagulls. Damn her, anyway—I explained the dangers of this place to her!*

You'll just have to find her and explain. And you'll tell everything this time. The deal, the money . . . the truth. You'll have to tell Wayland that there was no way around it, security concerns or not. Bloody hell, why don't you just tell Wayland the truth—that the light of his daughter's smile makes you so damn giddy, you'd risk life and limb and even your own precious honor to bring peace to her world again?

He actually laughed at himself then. Cor, now the infuriating sea witch had him paraphrasing *Don Quixote.* And, a smile tilting up one side of his lips as he admitted it, believing in the windmills he'd tilt at for her.

Until he got to Ramses' side.

And the windmills came crashing down upon him.

"Ah, Christ." He sank to one knee next to the spread-out flag with the familiar skull glaring from it. "Not this. Not—this."

He breathed in sharply several times. At last his hand extended out over the dark-red material . . . shook uncontrollably a few inches over it . . . then lowered and crunched an agonized, white-knuckled fist into it.

Only two words reverberated a nauseating chant in his head. *She knew.* There was no telling what she'd done now. Or where she'd gone. Or who she'd met.

Or what they'd done to her.

His other hand curled into the flag. With one violent wave of fury he ripped the fabric in half. "Dink!"

A rustling came behind him; a boot stepped tentatively on the ladder. "Ive?"

"Search parties." He tried to lick his lips, but his mouth hadn't a drop of moisture. "Please," he croaked, "organize search parties. Four men each."

The boards over his head started pounding with bootsteps before he was able to finish the thoughts.

But Mast didn't rise to join his men. Not yet.

Instead, he slowly lowered his other knee to the deck. He reached and gathered both pieces of the flag into his lap.

Then, for the first time in fifteen years, Mast Iverson lowered his stubborn, prideful head before his Maker . . . and prayed.

Seventeen

The lock in the door clicked. Golden tried to angle herself up from the bed to see who was entering, but she came to a wincing stop after a few inches. The cuff holding her left wrist to the bed frame allowed no more than that. Braziliano had ordered it that way, said the grinning henchman who'd shackled her there. "After all," he'd gone on to jeer, "that's what happens to wild little girls who try to break their windows and leave our happy home!"

She saw it was that same greasy henchman entering the room now. He was followed by a rotund, flat-nosed black woman who looked like she'd never smiled a day in her life. Golden tried to catch the native's eyes with the hope of finding a friendly light there, but all she received was an imperious glare that made her already-queasy stomach a pit of leaden despair.

"Well now, how's our pretty little missy after her rest?" Braziliano's man drawled. His patronizing tone didn't lighten the sickening feeling, which grew worse as he opened the heavy curtains on the one window that wasn't boarded up from her escape efforts. The late-afternoon sunlight streamed in to make slithering dark orange snakes out of the sweat rivulets on his scrawny chest. Golden gulped back a mouthful of bile.

"Cat snatched yer tongue, aye?" He turned toward her

again. " 'Tis likely for the best. Ye've a big night ahead o' ye." A gold tooth flashed as he cracked a lewd grin. "Damn, ye be a comely one. And a mighty juicy morsel, Cap'n Braz says, when yer piqued. Saints, I may even have to try my own luck on biddin' for ye."

Only her most supreme effort kept Golden from leveling a hiss and a good strong kick at the slimy bastard, despite the scant reserves of her strength and energy. But instinct told her that would only make matters worse. She must try her hardest to control her temper—and even harder, her impatience. She would escape this horrid mess; it was just a matter of waiting for the right opportunity.

Spirits help her, let that magical moment be soon.

The divine powers decided to answer that plea sooner than she thought. The henchman produced the long gold key which had sealed her in the cuff hours ago. He twisted it in the lock; Golden's numb arm fell and started to tingle with an ecstatic rush of blood. The rest of her body followed suit, her eyes rapidly searching for the quickest path off the bed and through the door, just when the time became perfect.

"This here be Lilly." The henchman spoke as if his previous overture were but a passing quip on sugar prices, though his expression still curved suggestively as he leaned closer. "Get it?" he whispered. *"Lilly.* Har! Sot was bloomin' drunk who named that darkie wench, I'll be wagerin'. Har!"

Just as Golden thought she was going to lose consciousness from the brute's stale breath, he stood up. But she continued to watch him carefully. She intended to take full advantage of the instant he turned away.

That was when he smirked as if knowing just what she wished for, and just how to dash that pinpoint of hope. The henchman curled a dirty hand around the back of Golden's arm and yanked her up next to him.

"Now did ye really be thinkin' I'd let yer lovely face out o' my sight, missy?" he taunted softly. "Tsk, tsk. Naughty wench. Besides, there be much too much to do with ye yet before yer big debut. Lilly's goin' to make that face o' yers real beautiful. Now don't that sound lovely? And o' course, ye'll need somethin' as lovely to wear."

He pulled her over to a set of double doors in the side wall. Golden had stared at the carved wood panels many times during the day and tried to distract her fearful thoughts by wondering what lay behind them. Now, standing here with the henchman's leer as her introduction, only a foreboding gloom gripped her at the imminence of at last finding out.

The henchman swept back the doors like a court escort showing her the grand ballroom. A walk-in closet was revealed, lined on both sides with satin gowns in every color Golden could imagine. A sight, she imagined vaguely, that would have taken her breath away in awe—if her mind wasn't screaming so frantically, *what happened to those other women?* What had happened to the women who once filled those sunset golds, coral reef blues and peacock greens?

She couldn't envision them. All she could see was herself attired day after day in the rainbow of dresses, awaiting a degrading fate.

She pulled away from the door. The henchman chuckled and yanked her forward. "Oh, here now, don't be shy, missy. Which one do ye fancy? Every lassie fancies satin. O' course—" his gaze fastened to her breasts in a manner that made Golden feel as revered as a brood mare on display, "you don't have the top hold we be accustomed to around here." The sly grin inched a little higher as the beady eyes roved back into the wardrobe. "Not a thing wrong with that, if ye ask me. I get bloody tired of all that bubby in the way sometimes—aahh, now this should do it!"

He reached in and pulled out a mass of blood red material. Golden barely had time to observe the off-the-shoulder bodice, richly-draped skirt, and lavish black lace flounces that trimmed the dress before the pirate pressed it against her and pushed in here and there for a crude fitting.

"Aye," the henchman purred. "Very nice. Very nice, indeed." He tossed the dress on the bed, nodding casually the same direction. "Put it on."

Golden forced herself to move calmly as he released her, though the freedom from his bruising hold and the wrist shackle made her feel light and strong enough to break down the door if need be. But her head reminded her she wasn't ready; her wits were going to be her greatest asset in the next few minutes. The minutes she saw forming into an escape.

Her plan came to her quickly. It would be imperative to give the illusion of complete acquiescence as she gathered up the gown and entered the closet. Then she would need to dawdle long enough in there for the henchman to become bored and distracted. Judging the dolt's attention span by what she'd observed so far, that would be the easy part.

The difficult part would be slithering out the door without so much as the peep of a field mouse.

It was close to impossible.

It was her only hope.

She had to try . . .

"And just where do we be thinkin' we're goin'?"

Golden's chest froze as she stopped in the middle of the room. "To change." She forced her eyes up with a strength that clearly daunted the henchman's bloodshot gaze for a moment. "As you requested." She issued the last as a challenge.

Surprisingly, she found her gauntlet riposted by a grin. A very slow and unnerving grin. "That's very nice o' ye, missy. But I'm afraid Cap'n Braz anticerpated the yen ye'd develop for that closet. He bestowed me with the most pleasurable command of makin' sure ye do this with me own eyes."

"The hell you will," Golden snarled. Never mind that the plan would fall through; the thought of his intentions made her skin clammy and her innards want to retch.

"Now, ducky. No need to get testy." Despite her defiance, Golden was compelled to shuffle backwards as the sweat-snaked chest pressed in on her. "Just be a good girl and put the dress on."

"Go drown yourself!" She was horrified to hear the slur crippled by her shaky rasp. The threads of her self-control stretched thinner and thinner, pounded by instincts of panic as she was trapped closer against the bed. The tenuous strands snapped completely as the pirate laughed and leered at her. The wicked chortle entered and echoed through her brain. The hideous face filled her vision. Golden hissed and raised a handful of fingernails at the revolting visage, but even as she dug into the grime-slippery cheek the smirk grew larger, taunting her with a life of its own.

"Lord love it, ye do have a hot flame." The pirate bastard jerked on both her arms then, hard. "Now put on the damn dress before I have to douse it out."

Golden said nothing. She raised her chin and curled her lips as if to spit straight into the bastard's eyes.

"Put it on," he ordered lowly again.

"Go to hell."

The battle of their stares escalated. Volleys of the pirate's fury exploded against Golden's counterattacks of topaz rebellion. The tally persisted an even score on both sides—

Until the whoosh of a knife from its sheath severed the silence. In an instant Golden felt the icy blade pressed to the skin at her throat. She froze, terrified even taking a breath would send one of her veins into the well-sharpened edge.

"I tried to do this nicely, ducky," came the harsh, stinking whisper. "I do apologize that ye wouldn't see it that way."

Then as suddenly as it had come, the knife left her pulse point—and gashed down between her breasts. Into the beautiful sky blue fabric of her gown. The gown Mast had loved, Golden thought with agony as the pirate tore the bodice from her; then the flounces, down to the bottom hem, and away into a ruined heap. She stared at the heap of blue tatters— feeling as if her soul lay there meaningless on the floor.

"Now." He shoved the mound of red satin into her arms. "Put it on."

Golden looked at her hand as she accepted the gown. But it wasn't her hand any more. The same way her legs were controlled by another as she turned to lay the gown out on the bed. The same way she heard the henchman issue a word of approval to her, but her eyes looked up and saw a faraway face with a disgusting smirk she didn't care about any more. The same way all the pain in this nightmare had violated her to the point of numbness. For that's what it had to be—a hideous, unreal nightmare.

She only prayed, as she pulled the cheap-smelling satin over her head, that consciousness would rescue her soon.

But nightmares never ended when one wanted them to. They only clamored louder and pounded harder, just like the throng Golden could hear somewhere in the building below her room. Ale mugs slammed together between shouted profanities and blatantly sexual jibes. A fiddle struck up a lively tune until a bottle crashed and halted it; a round of bawdy singing accompanied the mild skirmish that ensued.

Then Roche Braziliano's voice boomed into the din. Snatches of his speech escaped through the ever-increasing hoots and whistles. ". . . in the most excellent Braziliano tradition . . . finest wenches from the world over . . . a final sale that will render you speechless!"

The crowd was frenzied by the time he finished. A cheer went up that shook even the second-floor window across from Golden.

The clutches of terror sank their last inch into her nerves.

"Oh, God," she whispered, her eyes riveted to the white-knuckled wad of her hands in her lap. Lilly still stood behind her, strong black hands smoothing over the elaborate twists and coils she'd created of Golden's hair. But Golden knew better by now than to expect a word of encouragement from the voiceless woman.

She was truly alone.

Even the creature she raised her eyes to in the dirty oval mirror was a stranger. Lilly had rice-powdered her face until she couldn't stop sneezing, then hurrumphed in disgust and powdered her all over again. Golden had caught a glimpse of herself in the mirror and thought there surely must be darker ghosts in the world than she. Next came the deep red cheek rouge, which also got smeared into her lips, worsening her nauseated state. Then the patch box emerged. A small black dot was placed strategically at the top left corner of her lips and a heart-shaped patch was affixed below her right eye. And just when Golden thought Lilly was done, her well-exposed breasts were given the same treatment.

The skin and nipples ached now from the black woman's relentless pushing and poufing.

In the hall downstairs, the bride auction commenced. The bids rang out higher and higher with each wench brought to the auction block. "One hundred guineas!" "Three hundred creoles!" "Five hundred doubloons!" From the giggling and tittering starting to pass by the outside of the door, Golden surmised few of the new wives protested their newly purchased status, either.

The sounds didn't reassure her.

Her body coiled as hard and painfully as her hands. Her chest wrung a knot around her heart. Her legs cramped and uncramped without rhyme or reason. Her head pounded and her throat dropped leaden swallows of fear to her stomach.

She could bear this dread and shame no longer!

Like a cave falling in, the fear imploded on her, and Golden's wildest instincts burst forth like the dust from the rubble. She jumped up from the chair. The astonished look she provoked on Lilly's face alone sparked enough triumph in her to go even further. She dashed for the window she hadn't yet broken. Braziliano's man had removed every battering ram she could use from the room, but like a caged animal, that was her least deterrent. She flew at the window shoulder first and head down. The gashes that would come would be a flimsy price to pay for freedom.

But the joyous crash never came. The breath Golden held in anticipation of her freedom-giving leap instead burst out in a stunned gasp as she was grabbed back and thrown across the bed. Her senses barely had time to balance before she was dragged up again, her chin yanked high, her sights saturated with the black stare and somber frown of Roche Braziliano.

"Ah, *querida*. It seems I should be glad I decided to

come and escort you downstairs myself." One of his scarred
fingers slid down the bridge of her nose. "Beautiful, fiery
Golden. I shall truly miss you. And lovely you are in your
finery, as well. The man who brings you back here tonight
will be fortunate, indeed."

"Nnnnooo!" Yet the protest was little more than a moan,
for talonlike fingers still clamped her chin and jaw to keep
her gaze locked on the Brazilian. Golden lurched against
her restraints, as paralyzing terror attempted to claim a new
part of her body each second. She tried to kick her legs—
they were wrapped in fat arms. She tried to wrench her
arms—they were pulled and locked behind her back.

She tried to free her voice in a scream—all that sounded
was something like the dying wail of a seagull after its
wings had been shot off.

Images blurred by as the faceless arms carried her down,
down even further, descending Oriental-carpeted stairs, then
over dusty wooden ones. They passed doorways where
women with faces painted worse than hers laughed at her.
They taunted like derisive voodoo gods before more sweaty-
faced henchmen pulled them back, kissing them and fondling their writhing bodies. Then the singing started again;
more and more singing . . . oh, it was so loud.

*"Ohhh, what shall we do with the drunken sailor, what
shall we do with the drunken sailor, what shall we do—"*

"Gentlemen!" Braziliano's bellow was a thunderclap over
her ear. Somehow through the echoing cacophony in her
head, Golden noted the abrupt fall of silence—and the two
hundred pairs of ogling eyes that followed. Staring straight
at her.

"Gentlemen," the exotic accent said again, lower this
time, caressing the moment for all it was worth. "I now
present my prize filly."

A breeze sneaked in and brushed the room. No one said a word.

Until a single yowl pierced the air, long and loud and lusty. The rest of the mob followed the lead and echoed enthusiastically. If silence was the dam then pandemonium was the flood, each drop of the downpour a shout or a catcall, a curse or a blasphemy, and, for Golden, a pinch or a grab or a greedy pair of lips trying to get at her.

She was almost thankful for the armory of Braziliano's men who beat off the ruffians and closed in around her again. But she knew it was only to transport her across the din to the raised platform along the far wall, where their leader waited with the calm of an executioner at the block. Indeed, at that moment Golden understood the last burst of energy a dying person had, for she started to jerk and squirm and claw as the stage loomed larger and larger before her.

"No!" she thought she called, but it appeared not, for nobody even turned their head at her behest. She wrenched harder against her bonds. All that came loose was her hair, spilling everywhere as she threw her head back in the last rebellious screams of freedom. "Someone help me! Don't let him do this!"

"Oh, little chick," came an ale-slurred repartee, "that ain't half what I'll do to ya!"

She snarled in answer at the voice. Wild laughter slapped her back.

Before she realized it they had arrived at the auction block. Hands lifted her and turned her to face the crowd. A sea of staring, leering faces stretched before her. Golden squeezed her eyes shut and sucked in her lips against the clamoring sobs in her throat. She had danced naked with her tribal brothers and sisters and not felt as ashamed as she did in her half-clothed state now. A few lechers even reached out and pawed at her feet. Golden jumped and kicked as if their fingers were scorpions' legs.

"A fine *señorita* indeed, aye, my friends?" Braziliano's hand snaked around her waist and hauled her next to him. The handle of his pistol ground painfully against her hip. "Nearly wild, just as I promised. Behold such hair, and the spirit in those eyes!"

"But has she been broken to the whip yet?" somebody jibed from the crowd. Chortling voices seconded the question. Golden twisted in Braziliano's grip to snarl her answer to that. The laughter only swelled louder.

"As you can see, I've left that enviable task to her new master." Braziliano's voice was mild. His grasp on her was firm. "Now what do I hear for this fiery little filly? We will start the bidding at five hundred creoles. What man dares to take the challenge of this wench for five hundred creoles?"

The bidding went loud and long after that, the numbers doubling, then tripling what Golden remembered any of her predecessors garnering that evening. One thousand creoles. Two thousand. Three. Still the calls waged battle over her head, Braziliano's hand sweating wetter and wetter into her side with excitement, her dignity sinking lower and lower into humiliation and despair.

Finally the bidding eliminated all but two contenders.

An anticipatory hush settled in the hall. As much as she tried to contain her dread-filled curiosity, Golden's eyes dragged up for the stand-off that would seal her fate.

Her eyes fell upon the first rival—and recoiled just as quickly. The giant of a man hid nothing and wanted everything. He openly lusted for her from his six-and-a-half-foot height as he downed a stein of ale cupped in a hand that looked more like a bear paw. Golden gasped when the Neanderthal tossed away the empty mug and grinned a mouthful of triangular, razor-sharp teeth at her.

"Blood an' 'ouns!" he howled. "She's the most gorgeous thing I ever laid eyes on. My love!" He kissed his hand and waved wildly at her. "I'll be wi' ye soon, my love!"

Golden whipped her head away. Mighty Puntan, surely she shouldn't be worse off with the other bidder.

Her knees went limp and her mouth went dry when she discovered just how horrifically wrong that assumption was.

Unblinking black eyes probed into her from the opposite wall. The same eyes she'd seen just twenty-four hours ago, staring out over the rail of a pirate's frigate.

The emotionless eyes of El Culebra.

Her body desperately begged her to turn away. Pure shock chained her limbs just where they were. Her lips trembled when the Spaniard broke a calm, almost haughty smile. Her chest wrenched when he snaked his arms across his finely-dressed torso. Clearly, El Culebra already anticipated his victory over the Neanderthal.

But was it because he coveted her as the wench to warm his bed tonight—or something more? Had El Culebra somehow seen through the grime to recognize the sea witch who'd cost him a triumph over the *Athena* yesterday? Did he seek his retribution now?

She couldn't even consider the answer to that.

"Goddamn it, Braz!" the elephantine brute bellowed. His friends pounded their ale steins on the bar. "Let's get on wi' it afore ol' Mr. Tom here splits outta my britches!"

And Braziliano did, licking his lips hungrily as he recommenced the auction between the two men at five thousand creoles. The giant's calls countered El Culebra's into the six and then the seven thousands. The bids stretched into a harrowing, degrading, petrifying eternity. Golden's body grew so taut she thought she would break apart from the strain before anyone had the chance to claim her.

"We have seven thousand, six hundred, gentleman," Braziliano called next to her. His hands trembled with greedy exhilaration. "Seven thousand, six hundred. Do I hear—"

"All right, all right!" the Neanderthal yelled angrily. "Seven thousand, seven hundred!"

"Eight," came the disturbingly calm return from the other wall.

The bear paws coiled in slow fury. "Nine!"

For the first time in the evening, there was no reply. Breaths caught audibly across the room. Golden looked up to the corner where the finely dressed pirate now thoughtfully accessed first his rival, then her. Her heartbeat doubled. Was that the blackness of pure lust or pure vengeance fastened so intently upon her? Or, she thought with a dry gulp, both?

And still he made her wait.

The silence was eerie; like the surreal calm before a hurricane. But *calm* was hardly how Golden termed this maddening ordeal. She closed her eyes, concentrating on inhaling a deep, long breath . . . most likely, she conceded, her body's last before El Culebra claimed it as his property.

A rustle of silk from the Spaniard's corner bade her head rise for the words that would seal her wretched fate.

Instead her eyes flew open as wide as her lids would allow, to confirm that every fleck of those black pirate eyes had suddenly chosen to ignore her—in favor of the sultry, big-bosomed wench who was all but mounting him there before them all. Loud hoots and whistles punctuated every shameless undulation of the display, but the sounds were just whispers of wind behind the ardent prayers of Golden's heart . . . *please make him forget, please make him forget me.*

It seemed El Culebra had forgotten the whole blasted world as he sank away down a dark corridor behind the dark-eyed whore, waving a hand to Braziliano in promise of a sum he had clearly paid here before.

Golden gave a small cry of relief.

The giant and his friends roared in victory.

"We have a lucky *gringo* at last!" she heard Braziliano exclaim.

And her mind crashed back to the situation at hand. In her celebration of eluding El Culebra, Golden had let an portentous fact grow dim. *There was another pirate waiting for her now.* With anguishing swiftness her conscious seized in terror again; her eyes filled with the sight of the leering giant lumbering up toward her.

And the terror was worse because she knew very well what was to come now. She understood what a man did with a woman when they were alone in bed. But envisioning herself naked below this grunting drunk only made her knees grow weaker, her chest heaved harder, and her mind stab more painfully with memories. Mast's kisses and caresses, the glow in his eyes as he took in the sight of her body . . . the joy of moving with him, of loving with him . . . of drinking in the strength of him . . .

A pistol shot suddenly blasted into the air. The rowdy group halted into silence. The pictures in Golden's head froze to a startled stop.

No, she realized a moment later, the remembrances hadn't stopped at all. They'd come to life . . . moving before her eyes . . . pushing through the crowd . . .

It couldn't be.

She bit down hard on the overjoyed smile yearning for release at her lips. She wouldn't set it free until she was certain this was truly happening, that she hadn't collapsed and some grimy henchman's hand wasn't going to jostle her awake from this dream any moment.

"Roche. It's been a long time."

The familiar deep tone flowed over her charred senses like a douse into a cool island spring. For the moment, this one shining moment, it didn't matter why he'd come back— just that he had. Just that he was here, standing proudly before the Brazilian bastard, his spotless black jacket, silver-embroidered waistcoat and perfectly-tied stock rivaling Braziliano's finery, and his hand carefully resting on a pistol handle of similar opulence. Larger than life. Her lethal black panther in the flesh.

"Captain Iverson." Like the greeting Mast had issued, Braziliano's manner was so composed it mocked the apprehension in the room. "You are right, *amigo*. It has been a while. Barbados, was it not? *Sí,* I remember. The Sea Siren's Tavern. That little tussle about your "missing" cargo. So sorry about that ruby-handled dagger of yours."

"So sorry about the gash I left in your leg before you broke it. Hope the scar wasn't that bad."

A hearty eruption of snickers followed Mast as he stepped forward. Golden was certain that, if Braziliano's skin could show it, his incensed flush would be spectacular. Instead, the beast worked his fury into her, screwing his grip tighter until she winced. A nerve jumped violently in Mast's jaw; otherwise, all everyone saw was his straight-ahead stare and his spread-legged stance. But Golden saw the fatigued shadows behind his eyes, the weariness camped out along his shoulders and the fist of agony that screwed tighter and tighter upon his pistol handle. They were as clear to her as the aching emotion in her heart.

"Well, my friend," the accented voice slithered on at her shoulder, though an octave lower now with implied threat. "It is an honor to have you here with us this evening. But I am afraid you've missed the best part of our festivities, Captain. We have just concluded our final transaction."

"I'm afraid not, Roche."

Braziliano only smiled, slowly and wickedly, in reaction. His stubby brown fingers began to slide down along the satin of Golden's shoulder and low neckline. *Damn it,* Mast raged, the filthy cockroach was baiting him. Strongly. Which meant only one thing: Braziliano had a strong suspicion of how precious the lure was to him.

Which meant this was going to be harder than he thought.

"My apologies again, Captain Iverson, but I am afraid so," Braziliano stated. "This lovely lady was my prize sale of the evening—"

"This lovely lady was my property first."

He made sure to crack the announcement like a whip through even the outskirts of the crowd. Their combined huff of astonishment responded with perfect timing. From the block, Golden didn't utter a sound. Mast fought every muscle behind his eyes to keep from glancing at her. The accomplishment was agony. He'd only been able to gaze fully at her when he first came in, the rush of triumph at finally finding her twined in a sickening knot with the realization of where. Even then, in the dim light from the back of the hall, she'd looked like a different person—exhausted and frail and very, very frightened. Braziliano may not have laid a hand on her, but the bastard might as well have raped her already.

"You have papers to support this allegation, *amigo?*"

"I don't need papers and you know it, Roche. This room will stand testimony to my word. The wench is mine and I want her back."

Again there was no answer for a long while but a lazy, lurid grin. "Prove it," Braziliano finally drawled.

Mast responded with his own pause of silence. Finally he blew out a slow, but heavy breath. He had anticipated this; dreaded this. His chest clenched harder for every inch he started to raise his hand, but he lifted his arm high into the air without faltering. He snapped his fingers loudly. The corner of his eye caught Golden's jump of surprise.

"Come here." His stare was still imbedded into Braziliano, but he directed the command to her. *Please, Golden. Just come here . . . and understand.*

Golden moved to his side without a sound. The silence clung to and weighed down the air around them, making him all the more aware of her next to him, pressing the knowledge of her mercilessly into his skin, his senses. Pleading with him to take just one parched drink of a look, one starving swallow of an embrace, to make sure she was real and not some exhaustion-induced vision.

"Kneel," he ordered.

He could hear the gulp thud down Golden's throat. He yearned to echo with a hard swallow of his own. What he asked her to do made his gut recoil; to endure this humiliation after what must have been a degrading ordeal already. And to trust that he knew what he was doing by asking this of her. To trust him. The man with the Moonstormer's flag in his hold.

It was the most staggering request he could make of her. The most impossible.

Mast looked down at the softness suddenly brushing the

knuckles upon his pistol. It was Golden's forehead—as she knelt before him.

He hoisted his gaze like a victorious battle sword at Braziliano.

"This is bloomin' horse piss!"

The voice seemed to come from nowhere. And the hands that snatched Golden away with it.

"That's right, Captain Iverson! Did ya hear me? Horse piss!"

Mast spun in the direction of the ale-slurred insult. A wall of sweating pirate filled his vision. Pointed shark's teeth threatened from a mouth a head and a half over his. A neck with the radius of a mizzenmast erupted from a chest the width of a mainsail. Burrowed in the middle of that chest and nearly swallowed by one timber log of an arm was Golden, her face an amazing picture of calm even under the face paint they'd forced on her. She was the most heart-wrenching sight he'd ever seen.

She was beautiful.

"Get your hands off her," Mast gritted.

"Bugger off, Captain Fancy Britches! You lost 'er, I bought 'er. The wench is mine!"

"Get your hands off her."

"Gentlemen, gentlemen! Come now; we are all friends here!" Braziliano sounded as if he were merely breaking apart a scuffle between two schoolboys. The tone grated on Mast's nerves like glass against a grindstone, but he forced himself to stop and take a calming breath for Golden's sake.

"Fine," the giant growled. "Tell yer friend about the way we do things 'ere, Braz. Tell 'im I bargained for my bride in a fair and legal auction."

"Aye!" a voice in the crowd piped. "That he did!"

"Now wait a bloody minute," someone else interjected.

"Mast Iverson's always done right by me. If he lays claim to the chit first, I believe him."

"And I!"

"Gentlemen!" Braziliano had to shout again over the quarrel that ensued. *"Gentlemen!"*

He stood with hands outstretched for a moment to solidify the silence that finally fell, then he lowered each arm to its respective side as he looked to Golden and the giant at his left; Mast at his right.

"We seem to have a small *problema,* my friends. Two men, and one wench."

Again the richly accented voice slid over the crowd with no more effort than honey on a biscuit. Mast hated honey. And distrusted Roche Braziliano even more. The few unlucky times in the past he'd been on the receiving end of the infamous lunatic's treachery led him to believe nothing more now—and expect nothing less. What kind of depravity did the bastard have in his bag of tricks this time?

Mast didn't seem to be the only one pondering such a question. "We know all about the problem, Braz," a gravelly voice near the front of the crowd called. "But what the hell are you going to do about it?"

"Aye! What, indeed!"

"Stop piddlin' about up there!"

Braziliano waited sedately during a smattering of other catcalls, then at last stepped to the lip of the platform and placed a convincing finger of thought to his chin. "That is an interesting question, *amigo.* But alas, I am not certain how to answer it. The Brotherhood of the Coast has passed down many laws and agreements by which we live here, but even I, as one of the last original Brethren, cannot recall a mandate for such as this. Then again . . ." he glanced back at Mast. The thinning ends of his mustache lifted smugly. "I do not think the Brotherhood ever anticipated the day when Mast Iverson rode to the rescue of a female."

The implication of the slur opened a cloudburst of laughter through the hall. It was more than Golden could bear. Affecting a composure she didn't feel had become torture enough; suppressing the wild anger that erupted at watching Mast endure the vermin-bred barbs was inconceivable. She lurched against the giant's hold. He laughed and crunched her tighter. Golden growled and bit into his forearm. His yowl filled the air. She was able to dash free—only to be ensnared by the two henchmen who had "escorted" her down here.

"Mast!" Even in distress, calling his name felt glorious. But the next moment she watched as Mast, too, was restrained by a pair of Braziliano's men. Three henchmen held the Neanderthal in check on the other side of the stage. The crowd roared their approval of the unfolding drama.

"My friends!" shouted Braziliano, playing the scene for all the excitement it was worth. "I see no other solution for this untoward predicament but the dueling log!"

Only a single heartbeat of consideration passed before the verdict was rendered.

"Yes!"

"The log, of course!"

"Take 'em to da log!"

Within minutes, it was a frenzied, frantic, primeval chant: "The duel-ing log, the duel-ing log, the duel-ing log!" Bloodthirsty voices rose to the sky and perspiring bodies bobbed to the rhythm. The mob was no longer a collection of faces and colors and personalities, but one savage, insatiable beast. Golden stared unbelieving at the monster, hardly able to fathom what "the dueling log" could possibly be.

She looked to Mast. His expression gave no answers, either, though she'd expected that. The hard planes of his jaw were as tight and unrevealing as she'd ever seen them. His lips were set in a strong and serious line.

He was beautiful.

As if he'd opened up that special window he seemed to have to her thoughts, his head came up then. His gaze met and mated with hers. And for a moment the din around them died and the world was caressing, midnight blue velvet, holding her softly, safely; replacing all the hate inside her with patience and strength and—

Love?

Was that the incredible and encompassing feeling that Mast opened up in her?

As the throng parted and the henchmen began to lead them outside, the very real possibility hit Golden that she might never receive a chance to find out.

She felt like a stranger looking in on the shell of her body as it was forced to walk down a twisting dirt path by the light of ethereal, spirit-world-like torches. Weeping moss trees filled with sorrowful-eyed creatures mourned their passing into this muggy hell, though the eyes appeared fewer and fewer as the moist stench of swamp water became stronger and stronger.

The tree tunnel broadened and heightened after a little over two-hundred yards. As the crowd moved in around the circular area, Golden sucked in her breath. The massing of all the torches allowed her first look at this thing they called the dueling log.

She expelled a breath as puzzlement overtook her. It really was just a log—a giant tree of some sort that had probably been slain by a bolt of lightning, and fallen here, across the sides of a narrow, murky lagoon. The resulting platform was so wide and appeared so sturdy it could nearly be designated a bridge. Golden looked harder at the huge log, still seeing nothing in the least bit unordinary about the scene.

A glimmer of relief dared to find an opening inside her. Could the dueling log be just that—two men standing back to back in the middle, then, turn and shoot? Her mind called up the memory of that first night in the front hall on Saint Kitts, when Mast drew his pistol on the French soldiers. An eye's blink and the shot had been shaking Papa's Gainsboroughs on the walls.

The Neanderthal would fall before he'd ever begun a drunken search for his weapon.

Golden braved a small smile. She edged her lips up another notch as Mast entered the clearing behind Braziliano. Square-shouldered and steel-composed, he stood out like a Zeus among mortals. Her heart overflowed with pride. Pride and admiration and—a jolt sliced her chest with the admission—trust.

Oh yes, she admitted with a slow gulp, she trusted this man. If she'd been honest with herself instead of running off at the first suspicions that arose when she'd found the flag in Mast's hold, she'd have realized she did all along. And there was a perfectly reasonable explanation that she would listen to, as soon as Mast showed that Brazilian oaf what he could do with his bloody dueling log.

Wait. Why were Mast and the giant turning their pistols over to Braziliano? And why were they starting to remove their shirts? She'd never been to a duel before, but she knew it wasn't done this way!

"The rules be the same," a pudgy henchman stepped forward and bellowed. "Neither man will turn before the count of three be tolled. Neither man will employ any weapon in the contest but his own two hands and legs. Neither man will leave the log until Captain Braziliano 'as thus declared it. Do the contestants understand these dictates and agree to abide by them?"

The Neanderthal grunted. Mast nodded tightly. Golden swallowed back the fresh surge of panic attacking her bones. She should have known it was too good to be true! A hand-to-hand clash on the log, not a simple duel! She should have remembered just what kind of monster ruled this mob. It was just like Roche Braziliano to take this insanity to its limits, dragging the fight out as each man undoubtedly fell into the swamp, then had to pull himself out and do battle with the added weight of water and moss—

But there was something even more wrong about this situation. Golden sensed it with instinct as her eyes roved the swamp. It was something about the pattern of the bubbles along the water's surface . . . and the irregular directions of the currents . . . as if the bog were breathing somehow. As if it were . . . living.

Her gasp burned a horrified path up her throat just as the first pair of eyes broke the surface. Round, unblinking yellow eyes, staring at her across a long, dragonlike snout.

Alligators.

Eighteen

She had do something. The Neanderthal was already eyeing Mast like an elephant about to crush a mouse. A single sweep of either battering-ram arm, and Mast would be toppled from the limb without a chance.

Gone forever.

"No!"

Terror ripped the sound from her lips as Golden began to run. She couldn't let it happen. She wouldn't! She could feel the hands of the henchmen assigned to her grabbing her, but a powerful, unseen force took over her body, and propelled her across the log. All that mattered was Mast at the other side; Mast, strong and tall, his eyes fixed darkly on her as he stepped forward from the others. She rushed even faster, colliding into him at a full run.

"Hellion." His voice was low, but gently chastising as he cupped one hand around her shoulder. "What are you doing?"

"No." It was all she could say. All she could feel. Terrible, wrenching fear and denial. "Please, Mast—no—please." The start of a sob burned up her throat. Mercy, she was going to cry. Good little sailors didn't cry!

"Sweet." He lifted her chin. The sting behind Golden's eyes intensified as she took in the deep exhaustion lines bordering his face. "This isn't the *Athena*. I have no choice about this." His jaw tightened; a pulse thumped erratically beneath his scar. "So I need you to obey me. Do you hear me? Golden, listen to me. Go back to your place and—"

"No!"

"Yes."

"But—" She drew in a sharp gasp. "But I love you."

Time seemed to stop. Golden reached trembling fingers to his jaw, his cheek, his hair. She explored him, memorized him, absorbed the scent, the strength, the feel of him. Hating the torture of it. "Oh God, Mast, I do. I love you."

He swallowed deeply. Then again.

Golden gazed into his eyes and saw the turmoil raging there . . . the battle he waged not only against the situation, but himself.

His lips parted as if to say something, but he caught the sound in his throat and forced his mouth tight again.

Then as quickly as the precious moment had happened, it disappeared. Like a curtain drawn across the light through a window, Mast's expression hardened to the unforgiving scowl Golden hadn't seen since her first tumultuous days aboard the ship. "I said to stay back, wench," he ordered as imperiously. "And damn it, I said now."

With a long and labored breath, Golden lowered her arms and quietly stepped back. "I love you, you bloody stubborn ox," she whispered. "I love you."

"Enough! Let's get on with it!" Braziliano shoved her aside. Two henchmen waited beyond to prevent her from causing any further disruptions. They dragged her to the water's edge to one side of the log, clamping her arms and legs with their own like a medieval torture rack. Golden writhed against them, without an inch of success.

The Neanderthal bounded out first. The entire log shook with his weight. He laughed at that, pointing out his achievement to his friends on the shore like a tot discovering his shadow. They cheered him, though they quickly switched to hoots and jeers upon Mast's arrival.

The shouts that countered in Mast's favor did little to untie the twist of Golden's stomach or keep her from chewing her bottom lip. The agony went on as the two men approached each other, then locked stares for a long, appraising minute. She could see the muscles tense in Mast's shoulders as the giant bared a hungry leer at him. But when she looked to her love's face, nothing but the rock hard Iverson reserve filled her sights.

The two men turned back to back for the final count-off.

Golden squeezed her eyes shut.

"One!" Braziliano's voice called out.

Her heart skipped.

"Two!"

Her heart froze.

"Three! Let the contest begin!"

The roar of the mob was deafening around her. A horrible force pried her eyes back open again, forcing them to the battle unfolding on the log.

Mast and the pirate squared off in catlike crouches, stealthily testing the limits of the limb and each other.

Several minutes passed like that. The crowd grew restless, and so did the giant. He growled at Mast, emphasizing his point with a wide swing of his arm. Mast easily ducked the punch. The pirate bellowed disapproval. Mast didn't flinch from his position.

"Yes." Despite herself, Golden murmured a favorite encouragement Guypa would often give her when they hunted. "Play him against himself, Mast. Make him come to you."

And come the giant did—though so suddenly and so furiously, Golden wished she'd never thought the advice. Mast braced for the impact, but was smashed down like a reed in the way of a boulder. The pirate chortled in vicious cele-bration, raising a fist to his cheering cohorts.

Until Mast raised a shaking, but well-placed thump with his knee to the small of the giant's back. There was a loud yowl of pain; the gargantuan body fell back. Mast struggled free from the weight and stumbled to his feet, wiping the sweat from his face with the crook of his elbow.

"Oh, yer better'n I thought, fancy britches," Golden heard the pirate growl, in a tone much too calm for her comfort. "Much better. Too bad. I liked playing this game like a civilized pair o' blokes fer once."

To her dread, her instinct didn't prove wrong. The mon-ster's final word was a grunt that corresponded with the swipe of his hand around Mast's ankle. Golden gasped as he yanked mercilessly. Mast went down to the log again— this time with a spine-shattering *whack*.

She screamed. The crowd cheered. The giant laughed heartily as he rose on one knee, with Mast's leg still in tow. He scooped up the other ankle, using his grip to lower Mast over the side of the log, face first. Mast wrestled like a wild horse, head bucking, arms flailing. The pirate curled his arm high and punched him across the face. Golden screamed again as Mast's neck snapped back. Torchlight glinted on the blue streaks through his hair before his head fell over completely and came to hang an arm's length over the water.

At that moment, the swamp began to breathe again.

Golden's shriek dwindled to a terrified choke as the sur-face shimmered and snaked and slithered. The mob went berserk as an alligator snout appeared, heading straight for the easy target Mast presented.

"Bastard!" Golden lunged against the henchmen holding her. "You bastard—let him go!"

The Neanderthal broke into a silly grin as his gaze darted to the shore. "My love!" he cried in a voice more befitting a satin-hosed Renaissance poet. "Ye call to me?"

Golden looked away in revulsion as he puckered his lips at her. She spun toward Braziliano, glaring with all the burning, consuming fury inside of her.

"Damn you! That thing is going to eat him alive!"

"Ahhh. Temper, temper, *querida.* What would your dignitary father think about such unladylike behavior?"

"Tell that monster to put Mast down! Now!"

Braziliano threw up his hands in surrender, that maddening smile still spread across his face. "My friend!" he called jovially, waving to the giant. "She said she wants you to drop him!"

"No!" Golden protested. "No!"

"Drop him?"

"That's what she said."

"You insipid, lying beast!"

"Golden!" Mast's voice caught her by surprise, raw and exhausted, but still commanding. "Be quiet!"

"Mast?"

But if he had a reply for her, the giant cut him off, bouncing Mast's body up and down as he shrugged in mock innocence. "All right. Your wish is my desire, my bonny bride."

Terror annihilated even the scream in her throat. All Golden could do was gasp as she witnessed what everyone else did: the alligator breaking out of the water directly beneath Mast's head. The huge mouth opened, baring gleaming triangular teeth and a slimy pink throat beyond.

She wanted to die. She couldn't take her sights from the horrid beast. She couldn't take her sights from Mast—

though in the next moment she'd watch his head be ripped from his body while his strong arms and graceful legs would be shattered . . . bloodied . . . mutilated.

She wanted to die.

The snout crashed shut with a violent snap.

But it took everyone an instant more to comprehend the swift movement the Neanderthal had coordinated with the alligator's move. He lifted Mast high enough so all the animal slinked away with was an unappetizing snippet of black hair clogging its nostrils and snagging its teeth.

The contest continued.

The audience went giddy. The giant bowed and preened, even posed with Mast like a hunter displaying his prize kill. Laughter and cheers surrounded Golden as she struggled wildly against her bonds.

"You're all barbarians!" she shrieked. "You can't do this!"

"*Dios!* Shut that virago up!" Braziliano motioned two more henchmen in her direction.

The thugs started toward her with happy leers on their faces.

They suddenly stopped. Their eyes bulged. The crowd gasped. Golden raced her gaze after theirs—and emitted a stunned outcry of her own.

While his tormenter had continued to bow and bask, Mast had started to *swing* back and forth over the water—using his own weight and the pirate's iron hold to maneuver himself closer to the log. At the moment Golden and the others noticed what he was doing, he'd come near enough to attempt a daring twist in the air. He reached out and grabbed a tenuous hold around a sturdy outcropping of the tree.

And in the next moment, he actually bettered the incredible feat.

Mast used the Neanderthal's very advantages against him, employing the giant's unrelenting grip and mountainous size to flip him beneath the log while Mast rolled again to the top.

The pirate's outcry shook the treetops. He dangled wildly over the water, clutching only one boot of Mast's now; his remaining thread to life. Yet another murmur of surprise rippled through the gathering when Mast didn't give that leg the single shake it would have taken to conclude the battle. Instead, he strained and stretched his thigh muscles, trying to pull the brute back onto the log. When the giant was close enough, Mast flung out his hand to help. The brute's eyes bulged in disbelief, then peered up at Mast.

"Take it," Mast gritted.

"Y-you're barmy."

"Damn it, don't you get it? I don't want this. Let me take the woman and we'll both walk away. Don't let Braziliano win, blast you. Don't let that bastard have the satisfaction of your life."

A shaking moment of silence. The reptilian yellow eyes below slithered closer once more.

"Goddamn it, take it!" Mast yelled.

But just then his boot gave in to the inch it was threatening to slip. Then another. The giant shrieked. Mast lunged.

Too late.

Golden whirled in horror, clamping her hands over her ears against the tortured human screams, the hungered reptile thrashings, and the mixed howls and shouts erupting from the crowd. "Get your hands off of me!" she snarled at the henchmen who still held her, wrenching from the bonds she knew, even in her revulsion, no longer had any power over her. Because of Mast—because of what he'd done for her, even after she'd tried him, convicted him, and run from him.

"Golden."

And there he was, battered and dirty for her. A clump of hair, now dust-encrusted grey instead of black, hung over his tired eyes; another tuft stuck straight off the back of his head with the serrations of alligator teeth to its ends. His torso was sweaty and littered with bloody nicks and bruises.

She'd never seen anyone more perfect in her life.

He took a step toward her on his one booted foot and shakily lifted a hand for her. Golden sobbed as she walked past it and straight up against his body.

She lifted joyous hands to his face, kissing him, lifting the hair from his eyes, though the hooded blue-black depths weren't much for clearing at this moment. A wine-dark welt was forming under one thick set of lower lashes; fine-lined cuts surrounded the other.

But beyond the blood and the bruises, the core of Mast's stare was as powerful as ever, drawing her in, holding her close, blanketing her with his strength and life. Oh, yes, his life.

Mast was alive!

"I love you," she said against his lips.

Mast didn't answer. Golden tried a tender smile, but the only thing that crossed his face was a wince as he shrugged into his shirt again.

"Let me help you."

"No." He stiffened. Then somewhat more gently, "No." His glance at her was brief, even furtive. "Let's just go, hellion. Let's just . . . go."

* * *

The silence tormented her. The water was so calm beneath the ship, Golden would have thought herself staring listlessly at the ceiling from a bed on solid ground instead of from this bunk where she and Mast had shared so much passion. The decks and rigging were so quiet, she almost surmised that Mast had dismissed even the watches for the two days of shore leave he'd given his exhausted crew on the small island just beyond New Providence. But she knew Mast the ship captain better than that, so she tried to occupy herself listening for the footsteps of the men who stayed to guard the ship.

And there was her obstacle. She knew Mast better than that. Knew him . . . loved him. Had confessed it to him from the very space in her heart he had filled with understanding and joy instead of suspicion and hatred.

And received the biggest silence of them all as her reply.

She hadn't gotten a single summons to Dinky's quarters, where Mast insisted he was more comfortable when they'd arrived back at the ship. He had Ben tend his wounds there. Nor did an answer arrive to any of the questions that the hold across the ship from her still held.

And no hand answered hers across the ever-widening chasm of confusion and misunderstanding between them.

"You lookin' gloomy enough to frighten da death spirits."

Golden started. She hadn't heard Maya slip through the crack she'd propped open in the hatchway. She'd left it as a purposeful, hopeful invitation to Mast, but she nevertheless welcomed the sight of the native, who now eyed her with an expression of frustration and concern.

"Don't tempt me." She tried to joke but failed miserably.

Maya didn't rally with her normal comeback. Instead she descended the stairs then came to sit on the bed, taking Golden's hand and curling her own around it.

"Still nothing?"

The native lilt to her sister's voice was a soothing dose of home. In response to Mast's wall of icy silence, Golden had resolved to prove just how cold and indifferent *she* could be, but she found herself grasping the dark brown fingers back. Hard.

"No," she answered Maya. "It's been two days, and still I must answer you no."

"Perhaps, sister, if *you* went to *him*—"

"You don't think I've tried?" Golden's laugh was bittersweet. She'd lost count of how many times she'd stolen over to Dinky's cabin, softly calling to Mast, even breaking down to a plead at the door. Finally she'd screwed up the trembling courage to peek in the door. "Funny," she finished the musings aloud, "but he always seems to be asleep when I come visiting."

Again, Maya answered her only with steady silence. It was disconcerting. Golden's words reverberated back at her, and she heard the hint of anger in them just as it was in her heart. Oh, and it would be so easy to give in to that unthinking bitterness—that hatred so familiar it was as much a childhood companion as the Indian who sat next to her. Aye, it would be so simple to slip back into the haven of prejudgment and instant assumption, forgetting the fear and uncertainty of this fragile new Golden who had happened as surprisingly as a *pamperos* storm . . . and the man who had blown those thunderclouds of new ideals and dreams into her life to begin with.

"Sister," Maya finally asked with a soft tug at her hand, "what happened back in New Providence?"

Strange, but contemplating the answer really did fill Golden with anger. But this time, at herself. At Roche Braziliano. At any and all pirates like him.

Mast could very well be one of them.

"I told you yesterday," she replied quickly, rolling her head away as if she could avoid the onslaught of memories. "I was going to be sold into marriage. Mast found me just in time, but they made him fight for me——"

"No, sister. What *happened* in New Providence?"

Golden comprehended the tighter pressure of Maya's hand all too well. She swallowed. Somehow, the words frightened her now.

"Just before Mast went to the dueling log, I . . . told him I loved him."

Silence.

Golden looked back toward her sister.

"Maya?"

"Praise all dee spirits in dee sky and dee ocean!"

Papa had shown Golden a curious liquid called champagne once. She suddenly realized what one of the poor jostled bubbles in the glass must feel like. "Sister!" she cried and laughed at the same time. "Set me down! And let me go—I can't breathe!"

"No way," Maya retaliated. "I not lettin' any o' dat good sense of yours leak out. Glory to mighty Puntan, it be a miracle one of you finally got some!"

Nevertheless, the native pulled away enough so that their gazes met. The sienna flecks dancing at Golden narrowed to a more sober brown. "Sister," Maya prodded, "you mean it, too? You love him . . . truly?"

"I love him, Maya. Oh, I do. Truly."

"And he love you, too?"

Golden's smile faded. "I don't know." She glanced away. Tears nipped at the backs of her eyes again. It had become an agony battling them off since that night in the swamp. "There's still so much I don't know. So many questions without answers." She bit her lower lip. "I'm not certain—I may have fallen in love with a lie."

"And no other woman thinks da same thing?" Maya humphed back. "No, sister. There only be one way to know dat for sure."

"How?"

"Ask yoorself in *here.*" Maya took Golden's hand and placed it over her heart. Her sister smiled softly before adding, "I did."

"And . . ." It was Golden's turn to prod as she read the meaningful glow spreading across the cinnamon-shaded face, "Did Dinky tell you he loved you, too?"

Maya's eyes gleamed brighter with a light Golden recognized all too well. "He told me first."

"Oh, sister . . . that's wonderful. Just wonderful. He's a good man, and he's made you happy."

But Golden could see Maya's incomplete belief in the statement. She could sense her sister weeding through her words and picking out the forced overtones of cheer. "So where is Dinky now?" she asked hastily, hoping to change the subject by continuing it. "And why are you not with him?"

She was successful at her plan. Maya's smile returned as she moved back to the stairs. "Peabrooke get relieved at watch in a little while. Then we goin' over to dee island to watch dee sunset."

"Mmmmm. Sounds nice."

Maya suddenly straightened. Her eyes widened, springing tiny gold flecks again. "Golden, why you not come with us?"

A knot of discomfort twisted in Golden's stomach. "No—no, sister. I'd feel—well—" *I'd feel Mast. In every rush of wind through the trees. In every sensuous roll of the dark blue water. In every kiss, every touch, every caress you and Dinky share. I'd feel Mast. I'd feel horrible.*

"Ya'd feel fabulous." Dinky appeared at the hatch. He came down the stairs until he slid behind Maya, wrapping his arms around her, but he continued to look at Golden. "There's plenty o' room in the longboat. I think it's just what ya need, spitfire."

"Dink . . . I don't know."

"Well, I do. 'Tis a beautiful little island; why, Maya feels right at home there, right, lovey? See, I told ya. Lots o' birds 'n trees, flowers like the Queen's own jewels, water-falls 'n—"

"Waterfalls?"

Golden perked an eyebrow. How lovely a long soak beneath a cascading waterfall sounded. She'd indulged in such cool showers every day on Saint Kitts; now the grime and sweat that had caked her since New Providence had begun to feel as heavy and depressing as her continuing mindset.

"I know a very private cove I can direct ya to. Nice little bathin' pool at the bottom o' the falls. Some tantalizin' berry trees there, too, if I remember right."

Dinky's dissertation became a dull buzz behind the conversation Golden conducted in her thoughts. She was in a muddle, that was for certain. Perhaps getting away from the ship would be the very thing to clear her mind. Perhaps just getting away from *him* . . .

"Yes," she cut into the middle of Dink's discourse on the color of the island's water. "I think it's a lovely idea." She smiled. "Thank you, my friends, for inviting me."

"I'll tell Rico to clear another space in the longboat," Dinky responded with a grin.

Golden jumped from the bunk and slid behind the dressing screen to prepare. She had no way of seeing the conspiratorial wink Maya flashed at Dinky, or the long, wet kiss he planted on her in return.

"You were right, lovey," he whispered. "The waterfall idea snared her like a rabbit."

Nineteen

Golden closed her eyes in bliss as she breathed in the invigorating mix of sea salt, island flowers, and rich Caribbean earth. Opening her eyes again, she paused one more moment to watch a hummingbird flit by, suck the sweet tune from a trumpeting hibiscus bloom, and continue on its way. She smiled as she plucked the vibrant red flower and inserted it behind her ear.

She had to admit it. Dinky had been right. This was just what she'd needed to calm the turmoil of her mind and soothe the battered edges of her soul. Listening to the call of a spoonbill blend with the wind through the Caribbean pines, she felt, once again, truly at home.

The tunnel of bougainvillea was just where Dinky said it would be, and beyond that, Golden followed her own ears toward the waterfall's song. A few minutes later, she parted a curtain of thick-hanging fern—

And entered the most resplendent fairyland of nature she'd ever seen.

Where there weren't deep green ferns or trees, there were flowers—hundreds of them, an effulgent painting where the artist couldn't decide which color to use, so he'd used them all. The waterfall was a brilliant blue streak down the middle of the glade. At its bottom danced an enticing froth of white bubbles.

"Oh, Dinky," Golden murmured. She ran her fingers across a bank of yellow and pink flowers as she padded down an incline of velvety grass. "You didn't tell me it was this beautiful."

After skirting under an overhang of Spanish moss and past a curious family of raccoons, she finally stepped on a shelf of flat rocks that hung a few feet over the water. Congratulating herself on her decision to dress simply, she quickly tossed aside her shoes, stockings, and light cotton skirt, then walked to the edge of the shelf as she started to pull off her chemise.

She jerked the strap back onto her shoulder when her gaze hit the water.

A dark shape glided from beneath the waterfall. Fluid of motion, but powerful of strength. Long, bronzed arms. Long, bronzed legs. A torrent of black hair made a gleaming V between chiseled shoulder blades as they rose out of the water. A scraped-up hand wiped the water from a strong face turning toward her.

The same hand froze as Mast's eyes met hers.

"What the hell are you doing here?"

Instinct drove Golden's chin up, despite the nerve-stopping sight of that chest, with droplets shimmering through the thick chest hair and down the ridged stomach muscles. But Mast's harsh demand had set her indignation burning, and she'd be trampled by a boar if she let him dilute it with his beguiling state of undress.

"Don't look at me like that. I was about to ask you the same question."

He seemed to consider that, then glanced away sharply. "Dink promised me he'd keep you on the ship."

"He promised me you were sleeping the afternoon away. It was easy to believe him," she added meaningfully.

A thick pause. Then a resigned huff. "I suppose we've been set up."

"I suppose so."

The following silence was the emptiest of her life, even with the patter of the waterfall and the twittering of the birds.

She finally couldn't hold back from blurting, "Am I so hard to be set up with?"

"What are you talking about?" he snapped.

"You won't even look at me."

"Golden—"

"And that's the most you've said to me in two days." Her throat caught on the unexpected surge of emotion. "Damn it, you were a stone wall when I first stepped foot on the *Athena*. Block by block we tore it down, Mast. Together. Now you're a bloody Roman fortress again, and I—I don't know how to get through."

His head raised then, and his stare entwined with hers— and Golden dared to feel hope for a glistening, shining instant.

But only for that instant. She'd only inhaled once when the wet black head turned from her again. The awkward movement was underlined by a low, but intense growl. "None of this has been any easier for me, hellion."

Her lips released a caustic laugh as if the sound had been demanding release for an hour. "Really, Captain? I didn't hear *you* sinking to the boards outside *my* door, begging for but a short while to talk—pleading for even a few paltry minutes to decently explain ourselves to each—"

"Enough!" He cut her off with a violent downstroke of his tight-veined forearm. A wave of water washed across her feet. "Damn you, Golden. It's just not that square-sliced simple for me. There are circumstances I've had to think long and hard about. Feelings I can't just wrap up in a bow and present to you over afternoon tea. I just can't. I just won't."

"Well," she stammered, suddenly frustrated and angry and very, very confused. And from that unthinking confusion she snapped out the first furious blurb that rose to her lips. "Well, I just resent it."

"Oh you do, do you?"

The reply was too low and much too calm. The next instant Golden knew why. She had enough time to release an astonished cry before pitching forward through the air at the mercy of Mast's sudden lunge and jerk at her legs. He caught her without effort, but let the momentum of her fall carry her below the water, anyway.

"Now," he gritted in her face the second she surfaced, "you want to talk about resentment? All right, *my lady,* let's talk. Let's talk about people who share their body with a person one night then don't have the guts to share their trust the next day. Let's talk about assumptions. Let's discuss convictions before the trial—and guilt without a chance to prove innocence!"

"Proof?" she managed to sputter back through a spinning red haze of fury. "I'd say I had all the proof I needed in that hold, *Captain* Iverson!"

"I didn't hold that back from you on purpose."

"No?"

"I was bound to a promise, Goddamn it."

"To whom, pray tell? The devil?"

Nothing but the wind and the water answered her for a long moment. A moment that Mast Iverson's face transformed before her eyes. The heavy frown surrendered and receded. Those straight lips pursed, then attempted a wry curl. "Aye, your father can be a demon sometimes," he finally stated.

Golden opened her mouth; closed it to swallow. "So I guessed correctly," she said quietly. "You do know Papa."

"I know Papa."

"And Uncle George confined him to Abaco," she filled in with dawning realization, "so he sent you for the things that I found in the hold." Mast nodded. She watched the slow movement closely, sensing his second meaning. "And me."

Mast's hands gentled on her arms. He only used the pads of his fingers to prod her closer. "And you."

As wonderful as his body felt, the revelation opened up a slew of questions in Golden. She pressed her hands to his shoulders while searching his face. "But why didn't you tell me that to begin with? Why the French army disguise, and the stories? Why didn't you just tell me you were Papa's friend?"

"Because two countries are at war, hellion. A war of lust and greed for rule of these islands. He who returns home with the most prizes wins, goes the saying. And your father, as cantankerous a bear as he may be, would be quite an impressive prize for the French." His hands moved to her waist, his thumbs making soft circles through the wetness of her chemise. "So he asked me to make some promises and keep some secrets. And I did, because I trust him. It works like that between people who care for each other." He brought one thumb up to wipe a wet strand of hair off her cheek.

Golden shivered at the caress, but softly smiled. "I . . . suppose I didn't make things any easier."

His own lips struck an amused expression. "You made things hell." The touch on her neck now moved to her nape; the night-smooth voice lowered to a husky murmur. "Especially after I kissed you." His hands slid down her back.

He pulled her close against him, closer, into the realm of that beautiful, midnight-deep stare. "Especially after you'd started to turn my high-and-mighty propriety upside down with your snarls, and begun to turn my heart inside out with your passion." He inhaled shakily. "Oh, Golden Gaverly, after you'd begun to make me fall in love with you."

Golden stopped breathing. She blinked several times. "Wh-what?"

"I said," he murmured, "I love you."

"Mast—"

"No." He splayed three fingers across her lips. "No, don't say anything. I know the one question you have left. And I know it's why you fled the ship that day. Ramses showed me the way you left the flag in the hold." His touch moved across her cheek and brushed the curve of her jaw. Golden swallowed back a wave of emotion.

"I didn't kill your parents, Golden."

"I know." She stared deeper into his eyes, yearning for him to believe her. "Deep inside, I think I've known all along. It was just so easy to jump to conclusions. So easy to fall into the old hate—"

"I know," he repeated back to her. "But it's all right, because I'm going to find out who did kill them. I can't promise you much more at this time, but I make that single promise to you with every breath in my body. Can you—do you—trust me enough to believe that?"

She lifted her hand to cover his. "Yes."

The syllable coursed through Mast with a power that rivaled the nearby waterfall. "I love you," he told her again, swooping her off her feet until he suspended her above him and she shrieked at him in delight. "I love you!"

"I love you, too!" she giggled back.

He gripped her harder as the power of the words flooded him and threatened to explode into a primal shout of joy. "Louder," he commanded up at her. "Say it louder."

"I love you!"

"Louder!"

"I love you! I love you, I love you, I love you!"

She threw her head back, crying it into the treetops. And Mast just stood there and gazed at the joy on her lips, the swan's arch of her neck, the dripping white fabric of her chemise clinging to her body like diaphanous clouds around an angel. His angel. God, if only for this time, this place, this now, his free-flying angel.

He let her slip down then, down along his body. His lips began caressing her as she went, until they met with her mouth. Then he kissed her deeply, openly, needingly.

"You're the most gorgeous thing I've ever seen," he told her, suckling his way down her neck, breathing her clean, wet scent, capturing the vibrations of her low moan in his clutching throat.

He hooked his fingers to her chemise straps. Gently, slowly, he pulled the filmy material down her body. "Yes," he murmured at the sight of her bare breasts, their undersides dipped just below the water's surface, "so gorgeous."

The sultry smoke that clouded his stare made Golden tighten and ache inside, harden and squirm outside. "Mast." She tugged on his arms, urging him forward, yearning for the touch of his lips upon her again. "Please."

But he resisted her with maddening strength. Golden watched as he made a cup of his hands to scoop up some water, pour it over one breast, then the other. His fingers followed the rivulets that played over her flesh, circling each nipple, drawing out the trembling tips until they stood erect with deep red desire and Golden trembled with the need that filled her.

She could take the torture no longer. She cast Mast's hands aside while pressing against him, burying her erect crimson nipples in his thick-curled chest hair. She stole the groan at his lips with the hungry demand of her own. Her hands followed the ravenous cry. They went running down his back to his buttocks, then to his hips. Then they moved to the evidence of his passion and held it, caressing it, kneading it.

"Ah, God," he gasped against her mouth. "God, Golden, what you do to me."

"Show me."

And he did. Lifting her legs around him, he entered her there in the water. He loved her long and thoroughly in their wet and wild haven. The sun was making stars of the water beads across her body, his thrusts made stars out of the tears in her eyes.

Afterwards they splashed like nymphs in the pool, chasing each other, teasing each other. Golden inevitably outswam Mast whenever he seemed to have the upper hand. They kissed beneath the waterfall and caressed in the sundappled shallows. When they finally climbed out, exhausted and prune-fingered, they fed each other berries until Golden sucked one suggestively out of Mast's palm. Then he pushed her back to the grass, parted her legs as he knelt between them, and growled as he lowered his head, "So, we're eating little red berries that way, are we?"

Golden still flushed down to her toes remembering what he'd done then. She rolled on the bed of leaves Mast had made for them in a small alcove of hanging moss, hoping the late afternoon breeze would cool off those delicious, yet steamy thoughts. Alas, the glowing feeling only intensified, and found its way to a sigh at her lips.

"I'll take that as a compliment."

She jumped in surprise despite the new warmth to that low-thundered voice. "Mast! I expected you to return from the other direction . . ."

But she was only vaguely aware of the trail she left of her voice. He was her black panther more than ever now, crouched on a fat tree limb over her, elbows cocked casually to his knees. His dark eyes were relaxed, but they still devoured every inch of her at the same time.

He rose and leaned against the tree trunk. Now Golden felt her own eyes darken at the sight of those endless black-clad legs, the bronze-rippled muscles beneath the open white shirt.

"*I* expected me from the other direction." He folded his arms across his chest. "But things haven't been what I've expected lately."

Golden felt the flush repeat itself down her body with the implication of his brandy-smooth tone. She attempted to change the subject before she gave in to the urge to join him on the branch and perhaps kill them both with what she'd do to him there.

"How is the ship?"

"Quiet and under control," Mast replied. Then his eyebrows cocked. "Except the crew."

"The crew?" The men were giving Mast problems? Twinges of alarm bit at her. Golden knew they'd been upset about her being aboard the *Athena* at first, and she'd worked hard to conquer their fears—but that was before New Providence. Before she'd almost gotten their captain killed.

"All right," Mast said in a confessional tone, "I'd say the whoops of joy have calmed by now. But they were damn loud when their captain extended shore leave another day."

It took a moment for the words to take root. Another before their meaning grew and sent Golden sitting up, eyes wide. "Their captain—"

"Gave them an order. And expects it to be followed, no questions asked." He assumed a dominating stance on the limb, hands to his waist. "Does anyone have any problems with that?" His head came forward. "Your ladyship?"

Golden shook her head rapidly and giggled. "Nay! Nay at all, your Captainship."

"Then wipe that shocked look off your face."

"Aye, Captain."

"Lie back down," he commanded lowly.

Golden rested back on her elbows, reveling in the way she caused Mast's jaw to tighten as her breasts thrust up through her still-damp chemise. "Aye, Captain," she repeated sensuously.

Her anticipation heightened as she watched him swing down from the tree. His muscles bunched, then straightened, with his easy, but eager movements. But Mast didn't move to lie beside her as she craved. He stopped at Golden's feet—looked down the length of her sinuous pose, then back up again to her eyes. Neither spoke. The wind sang through the wilderness, lifting his hair off his face and the shirt off his shoulders. A muscle flexed in his jaw again, marking off another minute in this agonizing tug-of-war they played.

"You know, your ladyship, you're one hell of a misbehaved hellcat."

Golden bit her lip provocatively. "I know."

"Completely uncontrollable."

"Yes."

"Utterly untamed."

"Then tame me."

It wasn't a challenge. It was a plea, whispered as Golden slid across their sweet-fragranced bed and pulled Mast to his knees. "Tame me," she murmured against his neck, then his chest, then over and over as she kissed lower and lower, until she arrived at the top button to his breeches.

She unbuttoned it.

Mast moaned.

She loosened another.

His hand snaked into her hair.

"Don't stop," he grated.

She didn't. And as she freed his pulsing shaft, the very forest seemed to throb and beat around them, keeping time to the lovers' song they composed together. Mast's voice was a gently primitive murmur, then a gasp as he took her fingers and guided them to the most pleasurable places of his arousal.

But a single curiosity still burned hotter and hotter inside Golden. She had to succumb. She moved Mast's hand away and tentatively slid her lips to his hard length of flesh. His moan moved her, a powerful masculine outcry . . . yet the most vulnerable sound she'd ever heard. Golden clung to him, wrapping her hands around him. His buttocks trembled and bucked in her grip.

"Golden." His voice was full of sweet pain. "Golden, Golden, Golden . . ."

Suddenly she found herself lowered to her back again. Mast surrounded her. His lips were at her mouth, his hands fervidly pushing her skirt up. His fingers sensuously probed the junction of her thighs. Golden gasped, arching her hips into his touch as he caressed the folds of her womanhood.

"You're so wet," he whispered. "So wet and ready for me."

Golden kissed his neck. He tasted salty with sweat, musky with sex. "Tame me," she said simply. "I'm yours. Tame me completely."

Mast mounted her feverishly, cursing himself as he did. He'd vowed a slow and languorous taking, pleasuring Golden thoroughly as he had earlier in the afternoon. But the entreaties she'd just whispered in his ear were like a red flag before a bull and now he couldn't stop. The need was shocking, frightening, but he just . . . couldn't . . . stop . . .

He braced her hips as he buried himself inside her—to the hilt on his first thrust. He forced himself to stop there, shuddering on the brink of losing his control. "I'm sorry. Jesus, I'm sorry. You light this bloody fire in me—"

He'd never noticed how frenziedly Golden was squirming until she yanked him down by his shirt front and silenced him with a deep kiss.

"Shut your mouth and make the most of your shore leave, seaman, before I prove how uncontrollable I can be."

As Mast did just that, he marveled once again at what this brazen topaz-eyed creature could do to him—had done to him already. Love. Great God, he was as astounded as Golden when the words spilled from his lips. But she'd cut to the very core of him again, as she had that maddening way of doing, and he'd blurted it as unthinkingly as . . . well, the truth.

Yes, God help him, the truth. As unexpected as a summer storm, as startling as a lightning flash in the sky, love had ambushed and conquered Mast Iverson's lonely heart. It was the last blasted thing he'd been looking for . . . the only thing that had ever filled him so completely.

It complicated so much.

Come their arrival at Abaco, it would complicate everything.

"Golden," his lips begged silently as his body conquered hers, "forgive me."

Twenty

A brisk morning wind brought the *Athena* into Abaco Harbor an hour earlier than Robert had estimated. But instead of the pleased nod Mast would normally give that news, he retreated to the quarterdeck, alone and stiff-shouldered, to scowl at the awakening little town. He broke his silence once with a "bloody damn" muttered in response to the apprehension and remorse growing larger as the whitewashed buildings on shore did.

It was the sight he'd been dreading. The deep green hills and trees that signaled the end of their voyage. The lovely Lady Golden returned to her father by the dashing Captain Iverson. Dashing, he could hear the matrons cluck, but "very well *not* acceptable."

And so it meant good-bye. *The end* on a story that should never have had a *once upon a time.* She'd cry, but try valiantly not to. She'd kiss him, then slap him. And he'd take it. Then he'd touch her smooth, tawny cheek one more time, wishing he was the sun so he could kiss every inch of it.

It was real life. It had all become such an impossible net of emotion.

Mast swore again.

"Fine pretty sight." Dinky's casual tone contradicted the suddenness of his appearance. If the little man had overheard Mast's mutterings, he wisely gave no indication of it.

"Mmmm." *Pretty as a god-blasted funeral.*

"Nice little harbor. Good place to raise up some little ones, I'd be thinkin'."

"Mmmm." But he barely controlled his commentary below a growl this time. Dink's words called up the vision of Golden on one of those sun-drenched verandas, surrounded by laughing hellion children. Children with another man's features. *And maybe one lonely little tot with unruly black hair and a much too long nose.* He closed his eyes tightly against the sight—and the way it sliced his gut like a double-edged sword.

"I been thinkin' on things like that a lot lately," Dink obliviously went on. "Family. Home. Belongin' somewhere." But then he coughed nervously. "That's why . . . well, that's why I've asked Maya to marry me."

Mast opened his eyes.

"She said yes," Dinky prodded into the tenuous silence.

"That's . . . great, Dink." He finally forced a half-smile. "Great. I'm happy for you, my friend."

They clasped arms, each holding the other from the elbow to the wrist, eyes locking tightly, yet awkwardly.

"I'd be honored if you'd perform the duties, kid."

"I'd be honored in return." Again, the effort of response was torture.

Much to his relief, they broke apart and moved to their familiar, and now somehow comforting, stances at the rail. Mast tried to relax, tried to think about the sunshine and the crisp sea air, perfect heralds of a man's betrothal announcement. But all he saw in the bright gold rays were topaz eyes filled with passion and life. All he heard in the wind were musical laughs and whispered love words. All he heard in the surf were feline-inspired cries in his ear at the height of a crashing climax.

All he heard was wind that could tear a man's soul from him before he knew it was gone, only to return it to him, satiated, filled. Loved.

He took a ragged breath and closed his eyes again.

"O' course, we can't do the deed right away," Dink broke the silence again. "There's a few obstacles we have to hurdle first."

"Obstacles?" he responded half-heartedly. *Right, Dink. Tell me what you know of obstacles. Let's hear them all. I'm dying to know.*

"I guess ya could call 'em that." Mast heard his first mate resettling himself on the rail. "Ya see, I just happened ta set my cap for the daughter of the Arawak chief on Saint Kitts."

"Nice work, Mr. Peabrooke. Straight for the top, just like I taught you."

"Yer flammin' me, right?" Dink snorted incredulously. "Ive, don't ya remember we fancy white men aren't exactly invited guests of those people? The few hundred livin' Arawak would just as soon cage and kill us as we did them. Now just how do ya think ol' Chiefie is gonna take it that his little girl has fallen in love with one of us?"

Mast blinked. "The bastard might toss a spear through your heart."

"Yeah. He just might do that."

"What about Maya?" he snapped to that, an unexpected surge of anger driving his glare around at his mate. "She could be banned from her tribe, Dink. Severed off from her people."

"Yeah, she could."

"For the rest of her life."

"Ya don't have to shake it into me. I know. Maya knows. But we did something that may come as a shock to ya, kid.

We talked about it. We went over the risks, but decided they were worth takin'."

He stepped back then—though his feet felt far away with this body of whirling thought and comprehension atop them. "Maya's a strong woman." By contrast, his voice sounded utterly witless.

"Aye, she is."

"And she really loves you, doesn't she?"

Dink cracked a lopsided smile. "That she does." He reached and clasped Mast's shoulder. "And I'll tell ya, kid, that's worth a spear through my heart any day of my sorry life."

Mast nodded again, but more slowly. He looked down. A minute ago he'd thought himself the wiser of the men on this deck . . . the scarred, world-weary one. But the only wisdom he could claim was that of the stiff-spined books and the cold seas which had kept him company the last ten years. He knew nothing of the life he'd amputated himself from. The life—and the love.

He had so much to learn. And only one teacher he wanted.

He yanked his head back up, returning his mate's reassurance with a determined stare and a set jaw.

"Thanks, Dink."

The crooked grin flashed again. "Any time, Captain."

Spinning on his heel, Mast shouted for any more speed they could fill the sails with. He was suddenly very impatient to get to that dock.

He'd forgotten about the revelry that would greet them when they did. News traveled more swiftly than a court rumor among the two hundred British inhabitants of Abaco, especially when the Earl of Pemshire was bellowing the latest on his excited way down from his villa. Behind Wayland trailed a throng of everyone from queenly gaited matrons to delightedly leaping boys to wildly barking mutts, all come to see the much-awaited *Athena,* back with its precious cargo at last.

"Papa. Papa!"

Mast looked down at Golden from the helm as she shouted and waved from the main deck. He swung his attention back to the wheel just as rapidly. He was battling enough trepidation as it was without being distracted by her and that delectable thing of cream muslin she'd chosen to wear today—even if she was the entire reason for this self-imposed determination; this heart-thudding, knee-buckling foolishness. This fire he'd gladly walk through for the promise of their future on the other side. This fire that seared hotter as that bear of a man on the dock grew larger.

The crew secured the lines and lowered the gangway with speed, spurred by the bevy of young ladies watching the process with batting-eyed awe. Their counterparts, a cool, but cocky group of youths assembled at the opposite end of the dock, were *not* happy about the new distraction in the least. They eyed the *Athena,* its size barely fitting the sole dock Abaco had, with open envy. And they eyed Golden with open desire. Mast had to constrict every muscle in his body not to stride over and claim her before them all with a kiss to render her senseless.

He did the next best thing. "Robert," he called down the main companionway. "Bring Dack up. I want him taken care of first."

A few minutes later, Robert emerged with an emaciated figure. Mast barely recognized him as the once-happy, determined Dack. Glazed eyes peered out from a sallow face with thin lips that puckered and convulsed.

"Land?" the youth squeaked into the suddenly still air. "Land, please? So much water . . . so much loneliness. I'm trapped. Trapped! Get me out of here!"

Mast shook his head. He now saw that Dack's sickness had begun well before he'd brought Golden aboard the ship that fated stormy night. The sea could be a man's friend and enemy at different times. Dack had permanently cast it as the latter.

"Should've left him at New Prov, if you ask me," Robert grumbled. "Bloody bedlamite tryin' to kill us all behind our backs, not mention our spitfire."

"That will be enough, Mr. Chief Gunner," Mast replied evenly. Then in a voice loud enough for the gang of youths to hear, "You know it could well be you or I in his boots next month. Life at sea isn't what the fairy tales say."

"Nay. It's better," came a familiar murmur of seduction for his ears only. And like a priest tempted by a carnal goddess, he denied his earlier vow to turn to her. Ah, God. He alone had heard the whisper, but the tiger-eyed look Golden accompanied it with might as well have been a ten-foot-high banner telling exactly what kind of a fairy tale she'd spun with the now-squirming captain of the *Athena*.

But as much as he struggled and swallowed, a precious inner part of Mast loved the hell out of her for it. That section of his heart now warmed just enough to heat one side of his mouth into a smile. He bent toward her, pulled by that amber glow in those magical eyes.

He yanked himself back a half inch before it was too late. Christ. He had let his head fog over, after a minute near her. *Clear. Remain clear. Damn it, Iverson, you need*

*that self-control you're so bloody proud of now more than
at any other test in your life.*

"Go to your father, hellion," he forced himself to say.
"He's done a great deal to get you back."

"Kiss me good-bye."

He clenched his jaw to keep from doing just that. "No.
You remember our agreement about our behavior here."

"Posh. Nobody cares about all that honor and propriety
nonsense here."

"The hell they don't."

"I want the agreement changed."

"Golden . . ." he started to warn.

"Golden! Thank God, is it really you?"

"Papa!"

Mast exhaled in relief as Golden sped down the gangway.
He watched as she flew into Wayland's arms and then
mushed a wet kiss on his cheek. Wayland rocked her back
and forth and angrily wiped beneath his eyes a few times.
An uncomfortable knot formed in Mast's throat, but the
feeling wasn't a stranger to him any more. No, he realized,
he even welcomed the aching surge. It affirmed that he was
alive. He savored his renewed belief that anything was possible in this crazy world.

Even the miracle he prayed for now.

Golden had pulled away from her father and was talking
to him with hardly a breath between sentences. Mast found
himself laughing along with Wayland at the scattered phrases
that wafted up to him: "Nirvana . . . storm . . . I nearly killed
him . . . gowns . . . tons! He taught me everything . . . El
Culebra . . . New Providence . . . saved my life . . ."

Wayland's brows became a heavy grey blanket over his
eyes at those last words, but Mast could see him forcing
the twinkle to remain in his gaze until Golden finished.

When she did, sucking in a deep breath and laughing, he embraced her again.

"We'll talk more later, nug," his affection-filled voice drifted upward. "Right now I need to settle some things with Captain Iverson."

Golden flipped her head over her shoulder and looked up to Mast with a tender smile. "All right, Papa. But don't let him bully you around. He's all growl and no bite."

Wayland's eyebrows jumped into his hairline, but again all Golden saw were his wide smile and gentle wave as he sent her off with Dinky and Maya to the hilltop villa.

Mast tugged one more time on the bottom of his gold-edged blue jacket and set his jaw above the stock he'd tucked into it. Then one more time he prayed for strength and conviction.

His friend strode over the gangway, and stopped with one boot braced against the deck. "Permission to come aboard, Captain."

"My Lord Gaverly, that is a ridiculous request."

Wayland chuckled and strode onto the deck. He pulled Mast into a rugged handclasp. "God's glory, it's wonderful to have you back, lad."

"It is good to be here, sir."

Wayland's gaze curiously took in Mast's elaborate clothes, then widened to a perusal of the shrouds and sails, decking and rails. "The old lady looks splendid."

"Thank you, sir."

"You, on the other hand, look like hell."

"Thank you, sir."

Mast likened his friend's face to a rampaging bull now more than ever. As they locked gazes, Wayland's lips twisted and his eyes narrowed. "All right, Mast. What is it this side of Hades' gate you're holding up in that stubborn skull?"

Mast screwed his hands together behind his back. Hard. "I took the liberty of having one of the ship's prize bottles of brandy brought to my quarters, Lord Gaverly," he rushed out in answer instead. "Would you allow me the pleasure of sharing it with you?"

Wayland rolled his eyes. "Fine, fine," he grumbled. "I have a funny itch I'm going to need a drink for this, anyway."

Not as much as I, my friend. The thought echoed damningly as he escorted Wayland below.

Everything was as orderly as he'd arranged it before they'd docked, but Mast doubted he'd ever completely erase Golden's presence from the cabin. He wondered if Wayland noticed it. The fresh, salty scent of her in the air. The way she liked the bed pillows arranged, piled high atop one side of the bunk. The rainbow she'd created on his bookshelf by refiling his books according to their cover colors and not their authors.

He bade Wayland to make himself comfortable. His friend sank into the velvet reading chair to his side, not showing if he observed anything out of the ordinary.

But the stroke of luck was fleeting. Mast turned with the two filled glasses to find Wayland leaning forward and gaping at the floor. "Don't tell me *you* put that there," he queried.

Mast only followed his friend's puzzled gaze because he dreaded Wayland would catch his pained grimace. The small but dark dirt and oil stain in the corner had slipped his mind completely. He'd planned to have it bleached and polished out of the floor by now, but the memory of its creation was still too fresh and too treasured to let go.

"Nay," he answered. Then he glanced away, the remembrance a worse threat to his composure than Wayland.

"Your daughter did, my lord. We encountered a brief rain shower through the Windward passage. But Golden—*Lady* Golden," he nervously caught himself, "was determined to reassemble the double deadeye she'd pulled apart, rain or shine."

Wayland snickered. "She did that, did she?"

"She wanted to—"

"Find out how it worked," the other man finished with him in unison. Wayland laughed. Mast managed an awkward half smile. God, he wished he'd listened closer to the man's court gossip the first time he'd been in Abaco, on that fatal wind-filled night that had changed his life. Suddenly Parliment power plays and plunging bodice trends sounded incredibly engrossing. And wonderfully safe.

But he willed himself to pull out the chair before his desk, position it in front of Wayland and firmly sit. He handed a snifter to his friend, then cradled his own drink between his hands as they hung from his knees. Mast gazed into the dark amber liquid, trying to envision the more fortifying depths of another golden-colored intoxicant to push him past the empty blurb about Lord North and the Whigs pressing at his lips.

"I'm . . . going to be painfully honest with you about what happened on this voyage, Wayland." *He'd done it. The wheels of this debacle were in motion now.*

Wasn't there some way he could jump off . . . ?

"I appreciate your forthrightness, lad."

"You may not after I'm done," he returned. He took a deep breath. "But I've decided this is the best thing in the long run, cards fall where they may."

"Then deal them with a direct eye, Mast. I didn't pull a mollycoddle off that dock fifteen years ago."

He straightened in the chair. "You're correct, sir. You

didn't." He crossed a boot across the opposite knee and leveled his head.

But now what to say? Wayland's complete attention flooded him. Mast drew in another long, aching breath and finally began, "Your daughter is a very unpredictable person, my lord."

Wayland snorted good-naturedly. "That she is, Captain. That she is."

"Because of that . . . spontaneity, she managed to tangle herself into a few predicaments along the way. I—" The temptation to look back down into his alcohol pulled on him like a runaway anchor chain. *Don't do it, Iverson.* "I had to keep a bloody close watch on her, Wayland."

"She told me you saved her life."

The comment was not the disgruntled comeback of fatherly protection he'd prepared for. Mast recrossed his legs, unsure about how to answer this surprise of gratitude instead of resentment from his friend.

"We had to stop for repairs in New Providence for a day," he continued slowly. "We crossed paths with Roche Braziliano."

"Braziliano! If that sadistic son of a bitch—"

"Wayland, sit back. He didn't touch her. Fortunately he's a smart son of a bitch. He realized he wouldn't be alive if he had."

"Christ. I'm bloody glad you were there, Mast. I knew I couldn't depend on anyone else for this task. Would increasing the commission by a thousand pounds make up for—"

"For God's sake!" Mast's body carried through the vehement jump of his voice. "Stop it, Wayland, for God's sake." He drenched his rough croak in a sizable gulp from his glass. "I can't—I won't—even accept your original offer."

"What are you talking about? You can and you will."

"No, damn it. I won't."

He spun and pounded the wall. "Wayland," he grated toward the hard, polished panel, "after we cleared New Providence, I—I told Golden about the deal. I told her you had arranged my little rescue mission to begin with, and why I'd withheld that fact from her at all." He turned and leaned back against the bulkhead, dragging another long quaff of his brandy. "I broke our agreement right in two, my friend. Now can you see it is I who owe you the money?"

For a long pause his only answer was a heavy sigh against the nervewracking quiet of his near-empty ship. "You've never jeopardized your honor like that before," his friend at last stated.

"No, I haven't."

"Must have had one hell of a strong reason."

"Reason had nothing to do with it. I had no choice, that was all."

"Golden held a knife to your throat?"

"No."

"What, then?"

The moment had arrived. Mast burrowed deep within himself and tried to come up with the same courage that had helped him confront everything from cutthroats to crocodiles over the last ten years. But all he felt was the wish to be staring down the dueling log again instead of at Wayland. He'd rather be squaring his shoulders to that witless pirate giant instead addressing the man—the friend—who had given him so much for so little—who now eyed him so earnestly.

"I had no choice because—" He cleared his throat, set his jaw one more time. "Because your daughter and I had become . . . intimate, my lord."

An agonizing pause.

"I see," Wayland finally responded.

"I didn't maneuver for it to happen," he rushed on. "But it did, sir, and I'm not sorry about it."

"I see," Wayland said again. And once more, an excruciating silence. "But I still don't understand how that warranted your break of silence, Captain. Certainly one night's indiscretion with—"

"How dare you." He whirled, losing all cognizance of who he was talking to or who he was. "Damn you, she was not some groping, half-thought *indiscretion!*"

"Then what was she?" came the reply as if Mast was no more than differentiating between a barkentine and a brig.

"She—"

He stopped, breathing hard through his teeth, scrambling through the bedlam in his head for a single thought that made sense any more. He blurted the only truth that did. "She was the woman I'd fallen in love with."

A gull keened somewhere near the ship's rigging. Water lapped softly around them, marking the long seconds of the next endless minute.

"Ah, Christ, Wayland," Mast finally muttered. "I'm in love with your daughter. I'm damnably, helplessly in love with Lady Golden Gaverly."

"I see." That maddening, calm reply again. "And have you made Golden aware of this yet?"

"Yes sir." Involuntarily, his eyebrow arched. "I have."

"And what did she say?"

The man's tranquility was more unnerving than his gratitude. Mast's mind hastened to fall back into rank, searched for the order of coherent—and correct—words. "She said she loved me, too, sir."

"Well, praise the saints in heaven."

"Now I know this comes as a shock to you, but if you'd let me expl—sir?"

"And would you stop calling me that?" Wayland snapped. "What's say you try Father for a change?"

"F-father?"

"Sweet Virgin give me strength." The older man rolled his eyes, pinning the sharp green stare back to Mast when he was done. "Captain Iverson, did you break out your best brandy to stammer at me, or to do the honorable thing by me and my daughter with an offer for her hand?"

Mast opened his mouth—shut it. Restraightened his shoulders—surrendered them to the overwhelming sag of amazement. He paced to the small round stain in the corner, then back.

Finally he stopped and braced his feet before the man who bemusedly watched him. "Sir—Wayland—you would greatly honor me—I mean I would be most joyous—what I want to say is—" As Wayland chortled, Mast sank frustratedly back into his chair. "Bloody hell," he muttered. He looked up to his friend with a stare he hoped was transparent with all the ecstasy in his heart.

Wayland chuckled again. "Wipe that Goddamned grin off your face, lad, and help me share a toast to the blushing bridegroom."

Mast obliged, though he felt as if he'd already emptied his glass.

"You mean it, don't you, Wayland?" he asked after they'd clinked snifters. "You're really happy about this?"

Wayland's lips thinned and his jaw tightened. "I'm stunned you had to ask me that, Mast." The older man took a full swallow of his brandy then. But his eyes remained as sharp as twin cutlasses when he raised them back up.

"When I said I trusted only you with this commission, I meant it. By now I think you've come to determine why."

Mast nodded humbly. "Because the most important part of the mission was Golden."

His friend joined a similar nod to his. "As I told you on that night you first came, lad, she's the best thing that's ever happened to me. The jewel in my crown. Not the bloody earldom of Pemshire, not that frigid castle in those Godforsaken outbacks of England. Golden's uncle is perfectly happy taking care of all that. My life is here in the Indies, and I'm as proud of it as any Englishman is of his achievements.

"But I'm proud of Golden in a way I could never fathom. I'm proud of the woman I've helped her become in my small way." His hand came down to rest on Mast's shoulder. "I'm proud of you, lad, and the man I've seen you become. So did I mean I was overjoyed at the love you two have found?" He smiled. "I couldn't mean anything more, my son."

Mast took a deep breath. "I'm very glad to hear that, my friend."

Wayland withdrew his hand. "Then why have I not heard a more enthusiastic response, Captain?"

"Because," he rose and began to pace his well-loved groove along the floor again, "I'm going to ask more of you now, Wayland. Your understanding, and your help."

"My understanding? Understand what?"

"I'm going to take you down to the side hold to explain. It's a long story, but I'm going to tell it all to you. And after that, I'm going to ask for your help."

"You don't have to ask for that, Mast. You've got it. Even if you sound like you're trying to move a mountain."

"I may just be. But it's the mountain that's standing between me and the woman I love."

"Then what are you waiting for? Let's get to that hold."

Twenty-one

"You want to get dis over with, or not?"

Maya's face was as stern as her words, defying the lively, gold-edged pattern in the frame of the dressing mirror behind her. Though Golden braced her hands to the stays and ribbons at her hips and answered her sister with a resistant glare, she turned and obliged Maya with a deep inhalation.

The Indian cinched the final knot on the corset. Golden's eyes popped as she fought the urge to tear the horrible thing off and throw it to the dogs in the garden below. But it was "the latest style out of Paris," Papa had proudly stated when he'd presented it to her, with the elaborate gown that now hung against the wall. Golden hadn't the heart to do anything but kiss his tenderly gazing face with an affectionate, "Thank you, Papa. It's lovely." *No matter how mercilessly this brocade and stiff lace chafe my skin,* she now added.

"Now your hair," the native accent directed.

"No!" Golden snapped, sweeping the hairbrush from the dressing table and brandishing it like a sword. "No more fussing, no more primping. I want to get dressed. Now."

"You can't go out wit' your hair like dat."

"The hell I can't."

"You barely brushed it!"

"If you come near me with a hairpin, I'll stab your eye out with it."

"Gooll-denn . . ."

"No!" At that she whirled and plunked onto the pure white cloud of a bed with a long and frustrated sigh. "Oh sister, I just don't see the point of all this. I don't *want* a silly ball. I don't *want* to dress and paint myself like some—" She stopped, as images of Roche Braziliano's greasy hands on her barely clad body and El Culebra's lascivious stare on her rouged and powdered face came back to her painfully. "I . . . just don't see what all the fuss is about."

"You're nothin' to get fussed aboot?" Maya angrily jerked the folds of the copper-colored petticoat over her head. Golden stood again and helped her pull the shimmering fabric over the voluminous hoop and underpetticoats around her legs, then tie the petticoat in place at her waist.

"I'm not worth an entire ball, for mercy's sake," she countered through the layers of the swirl-patterned gold brocade top gown that now went over her head. "I feel like a fish out of water with these people. I can't laugh at things I don't find funny. I can't smile at people I don't even know." As her head reached air again, she grimaced. "And I certainly can't dance!"

"Bosh," Maya snapped. "You do too dance. You dance fine. You always dee best at dee celebration of Quisqueya every year."

Golden laughed despite herself. "I don't think Papa's friends want to see my ceremonial bonfire dance to the earth goddess, sister."

She sighed again and moved to the window. Beyond Abaco Bay, wind-swept feathers of clouds floated against the first bronze and crimson tones of the sunset. The sight, along with her and Maya's talk of all those past celebrations around the tribal fires, seemed to intensify that subtle tug-of-war inside her. The mannered and civilized Golden was straining and striving against the primal, rain-forest Golden . . .

It wasn't as if she was unaccustomed to the battle by now. The warring Goldens had flailed at each other for so long that at times she almost forgot the violent confusion, the sense of misplacement, and the painful conclusion that she would never really belong in one world or the other.

Until she'd met Mast. Until she'd loved Mast, and in his arms the two sides had come to a soothing harmony with each other. Accepting each other. Belonging with each other.

But Mast hadn't held her since their last powerful loving, in his bunk on the morning they'd docked. The two sides of Golden were restless.

And aching.

She'd barely been able to stand it at yesterday's supper, and that had been almost twenty-four hours ago. Just remembering the scene sent a languish of heat through her body; Golden sank onto the window seat as the shimmers of the Bahamas sky became last eve's muted twilight and magical candle glow.

Her heart had swelled with love and pride as she'd gazed at him across the table from her. She had admired his commanding profile as he conversed with Papa's invited dignitaries, and his charming, but cool half smile as he played the perfect gentleman to their ladies. And when he chanced to look her way, which she noticed was often, his gaze would cloud for a moment with a sultry smoke he knew only she understood . . . and heated her with that same secret fire. And she'd damned him over and over for that silly rule about public affection.

Then, when she was finally able to get away from the after-supper twitterings of the dignitaries' wives, the servants told her Mast had just disappeared with Papa into the night. Perplexed, she'd waited hours for her father and her love, but she'd fallen asleep on the veranda settee. All she could remember in the morning was a soft-whispered, "I love you, hellion," before steel-banded arms carried her to the bed now behind her, and cool lips gently kissed her back into slumber.

It was the last time they'd been together since they'd docked. As if some secret voodoo curse had befallen her, Golden was cruelly subjected to a day of lawn croquet and high tea, of inane gossip and even more inane questions until she pleaded a headache—a real one—and fled to the sanctuary of the *Athena*. But once she got there, Robert and Rico greeted her with shrugs and curious looks. They hadn't seen Mast since dawn.

The ache grew unbearable.

Golden jumped from the window seat. "Let's hurry up, Maya, please!"

"By dee sweet stars." The Carib rolled her eyes. "First she runnin' for dee hills, now she screamin' at me to hurry. I should just go now and leave you half done—"

"Maya!"

" 'I don't want a ball, Maya!' " the Carib mimicked.

Golden found herself laughing again, but this time the joy was doubled by a delicious anticipation bubbling its way up her spine and erupting in waves of shivering excitement along her shoulders. "And I still don't!"

"But now you thinkin' 'bout who gonna be there."

"I am not."

"If we were back home, I'd strap you for lying."

"Maya—"

"Don't push dat chin out at me, girl. You lyin' and I know it." But for all the threat in her words, Maya's fingers were gentle as she lifted them to Golden's shoulders. "Sister," she stressed in an equally soft tone. "Sister, it be all right to say how you feel. It be all right to show dee things inside you." Her eyes deepened to a maroon-tinted brown. "Stop sittin' on your heart like a lion protectin' her young ones. One day you goin' to suffocate it. Dee captain . . . he love you. He not going to hurt you."

Golden could do nothing for a moment but blink back an embarrassing rise of tears. At least a hundred times in the last few days she'd tried to tell herself what Maya had just lectured at her. But the words were too astonishing— too wonderful—to believe. But here Maya's expression was bloody well belligerent with how much she believed, and Golden's heart took a second look—opened just a sliver more.

"Now you goin' to turn around and let me finish?" came the renewed crack of command. "We got no time to waste like dis."

"Yes," Golden agreed quickly, swirling around in her new finery, feeling like a joyous flower waiting to bloom. "You're perfectly right, Maya. After all, I'm on my way to see the man I love!"

The man who took my soul by surprise and healed it. The man who showed me how to love instead of hate. The man who will never, ever hurt me . . .

Oh, Mast. My dark and magnificent and wonderful Mast.

So many candles were aglow at the Marston residence, that Golden had been able to see the grand two-story structure before she'd ever left the front door of the Gaverly villa with Papa. The setting for the ball shone out from atop the next hill like a star on a Christmas tree, sparkling with the promise of joy and music and laughter.

And dancing, Golden thought anxiously.

Nevertheless, she smiled bravely into Papa's face as they now stood in the foyer waiting to be announced. She was trying not to tap the uncomfortable high heels of her shoes against the polished wood floor. The prized hothouse roses Lady Marston had spared no detail in telling her about this morning spilled their redolent glory from urns and vases everywhere. They were complemented by smaller arrangements of hibiscus, heliconia, and freesia. The ball looked grand and opulent already.

Golden closed her eyes against a wave of nervousness and tried to think of Mast waiting for her within.

"Wayland, Lord Gaverly, Earl of Pemshire, and his daughter, Lady Golden!"

The baritone voice still sounded like a death knell. Golden clutched Papa's arm tighter as they entered to an onslaught of applause and faces. She hoped she remembered to smile; she was too numb to know for certain. Stiff white stocks and jewel-strung necks floated by, the faces belonging to them vague and indiscernible. Only one countenance mattered—the features she searched furtively for . . . the dark depths of midnight eyes, the proud, prominent nose, the blue-black hair falling in graceful waves behind a tanned neck and strong jaw . . .

Where was he?

"Lord Gaverly, Lady Golden!" came a trilling matron's voice. "Welcome to our home, as modest as it may be."

Modest? Golden stole an incredulous glance around the room. They called this sprawling, gilt-windowed place modest?

"Ahhh, the lovely Lady Marston," Papa greeted back, gallantly kissing the fleshy hand of the kind-faced woman standing opposite them. "And what a beautiful home it is.

The thanks of my daughter and I cannot find words in exchange for your generosity of this evening."

"Nonn-sense," Lady Marston crooned as the musicians struck up the first lively melody of the night. "Why, I haven't felt so alive in years. Not since we left Boston, just before the Revolution. Oh, I know the independence issue seems to have worked out with the colonies now; goodness me, who ever thought they'd all be sitting down at Versailles to discuss peace?—but could not there have been a manner of achieving it without bloodshed? I abhor bloodshed. Thank God we got out before Johnny—you know, our handsome and *available* Johnny, over there between Alexander Sutcliffe and William Deveraux?—got his head filled with some foolishness to join the fight and went off into some dreadfully dangerous battle or another! Oh my, oh my . . ."

"Come now, Lady Marston. There, there . . ." Papa moved to help the flustered woman to a high-backed chair in the corner next to a table filled with plates of imported English sweetmeats and local treats of fresh cassava and jam-filled *rôti* pancakes. Golden bemusedly watched Papa and their hostess for a moment, then, self-conscious of the way she stood alone in the open space, turned to find her own chair.

She whirled into a net of six meticulously pinned stocks tucked into six extravagantly embroidered waistcoats covering six proudly thrust chests.

"What in the world?" she blurted.

One of the stocks suddenly sprouted a face. A thin mouth smiled just below huge, puppy-like brown eyes. "Our profuse apologies if we startled you, my lady," the strange boy began. " 'Tis just—" he faltered, looking to his tittering friends for support, "well, we couldn't bear another minute waiting to meet you. We've all been smitten blind since yesterday morn."

"Yesterday morn?" She was confused. She heard the puppy's words, but nothing connected in her mind. And now she was beginning to feel hemmed in and restless.

Where was Mast?

"On the ship. The *Athena*," another voice supplied. At least that word made sense to Golden. She turned toward the speaker, a boy with fuller lips than the first, but beady, ratlike eyes. "Yesterday?" the youth prompted. "When you arrived on the ship?"

"Oh," Golden replied. "Of course. I'm sorry, I—"

"We were hoping you'd give us all the honor of a dance this evening," the first puppy interjected.

"I—I don't think so. Thank you for asking, but—"

"Just one dance." He caught her elbow.

Golden stared at the well-manicured paw on her arm. She was just about done conceiving her rebuff to the mongrel and was about to snarl it at him, when a hand at her elbow pulled her back another step.

"Really, Master Bromley. You ought to be ashamed of yourself."

But Golden suddenly yearned for the attentions of Master Bromley and a few hundred of his friends when she recognized that nasal female drawl. She lifted her eyes up into the pointy nostrils of Lady Penelope Fitzbottom and tried to smile.

"My lady." She dipped a quick curtsy. "My thanks for your concern, but—"

"Think nothing of it, my dear," the tall twig of a woman cut her off. Golden was beginning to wonder if she'd finish another sentence this evening. "Besides," Lady Fitzbottom went on while leading her to a raised dais where a gathering of other satin and silk-gowned ladies sat, "we never had the chance to complete our little talk this afternoon at tea. How *is* your headache, by the way? I get the most dreadful headaches from this Godforsaken heat at times . . ."

Drawing on the practice she'd gotten at the fete this afternoon, Golden let the woman's prattle become a single-toned drone in her mind while a soft and aching moan took over her heart. She anxiously looked over the couples on the dance floor between adequate smiles and nods to Lady Fitzbottom—but no long, lean-muscled legs guided any swishing skirts through the minuets, quadrilles, and contredanses. No powerful shoulders reached down to hold any of the brightly sashed waists. No hint of a smile jerked up just one side of any strong, male mouth.

Her stomach knotted and she hated herself for it. She hated Mast for this suffering even more. She passed one more disheartened glance around the room, then drew up her chin and excused herself right in the middle of Lady Fitzbottom's comparison of bowel irritation to gout.

Scanning the dignitaries at the back of the room, she set her sights for the jovial tilt of Papa's head. By the stars, Lord Gaverly was going to tell his daughter just what he'd done with Captain Mast Iverson last night, or she'd truly start a ceremonial dance to Quisqueya in the middle of the dance floor!

She jerked up her skirt to step off the dais.

Her pointy-toed shoe froze inches over the floor.

A gaze of darkest midnight velvet reached across the room and enveloped her.

Certainly the reason Mast looked like an oasis to her parched sights was the tormenting absence she'd endured from him today. It certainly couldn't be the way his shoulders seemed especially forceful beneath the perfect fit of his ink black coat, the sinful way his breeches hugged his long legs, the allure of his dark skin against his white satin stock and waistcoat, or any of the other tiny things Golden had never seemed to notice about him before such as the few rebellious curls of his hair around the bottom of his ears, and the way one eyebrow, just like one side of his mouth, tilted higher than the other.

It was then that her gaze expanded.

And she gulped down a stab of pain.

Ah, yes. Now she saw. As a matter of fact, she should have seen long before now. It wasn't his stare that sent her heart reeling . . . or his coat or his well-fitted breeches or even his bloody stupid eyebrows!

It was the way Mast stood out like a warm coal upon a blanket of snow among the powdered wigs and faces of the dozen young women who surrounded him.

She lifted self-conscious fingers to the unhindered and uncovered waves of her hair. Damn. Maya had, as usual, been right about doing something with her coiffure.

But her fingers clenched at her temple as a particularly stunning face from the crowd leaned up and murmured something from well-reddened lips close to his ear.

Golden recognized the beauty immediately. Her name was Penelope Farsquith. If but a fraction of the rumors flying about the girl were true, she'd have Mast out of his breeches and into her bed before the moon peaked in tonight's sky.

Golden swallowed again. Her lungs begged for a breath, yet she couldn't accommodate them if she'd wanted to. Her foot still hung suspended over the floor. Her eyes were riveted by the sight of Mast's face . . . Mast's ear—the ear she'd kissed and cried into with the culmination of her passion, how many times?

The momentary lull of the music only made the moment more agonizing—as if the rise of all her fears and self-doubts at one time didn't leave enough room for sound. Then the orchestra eased a soft, romantic tune into the air, and time began its excruciating surge forward again.

Golden observed Penelope tap her hands together delightedly. " 'Tis my favorite!" she seemed to exclaim, and yanked Mast toward the dance area.

He didn't budge. Penelope's high wig swayed precariously as she was taken aback. The beauty burned a glare into him as she settled the wobbling collection of hair and pearls and bobbles.

He didn't flinch. Then, calmly expressing all the dispassion he'd give a lobster that had clung to him, he pried loose the shapely fingers around his arm and let them awkwardly drop.

Penelope's ruby lips popped open in astonishment. Golden erupted with the laugh she couldn't hold in. Mast stunned her yet again by turning and grinning at her—the full, joyous grin she'd only seen him give Caesar before now. The charismatic power of that look bolted across the room and into her waiting heart. Golden closed her eyes for a moment, to savor the magical feeling and seal it deep within her so nobody would ever steal it from her.

She opened her gaze upon the sight of Mast pushing through the rest of the made-up faces without so much as a backwards glance. His eyes hadn't left her. He headed for her with a determined stride that sent her senses into leaps and tumbles.

He halted before the dais.

"Lady Golden."

She swallowed. His hands were fixed at his sides in a

pose of polite decorum, but the low tone of his greeting was like a thousand ardent caresses on her body.

"Captain," she managed to respond in a soft murmur.

"I take it you find the ball enjoyable?"

"Aye. At least the last few minutes."

The wayward corners of his eyebrow and his mouth tilted up, but his tone was commanding and serious as he raised his palm to her. "Come here."

"Well, I don't know, Captain. It could be dangerous. You're very . . ." She threw a pointed glance at the gaggle of maids still gaping at him, "popular this evening."

"And you're breathtaking."

Her eyes sprinted back to him. He wasn't smiling any more. The carved cliffs of his face intensified and the blue of his eyes now heated to a desire-smoked grey. Mast boldly stepped closer to her. The spicy clean scent of him teased Golden's senses until she had to hold her breath to stay the images the smell brought to mind.

"I believe this is the dance I had reserved, my lady," he said while bestowing a soft kiss upon the back of her hand. But his head didn't rise from the courtesy. Mast's mouth continued to nip and linger at her skin until Golden was forced to expel her breath in a shivering gasp.

"Dance?" she repeated in a daze.

"Aye. It's called a *waltz*. It's the height of fashion in Vienna, though it's still causing quite a scandal elsewhere." At that he gazed up at her. "You see, one dances it very closely, with one person only."

"Leave it to the Viennese," she managed to stammer.

He showed no sign he'd even heard her. His lips parted and his stare grew hotter. "Dance with me, Golden."

"No," she countered between locked teeth, "I can't dance."

"I don't care."

At that he slid his other hand around her waist, pressed his legs into the folds of her skirt, and whirled her off into the sweeping colors in the middle of the room.

Panic struck when they were nearly enveloped on all sides by other swirling couples. Golden stiffened and darted her head around for escape.

Mast's hand merely gripped her waist tighter. His thighs prodded hers harder. "Sweet," he said quietly, "haven't you learned to stop fighting me yet?"

She turned her face back up. Blast him, he looked perfectly at home out here. His features possessed a flawlessly correct composure, except for his stare, which still silently and subtly heated its way to her core.

"No," she quickly stammered back, fighting off the intoxicating warmth even as her body bent to his will and cried its blissful pleasure. "No," she repeated more firmly. "And I won't ever learn, either."

His hand started a gentle, yet maddeningly sensuous massage to the small of her back. "I'm certain I could teach you. We both know what an excellent pupil you can be."

"I said not ever and I meant it!" Merciful gods, this warm entrapment of his long, hard body and his smooth, intimate words only made it harder to stand her ground. But all the confusion and anger of this day was not so easily torn down, even by the deep-furrowed brow of perplexion Mast leveled at her.

"Never," she gritted again, proud of herself for the firm tone, even if her feet were so muddled beneath her skirts that she'd surely take a tumble the next measure or two. "Not when you disappear without so much as a by-your-leave to me, Captain, then reappear a near full day later with—" She hesitantly pursed her lips, then blurted her first choice of words, anyway, "with your harem."

"My . . . *what?*"

"You heard me. Harem."

If Golden wasn't wrapped so closely next to him, she'd never believe the reaction Captain Decorum-Above-All Iverson gave to her.

He laughed. Not one of his discreet snorts of mockery, not even a quick Mast-like chuckle of amusement, but a hearty eruption from his thrown-back head that sent stares raining upon them with more force than a sudden summer squall. To her further vexation, Golden found herself scowling back at the strangers' oglings in defense of the inconsiderate brute.

And he twirled her on through more gawks and gapes.

"Harem," he chuckled more quietly after taking a few turns to recollect himself. "Oh God, Golden, I thought you couldn't surprise me any longer."

She surprised *him?* Golden scrutinized his face, thinking few sights elsewhere had surprised her more. Creases she'd thought permanently rigid about his eyes and cheeks were now relaxed, even crinkled up a little around his smiling mouth. The scar that once pulsed tight and white with tension was now just another distinctive feature to his face. All this was after he'd roared with laughter in the middle of a waltzing dance floor.

She was beginning to wonder if this was the same brooding, angry man who'd ruthlessly cornered her in Papa's study back home. Not that she was sure she wanted to give this impostor back.

As if reading her thoughts, Mast bore a stare into her and murmured softly, "Oh hellion, have you forgotten so soon? Covers do not their books make, remember? Just as situations are rarely what you leap to conclusions thinking they are."

The scoundrel. He'd perfectly timed the lecture and he knew it. For just as Golden had summoned the perfect mixture of ire and frustration to lash in response to his gentle accusation, a fragrant outside breeze pulled the words from her mouth and replaced the comeback with a surprised, but delighted gasp.

She gazed about the moonlight-dotted terrace as Mast waltzed her farther out into the night. Golden's senses instantly came alive to the night-jungle scents and sounds that were floating along the glittering silver beams to dance with and around them.

"This—you—" she stammered.

"Like it?" he asked evenly.

"I—it's—"

"Knew you would."

"This is why . . ." she uttered with emerging comprehension, "This is why you asked me to dance in the first place."

Mast nodded. "Books and covers, my love. Situations and conclusions. They're not what they seem, even when the titles seem perfectly clear."

But then, as if somebody had jabbed a needle in him, his expression flinched. A strange cobalt moistness formed in his eyes. "Promise me," he whispered tightly, "you'll remember that this time."

She didn't say anything for a long moment. Golden still felt the slight swaying of their bodies as she and Mast moved together in a semblance of dancing, but at that moment, her world was his gaze, a dark and clamoring plea for her love and understanding and . . .

What? What did that other, desperate pain in his face call out to her for?

She raised her hand to his cheek, as if the answer would magically melt from Mast's spirit to hers through the touch. But like the hint of moonlight through the fluttering leaves of the trees overhead, she could only discern a hint of the secret he veiled from her, before a flick of the wind threw it once more into the deep shadows of his eyes.

A shiver coursed through her despite the balmy warmth of the evening. Golden stepped closer. She pressed the length of her body against the hard height of his. Suddenly she needed Mast as urgently as he reached out for her.

She burrowed her head into the bend of his neck. "Yes," she said to him, the word quiet and simple in the night. The satin of his waistcoat was smooth and cool against the fingers she raised to it—another of Mast's ridiculously deceiving disguises, she thought, to conceal all the true heat and passion and fear in the heart she spoke to. "Yes," she told him again. "I'll remember."

"Thank you," came his whisper at her ear. "Thank you."

He sighed again. Golden felt a tension leave his body along with the saturation of warm air at her neck. But as he breathed in again, another tightness returned to the muscular limbs fitted intimately against her. An urgent strain—a hungry need. "God," he murmured, his voice filled with true sanctification for the twinkling heavens above them. "God, thank you."

There was no mistaking the need that plagued him now. Golden felt it in the hands now grabbing instead of caressing her back. His thighs quivered against hers through the layers of her gown. His lips hovered over the arch of her neck, on the verge of kissing and suckling and spinning her into a freedom as beautiful and wild as the wind.

And the need sizzled and sluiced through Golden's excuse for composure. When she felt Mast pulling her farther from the light that filtered out from the ballroom, she followed his lead without hesitation.

Twenty-two

Neither spoke a word as he pulled her down first one row of hedges, then another, but their bodies cried out as deafeningly to each other as thunder to lightning. Their hearts were pounding like the wind to the sea. As Mast finally tugged her into an alcove big enough for two people and the small bench that occupied the space, Golden looked into his eyes to find the uncontrollable, unavoidable yearning of her own soul mirrored there.

She stepped into his arms.

He grasped the back of her neck and forced her face upward.

"Jesus," he whispered, eyes raking over her with a raw, primal voracity. He brushed his lips across hers, sending tremors through both their bodies. "You torture me, sea witch. You just . . . torture . . . me . . ."

Golden couldn't hold back the smile she beamed up at him. "Well, now you know how it feels, Captain."

A hint of self-deprecation fought its way to his lips. "I'm sorry. I know how today must have been for you."

"It was hell." Her smile faded then. She looked away to prove just how serious the allegation was, but that only gave Mast the perfect angle to assault the sensitive skin of her neck with his lips and tongue.

"I'm sorry," he repeated softly into her ear.

"It was worse than hell."

"Then I'm very sorry." His mouth descended along the neckline of her gown, nipped at the valley just where the gold brocade began to hint at her breasts.

"I wanted to knock Lady Trueglove through the wickets instead of that silly croquet ball," she murmured, trying, but failing miserably at keeping her breaths even with the sight of his dark head against her flesh. *Think of hateful things,* she told herself. *Don't think of how you become such pliable clay in his arms. Don't show him how good his fingers feel on the backs of your arms, on the inside of your neck.*

Make him search for it the way you searched hopelessly for him today.

"Tea," she managed. "Yes, tea. They poured gallons of it. You know how I hate—oh! Ohhhh . . ."

It was too late for searching, she realized then. Mast had found and conquered. Golden dug her hand into his hair as his tongue flicked its way under her bodice and over one willingly erect nipple.

"Yes," he murmured back against her breast. "You hate tea. I know."

"I hate *you.*" She gasped as he slid over to the other crimson-flushed tip.

"I know."

"You left me."

"I'm sorry. So sorry. Christ, your skin is so delicious."

"Where were you?"

"You talk too much."

At that he moved his head up and sank his tongue solidly into her mouth, parting her lips so they could take the full, dominating demand of his passion. Golden sank against him. Her knees had given out, with the torrent of hot desire the kiss undammed within her. Her back arched as Mast's hands clawed down the bodice of her dress, then feverishly set to work on Maya's handiwork of her corset ties.

When they broke apart they both labored heavily for air. Their gazes intertwined in the union their bodies screamed for.

"Don't do it again," Golden said, though the force of her need transformed the command to a plea.

And then it happened again. That same strange twinge of pain shot through Mast's features, the same sad and almost despairing black sea gathering in his eyes. "Don't do it again? Oh no, hellion," he whispered. "I couldn't leave you again. You see, I didn't leave you to begin with. No—" he kissed her swiftly, "no backlashes, no anger. Just listen. Listen. Do you hear it? That's my heart pounding, Golden. The heart that was frozen in place until you, you little heathen, came snarling your way into it, and even opened up a few compartments I never realized the damn thing had." Taking a weighted breath, he finished solemnly, "I never left you, Golden, because you never left me."

For a long moment, she didn't breathe. She didn't remember thinking, except the part of her mind which tried to digest the blinding, blazing beauty of his soft-spoken words—and, the hardest part, tried to accept them.

"Oh," Golden whispered. "Oh."

"You were with me all the time. In here."

She gazed at the dark outline of his hand, covering her lighter skin as he brought her palm to his chest. "Oh."

"And you were with me up here, in all my thoughts, in all my dreams. And you sure as hell were in every ache I had . . . here."

His voice rasped lower as he guided her to the swell at the

apex of his thighs. Mast shuddered. His neck arched back. Golden trembled. Her fingers closed tighter around him.

"Oh," she heard herself say again, but now the word was an affirmation, not a meaningless blurt. She reconfirmed it against Mast's throat as she felt him grow more hard and hot beneath her hand. He answered her with a low groan of pleasure as around her thighs his hands came up, gliding, then receding—stroking and grasping, dragging more and more of her skirtings with each journey that ventured closer and closer to her center of arousal.

And reality began its merciful slide away, banished to some frozen netherland far beyond this burgeoning starpoint of heat and need and love. Distant sounds of the ball's laughter and music now faded to this passion song of here and now, this primal tempo of bodies swaying, rocking, kissing one another. Mast licked her upper lip, Golden sucked his lower. A moan shuddered its way up his throat, a sigh trembled from hers. He recited every saint he could think of in slow, erotic thanksgiving. Golden responded with the corresponding deities in gasping Caribbee whispers. His hands climbed higher and higher on her legs, until finally Mast was gripping her bottom beneath her chemise and kneading it in time to the pleading, needing thrusts his tongue began inside her mouth.

"God help me," he grated between deep and heaving breaths. His stare upon her felt as if it could sear her skin away with its blue-flamed intensity. His palms rose to the sides of her face, demanding her own unalterable gaze on him. "God help me," he repeated, "because if you are a witch, I must cast myself freely to hell."

Golden opened her mouth, but the wonderful, confusing multitude of words that would explain just what cataclysmic miracle this man had wrought within her—those words refused to be spoken. Instead, idiotic tears welled and rolled from her eyes, adding a sweet, salty taste to the kiss she turned and gave one of his palms. "I'm just the hellion who loves you," she whispered.

A nerve flinched beyond the corner of his eye. He swallowed deeply as he brought his thumb across her cheek, wiping away the wetness there. "And I'm just the poor bastard who loves you."

And then he kissed her.

He kissed her deeply and thoroughly as his hands once more traversed the rumpled contours of her body, until his long fingers found the perspiration-moist softness of her thighs and gripped them, hungrily. He pulled her legs tighter, higher around him until suddenly Golden found herself lowered onto the bench. She watched Mast fall to his knees upon the grass in front of it.

He raised his eyes to hers.

Golden gulped back the stunned gasp that welled within her.

An animal, not a man, cast its gaze over her through the disheveled locks of brimstone-black hair. A wild and vanquishing animal, driven only by the deepest needs of his being, the wildest calls of his instinct. She'd never seen this beast . . . never, in her most outrageous musings, thought he existed. The finery encasing the taut-muscled chest over her was the only sign of the Mast she thought she knew.

For a strange moment, a scythe of fear sliced through her. This creature touched upon the vulnerable core of her in a way the dour, scowling-faced captain of the *Athena* never did.

Then she truly looked into the night-dark depths of those eyes . . . and saw Mast's own heart. The raw need, and reckless desperation.

The animal in her came alive in answer.

She moaned. Lowly and achingly.

His jaw clenched. He reached and jerked open the buttons between his thighs.

"Come here," he demanded. He yanked her forward on the bench until her bottom nearly fell off. In one stroke he was inside her, filling her with his hot and full erection, pumping urgently, driving with abandon. Golden cried out as his thumbs joined together and started to circle in the swollen folds of her flesh over the union of their bodies, coaxing the untamed creature inside her out of its civilized cage and into the wilderness of unthinking heat and ecstasy. She gripped his shoulders, throwing her head back as she began to meet his forceful thrusts. Mast pressed his lips and teeth to the hollow of her throat.

"If this is hell," she gasped to him, "then let me burn forever."

Mast stopped inside her for a long moment. Something close to a sob enveloped every inch of his face. "Oh, hellion, it quite possibly could be." Then, just as swiftly, raw passion overtook his features again. He began to move in and out of her with more passion and force than they'd ever shared together before. "So love me, please," he demanded in a rasp against her throat. "Love me like it's the last time before we die."

"No!" she protested, gripping his head as the spiraling inferno of heat flared hotter, redder, sweeter between them. "No. Not the last. The very first, always, with you."

He only answered with a cry that was pure primal lust and need . . . and pain. The moan reverberated through Golden, lighting fire to the tips of her nerve endings and setting the last of her inhibitions free. The spasms of her release were swift and overwhelming. They vibrated and

tightened around Mast's hardness until a few seconds later
he groaned yet louder and longer. His body convulsed like
that of a wild game animal gunned down for all of posterity;
caught in the midst of a glorious pounce against the heavens. Then his head came up again and he fixed his gaze
into hers as he spent his passion inside her. His eyes were
stormy and intense, his body hot and furious.

Slowly, very slowly, his breathing calmed, the tempest of
his body inside hers stilled, his features at last relieved of
the disturbing anguish which had attacked them. Nevertheless, Golden lifted the pads of her fingers to the tanned jaw
and nose and cheeks. She traced each carved angle to affirm
what her eyes told her. A tremor of joy overcame her when
Mast lifted his hands and started to explore her features in
the same way.

How long they remained like that, stares and fingers and
bodies entwined as if they'd never come apart, Golden
didn't know—or care. Even as the strains of civilized music
and conversation began to seep their way through the con-
tented haze of her brain, time hung suspended as an unreal,
faraway concept.

She didn't think she could be any happier.

"I love you," Mast whispered.

Nay, she *could* be happier.

She smiled and kissed him softly.

The last time her stomach had twisted so suddenly into
the next moment's alarm was when the French army's cannon blasts first shook across Saint Kitts. But the explosions
erupting into the garden tonight were twice as wrenching—
thrice as frightening. The voices first rose somewhere
within the Marston ballroom. They became more distinct

as the music stopped and the idle chatter dulled. The storm of shouting rolled yet louder as it advanced closer to the terrace, and gained the strength of more voices as it went along. Every bellow was detonating with one distinct charge: *"Captain Masterson Blake Iverson!"*

Mast jerked out of her and away from her in one movement.

"Mast?" Golden sprung up from the bench as he backed even further away from it. "Mast, what is it?"

"Get dressed."

For a moment all she could do was blink. His voice had suddenly grown icicles, dripping shock into Golden from their sharp, frozen ends.

"No," she retaliated through locked teeth, excruciatingly aware that she dictated it to herself as well as him. "No, I won't. Not until you tell me what's going on. Mast, share it with me and we'll face it together. Damn you, Mast, look at me!"

His shoulder tensed beneath her hand, but Golden refused to let go. He took a deep and ragged breath. She could feel the rage inside him.

His fingers came up and closed around hers—slowly—squeezing tighter, tighter.

"Get . . . dressed."

He flung her hand away and then bent to righting his breeches.

The din of voices grew louder as it progressed across the terrace, still calling Mast's name with accusing authority.

Golden didn't move. Motion would mean thinking. Motion would mean feeling. Motion would mean acknowledging the dread and alarm waiting greedily just beyond the realm of her composure, closing in on her with every moment as the voices grew nearer.

"By the great God Puntan!" Golden recognized her sister's voice and turned. Maya's arms and face were akimbo as she burst upon the alcove first, with Dinky a half step behind her. There was a flurry of movement; a cloak of some sort went flying off Dink's shoulders and around hers. Then Maya's voice hissed again, "I'll take care of her. Captain, Peabrooke, go dee back way; get out of here now!"

But the wind hadn't even a chance to carry away Maya's words before a bonfire's worth of torches irradiated the hedges and bench—and the twisted faces of the men who carried the blazing spears. The most prominent savage—one of Papa's dignitary friends!—pointed a gnarled finger at Mast and Dinky and boomed, *"These* are the fiends!" The others closed in and shoved them both into the waiting arms of two uniformed English soldiers.

It was more than Golden could bear.

"Leave him alone!" She charged with the unleashed strength of her outrage—and terror. She hurled several of the ugly barbarians aside before throwing herself at one of the startled soldiers and clawing mindlessly at him. "He saved my life, damn you! Leave him alone! Let him be!"

"Mary and Joseph! Get this bloody shrew off me!"

"Somebody calm her down!"

"Just slap the damn bitch!"

Mast's unmistakable roar silenced them all. Golden looked up to see a rage so severe on his face that even she took a step back. Veins bulged from his temples and sweat trickled down his neck. He strained out from the hold the two soldiers had on him. His arms were pulled back so tight behind him that his elbows nearly touched, and his ribs were visible beneath his shirt.

"If you so much as touch her—" his seething stare made

a complete circle of the surrounding faces, "so help me God, I'll kill every one of you."

A round of laughter was his answer.

Hot and blinding fury inundated her. Golden leaped toward the center of the mob with a snarl, but suddenly she found a pair of arms holding her back, as well.

A third English soldier stepped forward then. The gold decoration on his uniform declared him the leader over the other two. Still chuckling, the pompous man held his chin in his hand like he was nothing short of God. "I'm afraid that amazing feat will be quite impossible where you're going, Captain," he said contemptuously.

"No," Golden lashed at him. "What do you mean, where he's going? He's not going anywhere. You can't take him *anywhere!*"

The soldier turned and leaned over her. A knowing sneer crept into his shriveled lips. For a heart-stopping moment, Golden was certain he was going to throw open the cape about her shoulders, exposing her still-unbound breasts to them all and raising Mast's fury to a self-destructive pitch. But he merely smiled wider as he turned and declared, "My gentlemen and *lady* friends, the charges against the prisoners, one Captain Masterson Blake Iverson and his accomplice—"

"Accomplice!" Maya could barely say the word, but jumped forward with comprehension of the soldier's slandering overtone. "How dare you—"

"His *accomplice,*" the soldier sneered again, "one James 'Dinky' O'Dinkham, is also and equally accused of the following: Larceny of the high seas, pertaining to and including thievery, smuggling, and piracy—"

"No!" Golden screamed. "We *fought* pirates—El Culebra—Mast, tell him!"

"As a result of said larcenous acts, a second count of

high treason against the king and country who trusted him with their flag at his mast, and therefore, their honor."

The bastard knew just how to emphasize the last word to Mast. Golden watched his dark eyes squeeze shut, his tall frame tense as if dealt a physical blow.

"Liar!" she spat, lunging for the hawk-nosed bastard. "You filthy liar!"

The staid soldier cocked an eyebrow at her, adding an even more smug mien to him. "Lastly," he drawled, his eyes now fixed to hers, "the charge of murder on at least twelve proven accounts—"

"Nooo! Bastard! You treacherous, cruel bastard!"

"All executed behind the disguise of one criminal hereby termed 'the Moonstormer . . . ' "

Nothing beyond that charge made sense. Golden's hammering heart drowned out the rest. Slowly, so slowly through this underwaterlike murk of disbelief and pain, she watched Mast turn to her. His face was ghostly grim, his eyes such a dark and fathomless hue, that she longed to tear herself away from them forever.

But she couldn't. She opened her lips, remembered moistening them with her tongue though they still felt parched and dry, and uttered at Mast, "Tell him. Tell him he's wrong. Please."

Twenty-three

Mast said nothing.

Golden lifted a clenched hand to the burning pit her chest had erupted into. *This isn't happening!* her soul screamed. *This isn't real!* Fear and doubt, suspicion and hatred—they were the past Mast had helped her conquer and leave behind, not the searing, wrenching pain consuming her now! He had a flawless explanation for these beasts. Damn him, he *did*.

"Open your mouth," she hissed at him through trembling lips. "Defend yourself! Tell them they're wrong!"

The tension on his face only solidified; his jaw clutched so hard he appeared a shadow of the man who had passionately swept her into this nook only an hour ago—as a demon to the beautiful archangel who had taken her soul as he'd taken her body.

At that moment even the wind shunned the alcove, leaving an oppressive humidity that pressed the air from her lungs . . . the hope from her heart. Only the sharp click of steel against steel penetrated the thick air—the shackles, as the soldiers slammed them around Mast's wrists. With each jerk and rattle of the chain, Golden's teeth dug harder into her lower lip. She recalled all too clearly what kind of pain the brusque actions inflicted upon a prisoner.

But she couldn't imagine what kind of torment came with

the fight Mast gave to come stand before her one more time.

"Golden," he said softly.

Oh, how she tried to respond. She strained to heed the tension her spirit felt from his and battled to hear the strident supplication in his voice. But a slow and anguished fury continued to gnarl through her, planted there by his all-telling silence to the soldiers' accusations. She turned her head and closed her eyes against the sight of his pain-filled face.

"Golden," came his voice, soft and entreating again. "Golden, I lo—"

"Stop it!" She flung a shaking hand up. "Don't you dare say that! Not now! Anything but that!"

A long moment passed, until she finally had the strength to lower her hand and raise her eyes.

And then, for one wonderful, ethereal moment, it was as if a shaman had granted Golden a vision into her past. The leaping orange light of the mob's torches became the shifting shades of a Saint Kitts evenfall. They highlighted the face of a brooding and handsome French captain who paced like a panther and introduced her to a mind-exploding thing called kissing. And then he'd backed her into a corner and dwarfed her with his body, and surrounded her with himself just as he did now, until she was unable to comprehend anything besides him . . . his fathomless eyes, his dark and flowing hair, his bracing, sea-salty scent . . .

The shackles clanked again as the soldiers jerked at Mast. He asked for one more moment, in a tone that made his request a command, but their disdainful snorts said just how seriously they took that. They yanked harder on the chains.

An insane laugh burst on Golden's lips even as her body flinched at the painful sound. "It's come full circle, hasn't it?" she whispered with a frightening cheerfulness, only to struggle back a sob with her next breath. "You first found *me* in shackles . . . and now—now you—"

But nothing else would come. No more words, no more thoughts. Nothing except the deepest pain she'd ever felt in her life. The most mind-numbing anger. The most twisted confusion. She opened her mouth, trying to force some sound, any sound, out against this torturous bondage inside her, but the ties around her chest constricted tighter with each effort. So she stood numb and motionless in the middle of the clearing, watching the walls of her world come tumbling down . . . again.

"Golden," came a firm voice behind her.

"Papa," she gasped gratefully, running to the shelter of the hefty, outstretched arms. "Oh, Papa," she uttered into his shoulder, a sob finally breaking free at her lips.

"I'm sorry, nug," he murmured. "So sorry you had to see this."

Then suddenly she felt his hold stiffen. Golden looked up to behold Wayland Gaverly's profile as she'd never seen it before. The gentle lines of Papa's face were grooves of trembling anger. His eyes reminded her of a wrathful dragon from a fairy tale he'd told her once, flashing green fire as he stared over her head—straight at Mast.

Silence fell like a death sentence. The two men squared gazes for a long minute. At the same time Golden looked heavily at both of them. A discomfiting feeling overcame her as she did—as if Mast and Papa were exchanging an entire conversation, and she was the only one who couldn't hear it.

"Papa," she said again. Stony silence. She tugged more determinedly at him. "Papa?"

"Bastard," came his only response. "You God-damned

bastard," he seethed at Mast between tightly drawn lips. I trusted you with everything. Everything! Great God, my own daughter!"

"Wayland." Mast's voice was tight, yet desperate. "I can explain, for Christ's sake."

"Take him away." Papa slashed his arm once through the air and turned his eyes.

But Golden couldn't bring herself to emulate the action. Something held her gaze to Mast's imploring face. Something dark and uncontrollable, pulling her back to those eyes that now stared back at her with the black turmoil of a stormy sea. She battled to echo her father's condemnation at him. *Bastard!* her mind screamed. But unbidden and unwanted, the spirit behind those dark blue eyes reached across the clearing to her and pressed the word into tormenting silence.

"Books and covers," he said into the quiet. Calmly. Gravely. Nodding once, slowly and evenly, he engraved the phrase as if by a lightning bolt upon granite. "Books and covers, Golden."

And then the soldiers hauled him away.

True to precedent, the news traveled through every household in Abaco before supper the next day: at sunrise tomorrow, the Moonstormer and his conspirator would be executed by firing squad and then tossed to a watery grave among the coral, and eventually the sharks, in the Providence Channel.

The declaration was delivered to the Gaverly villa by a passing group of children. The youngsters laughingly proclaimed the event as if it were Carnival—a few even were dressed up and dancing. Golden squeezed her arms around herself as she leaned against the porch rail and watched the bright-costumed group go by. Her soul crumbled more with each youthful cry.

What the anguish didn't tear apart, a deep shame did, for she admitted it could have been herself she was watching. A mindless child, believing whatever the adults told her, growing up with blinders of superstition and hatred around her and never questioning why . . . until a courageous and patient sea captain gave her the astonishing knowledge that she had the ability to think otherwise. The ability to open her mind to a thing called trust.

Trust?

The bitter rebuttal screamed its way from deep inside her. *Trust in what? A fraud? A charlatan who passed himself off as a human being? You relied on someone who never existed, Golden. What does that make your "trust" now?*

But it was another voice that fought through the barrier of her memory to answer that question. A voice like gentle thunder, backed by an orchestra playing a new dance called the waltz . . . *"Books and covers, Golden. They're never what they appear, even when the title seems crystal clear. Promise me you'll remember that . . . promise me you'll believe . . ."*

The first presence inside her burst into jeering laughter. *Believe! In what?* In the silence a pair of grim-lined lips had thrown in her face after she'd pleaded for one word—one word!—of self-defense to the soldiers' accusations? In the incriminating sorrow brimming from storm-dark eyes as shackles were clamped and final charges issued? *Belief. Ha!*

Golden's hands clenched where they were wrapped against her ribs. *"Bastard,"* she rasped.

There. She'd finally said it. But the curse didn't feel as wonderful as she'd hoped. And it didn't relieve the torturous pressure still surging through her body, rising to a hot assault of tears as it mingled with the pounding ache behind her eyes.

"Why?" she choked into the merciless silence the children left behind. "You obstinant, prideful ass, *why?*"

She kicked angrily at the rail. Then again. The boards didn't even fray. True to the standard set by the midnight-eyed fraud they stood proxy for, their reply was nothing short of hard and unyielding silence.

The tears came harder. Golden began to punch at the boards with her fists. She struck again and again, faster and faster. The agony and confusion were pummeling in equal speed at her heart.

"Bastard!" Oh aye, it felt better this time, now propelled off her lips by a wrenching confusion she could no more control than understand. "You bastard! You told me you loved me. And I believed you. God help me, I still do! But . . . why? Why, damn you?"

But her only answer was that night-smooth voice in the forefront of her mind again, unbearably calm, self-sure. *"Situations and conclusions. Oh, hellion, don't you remember? One is rarely what the other accuses it of being . . ."*

"Stop it!" she hissed, slamming her hands to her ears. "I don't want to listen any more! I won't!"

". . . Even when your eyes tell you otherwise."

"Stop it! Stop it—stop it—stop it!"

The refrain wouldn't surrender. The words, now a haunting, echoing chorus, drove at her again and again until Golden ran from the veranda and down the hard dirt drive in desperate hope of escape.

Useless. The cacophony only grew louder as she neared the top of the hill the villa rested on. The ocean wind whipped over the rise and beat against her as its whirling music took up the cry, too. *"Never what they seem . . . titles just confuse . . . even when your eyes tell you otherwise . . ."*

She shook her head, moaning in protest, commanding her mind to release her from this torture. But the wind belayed every order, replacing her ultimatums with a petition of soft, soothing warmth, calling out to the deepest, most vulnerable part of her. The part of her that heeded essence, not substance . . . the core that heeded spirit, not mind . . . the heart that listened to love, not logic.

"Even when your mind tells you otherwise . . ."

"No," Golden gasped. "No . . ."

But despite how she struggled, her body and spirit began to still. She drew in a shuddering breath as she lifted her head. The wind lifted the tears from her cheeks with cool-fingered gentleness. The sky and sea filled her gaze with their brilliant blues and greens.

She slowly moved her hands to her face, where she peeled stray strands of hair from her eyes. Then her arms fell in surrender to her sides.

"This is insanity," she whispered, fighting back the strange, feather-light feeling beginning to suffuse her from the toes up. "Insanity." Even the damp dirt of the drive felt remote beneath her bare feet as she backed away from the rise.

"Golden Gaverly, you've really gone barmy this time. Voices from nowhere, spouting inane rubbish . . . 'though your eyes may tell you otherwise.' My eyes are fine, blast it."

She felt the unconvincing tremor of her voice down the length of her body. Golden spun on her heel and hurried toward the house. "Silly," she admonished at herself. "Rubbish. Books and covers. Promises and believing. Bosh!" She ignored the fact that her snort sounded more desperate than scoffing. " 'Tis more like—" she thought for half a moment, "trust without safety! Conviction without proof! Sheer stupidity!"

In other words, hellion, the quiet thunder countered from deep in her spirit, *a leap of faith.*

Golden halted in the middle of the drive.

"A leap of . . ." she whispered.

Faith.

Her skin began to tingle. Her blood began to pound.

"Dear God." She whirled around. "Mast . . ." Her eyes flew to the glittering blue strip of ocean just visible beyond the ledge she'd come from. "You weren't just spouting philosophy to me on that terrace, were you?"

The air answered with an unnatural stillness, as if nature itself saw the spectacular explosion of her thoughts and was standing back for the view. Golden's muscles eagerly joined the audience; she found herself unable to do anything but breathe as the scenes of last night whirled through her head, illuminated in an amazing and unbelievable new light . . .

She relived the solemn expression upon Mast's face as he danced with her under the moon and stars. Again felt the bafflement she'd endured trying to determine what that mysterious missing "something" was in his tight-set features. Then the tension which had practically been a physical presence between them . . . and the outright fear in his eyes as they'd made love in the garden. As if, in the words she recalled from his very lips, they were joining "for the very last time."

As if he were already imploring her to take a leap of faith.

To believe with every fiber of her being . . .

Golden began to laugh. And cry. Such an immense weight lifted from her heart that she swore she'd be able to fly any moment. "You crazy, damn fool scoundrel!" she joyously cried. "Mast Iverson, I love you!"

A footfall on the veranda turned her head back up the drive.

"Golden?" Maya stopped at the top of the stairs leading down to the drive. Her head tilted hesitantly. "What dee stars you ravin' aboot? You all right?"

"Oh Maya," she threw her head back and laughed louder, "I'm wonderful!"

Maya's eyes, fatigue-ringed from her own sleepless pacings after last night's drama, darkened beneath her suddenly lowered brows. "I'm going to get your Papa."

"Papa's not here. Which is just as well," she excitedly rambled as she ran back to join her sister, "because we're leaving, too."

"Golll-denn . . ." The alarmed voice trailed behind her as she rushed into the sitting room to grab the cloaks they'd thrown there last night. "Golden, I don't think dat's a good idea. Not at all—"

"Hurry into your wrap," she ordered. "There's no room to argue now. We've got a lot to do and not much time to do it."

"Do what?"

"Save the wrong men from being executed."

"What?"

"Stop staring and move! Please! There's so little time left."

"Wh-where are we going?"

Golden smiled. "To get help, of course."

The cocoa eyes widened. "Yoo're not goin' to the army—"

Now Golden laughed. "Oh, no, sister! We're going to the *Athena!*"

* * *

Wayland's features were as cold and harsh as the bars which Mast looked up at him through. A cockroach made its way up the steel pole to the left of his friend's face. It was the same bug which had just completed a thorough tour of the dank and smelly cell the soldiers had thrown him into last night. He supposed it was on its multi-legged way to Dinky's confinement a few spaces away. His first mate's earth-shaking snores undoubtedly offered a more interesting allure than the silence Mast had passed the morning in.

He didn't rise from his mud-encrusted pallet. He merely leaned his head back against the damp wall and concentrated on keeping his eyes open despite the sleep-deprived ache of his head. At least the goal distracted him from the shackle grooves in his wrists and ankles, and the assorted cuts and bruises tormenting the rest of his body.

But overcoming the agony of his body was a fraction of the effort required to battle the ache in his heart. "How is she?" he finally gathered the courage to softly ask of Wayland.

There was a long silence from the opposite side of the bars before the equally quiet reply. "Distant. Exhausted. Confused."

Mast's brows crunched in a silent wince. "Where is she?"

"At the villa."

"Alone?"

"Maya's with her."

He nodded again. "Good. She's not likely to go off on some half-cocked adventure now."

"She wasn't before. You broke her heart, lad. She can barely move."

Mast looked away. Silence weighed the air again, growing in malignancy like a gathering storm cloud.

Finally the low question came from over his head: "Well, then. Are you ready to die, Captain Iverson?"

Slowly, steadily, Mast turned his eyes back up to Wayland's taut, almost angry face. And he smiled.

Twenty-four

Golden allowed herself to breathe easily again as she and Maya scurried up the last few feet of the gangway and into the early night shadows along the *Athena*'s decks.

"We made it!" she exclaimed softly.

"I don't believe it," Maya retorted, bracing herself against a fife rail to stop and rub her foot.

Golden flashed her sister a scowl. "We couldn't take a chance on the main road and you know it. There were soldiers all over the place; any one of them could be the Moonstormer."

"And none of them could be."

"No!" she returned Maya's irritated tone in equal measure. "No, sister. They arrested the wrong men, and they did it for a reason: to take the punishment for the real criminals. Can you tell me, who but the army has enough power to do such a thing?"

Maya dropped her foot, but even in the dim light, Golden could perceive the skeptical expression of the Arawak features. She whirled on her sister, stepping into Mast's spread-footed pose without even thinking. "Masterson Blake Iverson and James O'Dinkham did not commit those crimes," she declared with all the determination swelling through her soul. "And I'm going to prove it, whether the rest of the world believes me or not."

Not awaiting nor wanting to hear an answer, she turned and started across the main deck.

Golden tried not to notice how eerie her footsteps sounded in the strange stillness encompassing the ship. Even the dock was abnormally empty—nobody wanted to gawk at the famous *Athena* any more. Well, all the better for her and the men to mobilize, she heartened herself. They had less than twenty-four hours to track the real Moonstormer.

Less than twenty-four hours left of Mast's life if they didn't.

So much for her vow not to be daunted. Golden sprinted across the deck with the fresh surge of panic that gripped her. "Rico?" she called urgently into the shadows. "Ramses? Where are all of you?"

She headed to the forecastle, straining her ears for any familiar voice or laugh, even a snatch of harmonica or flute music . . . Only the soft creak of the floorboards answered her from the dark space with the empty bunks. The gunnery deck and main hold yielded the same return.

"Is anyone here?" Golden called as she emerged back onto the main deck. "Hello! It's me, the hellion!"

Ropes and canvas obeyed the wind to clap out her only answer.

She looked to Maya. Her sister shrugged her shoulders. Golden whirled and started to move aft, refusing to surrender to the frustration and defeat that taunted her. She wasn't going to give up. She wasn't!

Her mission was cut short by a spill of bright lantern light over the deck ahead. Golden's throat caught for a second, but she expelled her breath in a smiling sigh of relief as she identified the stoop-shouldered figure emerging from the galley.

"Ben," she cried. "Oh Ben, I'm so happy to see you."

Ben's head snapped up with an alertness denying his wizened appearance. His owl eyes and thin lips formed three circles of surprise. "Milady—"

Golden stepped forward and hugged the lovable coot who had become such a good friend to her the last weeks. "At least *someone* stayed aboard," she said to him with more than a little frustration. "I should have known it would be you."

"Milady, what be ye doin' here?"

"And where *is* everyone else?"

Ben skirted his eyes from her to the dock. "At the tavern in town. I—I told 'em to go," he hastily added. " 'Tis been a tryin' turn o' events. The lads needed somethin' to think about other than when the ship'll be burned—"

"Burned!" Golden pushed aside her curiosity at Ben's abnormally rapid chatter to absorb the impact of his last word.

"One way or another, aye. If not the army, then likely the townfolk." Ben's head swiveled around again, as if the first lethal flames might have sparked somewhere in the darkness already. "So I suppose ye can see why this not be such a good place fer ye anymore." He gently grasped her elbow "Why don't ye ladies try to put this mess behind ye fer good? Join the others at the tavern, try to forget—"

"No." Golden grabbed Ben's hands and locked her feet to the deck in emphasis. "Ben, you don't understand. That's what I came here for. Believe me, my friend, this crisis is all but forgotten—but I'm going to need your help to prove it. I'm going to need everyone's help."

"Milady . . ." the old man's voice wavered with puzzlement. "What the saints ye be sayin'?"

She pulled her chin up and set her shoulders. "Mast and

Dinky aren't going to be executed. We're not going to let them do it."

"We're *what?*"

"Think about it, Ben! Don't you think Mast and Dinky's arrest, not to mention their conviction, happened much too easily? As if it were all planned . . ." Her grasp moved to his shoulders. "Because it *was* all planned—I'm not even sure Mast didn't know that at the time, but—"

"What!"

"But that's not the point," she drove on. "The point is, the true Moonstormer is still free, wandering about on this very night, and we've got to find him!"

Ben stopped then. His shoulders sagged; his sigh blending much too well with the lonely creaks and snaps of the empty ship. "Ye truly believe this?"

"With every instinct in my body and every conviction in my heart."

The wind gave the rigging an extra gusty push; the deck angled strongly starboard, then moaned its way level again. Ben slowly turned. His stare locked with Golden's.

"Ye fell in love with him, didn't ye?"

Golden struggled for a moment with how to answer that, but knew the answer was already evident in every expression of her face. "Yes," she said. "But that has nothing to do with it. Ben—" She pressed her hands harder to his shoulders. "The point is, your captain, a decent and honorable man, is to be shot to death tomorrow morning if we don't do something about it."

"Oh, *milady,*" Ben began, and faltered. His eyes almost frantically scanned her face. "Milady, I—"

A loud thump caused both of them and Maya to jump in startlement. Golden's hands dropped from Ben's shoulders as her gaze was drawn to the portion of the deck she'd been avoiding tonight, for fear of the bittersweet memories evoked by just looking—toward the hatchway of Mast's quarters.

Her heart seized completely as the door pushed open into the night—and a figure emerged from the cabin.

The face was an indiscernible silhouette against the backdrop of shimmering lantern light, but the man's shoulders, broad and straight, held the unmistakable mien of pride. And the towering masculine height . . .

"Mast?" she gasped in hope and disbelief, shakily stepping forward.

The figure turned and raised the lamp.

Golden choked and froze.

He wasn't Mast.

Dear God, he wasn't Mast.

"My Lady Golden," came the surprisingly refined greeting from El Culebra's placid lips. "At long last we have the *deleite* of meeting again. Ahhh Ben, you were so right, my friend. She is quite lovely when she's not covered in either grime or cosmetics."

"W-what's happening?" she stammered. "H-how did you . . . ?"

"Oh, dear," the Spaniard muttered. "Of course, what happened to my manners? Allow me the pleasure of introducing myself, my lady. I am Carlos Rudolfo José Nánchez, at your service. Or perhaps you'd prefer to address me by my other titles. Ben tells me you are well acquainted with El Culebra already . . .

"Or maybe the *Moonstormer* would be more suited to your taste?"

Golden cried out in pain and stumbled backward. "No. I don't understand—how could you know—"

Her gaze flew to old Ben with sudden and horrifying

comprehension. "Milady," he muttered fearfully, shaking his head at her. "Milady Golden, I'm so sorry."

She remembered whirling then, flailing her arms against the wrenching truth—*Mast betrayed by one of his own!*—and then running, everywhere and anywhere away from this Judas she had once called a friend—and the beast he was in league with.

But furious, iron-gripped hands yanked her to the deck. Maya screamed somewhere behind her. Then all sight and sound were bludgeoned to a halt by the blow at the back of Golden's skull.

Firelight danced before her half-open eyes. For a moment Golden stared in numb fascination at the mesmerizing flashes of orange and red, gold and black; then a knife of pain cut its way through her head, and the flames became the inferno of Hell.

Otherwise, she realized, consciousness.

A moan clamored for freedom from her throat, but instinct ordered her to gulp it back, an overriding sense of danger, of vulnerability, permeating her.

Where was she? Her sense of smell told her mist and moss. Touch told her wet and cold. Sound told her echoes of nearby waves. A cave.

How had she gotten here? And why? What had happened? Images crisscrossed through her mind. Torchlight was playing along hedges in a garden . . . the smirks of jeering soldiers, melting into the faces of laughing children dancing in the sunlight. Then darker scenes of a ship at twilight . . . another boat, smaller, being lowered into night shadows . . . oars slashing through midnight waters . . . midnight blue . . . deep blue eyes, loving her even as they were dragged away to a prison cell . . . *Mast! Oh Mast, they're going to kill you! No! God, oh God, no!*

Her restraint shattered beneath the weight of agony. A cry erupted from her lips; her body lurched frantically, yearning to bash everything in its way.

Her limbs met painful resistance. Not shackles, Golden discerned. This confinement entrapped her limbs tighter. Enraged her spirit more.

She dragged the leaden ball of her head upright as she forced the aching weights of her eyes open. She looked down to see thick seaman's ropes lashing her arms against her torso, and again around either of her ankles. The ends of the ties were secured around a heavy boulder for each leg. Next to her feet she recognized the top of Maya's head, disturbingly immobile, layered with the same damp dirt which covered her.

She swallowed deeply.

"Ah, the sea siren awakens at last."

The greeting was as calmly issued as a salutation at a garden party. And the voice sent a broadsword of dread down Golden's spine. She sent a slow, intense glare across the fire—into the cold, dark eyes of Carlos Rudolfo José Nánchez.

The Spaniard's lips curled in an expression that could, if a body was demented enough to see it that way, be called a smile. Tapered black eyebrows arched against the smooth dark brown skin of his forehead. A subtle laugh accented the nod he gave her.

"Buenos días," he said in a nauseatingly pleasant voice.

"You," she finally summoned enough composure to state.

Nánchez only leered a little wider.

"All this time." Golden swallowed again. "All these years."

He nodded at her. Serenely. *Proudly.* "All this time," he repeated to her. "All these years."

"You've masqueraded as both El Culebra and the Moonstormer."

"No, *amada,*" he gently reproved, "I *am* both El Culebra and the Moonstormer."

The nausea swelled to unbearable severity. Golden shook with the effort required to battle the wrenching sickness down. "You—you and Ben plotted against Mast—"

"Ben has nothing to do with this anymore!"

His exclamation rang with a frightening harshness. Nánchez jumped to his feet with a jerking agility and ordering, "If you are bestowing acclaim for my work, it goes to me. All of it."

Finality, Golden thought. The Spaniard's words echoed with such finality, causing the snakes of sick dread to coil tighter in her stomach. "Wh-what did you do with—" she stammered, but found her answer quickly enough in the sight of Ben's gaping-eyed, blood-stained body crumpled against the far wall of the cave.

"Dear God." Her sob haunted her from the dense silence that followed. Even more intimidating, Nánchez rose and paced as if she hadn't seen or said anything at all. Then gradually his lips widened into another smile. He broke into a small chuckle. Another. He burst into a full laugh. And another. The evil mirth filled the air, echoing through deeper caverns just as the taunting beast seemed physically to dominate the cave. His shadow was bouncing larger than life, on the surrounding rock walls.

"Stop it!" Golden screamed. "You're insane!"

Astoundingly, Nánchez did just that. His mouth pressed shut as his glare silently swept down upon her.

"Insane?" His slow snarl made Golden yearn for the

gloating laughter again. "Insane?" he repeated with a snort of incredulity. "Oh, my dear lady, who is the insane, the pied piper, or the vermin that follow him? Don't you know it's jungle brats like you that made me into the legend I am today? Oh *sí*, all of you, with your island ways and your stubborn native pride. I merely milked you fools for what all your blind superstition was worth. I *am* brilliant, am I not? Brilliant! Yes, yes, brilliant!"

Golden thought she was going to throw up into the rapid-breathing, glaze-eyed stare lunging closer toward her. Sparks from the fire popped in the air between them. Horror and shock exploded through her mind and soul. She thought of the hell she'd put Mast through—all the suspicions and doubts and the glares of half belief—even the night she'd tried to kill him in his own cabin with his own bedding. Oh, how could she have ever mistaken the unassuming courage and gentle patience she'd known with him for the raw evil she beheld now?

She drew a shuddering breath. The revulsion encompassing her made the rope bonds feel like gossamer strands. But no matter how vehemently she yearned to squeeze her eyes shut against the image of madness before her, a more commanding force kept her gaze affixed to Carlos Nánchez—kept her head screaming with the question she couldn't stomach to ask, couldn't bear to hear the answer to . . . but couldn't suppress from her lips any longer.

"Why?" she blurted. "Dear God, why?"

The Spaniard's smile dropped. "Why, indeed," he replied to her from tight lips and teeth.

She forced her gaze to continue on him as he crouched low to the fire again. The flames were far from becoming dying embers, but Nánchez took a stick and shoved at the logs, anyway. His arm jerked more violently with each crack and pop he set free, as if the escalating blaze were a manifestation of his thoughts. Golden squirmed as the sparks flew closer and closer, some trailing cometlike flames—as if the Moonstormer's merciless wrath were flaming hotter toward her, too.

"The first time I boarded the *Athena* was Mast's first time, too," he suddenly stated. Golden's eyes widened as she felt an eerie surprise along with her onslaught of apprehensions. Nánchez smiled smoothly at that before continuing. "We looked at each other and laughed—it was a bit like peering in the mirror, you see. We were both very arrogant, and very young. We both wanted it all. So, we both worked very, very hard."

His smile contorted into that angry twist of lips again. Golden watched Nánchez's hands tremble and curl into fists. "But who do you think always got all the praise? All the promotions? All the honors?"

A bitter snort and a Spanish oath blended with the curls of acrid smoke from the fire. "Our bastard of a captain even assigned us to a duty together, so I could learn from Mast. Do you imagine that? *Me* learn from *him?* All that concerned our good and fine Mast was doing it the right way. *Basura!* To hell with his right way! I'll do it my way or no way at all!"

At that he jerked up again and started to pace the cave. Nánchez's head swiveled nervously. His eyes darted into the mad-leaping shadows, the dark holes and corners. "Well, Captain Thompson didn't like that. Not at all. Carlos's independent thinking wasn't appreciated at all by good Captain Thompson. From the start, it was always, 'Mast, the Magnificent,' or, 'Mast, Wayland Gaverly's miracle man.' Soon it was, 'Mast, the boatswain,' and, 'Mast, the first officer.' " A loud pop from the fire marked a weighted moment of silence. "Well, little *amada,* you know what came next, don't you?" He emitted a guttural growl of anguish. "Mast, the new captain of the *Athena,* that's what."

Clay clumps flew from Nánchez's suddenly-halting boots. "Mast, the *gringo* glory-robber. Mast, the bastard who ruined my life."

"But—but you became a captain, as well," Golden interjected, taking heart-stopping care to forget that his commission was purely in the pirates' navy. "You lead a hundred men on one of the fastest frigates in the main—"

"But not the *Athena!*" The Spaniard whirled on her. *"Dios,* don't you understand, either? It was never good enough! None of it, not after the *Athena.* Not after the humiliation I suffered. Not after the shame. I had to prove them all wrong; all of them! No, no. No other compensation would be enough."

"So you left when Mast became captain," she supplied, "with the intent to plot against him." She didn't bother to hide the accusation in her tone any more. Her strange aspiration to understand this lunatic now crystalized as the hopeless cause it was. "You committed larceny and murder and planned to let your friend take the punishment all along. Created your beast, the Moonstormer, in his image—"

Nánchez's almost sensuous outbreak of laughter cut her off. "Oh, *amada,* that was the sweet beauty of it," he drawled. *"I* created not a thing. Your *amor precioso* Mast did it all for me!"

Golden snapped a burning glare at him. It only seemed to make the pirate happier. Indignant fury writhed up her spine and even into the locked teeth beneath her raised chin.

"What are you talking about?" she demanded.

"Hmmmm. Have your attention now, do I?"

"Stop it!" she yelled. "Just stop it! What the hell are you saying!"

Nánchez didn't laugh any more, but the Spaniard's self-pleased leer was just as intimidating. "What I am saying, my dear Lady Golden, is that your strong and mighty Mast isn't who you think he is."

She grappled to rise to her knees then. "You . . . bastard," Golden seethed. "How dare you imply Mast had any part of your madness!"

"But I insist, my lady, he did. He still *does*. Truth be known, I have him to thank for my—well, quite spectacular career, if I might be so bold to say. You see, Ben was helpful, in his own little way—*sí*. I would say the gambling debts he owed me were a wise investment in exchange for his helpful journeys into his captain's files regarding shipments, cargoes, and the like. But my true allies were Mast and Dinky themselves. If they hadn't said yes to King George all those years ago and created the Moonstormer to begin with, my vengeance wouldn't have been half the pleasure—"

"Wait! Stop!" Golden's mind finally found its way to her voice through the stormburst of astonishment inside her. "King George? I . . . I don't understand. Mast said yes to what? Created the Moonstormer himself?"

But Nánchez only chuckled lowly as he sauntered around the fire toward her, the obsessive sheen to his eyes shining brighter and the corners of his lips twitching erratically. "Oh, my little *fuego de pasión*," he crooned, "it matters not now. It does not matter at all." He stooped to her, lifting the back of his fingers to her cheek, and lightly rubbing. "You see, *you* are my helper now. *You* are the grand finale of my plan. Imagine that! Nobody else can say they were able to help the Moonstormer but *you* . . ."

All of Golden's most finely honed instincts were never tested more intensely than in this moment. Every beat of her heart screamed in repugnance, hatred, and an urge to strike out despite her bindings. But every muscle in her body dictated another command, an order to remain absolutely still. After weighing the circumstances of her predicament, she willed herself to listen to the latter directive. She ordered herself to stay calm, no matter how impossible the feat seemed.

"H-help you?" she barely managed to stammer.

"Oh, *si* . . . in the most wonderful way possible."

Nánchez's voice was even more nebulous and quavering than hers, causing Golden to suppose, for a shining, hopeful moment, this was all just a weird and awful dream. An atrocious trick her own subconscious was playing on her . . .

"Imagine this, *amada*," the low voice continued through the haze, "Imagine the glory of knowing, without a doubt, the person you hate most on this earth is finally dead. Ahhh, *si*, I know you have had such fantasies before. I can see it in your beautiful eyes now. Then how about . . ." he sidled in closer to her, on both knees now. His hand was moving to roughly knead her neck. "How about following it with the death of the one woman that bastard loved? How about watching all her dreams, her hopes, the seed she could be carrying in her belly . . . all be destroyed, too? How about that!"

Oh God, let this truly be a dream, and oh God, let me wake up now.

"Does it not sound *maravilloso?* Oh, love, would you not like to die for me today?"

Golden didn't say a single word.

She jumped up and ran for everything she was worth with no arm motion to propel her and two boulders tied to her ankles.

But she'd clunked only five or six steps when the gloating laughter engulfed her again, surrounding her from behind. Then the arms came like a ravenous boa constrictor—whirling her back toward the wild-dancing fire—squeezing all the air from her as she lunged away, then back again at the flames and the exploding sparks.

She screamed. Screamed and squirmed, even tried to kick and bite, but the arms—no longer human limbs, but the talons of a monster she knew only as enemy—grabbed her tighter and hoisted her off the ground, boulders and all. Golden threw her head back as she shrieked and struggled harder.

She was conscious that they passed Maya and the fire ring. They had started to traverse a wet tunnel. The sound of the surf grew louder. A blue-grey light cast a ghastly glow to the rocks and puddled mud floor.

The light was the breaking sheen of dawn. The surf, crashing against the steep rocks of the cove below them, was directly opposite the deserted Abaco dock and the strangely remote-looking *Athena* tethered there.

"Mast," she exclaimed toward the magnificent brigantine. "Oh, Mast."

"Shut up," the beast growled at her ear. "I've had enough of you, *bruja.*"

"Mast," she repeated with even more horrifying realization. "Oh stars, the sun's coming up! Mast!"

"I said shut up!"

"No! Don't kill him!" she cried out toward the people she could now see emerging from their homes, some carrying picnic baskets—picnic baskets!—as they hurried, so as not to miss the day's grand event. It seemed no matter that the execution would be private. The crowds merely jostled for the best "listening spots" along the yard's looming walls. She faintly heard hawkers shouting prices for the very best seats—those positions along the wall Mast would fall against.

"Nooo!" she shrieked again. "You've got the wrong man! Oh God, please! Up here! Listen to me! Help me!"

Something wet and dirty-tasting was shoved into her mouth, then bound there by a strip of cloth the beast tore from Golden's own skirt. But the true atrocity was having her head pinned as the monster secured bonds around her skull. They forced her to gaze at the calmly leering brown face—to endure the callous laughter slithering from between the smoothly curled lips.

"You stay just like that, my *amada precioso*," the monster gently grated. "I just can't wait to see your face when—"

A barrage of gunfire reverberated through the hills and across the bay.

Every muscle and nerve in Golden's body stiffened in horror.

Another crackling round echoed the first.

She didn't care that the cloth in her mouth reduced her scream to a pathetic mewl. The cry surged from the most complete and agonizing pain she'd ever known. Backed by the Moonstormer's howling cackles, the torment sliced through her sharper and harder and deeper until it was too much—*too much* . . .

She became numb, and sank into black, blissful nothingness.

Oh Mast, her subconscious sobbed before the final curtain of darkness fell, *I'll be joining you soon, my love.*

Twenty-five

"Golll-den!"

She rolled over, deeply perturbed. She was having a lovely dream. There was a waterfall, sparkling and clean, and her own smooth and sinewy god was emerging from the white foam at the bottom of it. He held out a hand to her and murmured, "Come here, hellion . . ."

"Golll-den," Maya's voice continued to prod. Her urgency lifted the tone. "Golden, wake up!" But Golden honed one ear to all the familiar sounds of home—the laughing water of the rain-forest stream, the whisper of the Saint Kitts wind, the snapping of the village fire. Everything was normal. The world was right.

"Mmmmph." She burrowed into a deeper ball.

"Golden, please—"

"Wake up, *bruja.*"

The hand cracking across her face coincided with the gruff command that replaced Maya's pleas. Golden's eyes flew open. Memory returned in a harsh rush. The rushing water was not the rain-forest stream, but the ocean against nearby rocks. The fire illuminated jagged cave walls, not a canopy of trees and vines. The wind didn't waft with the tang of Saint Kitts poinciana, but blew with the stench of rotting, stale things.

Dead things.

Mast! her heart cried.

No, a grieving voice inside her sobbed, the world was *not* right. It would never be right again.

"Up here, *amada,*" the low voice directed again. "Look up here at me." Iron-hard fingers curled beneath her chin and forced her obeyance before she could even think about defiance.

She gasped into her gag at the sight that filled her eyes. Not one deranged face leered down at her now, but two. Above her and next to Carlos Nánchez was a scraggle-haired, grubby-bearded mess of a scoundrel. He flashed a lascivious wink at her from his eye that wasn't covered with a tattered black patch.

"Well, my *amigo,* did I not tell you right?"

"Oh, ye told me right, all right!" The scoundrel's voice was the manifestation of his gritty, grimy, lewd appearance. "She's very perty. Aye, a comely wench, indeed . . ."

"You'd like to kill her while I watch, then?"

"Oh, aye! I'd like that very much!"

Maya wailed sharply somewhere behind Golden, but only Nánchez rose and went to her. "Mind yourself, wench, or I'll silence you, too!" Golden heard him snarl.

The new face stayed and continued its disconcerting stare at her. The wretch cocked his eye first one way and then the next in a thorough perusal of her features, even lifting a gentle thumb to the welt on her cheek and wincing when she flinched in pain. "I'm sorry," came the soft apology. "So sorry. I don't mean to hurt you, dearie. I just want you to trust me, all right? Trust me. I'll make it all better; you'll see. It'll be all over in a while. Trust me."

It was like a lullaby, the litany of soothing words washing over her . . . the perfect entrance into death, Golden thought wistfully. Aye, she could just give up, go to sleep, and she'd open her eyes and be with Mast again . . .

So why were her lungs heaving with the rapid breaths of terror, her arms sawing at her sides to slide free of the ropes, her feet churning into the dirt to push free of the weird pirate who wouldn't stop staring at her, or touching her?

The revelation beamed into her consciousness like the sun bursting through dark grey clouds. *Because I want to live!* it sang joyously.

Yes, she realized, she needed to live—for the very man she'd yearned to die for. For the man who'd crashed through the nightmare of her doubt and superstition, and given her trust and security instead. For Captain Mast Iverson, who'd taken her hate and turned it into love . . . who'd given her the greatest weapon of all to defy the Moonstormer with: her own life, lived in freedom from the hate that had given Carlos Nánchez his power to begin with.

Her life! Yes, she'd fight to have it now, but not as a weapon. As a gift, to the man who'd given it back to her. A gift to Mast.

Golden almost thought it was her exhausted imagination . . . but she felt a presence embrace her then. A strong, spicy-scented presence, as near to her as the quietly crooning pirate with his one leering eye. A mighty, unmistakable force . . . no, this couldn't be the work of her mind!

As if a physical force had climbed inside her and knew how to move her body in just the right degrees against the ropes, the heavy hemp binding her right arm began to slip, then fall. Golden bit back the gasp of elation at her lips. A few more squirms . . . if Nánchez would only stay occupied with Maya a moment longer . . .

Sucking in her breath and ignoring the rope burns of the last hard yank, Golden pulled her right arm free.

Pure instinct took over. Her first thought was to secure the nearest weapon—the dagger tucked at the dark-haired scoundrel's side. Before he could overcome his shock enough to challenge her assault, she snapped her knee up into the space between his thighs.

"Aaarrgh!"

That brought Nánchez whirling around. "What?"

"Aaarrgh! I—can't—move!"

The luxury of a few tiny seconds was all she had. That sole thought dominated Golden's mind as she raced to sever the remainder of her bonds.

But she'd barely freed her ankles and her other arm when Nánchez broadsided her. They went tumbling to the ground close to the fire. Maya's shrieks pealed through her ears as she rolled several times over with the savage-cursing Spaniard. The air was crushed from her chest each time she landed on the bottom. When she was on top, hunger-induced dizziness attacked. The heat of the fire menaced closer and closer.

With a sudden and vicious shout, Nánchez halted their gyrations by straddling her. His thighs clamped her legs to the ground. His hands locked around her wrists and slammed them to the ground on either side of her head. Golden only gripped the dagger harder; clutching it with every ounce of strength she had. Every muscle in her arm strained to its limit. The veins in her wrist felt about to burst with the pressure.

"Now, my lady," came the vicious rasp from the scowling face looming over her, "why don't you be a good little *niña*—" Nánchez grabbed her throbbing wrist and pounded it down again, "and give up?"

Golden replied with a low, feral snarl through the cloths still binding her mouth.

Nánchez cursed and ground her arm into the pebble-strewn dirt. Curiously, Golden barely felt any pain from the ordeal. She flashed a glare of radiant heat that seemed to blaze into her from nowhere. A defiant and victorious fire. As if an angel had touched her . . .

I love you, Mast, she jubilantly thought.

Until Nánchez began to laugh.

It was a low and soft and strange sound, an ominous growl even when laced with undertones of mirth. Like a cup of pineapple juice laced with poison.

Just like the laugh that had echoed through her nightmares since she was eight years old.

The snarl withered in Golden's throat. She closed her eyes, fighting the sound, but the laughter rumbled deeper around her, cutting off her breath, tossing aside the angel's touch, gusting at the boldness inside her until the defiant flame flickered, sputtered . . . died.

"Oh, little *bruja*," the chuckling monster said. "You must know, I'm secretly smitten with your feist and fire. Truly, I am! Especially when I lingered at Braziliano's auction just long enough to see Mast enter and look at you. 'Ah, *Dios*,' I said to myself, 'the wench who has finally put a fire in Mast's groin again.' And when Ben told me what he'd heard between Mast and Dinky one morning on the *Athena,* that you were a survivor of the *Gabrielle's Hope*—oh, little Golden, you cannot know my ecstasy, my delight at envisioning this moment!"

Gabrielle's Hope . . . Gabrielle's Hope . . . The words emblazoned themselves across Golden's mind as the face above her slithered into a wide grin. "Nuh!" she heard herself plea through the gag. "Nnnnuh!" She started to toss her head, resisting the horror and the fear . . . the sting of the remembered splinters cutting into her hands as she grasped a ravaged piece of driftwood painted with the words *Gabrielle's Hope* . . .

Mast . . . wherever you are . . . help me.

But the pirate beast above continued mercilessly on. "That was my very first victory, you know. I was extremely proud of it. I remember how obsessed I was about 'doing it right,' as my *amigo* Mast would say—about burning it all, you see. And I thought I did—" His grin deepened. "But you—you lovely little vixen, you proved me wrong, didn't you? Showed those idiots aboard that tub just how it was done. Watched them go screaming to their death while you escaped without a trace. Brilliant. Brilliant!"

Until that moment, Golden didn't realize how much pain a person could withstand and still live. Images collided one after another before her eyes. The leering face above her melded with impressions of burning bodies falling through the air like flame-tailed comets, the silhouette of a ruined ship sinking against a smoke-hazed moon . . . and then an even more petrifying vision, a nightmare she'd never had to endure before—the image of Mast's blindfolded face, plummeting to the ground. His body, lifeless and twisted. His clothes, riddled with bullet holes and oozing deep crimson blood . . .

Gone, something inside her declared with cruel clarity. The light beyond the cave entrance told her morning had become afternoon many hours ago, but the dawn of realization only now fully blazed upon her. *Bastard, bastard . . .* He was gone! He'd made her believe she'd never have to go through this mind-ripping, soul-slashing loss again, but now he was gone, and the misery twisted her until there was nothing left but lost, helpless grief. Golden had no more will left to fight the tide.

She felt the gates of her heart rip off their hinges as the

anguish laid full siege to her. Felt the familiar fury enter her bloodstream, her muscles, her bones. Felt her limbs obey the primal call, lashing out in an unthinking flurry of kicks and writhings. Even as she slammed against the resistance of the monster who bound her, Golden thrashed again and again, yearning only to release the seething monster inside of *her,* needing only to appease this blinding, exploding frenzy of grief.

"Ahhh, that's it," came the evil laughter again. *"Sí,* my little witch, I knew there was some fight left in you. Oh! That's a lovely move you have in that right knee, *amada.* So perfect in the middle of my back, too—I might even get a welt. But it will be worth it." The grip around her wrists constricted tighter. "Oh, yes, well worth it." The laughter dropped to a gloating growl. *"Caramba,* I can't wait to see you die. First Mast, and now his sea-witch whore. My dreams have finally come true. At last, come true."

Many times in her life Golden had looked to the sky at rolling storm clouds, wondering what kind of downpour could so possibly be worth holding such awesome fury in check until the moment was right. Now she no longer pondered that mystery. Her body shook with the effort of channeling every drop of strength along her right arm, into her wrist, which shuddered like an antagonized cobra as it coiled back and up, the dagger a poised fang. Then, in a rush of adrenalin, she made the strike. The blade sliced fast and hard into the beast's forearm.

Just as swiftly, Golden jerked the dagger back and scrambled free. She struggled to stand as a fierce howl of pain echoed through the cavern.

"Golll-den!" Maya's cry broke into the curses that followed. "Dee other pirate—ayyee, behind you!"

Golden whirled, but dizziness caused her to overcompensate her balance. The stranger pirate's face wobbled before her eyes. She was so disoriented that she even thought, for one disconcerting moment, that true concern burned from the wretch's exposed eye.

She planted her feet and boldly brandished the dagger at the wretch. A drop of blood wobbled for a second on the tip of the blade before splattering into the dirt. Golden commanded away the surge of bile in her throat.

"Back," she hissed. "You already know I'll use it."

"Now, little hellion, let's talk about this. Why don't ye put down the knife and—"

"Don't call me that!" Her voice caught and broke. "You have no right to call me that! Damn you, get back!"

"Fine. I promise I won't call ye that. Put the knife down, dearie."

"Put the knife down, *bruja!*"

She realized her mistake the instant she'd made it. Whether she admitted it or not, in a strange way she believed the gentle words of the grimy stranger, and didn't think twice about turning her back on him as she twirled to reassess Nánchez. She recognized that delusion quick enough and turned back—but the stranger was already waiting with a determined gleam in his eye.

"Trust me," he gritted at her in what she swore was an imploring tone, just before grabbing her arm. Unlike the bedraggled rest of him, his grip was like steel. But Golden didn't pause to contemplate that irony. She tossed the dagger to her other hand, which continued up toward the wretch's face. He saw the assault and dodged—quick enough to avoid the blade, but not the force of Golden's blow. For a stunned moment, Golden stared as his eyes rolled back and he crumpled to the ground.

It was all the moment Nánchez needed. "Well done, my

friend," he growled to his unconscious mate as he grabbed both Golden and the knife with a vicious jerk. She gasped as he slammed her back against his chest and his arm fastened around her middle. "You're going to pay now, *ramera,*" came the moist murmur at her ear. "Oh, you're going to pay."

Then there was only the laughter. The low and husky and sensual laughter, building with every breath, intensifying with each pass of the knife before her face, until that evil sound started to inundate and echo through her. He was invading her—slithering into the deepest reaches of her, refusing to stop until the Moonstormer found what he had stalked all these years: her heart. Her spirit.

Her soul.

"No!"

She cried out with the shriek of thousands of her nightmares. She burst into the fight which her subconsciousness knew by heart. "No! Get away! I won't let you! I won't—let—you!"

"I'm so sorry, *amada,*" came the hard-breathing growl at her ear, "But I don't think you have any say in the matter."

Firelight flashed off steel as a white-knuckled hand veered the dagger in at her. But the gleaming edge wasn't what Golden thrashed wildly back and forth against, wasn't the pain she feared beyond anything else. With all her might she combated the anguish and torment of the voices suddenly erupting around her . . .

"Golll-den! Great Puntan, have mercy and help her!"

Maya. My friend. My confidence. My sister.

"Golden? Oh, Golden. My little girl. My life."

Mummy! Oh Mummy, you're on fire! Don't die . . . don't die!

"Golden. Ah God, Golden!"

Mast.

"Oh, no," she cried out then, wrestling harder and faster. She couldn't listen to the pain cracking that once-invincible voice now. Worse, she couldn't bear the way it sounded as if Mast were across the *Athena*'s main deck from her again, yelling some ridiculous, overbearing, wonderful command at her. "No—no!" she yelled.

"Oh, yes, yes!" the voice at her ear hissed. "Just one more moment, love, and it will be over. Are you excited? *Sí?* Oh, me too. Me too!"

"Mast. Mast, I love you!"

"Mast is gone," he jeered. "Yes, finally, gone! And now, my love . . . so—are—you!"

But the rasping words were a blur in Golden's ears as her mind finally collapsed beneath the weight of emotion. Without their center of command, her nerves and muscles followed. Her entire body gave way, slumping to the side— just as the big hand in front of her swooshed the dagger down.

There was a strange, sickening moment of silence. The hand around her middle went unnaturally rigid, then completely limp. The laughter stilled. Now there was only a single deep-throated gurgle, followed by a ragged gasp, exhaled in a weak trickle of air.

Silence again.

Golden summoned the strength to turn her head.

Carlos Nánchez's lifeless eyes bulged at her. His nostrils were spread wide. His smooth-lipped mouth opened far enough to release a thin river of blood that rolled to join the flow from where the dagger lay buried in his throat. His hand was still wrapped, white-knuckled, around the weapon's hilt. The point of the blade jutted out the back of his neck.

Her chest seized. Her throat wrenched in a hoarse sob. Then the death stare began to fall toward her and she screamed. Wild bolts of strength shot through her again. She shoved free of the body. It fell at her feet.

The Moonstormer was dead.

Golden couldn't stop staring at the wild-eyed corpse. "I killed him." Her whisper was an icy wind on her lips—her swallow like a chunk of a glacier. "I killed him. Oh, Ghede, great god of death, forgive me—"

"Golden!" Maya's cry brought her out of her stupor too late. Golden looked up to see Nánchez's cohort, newly awakened, dazedly stumble his last two steps toward her. Before she could move he captured her elbow.

"Don't," he ordered to her renewed struggling. "Don't. It's all right. It's over. Ghede wanted that bastard for a long time."

Golden narrowed her eyes at him. The hoarse edges to his voice persisted—but where was the irritating, high-pitched tone? The one exposed eye maintained its unsettling fixation upon her, but why did that singular stare now glimmer, flickering with a deeper, more intense kind of light? Why did she feel as if she were being opened wide . . . stripped naked . . .

Her eyes exploded with comprehension. Golden flailed against the pirate with any remaining strength she could summon. "Get your filthy hands off me!"

The wretch muttered something in irritation. Snatches of ". . . God's sake, hellion . . . this is enough . . ." flew by her ears and consciousness. But Golden allowed the objections no room to stay and linger. She was too panicked by the other steel-gripped arm grabbing her corresponding wrist and pinning her back against the cave wall. Wiser from his groin's previous encounter with her knees, the pirate shoved both his thighs against hers, rendering them helpless, as well.

"I'll kill you," she seethed between locked teeth. "You know I'll do it. I swear to every god in the heavens, I'll kill you before your diseased stick of manhood crawls inside of me!"

The wretch didn't say anything. He just watched her writhe and swear and spit at him, and then smiled. A slow, sensuous smile, tilting up just one side of his mouth, lifting up just one dark and dirty eyebrow.

For one shock-filled moment, Golden went still.

The pirate bent his head and kissed her.

Terror returned her senses to her. She clamped her lips against his invasion and bucked against his body, now pressed completely upon hers. *I'll die first,* her soul screamed. *I'll die . . . I'll die!*

But to her mortification, the chant in her mind became a pulsing backbeat to the primal rhythm her mouth began responding to, dancing with the lips that seemed to know just how to coax and caress her. The mouth knew just where hers parted the easiest. The tongue knew just how to graze hers, just how to stroke, exactly which soft spots of her mouth produced the most exquisite shivers down her body—things she thought only Mast knew . . . only Mast had discovered.

Only Mast.

No, she thought wildly, disbelievingly . . . desperately. It couldn't be.

Only Mast.

It couldn't be true.

Only Mast.

She began to weep. The hands that shackled her now and slid around her. She wrapped her arms around the corded neck, ran her fingers down the familiar muscles of the powerfully graceful back, joyously clutched the straight and strong shoulders. Mast's shoulders. Mast's living shoulders, here beneath her hands!

Golden wept harder.

"It's all right, sweet," he murmured against her lips, her cheeks. "It's all right."

"It's you." She pushed the eye patch, and his hair, off his face, gaping at the features that now made perfect sense, excited the deepest realms of her heart. "Oh, God. Mast . . ."

"Yes. I'm here. And I'm never going to leave you again."

She pulled away and gazed at the astounding sight of him. For this one miraculous moment, it didn't matter what had happened, or how. He was here. He was alive. That was all.

Then she took a deep breath and slapped him. Just once. Very hard. "Bastard! Why did you leave to begin with? Stop laughing! Do you know what you put me through? Stop that, right now! I thought you were dead, damn you! Dead! Do you know what that did to—"

Mast retaliated in the only way he could—by kissing her again, deeply and thoroughly. "I'm sorry," he told her, in a voice that was mostly command. "No, I'm not going to repeat it. And no, I'm not ever, ever going to leave you again."

He lifted his hand to her cheek, underlining just how much he meant it with the ferocity of his stare. Ah, God, he thought, how wonderful—and surprising—love was. For so long he'd closed off feeling, living, because he was so damned afraid of being left alone. Now, in order to regain his life, he was promising not to leave. And he wouldn't. Not ever. He loved her. Oh, how he loved her. If he'd had to endure this ordeal a hundred more times over, the love and passion of this stubborn, fiery, impossible woman would be well worth it.

"Ayyee!" came a cry that brought both their heads up. "What under dee stars is going on?"

Golden gasped. "Maya. Oh Lord, I forgot Maya. She's still tied up—"

"And just where do you think you're going?" Mast wrapped himself tightly around her again and kissed her soundly. "Don't worry. I think Maya will be just fine."

He tilted back his shoulder to allow her to view Dinky rushing into the cave, whooping with joy as he beheld Maya squirming impatiently on the hard ground. The delirious man sliced her ropes free between the fervent kisses he showered on the native's face and lips.

Mast looked back to Golden. A smile inched across her dirt-smudged face as she watched the pair across the cave. His heart burned fiercely in response—just beneath where her hand lightly rested on his chest.

"What happened?" she softly asked him. "How in the world did you know I was here? And how did you—"

"Wait! Hold your sails, woman!" he laughingly protested. He brought her fingers to his lips. "I'll explain everything after I get you out of here."

Golden nodded. Mast noticed the waver of her chin and the flicker of fright still glimmering in her eyes. When she wobbled on her first step away from the cave wall, he took no more chances. He swept her up into his arms and carried her toward the daylight himself.

He happily noticed that for once she didn't fight him.

The scene he brought her out into couldn't have been more perfect if Mast had dictated the menu to God himself. Sea gulls swooped over the shimmering water. Its blue-green hue was surpassed only by the deep cyan sky. Lace-sheer clouds were draped luxuriously on the horizon. A gossamer-light breeze sprinkled the air with the enticing aromas of cascarilla, orange blossoms, and hibiscus. Brilliant diamonds of water twinkled in the air as the tide crashed against the rocks in the cove below them.

But nature's splendor refreshed his weary body and exhausted senses less than did Golden's face at his shoulder. The wind was lifting her hair from her face. The sunlight was sparkling in her eyes as Mast caught her gazing, still disbelievingly, at him. For a long time he stared back, not knowing if he remembered to breathe or feel anything . . . but Golden.

She slowly brought her fingers up to his face. "Sky in his eyes, wind in his hair . . ." she softly murmured, sliding both touch and gaze along his cheek, "catch the brightest starbeams, and you'll find him there."

Mast laughed at her affectionate revision to the island verse. But Golden's features pursed into a tense scowl. "To think I lived so many years by that silly rhyme," she said. "Words. Just words."

"No," Mast countered. "Not just words. They were a part of you, Golden Gaverly. The part that trusted and believed and risked something. The part that chased dolphins off my bow and robbed El Culebra's crew of their body functions with her dancing." He pulled away the hand she'd thrown over her face in embarrassment. "The part," he asserted softly, "that showed me the magic of a human touch again. The part that taught me how to feel again."

"The part that made you beet red with fury, you mean."

"Yes. That, too. But that's part of living, sweet. The anger, the frustration . . . the stormy times, and, well—" He glanced around them at the water and the sky, "The bright times. Life and love include them all. And Golden . . . I do love you."

It stunned him that the simple quivering of her top lip

in response could move him so deeply. Shaking with the sensation now himself, Mast pressed his own mouth to that moist coral softness, with a long and loving kiss.

"But it's not true, is it?" she ventured tentatively when they'd parted. "The words themselves; the verse. The whole Moonstormer legend. Carlos Nánchez was the killer, not you. He admitted it to me, Mast. He was proud of killing my parents and all the others."

"I know. And I'm sorry you had to hear it like that. But it's done with, and—"

"No. No, there was more," Golden rushed on. "He told me more. He told me he did it to get revenge on you—because you created the Moonstormer in the first place. He spoke of King George and the Royal Navy, and that he blackmailed Ben to spy on you for him so they'd know where all the best ships and cargoes would be . . ."

Mast made haste to avert his gaze as her voice dimmed, but he came face to face with the realization that he didn't want to. Damn it, be told himself, it was over. All of it. The secrets, the sneaking, the hiding. Never again. He met Golden's widening eyes with the promise to himself it would be this way from now on—no matter how agonizing a truth he had to tell.

"Then it's true," she blurted.

Mast took a deep breath. "Aye."

He didn't know what to expect then. He waited in tense silence for Golden's next move."

"Tell me," she said.

He gently placed her back on her feet. "All right." He slipped his hand into one of hers and said, "Walk with me."

And as they descended the narrow path around the cove, he told her everything. The fifteen-year story of a young, proud sea captain, his cocky braggart of a first mate, and their dreams and desires of furthering England's "divine cause" in a faraway paradise called the West Indies. Thus, the Moonstormer had been born by the dim lantern light in a London tavern, nurtured by a wildfire of rumor along every dock and warehouse in the country, and matured to full infamy long before Mast and Dinky ever took their first sights of palm trees and coral reefs.

"The idea was more successful than we ever imagined," he stated as they made their way onto the small beach below the rocks. "Whenever we replaced the British jack with the Moonstormer's flag, the water seemed to part for us. England's top-secret communiqués were safer than a babe in its mum's arms."

Golden maintained her quiet. He dared a glance in her direction. Her eyes were focused out over the water, but she held her attention to him, as if she were trying to envision him as the arrogant young rooster he once was. Mast stopped, grasped both her hands in his, and pulled that faraway topaz stare back to him.

"I had no idea, sweet, of what Carlos was doing with our secret."

"I know."

He found himself taking a breath he didn't know he was holding. He lowered their hands and began to walk again. "From the beginning, I'd always sensed something from Carlos," he confessed. "Jealousy. Maybe resentment. Mostly just anger, even on the day we first met. But I never thought, in my wildest imagination—" The shock and hurt crashed through him as if it were the first time he was experiencing them again. "Until that night—ah, that wonderful night when we first made love, hellion, and you told me about your parents, and about the flag you saw as they were destroyed with your ship. My flag, I realized. The flag of the fake pirate I'd created.

"Christ." He stopped, clenching his fists at his sides, shaking his head. "I couldn't believe it. The stories Dink and I had laughed off as tavern gossip over the years weren't stories at all. They were real events, carried out by some real bastard . . . Bloody saints. What had I done?"

Only Golden's fingers, biting into his arms as she circled in front of him and grabbed him on both sides, brought his head up. "Stop it," she snapped, eyes flashing gold shards at him. "Captain Iverson, you are guilty of nothing but answering the call of your king when he needed your help, and thereby honoring your country and all your countrymen." Her hands slid up beneath his shirt collar to stroke his neck. "That means me, too, you silly oaf."

Her smile permeated Mast's senses until he found his lips tilting upward, too. He shook his head at her in amazement. "You take my breath away, Golden Gaverly. You take it away until it hurts. And that's why," he continued on a hard, deep breath, "I decided it was time for the Moonstormer to die at last."

Golden's hands stilled over his nape. Her head cocked in the curious, kittenish frown that set his heart to leaping and his manhood to pulsing. "Because of me? I don't understand."

"Of course, you. Golden, you beautiful creature of my heart, do you want to know something? In the beginning, in those first stormy days we were together on the *Athena,* you terrified me. Yes, woman, you did—and how I hated you for it. How I damned you for daring me to feel again. How I vowed you'd never succeed.

"But something happened along the way. Somehow, in some way, you never gave up on me. You didn't stop until every last block of me came crumbling down, and I could do nothing but concede defeat—and my love for you." Mast dropped his eyes and turned toward the water. "I just didn't realize it until we discovered you missing in New Providence. Terror," he laughed, "that was when I realized terror and I weren't even remote acquaintances yet. That fear stunned me, Golden. It drove me to my knees in prayer. The thought of losing you—" He swung around again, as if just invoking the nightmare of a possibility might make it come true, "I never, ever want to feel it again."

"You won't." Golden's touch on his shoulder was like a cleansing wind on his senses. "You won't."

He took that slender hand and squeezed it. "No," he confirmed, "I won't. But I knew I'd never be able to say that with certainty until the Moonstormer was done away with, both the myth I'd created and the murderer hiding behind it. I couldn't begin to hope for a life with you if I didn't. The danger I'd be exposing you to—"

"I'm not unacquainted with danger, Captain Iverson." She jutted her chin defiantly.

"A problem we will be discussing in the near future, Lady Golden."

"Problem? What do you mean, problem?"

But he just turned and began to lead her over the small outcropping of rocks which marked a sharp turn in the beach. "Dink and I had begun to uncover some trails of very troubling facts by the time we docked at Abaco," he continued on with his explanation. "Starting with dozens of testimonies we'd gathered in New Providence, then confirmed by the small files of information your father helped me obtain from the army here."

"The army?" she shouted, jumping down from the last rock cluster to come standing breasts to chest with him.

"And Papa? They all nearly had you swinging from Lady Marston's poinciana tree the night they apprehended you!"

"I'm pleased to hear you enjoyed the show, my lady."

Golden's head snapped around at the strangely familiar voice which responded to her instead of Mast. The next instant she bared a snarl. Even serenely smiling, the tall, bony soldier who'd led Mast's arrest made her think of a hawk hovering for its kill.

"Hellion." Mast's voice in her ear matched the reassuring imprint of his hand around her shoulders. "Put the claws away. It's all right."

"Bloody hell, it's all right." But she found herself pulled forward until Mast was close enough to lean forward and actually shake hands with the detestable cur.

"Captain."

"Captain."

"Your time was almost up in there," the hawk asserted. "My men were starting to load their guns."

"Tell them they can unload," Mast replied in a business-like voice. "It's over. Carlos Nánchez will no longer be spreading terror on the main under any of his disguises."

As if knowing the chill that coursed through her body at the announcement, Mast squeezed Golden's shoulder and pulled her closer to his strength and warmth. Even so, her instinct wouldn't allow her guard down. She was stiff and tense beneath his affectionate caress as her gaze continued to scrutinize the tall soldier before her.

"Ah, well," the hawk said with a tone of understanding. "Then, 'tis good to see you still alive, Iverson."

"I can assure you, it's good to be alive." Mast squeezed her shoulder again. "I believe you and Lady Golden have met?"

"We have. A pleasure to see you again, my lady."

Golden only glowered from one to the other of them. Why didn't they just break out the cakes and tea and make the bloody soirée official?

As if their sudden fraternity wasn't unsettling enough, the pair joined in a soft chuckle at her. She could feel the temperature of her glare rising.

"Golden—sweet—" Mast emphasized the latter endearment—wisely, Golden thought. "Whether you choose to believe it or not, Captain Merrick was the most invaluable part of our plan."

"Plan?" she huffed indignantly. "Plan? Oh aye, one just plans to have a pig like this drag one away in chains every day. One just plans to have people spit on them as they walk through a ballroom in disgrace. One just *plans* to—"

The warmth of Mast's gaze provoked the first indecisive catch to her voice. The knowing gleam in Captain Merrick's eyes brought on the second. The third never came. Golden's throat broke free with an astonished gasp, instead.

"You hoped I enjoyed the show . . ." she uttered with newborn comprehension. "The show."

She whirled an impaling stare at Mast.

"Great God Puntan, you planned all of it beforehand!"

"Now, Golden, just calm down and listen—"

"Everything," she exclaimed. "The guns and the torches and the shackles . . . You knew they were coming to arrest you all along. You purposely let them drag you away before everyone in Abaco. You *wanted* everyone to despise you." Her head moved in a slow, painful nod then. "Congratulations, Captain. You were very successful. They loathed you, all right. Everyone but me. My heart was too shattered to feel anything."

Silence swirled between her and Mast just like the increasing wind of the coming evening—just like the turmoil in her chest—just like the storm she could see gradually building in the gaze he wouldn't relent from her. It seemed that time had suddenly reverted. She could fathom less of what he was feeling than when they'd first clashed wills in Papa's study. Then, the sensation was a curious challenge. Now, it was a foreign and frightening fear.

Mast stepped forward. His eyes didn't leave hers as he said over his shoulder, "Begging your pardon, Captain Merrick."

"By all means, Captain Iverson," came the answering chuckle.

Then in one furious sweep he yanked Golden off her feet and into his arms again. She reacted with equal fervor, biting out a Caribbee oath and squirming. But his grip clamped harder as he growled, "I wouldn't if I were you."

Golden cursed herself profusely as she obeyed. The world went by in a blur as Mast tromped back to the rocks they'd just came from. With a grunt, he set her down and pointed to them.

"Sit," he ordered.

She stood exactly where she was.

"Sit down, Golden. Please."

With a slew of silent curses, she sat.

She tried to think about anything but his alluring presence so close to her. Mast sank to his knees in the sand and moved in until he surrounded her. His hands cupped her face and brought her gaze level with his own.

"Hellion . . . I'm sorry for what you had to go through." He kissed her. "I am." He inhaled deeply. His eyes flashed intense blue heat at her. "But sweetheart, you have to see I had no other choice. You can't imagine what Dink and I felt when every trail of evidence we uncovered kept leading back to the *Athena*. To have to admit we had a spy or even a killer under our noses the whole time—a member of the very crew we were relying on to help flush the real criminal out—*my* crew, Golden. The men I trusted with my life thousands of times." His gaze hardened and he looked away, his jaw clenching so hard she could make out the tense whiteness of his scar even beneath his several days' worth of beard. "I felt like driving my fist through a few hundred walls at once."

"Aye," she replied softly. "I know the feeling well."

He looked back to her. "I imagine you do."

The tingle of a smile tugged at her lips. Mast's own mouth responded with a tentative tilt.

"I think I understand now," she told him. "You knew someone on the *Athena* was the criminal, but you didn't know who. At the same time, you wanted to destroy the Moonstormer legend altogether."

"Exactly. But we were damned if we knew how to do it. Downing two pheasants with one stone seemed impossible—until we came up with the plan."

"To fake your own arrest and execution."

"Aye. As a matter of fact, we realized that killing me off might be the only way to trap the real murderer. With the Moonstormer brought to justice, the bastard had nothing to hide behind any more. He'd try to disappear as fast as he could, with as much as he could get his hands on. We simply made sure that it became as easy as possible for him."

"A trap," Golden gasped. "Of course."

Mast lifted a half smile at her and tapped the end of her nose. "That, my dear, was what kept me away the day of the ball, not Penelope Farsquith." He gave a small laugh at her reddening cheeks, then lowered his hand and entwined it with hers. "Captain Merrick helped us create false documents pertaining to a lucrative shipment of Oriental silks and carpets supposedly passing through Abaco the day after the ball. Dink and I just happened to leave the papers lying about my cabin when we left for the Marston villa. When I was conveniently shot and out of the way two days later, we knew it was just a matter of watching the *Athena* to see who took the bait."

"Ben," she said softly.

Mast nodded tightly. "Yes. Old Ben."

They passed the next moment in a moment of mourning for the old sea dog they'd both loved well. Then suddenly, Mast's features crunched into a foreboding frown at her. "There was just one important factor in this whole game we hadn't taken into consideration," he said ominously.

She straightened in perplexion. "What?"

"You."

"Me?"

"Don't flash those gorgeous eyes at me in innocence, woman. Aye, you. We'd foreseen every hitch the scheme could have had, except you getting to Nánchez before us. Fortunately, after a night in prison and a few hours playing the perfect corpse, I was well on my way to appearing the ideal partner Carlos was seeking when he came into the Rusty Starfish Tavern in Abaco for the last time. It took every ounce of my limited theatrical ability not to go through the roof when he asked me if I wanted to help kill you."

Golden blinked at the grating tone his voice had abruptly taken. She twined her fingers with Mast's and gave a tight, understanding squeeze. He looked to her and smiled again. "I just thank God Captain Merrick and his men were waiting to follow us."

A strident, high-pitched squeal cut him off then, drawing both their gazes out to the sunset-glinted waves. "Well, all right," Mast confessed in a mock tone of reluctancy, "we had a little help in that phase of the operation."

Golden laughed as the familiar grey snout poked its way free of the water and circled merrily for them. "Thank you, Nirvana!" she called.

But the happy amusement was a trickle of emotion compared to Golden's joy when a second nose popped up next to Nirvana and bobbed confusing, yet enthusiastic circles around him.

"Don't worry, Nirvana," Mast quipped, "I have problems getting my wench to follow a lead, too."

Golden giggled and jumped against him, forcing him to take a step back with the ardent power of her embrace. "I love you," she murmured against his neck.

"I love you, too, hellion." He pulled back just enough that they locked stares, and Golden looked deeply into that midnight sky she didn't think she'd ever fathom or conquer completely. Oh, but she'd try. With all her heart and soul, she vowed, she'd spend the rest of her life trying.

"The Moonstormer is dead," he told her quietly.

"Aye."

A flash of hesitancy furrowed his brow. "But I . . . am very much alive."

She smiled and touched the edge of his jaw. "Aye."

"My Lady Golden Gaverly, do you think you could spend the rest of your life with a simple man, and not a sea demon?"

Golden laughed again, then kissed him with all the passion and joy in her heart. "Mast Iverson," she uttered lovingly against his lips, "there's nothing simple about you."

Epilogue

Golden never wanted this kiss to end. She wound her arms tighter around Mast's neck and felt a thrill shoot down her spine at his answering groan of pleasure and his lips' increasing rhythm against hers.

But the world wouldn't leave them alone. The applause around them was impossible to ignore as it grew louder and louder. Reluctantly, Mast released her so they could turn and wave to the throng gathered in the Saint Kitts glade to hear the vows—with Guypa emotionally officiating—that had bonded them as man and wife.

Golden obliged her people and waved, but she couldn't take her eyes off Mast. He was the most spectacular sight she'd ever seen. His dark skin, hair, and eyes were a breathtaking contrast to the heroic white of his new frock coat and matching stock, slightly offset by a cream-colored satin waistcoat, light fawn breeches, and, for once, shiny gold-buckled shoes instead of his beloved boots. She smiled gratefully at him again as he stole a glance at her. That look became another long and enthusiastic kiss, resulting in louder applause. Again they forced themselves to release each other.

"Well, it do not surprise me!" Maya exclaimed, securing

hands to hips from where she stood on the flat rock before the pond next to Golden. "By dee stars, you two wait longer than dee elephants to come together!"

"Now, lovey." Dink poked out from behind Mast on the opposite side of the rock. He assumed the same stance as Maya, noisily rattling the string of shells and beads around his neck and setting his traditional Arawak loincloth to an almost indecent angle. "Ya promised me last night in the hut ya weren't gonna harp on that. Mast was busy helpin' England reclaim this island so we could all live in peace again. He can't help it if the blasted job took forever."

"Thank you, Mr. Peabrooke—I think," Mast cracked. He turned and gave Golden a private wink and a dazzling smile, which sent a renewed flurry of excitement down her spine—and through her lower abdomen. She ran a hand over the white brocade of her wedding gown there, and smiled secretively.

"What are you thinking?" Mast leaned over and asked her.

She just scooped her hand beneath his arm. "About how much I love you."

That brought a soft smile to his lips. "You're beautiful today," he murmured, fondling the ring of hibiscus, oleander, and orchids that supported the white lace veil flowing down her back. "But I prefer that shell and loincloth ensemble of yours better."

She giggled. "It's in the closet on the ship."

"Then what are we waiting for?"

He grabbed her hand and they hurried down the aisle of palm fronds and heliconia petals, ducking the shower of more flowers and good-fortune herbs tossed at them along the way. Mast led her through a tunnel of fern before the forest opened to the wide white beach. More well-wishers cheered for them there. Beyond them Papa proudly waited next to the flower-decorated boat which would take them to the *Athena,* now unfurling sails in the deeper waters.

"Nug," Lord Gaverly mumbled, angrily wiping a tear. "You look radiant."

"Oh, Papa." Golden rushed to embrace him. "Papa," she uttered to him, "thank you."

His bushy eyebrows lowered. "For what?"

"For making Mast come to get me even when you knew I could get back to Abaco alone."

Wayland Gaverly chuckled heartily and kissed her on the forehead. "Of course," he answered indulgently. "Now go on. Barbados awaits you. Besides, I don't know which is more impatient, your husband or the tide."

She glanced over at Mast. He suddenly appeared very uncomfortable standing beside the boat and staring longingly at her. Golden laughed. She turned and hugged Guypa, Maya, and Dinky, murmuring words of thanks and love to them all, then determinedly walked to her husband's side.

"Barbados and Iverson Shipping, here we come," she whispered to him with a smile.

His answering grin was more resplendent than the brightest sunbeam she could imagine. His chest puffed just a little more proudly as he helped her into the boat. "First Mate Rico Salvadore, are we ready to cast off?" he boomed.

"Aye, sir!" Rico replied while scooping up the oars and flashing a wide grin at Golden. "The *Athena* is ready and waiting for you and Mrs. Iverson."

"Mrs. Iverson," Golden murmured in wonder. "Mrs. Iverson."

"We could use 'hellion' if you prefer." Mast's mouth was dead serious, but mirthful lines around his eyes twitched with betrayal. Golden playfully snarled while proclaiming, "Never! Never!" and threw herself against him in a deep and languorous kiss.

Standing witness to their embrace was a throng of black and white Kittians, standing together on the sunset-washed shore. No one wanted to break the magic of the miracle that was sealed here today. A magic, they knew, that was so special, it only existed in island sunsets and summer storms, in rainbows and shooting stars . . . and, if one was very, very lucky, in the whisper of true and everlasting love.

And so they watched as the small boat sidled up alongside the majestic brigantine, and the captain, with his gaze still riveted to his bride, swooped her up beneath one arm— despite her well-heard protests of, "I can do it myself, damn it!" He held onto the ladder with his other hand. The crowd continued to watch as the anchor came dripping out of the water, the crewmen scurried up and down the masts and shrouds, and the proud sails were secured.

And then, the warm rush of a trade wind came from out of nowhere to fill those eager sails, propelling the *Athena,* and her precious cargo, to a new life in a new land.

As the ship faded to a dot on the horizon, they began to disperse. But the very few who remained smiled softly as the trade wind favored the little beach again, carrying a distinct Caribbee whoop upon it, followed by the excited shout: "A baby? God help me, another sea goddess to tame!"

Dear Friend,

Mast and Golden are a pair of very special people to me—so special, in fact, that they were "born" in the middle of Texas, nowhere near water or sailing ships. I turned on a hotel television to see a dolphin, much like the inimitable Nirvana, frolicking on a wave somewhere in the Caribbean. Well, once Golden bloomed to life in that scene, Mast, in all his dark and brooding glory, didn't take long to follow.

Star-crossed lovers? I'll let you be the judge of that. But as *Trade Winds* exploded in my head that night, I learned a lesson I don't think Mast, Golden (*or* me) will soon forget: happiness, like the trade winds, often comes whenever and from wherever you least expect it.

I thank you for letting these two maniacs into your life for a few hours—and do hope you enjoyed the adventure.

I'd now like to invite you over the Atlantic and ahead one hundred years to late Victorian London, the setting for my next Denise Little Presents historical romance, *Surrender to the Dawn*. It is here, at the height of a rainy winter in 1891, that Miss Gwendolen Marsh and Lord Taylor Stafford lock horns for the first time—and permanently set that dismal London sky ablaze.

Yet a word of fair warning—I exhausted myself when writing this book. Gwen and Taylor grabbed on to my heart and my soul, then ran. Gwen, the only surviving victim of a Jack the Ripper copycat serial killer, doesn't just carry a scar on the outside. Yet two years after her attack, just when she thinks her life returned to some semblance of normalcy, a vengeance-driven Taylor shatters her world again with his demands for aid to his quest—not to mention the bittersweet pride in his warrior's stance and the raw pain burning in his hazel gaze.

Needless to say, this is a story about healing. It is about trusting again, feeling again, fearing again, *living* again.

And again, it features two very special people to me.

I sincerely hope you like them, too.

The book will be released in January of 1996. Until then, I wish you many happily-gusting "trade winds," bringing lots of life surprises. I'd love to hear about them, too. Please feel free to write me in care of Pinnacle Books.

Annee Carter

If you'd like a hint of what Annee has in store for you in her next book, turn the page—and watch for *Surrender to the Dawn,* coming in 1996 from Denise Little Presents.

Denise Little

One

February, 1891
The Saint Jerome's Home for Needy Orphans,
London

"Miss Gwen? Miss Gwen, I'm sorry fer bargin' in so early, but—"

"It's all right, Tessie," Gwendolen Marsh assured the child, turning away from the rain-splattered window three floors over an empty East End street. "I'm awake. Come in."

She forced a smile to her lips for the dark-haired girl still fidgeting in the doorway—thankful the action also helped whittle the tearful lump swelling her throat.

One would think she'd have learned by now, she reproached herself. As many times as she'd insisted on extending her volunteer's duties at Saint Jerome's for a fevered or needing child, that was how many times she'd had to endure dawns such as this. Grey. Silent. Solitary. Nothing for company but her breath on that window's glass and memories of a blissful life she envisioned in that haze again.

Yes, that world had once been hers. She had not just dreamed it, no matter how faraway the fairyland seemed now. No matter how distant the ballroom where she'd met a dashing rogue named Lloyd Alexander Waterston; no matter how fleeting the sweeping waltzes, balmy summer walks and romantic hand squeezes of his courtship. No matter how much a stranger the laughing, flirting Gwen of those days seemed now.

She wiped the mist away, swallowing against the flood of pain, then left the window behind. "What is it, Tessie?" she asked. "What do you need?"

"Well, I—well, there—" The girl twisted her index fingers together. "There be *visitors* here for ye, Miss Gwen."

"Visitors?" Gwen glanced at the clock on the wall. The early hour of seven-thirty didn't amaze her as much as the fact that she had guests. No one had formally called on her in more than two years. Not since the "incident," as Aunt Margaret tersely phrased it. Not at the town house Gwen shared with the somber woman on fashionably proper Devonshire Street, much less here at Saint Jerome's, where, Aunt Maggie further humphed, Gwen persisted in "consorting with who-knows-what-kind of rabble in the name of Christian charity."

"Aye, miss," Tess blurted on. "Visitors. Two gentlemen." A shy smile flitted across the girl's lips. "And one rather comely, if I may say so. He smiled at me, and bowed. Like I was a lady, I was. He bowed like this."

During Tess's demonstration, curious pricks alternated with tense knives down Gwen's arms and legs. *Lloyd,* a secret, special voice whispered from inside, *are you at last here, finally here, finally back? Is God at last listening— and answering—me?*

Her right hand flew to her left, straightening the meticulously-shined engagement ring there. For the first time in months, the emeralds appeared to twinkle, not taunt. Gwen felt her lips curl upward of their own volition.

Her smile dropped at the same moment as her hope.

Two men. Suddenly, she remembered Tess had said two.

That eliminated Lloyd, leaving behind only one terrible conclusion.

Helson. It had to be Inspector Helson.

Her heart climbed to her throat again. Why couldn't he leave her alone? She'd told him—and what seemed half the Metropolitan Police—everything she could recall before her world had been changed in those black, blank hours on that cold, foggy night. And now she didn't want to remember any more. She wanted to forget the night of January 5, 1889, had happened at all.

In short, her heart retorted, *you want the impossible.*

A touch beneath the curls at her right temple served testimony to that fact well enough. Yes, she discovered with the usual jolt of dismay, it was still there. Almost as thin as the strands of hair hiding it, just over three inches long and hardly discernible to an eye not looking for it, but there. The reminder. The scar, and the event it represented, that might as well have been spots of leprosy to the people she'd once called friends.

Gwen forced her hand to her side. She spread her fingers into the skirt of her burgundy gown instead. Pausing a moment to check on Gertie, her now peacefully-resting patient, she followed Tess down the main stairwell, commanding each step to restore her composure in place of the fuming frustration. The bitterness only tangled her up like iron shackles when she was trying to escape the torture of Inspector Helson's calls.

She stopped at the door to the parlor, fidgeting again in an effort to hoard a moment's more time. "Dear Lord," she murmured, running a nervous finger along her lace collar. "Dear Lord, help me through this ordeal . . . again."

She took one more deep breath and pushed the door open.

She almost laughed when she saw the real ogre she'd been dreading to confront. With his top hat cocked a jaunty angle over his sandy hair and a mustard yellow suit tailored well to his lean frame, Bryan Reginald Corstairs presented as opposite a picture from stuffy Inspector Helson as anyone on the earth could. His light blue eyes sparkled when he saw Gwen; a lopsided grin formed beneath his mustache.

How many times had she turned to that smile for support and reassurance in the last two hellish years? Gwen lost count long ago. Yes, despite Aunt Maggie's scandalized declarations of, "But a reputable young lady is not just *friends* with a *man*," Bryan Corstairs was the best of the few remaining friends she had.

"Ah," he exclaimed with a dramatic sweep of his hand, "What light through yonder doorway breaks? 'Tis certainly the east, and sweet Gwen the—"

"Bryan, you incorrigible fox." She approached him with fingers wagging in admonishment. "You nearly had me slinking down the drain pipe like a housebreaker. I feared I was doomed to Helson and more of his horrid quest. . . ."

Her statement fizzled away as a form shifted just beyond the realm of the room's single gas light. The form emitted a cough, low and controlled. Gwen leaned and peered into the shadows.

She gasped and jerked a step back.

The man was still dressed in his heavy black rain cloak, one unbuttoned flap pushed behind the crook of his right elbow. His other arm leaned at a dominating angle across the mantel, almost blocking the shelf completely. An errant lock of dark brown hair brushed at his shoulder, trailing from where he cocked his head at her, features still a teasing inch from the light. Silently, steadily, he continued to appraise her.

Just as she stood in numb shock at the sight of him.

Her arms succumbed to the impact first. Her hands plummeted into the folds of her skirt. She felt the smile drain from her lips. The air whooshed from her lungs as she struggled to speak.

"Oh," she finally blurted. "Oh, Lloyd."

The relief, the utter victory of comprehending that he stood here waiting for her, filled her like the glory of a bower of roses on May Day. For a long moment, she didn't move. Then she laughed. She laughed freely and joyously.

"I knew it," she cried. "I knew you'd be back. I knew you were bigger than those ridiculous rumors, darling . . . I knew you wouldn't listen or care! We're going to show them, Lloyd; we're going to show them all what they can do with their gossip and their lies—"

"Gwen."

Bryan's interruption echoed his soft, but insistent touch at her shoulder. As distant thunder rumbled outside, she felt the May Day roses sagging.

"Gwen," Bryan continued, "I believe there are some introductions to be made."

"Introductions?"

Long, booted legs stepped from the shadows.

Gwen looked up.

The peaceful lake blue of Lloyd's eyes didn't meet her scrutiny. Instead, an explosion of color seared her: a riot of gold, green, copper, and even touches of black bordered by unblinking dark lashes. Where Lloyd's features made a noble, aquiline profile, this stranger's nose jutted out to a prominent edge—too prominent. His jaw rose so rugged above a neck three shades too brown, even beneath a cravat the color of creamed coffee, Gwen wondered which dock Bryan yanked this man from.

Indeed, the only trait Lloyd shared with this person was the thick dark brown hair which had fooled her in the first place. Now Gwen perceived the incongruities even in that presumption. Her betrothed never missed his twice-monthly appointments with the barber; the shoulder-length waves before her now only deepened the conception that she confronted a half-blooded Celtic warrior . . . perhaps a full-blooded one.

With horror, she realized she still stared at the stranger just as he examined her: curiously, intently—brazenly. She ripped her gaze away and fixed it to the safety of the wall, before managing to blurt, "Wh-what's going on?"

His scrutiny only continued in intensity, making her abnormally self-conscious . . . disturbingly warm. By high heavens, one might even think the reprobate *liked* the way she looked.

Nonsense. How in the world could she think he'd ogle anything than what everyone else gawked at? How could she think the long-haired infidel was interested in anything but *that?*

She should be used to such leers by now. She *was* used to it, she corrected, even if she no longer chose to endure the perverted distraction she provided people at parties, the probing glances trying to violate the coiffed curls at her temple, struggling to make out the man-made damage from her natural hair line. Even if she no longer battled to ignore the pointed fingers, the arched eyebrows, the whispers and the gasps—some discreet, many not so discreet—as if on January 5, 1889, she'd been transformed from a human being into a circus side show freak.

"Gwen," Bryan interjected, "it's all right. I'm sorry we startled you. We were on our way back through this neighborhood, and I remembered your aunt telling me you were here tending one of the girls for the week—"

"On your way through?" She reclaimed her voice to aid her perturbed thoughts. "At seven in the morning? Just blocks from the most popular brothel in the East End?"

At *that,* the stranger's eyebrows shot up. Bryan cracked a knowing smile. "What did I tell you?" he said to the warrior. "Now do you think she's strong enough to do it?"

"Do what?" Gwen demanded—more than aware of her suspicious tone.

An uncomfortable pause stretched as her only reply. Gwen coiled her arms across her chest and threw a glare from the stranger to her friend.

"Bryan, if neither you nor your stone-faced lackey wishes to let me in on your dandy little secret, I've got a sick girl upstairs who cares about what I do with my time." She set her sights on the door, following quickly with her feet. "Good day, gentlemen."

Only a step more separated her from escape when a voice stopped her. A gripping voice; the man's power came from conviction, not volume.

"The Lancer attacked his eighth victim last night, Miss Marsh."

Her knuckles went white around the doorknob. "God have mercy. Is she . . . ?"

"No. She didn't survive."

"Dear God."

She slowly turned—to where the tall stranger's gaze awaited her. "Who?" she heard herself rasp.

"Lady Veronica Spencer, of Middleham," Bryan supplied. "I believe you knew her, Gwen."

She stumbled, watching her hand grasp for something, anything, to steady herself against the flood of pain. One of the room's spindly chairs reeled into view. She fell onto the seat with a shudder.

"We played together as girls," she murmured. Her voice echoed with memories too long neglected. "We'd take turns pretending to be Queen Victoria. There was a medieval bench in her mother's garden. It was our throne. Oh, Nicky—" Her throat caught on the nickname. "Dear Nicky."

Out in the front hall, Saint Jerome's prized table clock called out eight o'clock. The last knell faded away into a heavier deluge of violent rain.

"Eight bells," came the stranger's voice again, a soft, muted sound when set against the torrent outside. Gwen looked up and concluded the same softness didn't hold true for his feelings. His eyes glared out the rain-soaked window; his jaw line grew even more harsh as he clenched and unclenched the muscles beneath. "Eight bells for eight victims. Eight women defiled by that bastard."

If Aunt Maggie were here, Gwen would have been dragged from the room at the first syllable of such language. But in this moment, she found herself silently thanking the man for the words she'd yearned to scream herself so many times in the last two years.

She supposed he sensed that, for he turned back then, straight eyebrows lowering in a more profound study of her. Every ounce of reason told Gwen to look away, to escape that disturbing, disconcerting, even crude scrutiny from across the room. . . . She couldn't. In his gaze, she saw something she never thought she'd find in another human's eyes.

A pain as deep as her own.

"Eight victims, Miss Marsh," he repeated, "and you, his third, still the only one of them who survived."

She didn't know how to respond to that. She gripped her

hands together in her lap and watched the warrior stalk across the rug, shined leather boots reflecting the lamp light with each measured, steady step.

As she dreaded, he stopped beside her chair. Gwen closed her eyes, alarmed by the effect his nearness had upon her. The shivers from the scratch of his coal-colored trousers against her arm. The unfamiliar scent of spiced men's cologne mixed with early morning rain.

But worst of all, dear Lord, the feeling that despite his size and strength and strangeness, she . . . she trusted this man. Despite the screaming dissent from her logic and sense, her heart flew effortlessly into the security of his presence, the broad strength of his nearness.

She was in trouble. And she had no will to struggle away from the danger. When he took her right hand, pulling her to her feet, she went without thought or protest. His fingers surrounded hers, warm and large. Her left hand, and Lloyd's engagement ring, felt cold and far away.

"Miss Marsh," he told her then, "my name is Taylor Stafford. My wife, Constance, was victim number four."